Darkess and the Purple Mist

Red Dobbs

authorHOUSE®

AuthorHouse™
1663 Liberty Drive
Bloomington, IN 47403
www.authorhouse.com
Phone: 1-800-839-8640

First published by AuthorHouse 7/6/2010

ISBN: 978-1-4520-2273-4 (e)
ISBN: 978-1-4520-2271-0 (sc)
ISBN: 978-1-4520-2272-7 (hc)

Library of Congress Control Number: 2010907316

Printed in the United States of America
Bloomington, Indiana

This book is printed on acid-free paper.

This book is dedicated to the memory of my mom, Barbara.

Preface

For five hundred years, the planet has been dying. Even the oldest souls cannot remember the bounty and happiness the planet used to produce. Each season changes ever so slightly for the worse – dryer summers, colder winters, and damaging floods in the spring that tear at the soil and bury the seeds, rendering them useless. Early autumns bring smaller sized fruit in lesser numbers. Some of the oldest and more secluded tribes remember some of the old ways, and their crops are more abundant than most – but even they can hardly produce enough for every one to survive the winters that follow. The world doesn't know it is dying...or that it has been waiting five hundred years for someone to save it.

The magic wars have destroyed the planet, and the creatures that care for it are either dead or in hiding. It will take great magic to heal the planet. What has been secret for so long must finally be revealed. What every one most fears is their only salvation. Three corrupted eggs lay in wait, wanting again to be reunited. What will find them? They hold the key to life and death, but who could possibly wield them? Even the wisest of Elders keeps them at a distance, for in their presence lies, deceit, obsession, and madness.

Magic has been hidden away for far too long. It needs to once again be in the open. The fears must be laid to rest. Will the humans accept the magic that can save the world? Or will they condemn it, allowing evil to finish off the world for good. Follow the girl with the flaming red hair to find out. She is the key.

☼

Do you see that girl over there on the hillside? The one holding the single, long-stemmed red rose with tears streaming down her face. Her expression is almost blank. Her long flaming red hair is tied with a black ribbon, and her cloak has braided leather rope following the edges. Until three days ago, she was a happy young lady – excited all the time and always ready to learn something new. Now, all of that has changed. Her grandfather, the man who taught her almost everything, is gone, and she has no idea what to do next. She stares with a stony face at the casket covered in a blanket of white roses. A single tear escapes her eye, falling on the rose she has in her hand. Seeing it land, she looks closely at it. The light from the setting sun hits the tear and glistens like a shining star. But even life's simple pleasures fail to impress her today. As the eulogy continues, and friends and family say their peace to their beloved patriarch and leader, the girls face remains unchanged. She feels lost and empty, without a lamp to light her path. It wasn't always this way.

This isn't the beginning of the story, but rather nearer to the end. Perhaps the story should start earlier, much earlier, so that you will also feel the loss of the loved man in the casket. Then maybe you will know the loneliness of that broken hearted young girl. The man in the casket is Richard Vallencourt. And that young lady is his granddaughter Darkess of the House of Goodspeed of the Vallencourt Clan. To most of the world, they are wealthy landowners, almost royalty. Most considered them the stewards of the sick and the poor. To us, they are one of the most powerful of wizarding families that has ever lived in the land of Xyloidonia. But even this isn't the beginning.

When Richard was young and newly in love, he was courting the then young Angela – also from a wizarding family. She would later be known as Grandmother. They made a vow to each other. That vow was to teach their children all that they knew, but not necessarily about the craft. Why? Well, as we all know, some children aren't born with powers, which can cause great pain to the child. So, until their children showed any sign of magic, or interest, they would not tell the child the secret.

When they had their daughter Silver, they waited patiently for signs of her power, and it seemed like they were going to have to keep their secret from her until she was wise enough to handle it and not accidentally expose them. Maybe with age, she could understand why they were protecting the world from danger and why they were keeping the humans in the dark. Hopefully she would show signs of power and they wouldn't have to keep their secret forever. But they would cross that bridge when they came to it.

Silver looked remarkably like her father with soot black hair and shining blue eyes, but they couldn't be more different in personality. She was more like her mother, always making or fixing something. She loved her schooling, especially art and the museum. In her teenage years, Silver visited the Crystal City's Kings' Museum as often as she could. This is where she met a boy…a human boy, which was a source of great tension with her father. Richard and Angela often had heated discussions about the pair, but Angela always won the battle, saying, "She is a girl and in love, what harm could it bring?"

One day Silver came home with an announcement that her beau was coming to the castle for dinner. Roxy, the family cook, who was also a witch, was delighted, as was Angela. However, the same could not be said for Richard. He had so wanted a magical child, and he was upset that she cared nothing for something he loved so much. Richard did agree to meet the boy, and to his dismay, he liked him. Daniel was his name, and he became a regular visitor to the castle. He took Silver to the museum where he worked as often as he could, and he spoke of the old country across the sea where he was from.

Daniel came from a wealthy human family, the House of Goodspeed, and he came here in search of treasures, art and adventure. He loved the different kinds of structures that were ordinary to the Xyloidonians. Daniel said that he had felt drawn to Crystal City. Daniel and Silver explored the city together, and after a year, Daniel asked Silver to marry him. Everyone was happy, but the secret was still a secret.

Daniel and Silver stayed blissfully ignorant of the family line and its powers, 'til one very odd day. Silver wanted some more salt, and the bottle moved into her hand. She dismissed it, thinking the steam from the food had caused her eyes to play a trick on her.

Then, later that afternoon, she said aloud, "I'm cold."

The logs in the fireplace shifted, and the blaze kicked up. Once again, she dismissed it, thinking that logs settle all the time and she went back to her reading. The clincher was when she grabbed for the pitcher of tea. Silver gasped, her body went rigid, and her eyes clouded over. Angela witnessed this.

"Are you alright?" Angela asked.

After a couple of seconds, Silver's eyes cleared, and she said, "The oddest thing just happened."

Angela waited for her daughter to get a grip on herself, and then she asked, "Well?"

Silver looked at her mother, and with a confused look, she said, "I saw myself holding a bottle of some sort of liquid. It was bright pink. And we were in a weird room of antiques that I have never seen before."

Angela grinned at her daughter, and asked, "Are you pregnant?"

Silver wrinkled her forehead, and replied, "I don't think so, why?"

"Has anything out of the ordinary happened to you lately?"

After a silent moment, Silver remembered the salt, the fire, and a couple of other things, and she said, "Come to think of it….yes. What is happening to me?"

Angela's eyes were bright with excitement. She stood up and said, "Follow me."

Angela was bursting with excitement. It was finally time for a trip to the tower.

As with any castle, there are many passageways and secret hiding places, but this one had more than your ordinary one. At the end of the hall, on the second floor, there was a painting of this very castle, with a completely different landscape. Directly on either side of it were sconces. Angela smiled at her daughter, and pushed the left sconce up. Silver looked at her mother with confusion, until the painting moved back a few inches, and then slid into the wall off to the right. Surprise crossed Silver's face as she noticed there were two sets of stairs hidden behind the old painting. One led up and the other led down.

Silver looked down the stairs with curiosity as Angela led her daughter up the small stone steps to a short wooden door. Silver looked at the door, and she could see marks of age on it – spots where the color had changed from hundreds of years of hands touching its smooth surface. From her studies at the museum, she realized that this door was ancient, much older than the doors in the rest of the castle. This door had been hanging here for centuries, and was well used.

Angela reached for the door, but it swung open before she could reach it. Richard was standing on the other side, and upon seeing his daughter, he held out his hand in a welcoming gesture. "At last, my dear, at last." Richard said, as his wife and daughter entered the room.

There was a look of complete awe on Silver's face as she looked around the circular room she had seen in her vision only moments before, down in the library. There were things here from so many eras that it was essentially a museum in its own right. She looked around the room, and the first thing that caught her eye was a wooden chest. It was encrusted with ruby, amethyst, moonstone, and maybe lapis or some sort of blue stones. Behind the chest was a podium or altar, with a thick book lying on top. The walls behind the podium were lined with books of all sizes, shapes, and colors. The bindings to the books ranged from recent to antique. There were large cabinets and hutches, a shelf filled with candles, and still another filled with crystals. Knives, swords, and other unusual items were hung and laid around the room. Chairs and stools were scattered about, with one large table in the center at one end of the room. Hanging from the ceiling was the most spectacular iron chandelier with nine pointed spires, each with a huge crystal hanging from its tip. Silver imagined that she could spend weeks exploring this room and still see new things.

Several minutes of quiet were shared between the three family members before anything was said. Angela had her hands clasped in anticipation as she watched different expressions cross her daughter's face. Richard watched her closely, waiting for her reaction, with the corners of his mouth twitching. Finally, Silver looked at her parents and asked, "What is all of this? Family heirlooms?"

The corners of his mouth broke into a full smile, and Richard said with a twinkle in his eyes, "Well, yes and no."

Clearing his throat, he inhaled deeply. "Several hundred years ago, our family realized just how special we were. Some of us had the ability to see the future. Others could move things with their minds. One of us could hover above the ground, and some had the power to heal. A few could talk to animals, and even fewer could turn into them. There have been some with power over water, and some that could control or even produce fire. After some years, one of the more educated members of our family decided to invite all of the relatives that they could find and have a sort of census. The related lines were written down so each could be traced, along with their powers, or lack there of. There was some of the family with only the ability to make potions or fight with a sword or bow, but had no actual magical power at all. Each and every one added to the family line."

Richard took a seat as he talked, and his expression changed to one of pain, but he continued. "There were problems with some of these members, the powerless ones. They felt cheated, some even despised the members with power, and they stayed away from or even fought with them. This caused a great rift in the family, separating us. So...when it became our turn to continue the family line, we made a decision to keep the magic a secret. We didn't want you to be in pain, or to hate us, possibly. And you would not be here today, had you not shown some sign of power...for your own safety, of course."

The women took a seat as Richard took a drink and watched his daughter. Silver's expression was that of shocked awe and disbelief. Then Richard continued.

"My dear, what we are dealing with here in this room is that of the utmost importance. The knowledge in this room alone could cause mass chaos should the humans see what we do here."

Before he continued, he saw a look of horror cross his daughter's face, and he quickly explained himself. "Oh, dear, by that I mean the mortals. You see, what we do here is save the innocent and destroy the wicked. We protect what needs protection. Your ignorance was for your safety. I do hope that you can forgive us."

Silver sat, taking all of this in, when realization hit her. I'm either a witch, I'm pregnant with one, or am I hallucinating this whole thing, she thought. Angela grasped Silver's hand, and said,

"Love, we are here to help you during this confusing time, in ways that you may not believe."

Standing up, Angela crossed over to a cupboard, opened the front, and started to dig around inside. There were packets of herbs and bottles of liquid. Angela mumbled to herself as she dug through the cabinet. It had been quite some time since she had made this potion. Returning to the table she had a large and a small bottle along with some herbs. Angela poured some liquid from the large bottle into the small bottle, filling it only about half full. Then, pulling out a mortar and pestle, she ground the herbs up, making a fine powder. A fragrant smell filled the air when she added herbs to the liquid. Putting a small cork into the bottle, Angela shook the bottle until it turned a purple color. All the while Richard sat in silence, watching his wife in action. Then, he would check out his daughter's reaction to see how she was taking all of this. Angela looked at Silver with a look of sympathy and said,

"Hold out your hand, this may sting a little. I need some of your blood."

This time, Silver looked more horrified than she had before.

"My blood? What for?" she demanded.

Angela exhaled harshly. "In order for this potion to work, I need your blood for the last ingredient. This is our version of detecting pregnancy much earlier than the average mother."

Silver's hand was shaking when she held it out towards her mother. Her thoughts were racing. Her mother had never hurt her before, this can't be that bad. There was a tiny knife in Angela's palm, and she pricked Silver's finger quickly. Silver winced, but the pain was brief, until Angela squeezed out three fat drops of blood into the small bottle. Returning the cork to the bottle, she shook it vigorously for the time of sixty heartbeats.

"If the potion changes to black, there will be no baby. But, if it turns pink, then…you, my dear, are having a baby."

Waiting for the color results, no one took a breath for a few seconds. The potion swirled in the bottle, with a life of its own. After what seemed to Silver to be an eternity, the potion started to brighten, and turn a bright shade of pink. Every one took a shaky breath and looked at each other.

"This changes everything. You are 19 years old, and you have never shown any signs or interest in magic. We have let you lead the life that you wanted. But now…you will have to learn the way of a different world. For you, my dear, are going to bare a magical child who will need your guidance, as well as ours."

Silver was silent, soaking in all that she could, while at the same time thinking that this must be a dream. Her father continued to talk, and she did her best to catch all that he was throwing at her, and at a very fast pace indeed.

"We will teach you about all of the herbs, both magical and practical, and the powers that they hold. You will see and know the Vallencourt family line, and the powers they held. And you will be able to help your child with control of active power or powers, because while you are carrying, you will be able to use them from time to time. You will hear the stories of our ancestors, and you will add to them, as will your children. All that we have will be passed on to you, and the next generation of Vallencourts."

Richard patted his daughter on the back and returned to his tutelage.

"Come my dear, let us tell your husband the news. I can see that you are in a state of shock. So, let us keep this little secret for the night. Tonight, we celebrate. Tomorrow, we will talk more, for it is a deep subject, taking years to learn, and even longer to master."

"But Father…" Silver started to say, but was cut off.

"No 'but father's' today. What you know of magic is the silliness written is books, by mortals who have no real knowledge of magic. Trust us now, and celebrate, as if it were only a baby. Let us forget magic for the moment. Now you are still safe, you still don't know enough to be in any real danger. I promise, tomorrow we will talk."

Silver was upset, happy, and a completely confused mess, so she relented and let her parents lead her back down to the part of the castle that she knew.

When Daniel returned home, Silver told him the news of their new arrival but left out the part about being a witch. She was, after all, still trying to stretch her own mind around it. The four of them had a happy dinner, talking about names, the cradle, and the like. The entire night seemed happy, but in the back of her mind, Silver could only think about what's next.

"What will happen to me?" she thought. "Will I lose my new husband?"

She limped her way though the evening as well as she could.

They all stayed up late talking, but sleep finally claimed Silver. Her sleep was fitful, as she dreamt of potions and crystals and odd ancient items. Dawn came in bright and sunny, with a tinge of fog in the air. Daniel woke Silver with a kiss and asked what her plan was for the day. With a wry smile on her face, she said, "Today, I learn of my destiny. Today, I will learn about my family history so our child can have the best chance of being well educated, strong, healthy, and happy."

☼

Silver was so anxious to find out what was going to happen today she could hardly contain herself. She felt as if she could vomit. Was it the baby? Or was it her nerves? Anticipation filled her, and every step brought a bigger knot to her throat. Staring at the door, she thought, beyond that door, everything changes.

On the other side of that door is a world few know and fewer still understand. The sake of her child was in that room, and the fear she had would not stop her from making sure her child had the best possible opportunities. She must learn all that she can. Silver entered the tower room ready for the unexpected. In her heart, she had the feeling that she was going to like this.

During months of studying books and making potions for everyday use, charting the family history, learning the differences between spells for darkness and spells for light, and reading through almost half of the family book, Silver had a premonition. Everything around her grew foggy as she saw this image of herself sitting here at this very table with a child. It must be her child, and she was learning from the same pages she was currently looking at. She even heard herself say her daughter's name. She was going to have a girl, and her name would be Darkess. Her hair was the most brilliant of reds. Her eyes were deep blue. Silver imagined that her smile could light up the darkest of nights. She will have an ancient heart, and an old soul that reached way beyond her years, even as a young child. Old wisdom, she will be born with it. She will be quick to learn, smart as a whip. Oh, what a handful she will be, thought Silver. She was amazed at the depth and clarity of these premonitions. She was going to miss them when Darkess was born and took the sight with her.

Mist clung to the windows, the sun had set, and the sky was now tinged a shade of gray. The stars were starting to shine brightly when Silver looked out the window. She was looking to see what constellations were visible when a shooting star streaked across the sky. Darkess would be born tonight, she thought.

Angela and Roxy would be helping with the delivery. Roxy had brewed a special tea consisting of Borach tree leaves, which induce labor and relax the muscles. And after a birth that was much easier than expected, the baby was born shortly before the moon had reached its pinnacle. Darkess took her first breath and never cried even the tiniest whimper. She looked into her mother's eyes as if she knew the power that they possessed. As if she knew of the greatness of the life ahead of her. She seemed to stare life down with no fear. The happiness was almost tangible as Richard and Daniel entered the room.

After the baby was cleaned up, Roxy suggested a trip to see the doctor in Crystal City. Wrapping the baby in a special birthing suit, Roxy handed Darkess to Silver. Silver reached over and put her finger in her daughter's hand and the flames in the fireplace flared up for just a moment and then settled back to normal. It wasn't a storm blowing in and none of the logs had shifted, it was the power of the family line recognizing a new member. It was magic.

"This is a powerful one." Richard said.

As suggested, they did visit the doctor in the city, and on the way home, something happened. A runaway buggy was careening down the road at an alarming speed. Daniel tugged hard at the reins, trying to pull the team off the road in time. Suddenly, the other buggy – horses and all – was lifted off the ground, sailing clear over their carriage, and landing on the ground safely behind them, continuing on its haphazard way. When Daniel finally got the carriage to a stop, he looked down at his newborn daughter, checking to see if she was all right. He saw her hand was pointed into the air. Her tiny fingers were splayed open, and there was a smile on her face. Daniel said, "I thought you said that infants can't smile? And what the hell was that? It was almost as if she did this."

A knowing look crossed the faces of Richard, Angela, and Silver.

"I think that she did." Silver said, mildly confused.

Daniel laughed uneasily, then looked at his wife, saying, "Don't be silly, it couldn't have been. She is less than a day old. And that….that was impossible."

Daniel rubbed his face and shook his head, trying to clear it. Richard leaned forward, grabbed Daniel's shoulder, and said to him, "Son, I think we need to keep going. We can talk about this when we get home."

Daniel was dumbfounded, but Richard insisted that they continue on home, and Daniel obeyed. All the way home, Daniel's mind was a buzz with questions. Was that possible? What the hell made that happen? There was no way his infant daughter had done that…. could she have?

The castle wasn't too far now, and he urged the horses on faster. It took a few more minutes to get back to the borders of the Vallencourt lands, but to Daniel, it seemed like an eternity. In the seat behind him, his wife was holding the new baby, cooing, and murmuring to her all the way home. And without a glance at him, he noticed. What was going on here? Still in a state of shock that their lives had been spared because of something mystical, let alone that his tiny, day old infant may have performed it, Daniel wondered how could this be? He had married a beautiful young girl of the same class, with a good education in art and histories, with nothing like witchcraft anywhere in their lives. Now he was wondering if he had married into a family of disturbed individuals. Darkess, a witch? This just had to be a joke.

The next few hours were quite intense for Daniel, and they talked the entire time, even after Silver and Darkess were fast asleep. Daniel threw question after question at Angela and Richard, until they finally gave in and took him on a tour of the hidden parts of the Vallencourt castle. Angela kept a sachet of befuddlement potion in her pocket, just in case there was a panic attack some where along the way. She also had a sleeping potion if needed. Together they showed Daniel nearly everything – partly because of his appreciation for art and history and partly because of love. They finally convinced him that his daughter was indeed a witch, from an old prophecy made a very long time ago. With a starry sky as the perfect backdrop, Richard sat Daniel down at a table under the window and they told him the prophecy.

"Centuries ago, Wolfbane Vallencourt made a prophecy in front of his entire family at the yearly festival. The prophecy was recorded and passed down through the generations. It goes like this: A babe born with extraordinary powers, which will grow infinitely through out her life, a babe with hair aflame, with curiosity and wisdom well beyond her years.

She will have a heart of love and strength. She will be born to our line and will become a powerful woman in many ways. She will be the greatest force against evil to be born in more than five hundred years. Her burden will be heavy, and she will be tested greatly. However she chooses to act, the results will be astounding. Her path will be revealed on the night of the blood moon, soon after the passing of a loved one. Train your daughters well, for they will be the key to their salvation."

Daniel thought for a moment and asked, "Are you telling me that you knew this the whole time? And you never told us this? Why would you do that?"

Angela decided that it was her time to do some explaining about the truth, the truth that Silver had only just learned. She raised her hand to her husband and took a breath to speak.

"Every female, and most males in our family line, have been told this prophecy for over four hundred years. Every member that has any interest or gift has been taught all that we know, and each generation adds to the knowledge that we pass on. Honestly, we had no idea that it would come in our time, or we would have forced Silver to learn at a much younger age. Actually, we only found out that the prophecy child would be born when Silver had a vision about a month ago. Of course, the near wreck on the way home, well...it was the shining moment of proof. Neither of us has seen or even heard of a day old child performing such strong magic. And with the safety of the family involved, it's as if she already knows that she must protect people. In our hearts, we believe, that she is the one."

Angela rubbed Daniels back as he rubbed his forehead. Then, Daniel looked from Angela to Richard, and finally he said shakily, "I believe you.... it's just...gonna take some time to get used to all of this. I need some sleep. We will talk again...tomorrow."

And with that said, he got up and walked to the door. Turning back to them, he added, "One more thing, about this loved one that passes on, who is it?"

Richard stood up, walked towards Daniel, and said, "Son, I am a wizard, but I cannot tell the future. No one has ever mentioned a name or even which family member. No one knows, as far as we know. You are more than welcome to listen to or read the prophecy if you like."

"Not tonight. I have enough to chew on right now, thank you. Good night."

Angela added, "When Darkess is old enough, you can ask her. She will have the power of sight."

Daniel slipped quietly out the door, and his footsteps became steadily softer. Angela looked at the book under her husband's hands. So much past, present and future – all in one place. It was again time to add to the book. The prophecy has now become a reality. She got out her favorite quill and sat down. Richard knew just what she was doing, so he kissed her on the forehead and headed towards the door himself.

"Don't be here too long," he said.

He knew full well that she would be here for as long as it took to add all that she had seen and learned over the last day or so. Angela heard Richard chuckling on his way down the stairs, but she was so excited that she only said, "I heard that, you old goat."

Angela's eyes sparkled as she pulled out the space in the book left open for the child. She could hardly believe it. Every girl who hears of the prophecy wants to be that child, or the mother of her. And I'm the grandmother, she thought. As it turned out, she wrote for quite a while. She went to bed exhausted but happy, for this was the adventure of a lifetime. As she drifted off to sleep, she had never known such a feeling of exhilaration.

☼

Five months later Silver awoke to her baby daughter's giggles. At first, she thought the crystal her father had given her was where the sound was coming from. The crystal was under a spell, so whatever sounds came from Darkess' room were transmitted from the crystal in her room to the one that Silver carried. Silver always left it on her nightstand when she slept. When she rolled over, she discovered that Darkess was indeed on the floor next to the bed. Darkess was playing with one of her favorite dolls.

"How did you get out of bed?" Silver asked her daughter with a huge smile on her face and a questioning tone to her voice. Daniel came around from his side of the bed, and said, "Well, it wasn't me."

"Hmmm, well she seems alright. I'm going to check her room."

As Silver took Darkess back to her room down the hall, every thing seemed just fine. Perfectly normal, in fact. The only thing was, the bed rails were up, so how did she get out? She was too small to get over the bed and too large to fit through the bars. Silver looked at her baby, smiled and asked again, "So, my little one, how did you get out?"

Darkess smiled at her mother, as if she had a secret, and squealed loudly.

"Not telling me, huh?"

Silver decided there was no problem, and the day proceeded as normal.

The next morning, the same thing happened again. Darkess had her doll and was playing on the floor. This time it was Daniel that said,

"Okay youngin' how are you doing this? I think we need a little magical assistance, via your father. I think tonight we have your father devise a way to see through walls or something. Anything he can come up with to help us find out what is going on here? What do you think?"

Silver rolled the crystal around in her hand, then looked at her husband and said,

"I think you are right, and I think she is smarter than your average tike. We are going to have to be one step ahead of her, always. Or she is going to get hurt. I will have a talk with father when he comes down for lunch."

At bedtime that night as Darkess snored her baby snore, Richard put a bewitched hand mirror in the arms of one of her dolls. The doll sitting next to her favorite doll, so it would provide the best view. Richard snuck out of the room, careful not to wake his granddaughter. Then he whispered to Silver and Daniel out in the corridor.

"This will show you a picture of what is happening, but no sound, so you will have to sleep in shifts. Obviously she isn't making enough noise to wake either of you."

Daniel let his wife get some rest, and told her he would wake her for the early shift. Daniel carried his half of the mirror set with him as he took a walk around the darkened castle, checking it every few minutes. In his pocket he had the sound crystal, but all he heard were gentle snores. Down in the deserted kitchens Daniel found a snack and was munching away when he heard a muffled sound coming from his pocket. Grabbing the mirror off the table, he looked for his daughter, but nothing was there. Well, not exactly nothing. Something was blocking the view. Daniel hit the stairs at a run, jumping two and three steps at a time. By the time he reached Darkess' room, it was too late. She was already on the floor, favorite doll in hand, and giggling at her father with a glee only someone playing a joke can have. There was no one or thing in the room anywhere. He scooped his baby and her doll up, and put her back into her bed. He rubbed her belly, and sang a little to her. Her eyes began again to droop. Soon she was fast asleep, and it was Silver's turn to watch. Daniel checked the angle of the mirror, re-aligned it, and went to tell his wife what had just happened.

So began the second watch of the night. This time Silver was determined to catch her daughter, red handed, so to speak. She put a spell on the mirror to freeze it exactly where it was. Then she changed its location. The stone wall opposite the baby's bed seemed better. Silver snuck from the room then checked the mirror. Good, she is still asleep, Silver thought as she pulled up a bench and sat in the hall outside the room. Just when she started to get comfortable, a noise came from the room. The sound was all of the stuffed animals and dolls falling from the shelf to the floor. Silver rushed into the room, trying to catch Darkess at her magic. As she cleared the door, she thought that she saw Darkess touch down on the floor, but she was not sure. She missed catching her again. That made three times that her infant child had fooled them in the same day. Silver picked up her child and was going to go back to her own room when she heard footsteps in the corridor outside. It was Richard, closely followed by Angela. "I've seen it! I caught her!"

He pulled out a third hand mirror from his pocket.

"She levitated her favorite doll to her in the bed then she actually floated out of her bed to the floor. Then she waved her hand at the shelf and all of the other dolls fell to the floor. She must not have realized that you had moved the mirror to the other wall. I think that she was trying to find it."

Daniel had heard all of the commotion in the corridor and came running.

"We are going to have to do something to make sure she can't get out of the castle or get a hold of something dangerous. Who knows what the next thing will be that she wants to examine. She can't just have anything she wants. Why, she could get killed. We have to lock down all of the windows, so she can't just float away!"

Daniel was in full panic by the time he had reached his family in the hall. Angela grabbed his hands and looked into his eyes. With a soothing voice, she said,

"Daniel dear, calm yourself. There have been many magical children raised in this castle, and each one was taught how and when they were allowed to use their powers. Besides, the use of powers can be very draining. Don't worry yourself so. Look at her. She is about to fall asleep already. We will be strict with her, and it will work. Wait and see."

Angela and Daniel looked at each other for a minute. Daniel looked at his daughter, calming more with each breath.

"You are correct. Though she can't walk, she is an escape artist. We must be careful for a while, until she understands us, for sure. That is all. Okay?" Angela smiled at Daniel.

☼

The following few months were definitely more exciting than most new parents would have ever expected. Darkess began to walk and murmur gibberish constantly. She levitated anything and everything, so they had to be stricter with her. She had to ask before she levitated anything to herself. This became a problem, because she wanted to talk and really couldn't yet. It just never came out the way she wanted. The only things she could say were, please, thank you, and ma, and pa. And even these were hardly considered words. Then came the no stealing rule. The no magic in public rule came about when Darkess saw something she wanted at the market. So they decided she could only be around magic folk for a while. It just seemed safest, until she could communicate more clearly. All of the people who worked at the castle were from magical families themselves, so there was no problem staying home.

On Darkess' second birthday, she was starting to outgrow the baby fat in her cheeks, and her manners were that of a much older child. Her powers were growing, and she was so fast now that even when she did magic without asking, she was almost never caught. Except by her grandfather. He was far too experienced for her, which gave them a special bond. He would usually just wink at her to let her know that she had been caught.

The birthday cake that Roxy made for Darkess had a unicorn magically drawn on the top, and there were two purple candies to signify her age. When she was told to blow out the candle, she puckered up like a five-year-old and blew out the flame. Then, to everyone's surprise, she pointed at the candle and the flame reignited. Daniels' first thought was that the flame had not gone out completely, so he bent over and blew out the flame. Darkess smiled brightly, pointed at the candle, and again it reignited. There was a slightly devious chuckle from Richard, before he said, "Oh-ho-ho, you are magnificent."

Silver was startled with this new development. They all knew that Darkess' powers would grow, but a fire starter? Now they would need extinguishing powder, and a lot of it.

Darkess was responsible with this power, and she seemed to know that it was dangerous – a defensive power only to be used with caution. The next amazing step was when she proved that she really could control the flame. She simply held out her hand, palm up, and closed her hand up in a ball, and out went the flame. It was quite amazing to see.

☼

Some years later, Darkess was climbing a tree at the far end of the castle yard. This was an old oak tree that must have been well over 300 years in age. The trunk was thick with limbs that were close to the ground, making it easy to climb and strong enough for even the largest man. It had a kind of nest in the center, Darkess' favorite spot. She spent hours sitting up there. She practiced her powers there, wrote in her journal, and practiced whatever new thing her grandfather had taught her. She also watched everything she could, from nature to the workers on the grounds. She was eight years old now, but she acted twice that – most of the time, anyway. If not for her small size and the fact that she had her mother stitch magical creatures to her nightclothes, she could have passed for much older.

She kept two journals, at this young age, one for magic, and one for ordinary things. She wrote down everything, from her progression in strength to how she tested her powers and if they changed over time. She kept notes on her ideas, no matter how silly they sounded. One day she was so engrossed in her journal that she didn't hear her grandmother calling her. When Angela tried to climb the tree to see if Darkess was all right, suddenly she stopped climbing, and started to scream. Darkess immediately jumped up, saw what was happening to her grandmother, and threw her hands up. The bees were frozen midair, some even stuck to Angela's skin as they were stinging her. Darkess hopped over the limb she was on and used her power of levitation to float down. Angela and Darkess were pulling the bees from Angela's arms and legs, when Angela said, "There seems no end to your powers, child. Hmmm…let's try something. Hold my hand and concentrate on the stings. Hold your other hand out, and let my power work through you."

Slowly the welts receded, and their color began to fade. Then they were gone. Darkess knew that her grandmother's power was to heal, but she hadn't realized that she couldn't heal herself. When the two witches let go of each other, they both had a wonderful feeling. The stings were completely gone; however, the bees were still hanging in the air. Angela looked at her granddaughter with a look of love and appreciation, and said, "I think we had better go. I'm not sure how long they will stay that way," Angela said, pointing at the bees.

Darkess levitated all of the things into her pack, then down to her. Together they ran for the safety of the castle. Once they were behind the glass window, they watched to see how long it would take for Darkess' new power to wear off. It only took a few more seconds before the bees were moving again. They seemed confused, then scattered off in different directions.

Angela asked Darkess, "Is that the first time that you ever froze something?"

Darkess remembered something that happened that morning and wrinkling her brow said, "Yes, well...this morning when I was getting cleaned up, I reached for the brush and knocked it off. I tried to catch it, and I missed. The funny thing is, I thought that it slowed down just before it hit the floor. It was like it knew I wanted it to fall slower so I could catch it. I thought I had soap in my eyes, guess not, huh?"

Angela grinned broadly as she remembered the first time that she had healed someone.

"When I was your age, I was helping in the kitchen after my studies one time, and we were boiling potatoes for dinner. When my mother turned around, her apron caught the pot's handle. Hot water and potatoes went everywhere, including the back of her legs. I had a wet rag in my hands, so I put it on the burnt spots trying to remove any bits of potato. When I removed the towel, some of the welts had started to get smaller. My mother also noticed a considerable loss in the amount of pain she was feeling. She had me concentrate on her welts. The more painful I thought they looked, the more they healed. We were both astonished. I was just about nine years old when I found out I was a witch. You are a very lucky girl. You have already manifested four powers. You know that I only have one active power. You were born already knowing what you are, didn't you?" Darkess gave a wicked little smile but said nothing.

"That gives you an eight-year head start on me. Still my power has come in quite handy."

Darkess' face wrinkled in confusion.

"What do you mean by four powers?"

Angela found a seat and sat down to answer Darkess.

"Well, let's see here. You can levitate yourself and objects. In a way, that is two powers – but for this case, we will call it one. Second, you can start fires. The third is, you can freeze things in motion. And last, but certainly not least, you can channel other people's powers. Channeling is a remarkable gift, a gift that some would kill to acquire. This power is a multitude of powers rolled into one. You can borrow any gift from anyone around you. You must be careful when you do this, as it will anger many people if you use their power without their knowledge. Each person considers their gift special, and theirs alone. You must only do it when it is truly needed. And try not to do it by accident. Some powers are so dangerous that they are more than doubly dangerous in the hands of someone that doesn't know how to use them. We are lucky that your first channeling was my healing power."

Darkess hadn't even realized that she could channel powers. She didn't even know that channeling was a power. The freezing power she had heard of, and that would come in handy. This power and the levitation power would keep normal accidents down whenever she was around. She liked that. Freezing in public would be a lot harder to explain than levitation. She would have to practice and be in control, she thought. How large an area can I freeze, she wondered. Can I freeze a charging horse? Or a room full of people? Her eyes began to glow with her thoughts, until she realized that her grandmother was staring at her.

"Practice, I must practice."

Darkess ran for the stairs. Angela made a mental note to have the grounds keeper, Tanner, destroy or move the hive of bees to a safer place. Next she had to tell the rest of the family what she had just witnessed.

Angela found Silver and Roxy in the kitchens cutting up hard-boiled eggs. They were having a cold dinner tonight due to the heat wave. There were a couple of knives sitting next to a bowl of fruit, so Angela grabbed one, deciding to help. Reaching for the same item in the fruit bowl, Angela and Silver's hands brushed. Silvers eyes clouded over, and she was jolted by a vision. Angela recognized the signs of a vision, and she looked around for danger. Upon seeing and hearing nothing out of the ordinary, Angela looked back at her daughter and awaited an explanation. Silver hadn't had a vision in nearly eight years. She seemed to know when things were going to happen, but no visions and nothing specific. She said she felt things. This, however, was a full-blown vision. Everyone had assumed that the visions would be Darkess.' And since Silver hadn't had one since Darkess was born, and Darkess had never had a vision that anyone knew of, they had assumed it would come to Darkess at an older age, or that it was one of those peculiar magical pregnancy effects. Finally Angela asked, "Silver, are you alright?"

Silver held her hand palm out toward her mother and gently waved it. Angela took it as a "hold on" gesture, so she waited, brow furrowed. When her eyes began to clear, Silver cleared her throat, and said,

"Whoa, that was different. I saw father making a potion. There were bottles everywhere. A book lay open in front of him, and he was adding rose petals to a smoking pot. Then he added willow tree bark."

Silver paused, and Angela interjected.

"That sounds like the potion we make for old age. It helps to relieve joint pain."

"No, this is different. Then he added some silvery powder, unicorn horn, I think. Then there was an explosion. A cloud billowed around him, and I couldn't see him anymore. I don't know what happened. Where is..."

Before Silver realized it, her mother was running towards the secret passage. As fast as her feet would carry her, Silver raced after her mother. There were old brooms and a mop hanging in the back of the closet. Angela pulled the mop handle down, and a small door opened. Angela darted up the stairs, two at a time, with Silver hot on her heels. Bursting through the door at the top of the stairs, Angela yelled,

"Stop! Don't put anything else in the cauldron!"

Both out of breath, and gasping, they watched as Richard lay down the bottle in his hand.

"What's the deal with the warning light? And telling me to stop? I'm trying to find the potion that recreates my power, and I think that I am close."

"Hmmph, is that what you think?" grumbled Angela.

"What are you talking about?" Richard demanded.

"Well, I'm not exactly sure, but I think that you were about to blow off your own head."

"And why would you think that?"

"For starters, Silver knew the items that you were holding, and she saw you add them, and she saw the cauldron erupt in a ball of smoke, and then you disappeared. So, naturally, I thought you were in danger, what do you say to that?" Angela answered.

Richard sat down with a thud and said to his daughter,

"Well, well, well...so the sight was yours after all."

Silver sat down, stunned. She thought that the magic had skipped her. Now, maybe she could help more. A real power. She felt incredible. The sight wasn't like other powers, it took a lot longer to get control over, and still it worked only when it wanted to. But, she could try anyway. Her heart was full of excitement. She would have to tell Daniel and Darkess. She would get to write in the family book. This changed everything for her. Someday she could be the one that told her daughter what she would have to do to save the world from evil. I could be the one to save Darkess' life. It was time for her to study up on her power. Once again she was going to be the student, and she was happy.

Richard took his cauldron over to a drain, dumped it, and rinsed it down with a bucket of water. With some disappointment in his voice, he said,

"It is entirely possible that my power can't be recreated. Sometime I will try again. Maybe I should write to Harlow to see if he could give me a hand."

"Who's Harlow?" Silver asked.

"Who's Harlow? Oh, what a long story that is." Angela said.

Together the three of them put all of the ingredients away, and Richard began to explain the story of Harlow.

"Harlow is the world's oldest wizard. He has more spells, potions, and tricks than any other wizard I know. He is connected to all of the major covens of the world in one way or another. He talks to only the highest-ranking elder from the clans, and he is highly respected. He is very good with different kinds of magical assistance."

Richard got up stiffly from his chair and picked through a stack of dusty old books.

"Here, read this. You and Darkess. He has been a friend of the family for several generations. He hides on an island with his mate and an oracle. All locked away, hidden from the world and its constant action. He is knowledgeable about all sorts of demons and magical creatures. He knows several languages. Hell, that man has seen things that no longer exist along with things we all wish didn't exist. Read the book, you'll like it. The only way to reach him is by carrier birds. In addition to that, his island is protected from being found. Only with his help could you even get within miles of it."

Angela had a lot to tell the family, and the day was coming to an end, so she said.

"Why don't you get everyone together for dinner?"

Silver looked at her mother to object, then saw the look on her face and decided other wise. She knew that they wanted to talk, so she headed for the door and slipped quietly out. Once the door was latched shut, Angela said quickly,

"What a day…whew. Darkess froze bees in the yard then she channeled my power and healed me. Then Silver has a vision. Mind-boggling."

Richard's brow furrowed in concentration.

"Two powers in one day. Harlow would love to hear this. And Silver! Who would've guessed? I'll have him talk with Oracle and see what she may see about our little Darkess."

Angela got up to leave the tower.

"Don't be too long. Dinner is probably ready," she said.

Standing in front of a dresser with about a hundred drawers, Richard opened one of them and pulled from it a small stone bird. It looked ancient and was a little dusty. The carvings were very lifelike. Taking the bird over to the table, Richard took out ink, paper, and a quill. He wrote a short letter to his old friend as quickly as he could:

Harlow-my old friend, how are you? Very busy here. Darkess gained two more powers in the same day. Silver regained her power of sight. Still having trouble with the potion to recreate my power. Need your help. Have a talk with your seer about my family. Send me word soon, we should have a visit.

Always your friend, Richard

Once the ink was dry, he tore off the written piece, rolled it tightly, and slid it into a small metal tube on the bird's leg. Rubbing the bird's head gently, he murmured,

"I need to talk to Harlow. Please take this to him."

The bird sprang to life at once, twittered, and shook the dust from his feathers. Hopping on Richard's hand, together they went to the window. Opening the window, the bird took to wing, soaring up into the darkening sky. Richard watched as the bird soared ever higher. Then, all at once, the bird turned into a diamond point of light and disappeared.

"That, as they say, is that."

I wonder how long it will take to get a response, Richard thought. Harlow does everything in his own sweet time. Darkess is still young. We have plenty of time. I hope.

☼

Two days later Richard and Darkess were in the tower looking over the family line for relatives who had the same powers as Darkess. They were surprised to see that about every fifth member had the power to freeze. It was fairly common. About 120 years ago, Richards' great-grandparents had nine children. At this time, there were five members from three generations living in the castle who had the power to freeze. Darkess looked for her other power – channeling. She was starting to get desperate in her search when she came to the name Virginia. It was high up on the list, or very far back in time. Darkess saw that there were twenty-five or so names written through five generations in the same hand. As she continued looking, she saw that there were blank spots on the map, and there were a few names crossed out but still readable. Richard was paying close attention to where Darkess was reading. He said,

"Ah, yes, the blank spots. Hmm, they are from the times when our ancestors couldn't write, were nomadic, or uneducated. Sometimes they weren't sure who family members were, where they went, and there were all sorts of orphans and such. It was more than 500 years ago."

"But what of the crossed out names, grandfather?"

Richard knew this day would come. He just hadn't expected it quite so soon. Richard raised his eyebrows, blew out a blast of air, and said, "You can teach a child almost anything, but some go bad anyway."

Darkess looked confused, so she replied,

"Go bad? What do you mean by go bad?"

Richard sighed then he explained.

"It hasn't happened in some time, not in our family anyway. Unfortunately sometimes people see the power their magic holds, then they see what they could do if they use dark magic. At first, they try something small, but before long, the rules get bent a little further. The lure of more power makes them try more until they believe that they are beyond the rules of magic, beyond death even. Their use of dark spells, and potions eventually drives them to the most extreme measures to keep the new found power."

Richard got up from his chair, pulled a small silver key out of a hidden pocket in his cloak, and unlocked a small wooden chest that was inside one of the hutches. He pulled out a few velvet pouches, a couple of bottles, and a small leather book. Holding out the book in front of him, it looked as if it had dried blood all over it.

"This is a dark grimorie used by the son of Virginia Vallencourt. He is one whose name has been crossed out."

Leaning over the family tree map, Richard pointed to a name below Virginia's. The name was virtually unreadable from the lines that marked it out.

"He was Victor, Virginia's first born and favorite of all of her children. At least until he turned into a teenaged wizard. This book was Virginia's. She used it to see what she was up against. Since she only ever had one active power – a small power in some ways, but very large for a good defense – she wanted to know what to do should she ever have to do battle with any dark wizards. Her power was to channel. She couldn't freeze, heal, levitate, or disappear. In her mind, all she was good for was defense. So she studied both light and dark magic. Unknown to Virginia, while she was out one day, Victor found the dark book. He liked what he found. He started doing in-between lessons, dark magic lessons. On his own time, of course. He always made sure to leave the book where he found it, so no one would be the wiser. After what may have been a year of reading, testing animals, and brooding alone about his talents, he decided to try some spells on a human subject. Nothing at the castle, at first, as his mother would catch him. He found that he could control people against their will, under the correct circumstances. And he could do it so well, in fact, that he could make them do things they hated to do but were powerless to stop. The more he experimented, the more dark spells and magic he began to do.

"Virginia had started to notice a change in her son. All of the housekeepers, cooks, and stable hands refused to go near Victor with out a direct order. And then, only if there were another witch or wizard present. Things were much different back then. There were many more servants and the family was much larger. Victor was still too afraid of his family to let them see what he was doing. The help knew that he was bad, for he had begun to use spells on them. Sometimes they would wake up in the wrong place, not knowing how or why they were there, or what they had done. Nevertheless, they knew that Victor was behind it somehow, and it was not good. Even the animals around the castle would have nothing to do with him, shying away. It only took one follower, one cousin, to make him go deeper into the dark arts. As the story goes, it was a winter day, and the two boys were playing in the snow, terrorizing the animals, when they were seen by one of the housekeepers. She leaned out the window to yell at them. I'm not sure if it was the fact that he had someone to impress, or the fact that he had been seen, but it was a serious case of bad luck for that poor woman. Victor made her jump from the third floor, against her will. Fearing someone else from the castle would see or hear what had happened, he used his power to close the windows. Only in his fear and anger, he used too much magic, and the window exploded. The falling glass finished off the mangled housekeeper that lay on the ground beneath. The shattering glass was enough to draw attention, more attention than Victor ever wanted. Young Samson was a coward, hiding behind Victor and agreeing with everything Victor said. Virginia asked Victor what had happened to the woman. Victor's reply was that the woman had jumped to her death of her own accord. With Samson in such a state of agreement, the whole mess was supposedly solved. In spite of this, Virginia did not believe her son. She decided that publicly she would let sleeping dogs sleep, so Victor would believe that she believed his suicide story. Privately was a different matter. She knew her son was a killer, but she had no proof.

"She began to watch her son more carefully. Victor knew it wouldn't be long before his mother figured out what was going on. Victor had chosen the dark side and fully intended to leave the castle. He needed a plan. He'd steal what he needed, and make his escape. For one full moon, he saved and wrote from the family books, knowing that he couldn't get them out of the castle. The books, then as now, are protected. Only an elder or the bookkeeper can remove them from the castle. Someday you will learn the spell to reverse this. For now, though, let us continue with the lesson.

"He did intent to try to steal this book. Fortunately for us but unfortunately for Victor, Virginia had noticed that some things had disappeared. Some gold from her purse, some magical stones, not to mention a locket that had the power to make the wearer invisible were all missing. Virginia began to cast spells all over the magical items from the room we are in right now to protect them from further loss. The crystals that hung in the windows and scattered about the castle, the ones that detect evil, they were put in place by her to follow the movement of evil around the castle. This crystal here…"

Richard pulled out a necklace that had a crystal in it, and showed it to Darkess. "…it is connected to all the other crystals by magic. When evil gets near it, this one will glow. This crystal fits in the head of my staff. They are interchangeable. Anyway, as Victor changed more and more, the crystal began to glow slightly in his presence."

Darkess held the rare moonstone crystal in her hands and felt its coolness against her palm. She had never had a chance to see it this close before, and she could feel the power pulsing in it, as if it were alive.

"When Virginia died, she passed on this crystal with the family book. If something evil comes too near the borders of the castle, the crystal will glow blue. If they actually gain entry to the castle, then it will glow red. As a last addition, the closer evil gets to the tower, the light pulsates. The closer to the room, the faster the pulse. But, again, I'm getting off track. Where was I? Oh yes, we were watching Victor more closely. Virginia knew both white and black magic better than anyone in the family at that time, and she plotted to catch her son doing some sort of evil any day now. She fully intended for him to reveal his dark side and then catch him red handed. She had several vials of a potion that would strip him of his powers for punishment. She kept them with her always. Misuse of magic is a serious offence in our family. Biding her time, as nothing else had happened, Virginia watched Victor get more skittish and waited for him to prove his guilt. One late night, Virginia was getting ready to head off to bed when the steady red glow of her necklace began to pulse ever so slowly. Grabbing her bag, she ran off down the hall towards the secret passage. Virginia's sister Shannon heard the footsteps in the hall and stepped out to see what the commotion was all about. Virginia, being the elder, told her sister that someone with evil intentions was headed for the tower. The sisters ran for the secret passage and up the stairs. Arriving at the tower door, they found it was slightly ajar. Footsteps and rustling papers could be heard from inside the room. A drawer opened and closed, followed by a murmured curse. Some one was very angry, and Virginia knew who that someone was. Virginia held up her hand to keep Shannon back, then clasped hands with her, and channeled her power of projection. She used this to distract Victor in the room beyond the cracked door by appearing there. At first, Victor was so intent on his search he hadn't noticed his mother was behind him until she said, 'My dearest son, what is causing your angst?'

He mumbled that he had lost something but wouldn't say what. Behind the door, the sisters watched as Victor talked to a projected image of his mother. Virginia handed an extra bottle of potion to her sister. Virginia then stuck her hand in her pocket and projected the book into the room.

'Looking for this?' she asked her son.

Victors' eyes nearly glowed red with excitement, and he twitched. A sad and pained look crossed the faces of both sisters. They held hands tighter. Shannon whispered to her sister.

'Save him if you can. Use the potion first.'

Victor eyed the book with an excited expression. His temper rose, and he yelled at his mother.

'You don't deserve that book. You don't appreciate it! Give it to me!'

Virginia stared deep into her son's eyes from the opening in the cracked door.

'No son, it is you who does not appreciate this book, for you are the one who is using it for yourself and not the protection of the family. You don't deserve this book. You don't deserve your powers. I think that I may even wipe some of your memory. I am sorely disappointed in you.'

Victor's eyes darted from his mother's face to the book in her hand. Then with a flick of his hand, he called for the book. Nothing happened, for the real book was being held by both sisters in the stairwell. Virginia smiled a sad little smile at her son, because her decoy was working. The tension was getting thicker in the room by the moment. Virginia was nervous, the next few moments would require all of her power, concentration, and most of all, her devotion to good, and her family as a whole. Victor's face contorted into an evil mask of hate, and he screamed.

'Give me that book!'

This time there was a truly evil glint of red glowing in the centers of his eyes. Virginia put the book back into her pocket. Victor was losing his temper. He called for the book again. Again nothing happened.

'How are you doing that?' Victor screamed, a vein in his forehead began to throb.

'You have no power over me!' he wailed.

He extended his hand for the book, and nothing happened.

This time Victor had had enough, and he took action against his mother. Making a fireball, he threw it at her. To his surprise, it passed through her, hit the wall behind her, and burned a nasty mark. Together the sisters winced at the explosion, and they used the sound as a diversion. Shannon tried to freeze him, but he was too quick, and a fireball narrowly missed her head. The second fireball was frozen in midair, glowing only a few inches from Virginia's chest.

'Those were kill shots Victor!' Shannon screamed, as she shoved her sister out of the way.

Virginia made up her mind, and with the next fireball, she used Victor's own power against him. Virginia tapped into Victor's telekinesis and deflected the fireball. However, at the same time he threw the fireball, he immediately called for the book. The book reached Victor's hands, and for a split second, there was a gleeful glint in his eyes. Then the fireball he had intended to kill his own mother with flew directly dead center of his own chest. He fell to the floor, clutching his demise in the form of a book. There was a complete look of bewilderment on his face as his last breath escaped him. Virginia had killed her son, but she had saved the family. A few days later, she sat down and went to work writing down Victor's story. She wrote about how to prevent it, or try to, and how to defend against it should it happen again."

Richard had been talking for a long time, and he was nearly finished, but he had a few more important points to add. He took a drink, measuring his words before he spoke.

"The blood on that book is Victor's. It was kept there as a reminder. A reminder to anyone in this house that decides to pick the love of power, money, and dark magic over the love of family, goodness, and doing what is right. It shows all of us that we can die for taking the wrong path. Anyone of us could die at the hands of our own blood, should we betray them and follow the dark arts."

Darkess was totally absorbed in what her grandfather was saying, and she held her breath when he stopped talking to get another drink. Richard reached over and grabbed his granddaughter's hand as he told her more of the story.

"It is also a reminder that we are mortal. We can sometimes be swayed or tricked into doing things we know are not the best for us or our family. Virginia checked into demonic possession and potions that could have meant that he was under someone else's control, but it seems that he was doing all of it on his own. When Victor died, he was only in his fifteenth winter. Killing her son changed Virginia, and she dedicated all of her time to her family and fighting evil. She rarely left the castle unless most of the family was going somewhere. She also made a list of rules for the family to follow. Virginia was the one that put the spell on the book so it can't be stolen. She made the crystals that warn us. Her research has helped generations of us in our zest for knowledge. She lived to be a wise old witch. There are many more stories about her and her family that will come up in our studies."

Richard put the book down on the table, far from Darkess' reach, and then pointed back to the family line, and said,

"Now let us look here on the map and see if there is any other member with the power to channel."

Darkess was amazed at her grandfathers' memory – the way he went from story to teaching and back again so seamlessly, making the lessons so much fun. She loved her lessons with him. He made her crave to know more.

Trickling water ran over crystals, some hollow wood, and down into a pile of stones in the magical waterfall that some witch or wizard had made. They continued their search for other people with the power to channel. The sound from the waterfall was soothing, and seemed to help in the search. Richard was skimming down the page with his finger, checking the powers written beneath each name. He found one.

"Here's one…very sad. This young lady here could channel, but regretfully she died of Cholera when she was but twelve. That makes two, are there any more?" The parchment that held the family line was huge, taking up most of the twelve-seat table at one side of the room. Darkess, being only eight years old, had to walk around the table to see it all. Together they looked the entire tree over but never found another person who could channel.

"So, in all of our recorded history I am the third one in our family to receive this power. It must be very special."

"Indeed it is. So special. You won't believe what you can do with it. Any entity having magical powers will be powerless against you, IF you know how to control their power. Remember how grandmother showed you how to look at and concentrate on her stings? How she had you hold her hands?"

Darkess shook her head yes.

"She was using touch to channel her power through you and your other hand to direct that power towards the damaged skin. Of course, the more that you practice, the better you will get. Virginia was so powerful that she only need be in the same castle to channel someone else's power. Power and practice are only two of the key elements in your channeling power. The third is the trigger."

Darkess squished up her nose and forehead in confusion.

"Example, when you channeled your grandmother's power, you used love and pain as the trigger. Number one, you love your grandmother, and number two, you empathized with her. You saw that the pain was tremendous, and you in a way felt it. That is what made the power to heal run through you. Understand?"

Darkess nodded her head, but it was obvious that she needed a little more information. Her eyes were clear, and watching her grandfather's every move.

"Okay, when you froze the bees that was a fear response, or worry maybe. Sometimes the trigger changes. Anger can also be a trigger for freezing. Every power has a trigger, and you must find it. Be careful, though. Powers can be, well, wonkey for lack of a better word. When Victor threw those fireballs at his mother, that had a hate response. If you accomplish this power as quickly and thoroughly as you have the others, and you find the trigger...channeling will become second nature to you."

Richard began to roll up the family tree and was placing it in a hard leather sleeve specially made to protect it, when a tapping sound came from the window. Darkess jumped to her feet and ran to see what it was. A little bird fluttered waiting to be let in. Once the window was open, the bird darted inside and landed on the back of the chair where Richard normally sits. The heat that blew in with the bird was stifling, so Darkess closed the window hastily. The bird chirped then held out his leg. Inside a small metal tube was a rolled piece of parchment. Darkess had never seen such a thing. Pulling out a small bowl and a vial of something clear, Richard pulled the letter from its tube and let the bird perch on the bowl. Richard poured the vial out into the bowl and the bird gulped it down. When the bowl was nearly empty, the bird chirped a few times and ruffled its feathers, preening itself. Once the bird was finished cleaning up, he straightened up and promptly turned to stone.

"That was amazing!" Darkess said, smiling from ear to ear.

"I thought you would like that. Now, let us see what this is."

Richard unrolled the parchment and begun to read.

Greetings,

It is good to hear from you. Still can't find the correct ingredients? Maybe you should try some dragon horn and blood-root. I hear that you nearly blew off your own head. Oracle saw it, and she checked on Darkess. All we have from the reading is stone walls and purple mist. Nothing more. It's still too soon. Give it more time. We may be getting old, but she has plenty of time on her side. Give my love to the women of your house. Write me again when something changes.

    Until the next time.

    Your loyal friend and servant,

    Harlow

Richard read the letter twice, making sure he hadn't missed anything. Then he rolled the parchment back up and tucked it into his pocket. Darkess waited patiently for her grandfather to explain, and when he didn't, she asked him.

"What was that? The bird, the letter, who was it from?"

Richard explained the bird, the potion that returned it to stone, and that the letter was from Harlow.

"Harlow?" Darkess' eyes practically popped out. "You mean the legendary wizard that can read minds, the one from the book?"

Richard chuckled in amusement, "Yes, my dear, what do you think of him?"

"I'm almost half way through the book already. He seems just brilliant. And you know him?"

Richard's eyesbrows shot up, he gave a long belly laugh, and answered.

"Yes, I know him. Don't sound so surprised. Do you think that I only know the people that live within our grounds?"

Darkess' face turned a bright shade of pink, and her skin showed her embarrassment.

"You almost never go to the city, and then only if it's a family outing. Heck, you almost never leave the castle."

"Yes, well, my young granddaughter, there is much you still need to learn about magic. And me. For now, I'll just say this…I am a master potion maker. I've had the gift since I was about your age. I can reproduce nearly every power this family has ever had, and some it hasn't."

A wrinkle crossed over Richard's brow, and he gave her an honest look.

"But I have had trouble with a few. I can't reproduce channeling, or my own power, chameleon. Mind-reading potion is very tricky. Truthfully, it doesn't always work." Richard rubbed his chin, pulling on his whiskers, thinking very hard about something.

"The potion to teleport, I made that when I was but ten winters. I used to play tricks on your grandmother. I'm sure you'll hear them one day. Any way, I used to teleport myself to where she was, back when I was trying to win her heart. Got me into some trouble, I'll tell you. My mother took away my unicorn horn powder until I was seventeen. They thought that would keep me from harassing your grandmother. Didn't work. I did have to come up with new ways of getting into trouble for a while, I'm afraid. But needless to say, I leave the castle frequently. By potion, if you will. I usually leave and return to this room. Safer. And I got into the habit when your mother was young and didn't know the secret. And I usually leave at night, when you are fast asleep. Have I overwhelmed you yet?"

Darkess shook her head no, but her eyes told another story. She looked tired.

"Off you go anyway. Finish that book on Harlow. He is indeed a great wizard. Read closely, for you may know some of the other characters in that book…some of the people that helped on his way to greatness."

Richard smiled at his prodigy and gave her a wink. She returned an upturned eyebrow and a cocked grin.

Richard opened up a journal that he had lying on the table, flipped to the next empty page, and began to write. He wrote out a list, titling it 'clues'. Then he wrote 'stone walls, cave?' The second line said only 'purple mist.' Then he closed the journal and placed it on a shelf with several others.

"Well, no news is good news, I guess." Richard said, as he touched the letter in his pocket and headed toward the stairs.

☼

By the following summer, when Darkess was nine years old, she had mastered her power of freezing, and was doing well unfreezing also. She even had the partial unfreezing down pretty well. She was using the farm animals to practice on, and they didn't seem to mind. Darkess used the stray dog that hung around usually, because the mutt chased her familiar Chakra, which of course was a cat. Almost everyday when Darkess made her way to the old tree, she had to freeze the dog to let Chakra escape. This happened so often that she started unfreezing the poor dogs head, and reprimanding the dog soundly, then releasing him. Richard watched her from the front tower window quite a bit, and he had to chuckle at her every time she did it. But the dog never left, and he took to following Darkess around. Sometimes when she would climb her favorite tree or go up into the barns loft, the dog would wait patiently for her at the bottom until she came back down. It seemed like a peculiar kind of partnership. The dog was perfect for magical practice, and it seemed to give the poor old thing a daily purpose. The dog never got hurt, and he seemed to think it was some kind of a game.

After some weeks of watching this little scene play out, Richard asked Angela to come up to the tower.

"Have a look at this…I think that you will find it interesting."

Richard pointed out the window, and pulled up two of the tall stools, suitable for snooping out the window. Together they watched nearly the exact same scene unfold again with Darkess, Chakra and the stray dog.

"That's peculiar." Angela said.

"Not half as peculiar as seeing it for two weeks in a row."

"More than two weeks? Chakra runs off every time? And the dog follows every time?"

Angela sounded completely confused, but Richard had an idea.

"Yes, yes, and yes. At first I thought that Chakra was luring the dog to teach Darkess. Then, I thought that maybe the dog wasn't really a dog."

A mixture of shock and horror crossed Angela's face.

"Really now? Do you think that I would let her come to harm so easily? I've tested him. He is just a normal dog. And he hasn't set off any alarms. No, what I was thinking next was…maybe she is getting another power."

Richard raised one eyebrow at his wife, waiting for her reaction. Angela looked at her husband with no expression at all.

"What power?"

Richard raised his shoulders in bewilderment.

"She already has four powers. She's only nine. Don't you think that it is too soon for her to be getting another power already?"

"Maybe. It is possible that the dog is sensing a change in her. Let's ask Silver to see if maybe she can get something from the dog by way of premonition?"

By the time they reached the castle lawn, they found Silver doing what she called a normal hobby: basket weaving. Daniel was reading from a book that looked ancient. Tea was sitting on the table, and Daniel poured them both a cup as they walked up. Richard repeated the story about Darkess and the dog to Silver and Daniel. Silver said she had seen the dog, and Daniel thought he was a friendly mutt. However, both parents eyed the dog warily. Daniel was preparing to go get the dog and check him out when Angela stopped him.

"No, son he's not dangerous. Richard has checked him out. What we were thinking is…we think that Darkess may possibly be receiving a new power, something that the dog may sense in her. Chakra does nothing to warn or defend Darkess from the dog…as if she would need any help. What we want to do is see if you can get a reading on the dog."

Silver stopped her weaving and gave her mother a confused look.

"You want me to try and read a dog? Well…okay."

Silver put down her reeds and went over to the tree where the dog sat patiently waiting.

"Hey Dee, who's your friend?" Silver called out to her daughter as she knelt down to pet the dog.

Leaning over the limb of the tree, Darkess called down.

"He's not my friend, he's my shadow!"

Darkess slipped back behind the limb, ignoring the dog. Silver scratched the dog's head and got a small flash. Silver's eye clouded for an instant. She smiled at the dog, whispered "good boy" and wandered back over to her parents.

"I got a reading, but it was more like a feeling than a vision. I got this burst of love. Plain old love. He thinks she is wonderful. That's it. That's all that I got."

Richard looked disappointed, and he rubbed his chin, pulling his whiskers and twisting the end.

"I still think that dog knows something that we don't."

Daniel, being non-magical, couldn't understand why they were all expecting a cat to defend his daughter when the dog was three times its size.

"How and why would Chakra defend Darkess against a dog?"

Richard knew this would come up sometime, and he was kind of amazed that it had taken this long.

"Chakra is a magical being. Harlow sent him as a gift for a special child. Darkess is meant for something wondrous, and she doesn't know it. She is too young for that kind of pressure. So we must protect her every way that we can. Chakra is a familiar, or watcher, for magical children or persons new to their powers. Have you ever seen Chakra's eyes glow red? Well, if you do, he has sensed something dangerous or evil to Darkess. His job is to ward off evil or warn his charge of danger. Only after Darkess is warned will Chakra warn anyone else. For that reason, you should always pay attention to the cat's attitude. He may just save your life."

≈

Richard kept a closer eye on Darkess for the next few days. Nothing new happened. Doing research on the purple mist from the Oracle's vision, he asked every witch, wizard, and magical creature he could find if they knew anything about purple mist. So far, he had drawn a blank from every single one. Stone caves on the other hand, were unfortunately a centime a dozen. There were caves in every land of the world, surely even uncharted ones in Brumalia and the Isle of Ardor. Add together the cave and the purple mist, and he had absolutely nothing. He was stumped. This is getting old, he thought, and so am I. Here we are again, at the same place as before, waiting. Only time will reveal the secrets of Darkess' future.

☼

The yearly festival had arrived, and the whole family was in on the celebration. And since it was Darkess' birthday, she celebrated extra hard. The entire first floor of the castle, the main entrance, and the courtyard were all decorated for the party. Quinn, a friendly ghost and one of the family members that had passed on long ago, flew about the castle talking to the guests and scaring the new arrivals, if he could. The shrubs in the courtyard were bewitched to grab at the guests as they went by. Lanterns floated in the air along all of the pathways. Darkess' favorite tree was enchanted as well. It swayed and creaked, as if in a ferocious wind. Chakra yowled and darted out from his hiding place on occasion, just to add atmosphere, and he loved to do it.

The atmosphere was pure excitement, for tonight was the biggest party of the year. Darkess was so excited that she could scarcely contain herself. Costume parties were all the rage with the mortals, so why not the magical world? The idea seemed absurd to them until they tried it. Richard and Angela were known for their extravagant parties, and this one was no exception. Darkess had dressed as a banshee, all pasty white and wearing a dress of white rags. She even had the perfect high-pitched squeal to go with the costume. Levitating down the staircase, it looked as is she could fly. All of the guests were from magical families, so the costumes were out of this world. The food table was somewhat of a show in its own right. There was brain dip, eyeball salad, severed fingers, sugared spiders, and much more. Some of the food was alive, or seemed to be. The sugared spiders for instance, got up and walked around your plate on their own. And there was a covered dish in the center of the table that, when uncovered, would scream, 'It's not time for me yet', forcing whoever had uncovered it, to recover it quickly. On the veranda, there was a palm reader and a 'haunted room' with a thick wood door guarded by a man in a tattered black cloak holding a sickle. The door would open upon the guests' arrival, and inviting them in was a wizard with a smile and a warning: You may not return…and if you do, you may not be the same.

Darkess simply loved this evening, whether it was her birthday or not. She saw new kinds of magic and met all sorts of new people and sometimes creatures. One of the guests happened to be a doctor with the power to freeze. She told Darkess that her success was split: half to her training as a doctor and the other half to her magical training. Since few women made it into this line of work, she was lucky to be doing what she does. She was considered one of the best doctors in all of Xyloidonia, and Crystal City has some of the wealthiest people to call on her services. However she was a kind-hearted witch, as well as doctor, and she saw any patient who needed her. Her name was Emily, and Darkess liked her very much. Darkess didn't remember that Emily was the doctor who checked her over the day she was born.

Another impressive guest was a magistrate from Crystal City, James. His power was what he called 'his sixth sense'. He knew if anyone was lying or hiding something. He also knew if there was a demon behind the person charged or if it was a demon in human form. Darkess liked him, but he seemed more interested in his wife, so she moved over to a group of children, some of whom were her own age. Two boys were making small spheres. The first one made energy balls, and the other made fire. An older girl was juggling them in the air with her power. Over by the wall, a young girl was running back and forth through it, teasing her smaller brother who was trying desperately to catch her. Children her own age rarely held her attention for longer than a few minutes. She never seemed to learn much from them, and beyond their powers, Darkess found them boring.

A beautiful woman of Asiattican descent by the look of her face was dressed as a vampiress of the old world. She stood alone in the corner, watching everyone and sipping from a silver goblet. Darkess looked closely at the goblet and had never seen it before. It must have been the vampire's private cup. Darkess wondered why would someone bring their own cup to a party? Who was this woman? Why was she standing alone? So Darkess, not having a shy bone in her body, strode directly up to the woman.

"Hello. My name is Darkess Goodspeed, and what might yours be?"

Black hair partially concealed the intensely purple eyes that were focused on Darkess. Slowly a smile crossed the woman's face revealing sharp fangs.

"Hello dear Darkess. I am Jori. I've heard quite a lot about you."

"Are you friends with my grandfather?"

Jori cocked her head to one side, as if listening to something only she could hear, her eyes locked onto Darkess.'

"I am a close friend to Harlow. Harlow and your grandfather have been friends for almost sixty years. I was sent here at Harlow's request to meet with you. To see what you are made of."

Darkess stared, very trance like at Jori, than she mumbled.

"W-what I'm made of?"

"Come, come dear, your attitude, abilities, what makes you, well, you."

Jori looked at Darkess, a small smile creeping again across her lips, showing the tiniest points of her fangs. Then she asked,

"Are you afraid of me?"

"Afraid of what?" Darkess asked in a slightly angry voice.

"Of me?"

"My grandfather would never invite someone here he thought was dangerous to me. I know lots of people with powers. What makes you so different?" Darkess demanded.

Jori realized that her clothes had been mistaken for a costume. She knew that she had better explain why Darkess could, but shouldn't fear her. Jori could hear Darkess' heart pounding. She was getting angry. Jori locked eyes with Darkess once more and said.

"Stay calm Darkess, and let me explain…"

Darkess' heart began to slow its pace, but only a fraction.

"I am a vampire, not in a costume. These clothes are mine, ancient… yes, but mine. These teeth are also mine, not a spell or potion. But…you need not fear me. Harlow and I are also close. Do you know him?"

The beating of Darkess' heart had returned to normal, and she said.

"I have heard of him, but I have never met him. I would like to though. Why didn't he come here himself to see what I am made of?"

Jori snorted a little laugh.

"What the book failed to mention is that Harlow doesn't read minds. He hears thoughts, every one in the same room with him. Look around you. There must be over a hundred people here tonight. The confusion would nearly drive him mad. Then you have the psychic imprint that people leave behind. That would cause him pain for days after this was all over. No, no, Harlow stays where there are no people."

"So you can shut off your mind?"

"Vampire minds are not like those in a human. I have to let him in, or he hears nothing from me. When a vampire bites its victim, the vampire sees all of the victims' memories; their very thoughts flow with the blood into the vampire. Accomplished vampires can read minds as well. So, you see, Harlow and I are very close. He can see what I see…halfway round the world."

Jori waited for Darkess to say something, but she seemed to be waiting for more.

"Do you see why he sent me? I can get impressions off of you, the same way as him. Except I can only read one mind at a time. It's less messy that way."

Darkess looked at Jori for a moment, then said,

"I still want to meet him for myself."

"Some day we will go together and meet with him. Have you read any about my kind?"

"I have heard some, but I'm still learning about magical creatures, non-humanoid, their powers and uses."

Darkess looked upset that she didn't know more about the subject at hand. Suddenly there was a book in Joris' hand.

"Where did you get that book? Can you conjure things?" Darkess asked.

Joris' eyes flashed as she looked at Darkess.

"Being a vampire has its advantages. I can move faster than human eyes can see, walk up walls, and fly. Your grandfather told me that you're an avid book reader, so I brought you one…a special one about vampires that can't be found in any library for the populace. It's from Harlow's private library, and a truer description of vampires than you will find anywhere else."

Darkess' eyes grew large as she smiled and took the book.

"Thanks."

"Do you know that I am the only truly accepted vampire in the world of white magic?"

"Why is that?"

"Harlow was the biggest reason. And the fact that I rarely need to feed any longer. Usually only when provoked, usually by someone evil."

Darkess' eyes seemed to dilate, and she swallowed a lump in her throat.

"You mean that you eat people?" Her heart skipped a beat.

Jori saw the girl before her shrinking away and it was reversing the progress.

"Mercy no child. But I can suck out their life force…the blood in their veins."

Staring at Jori, Darkess seemed to be sizing her up, as if she were going to battle.

"You need not worry, for your body would be cooling in death's grip if I wanted you. I believe that you and I will be good friends some day. Why not start off on the right foot?"

"Alright, so you aren't going to eat me, but good friends?" Darkess pressed.

"Oracle has seen it."

"Oracle?"

"She is the seer that works for Harlow, and she saw us together as friends. She is the greatest seer of our time, and she is the reason that Harlow sent me. When I return to our castle we will link, and she will try to catch a glimpse of your future. Plus, your family believes that your education needs a new direction. I decided to pick today to come here because of all the other costumed guests. I thought that it would be less of a shock. I am sure that the people here who don't know me think that I worked up a wonderful spell for this getup. And with a little mind control, they all believe this is a costume and that I am a witch."

Jori smiled and lifted one eyebrow in a knowing fashion at Darkess. An oldish looking wizard dressed as a vampire sauntered up. He asked Jori to dance, and off she glided in his arms.

"I'll see you later, enjoy the party." Jori said as she spun around the floor.

With a bewildered look on her face Darkess watched them dancing, until they got lost in the crowd. Then she saw her grandparents dancing on the floor, both dressed in their finest wizarding clothes. Every creature known to the magical world, even some that were imagined were out on the floor and standing around the room. The crowd had grown quite a bit over the last hour or so, and it was hard to keep an eye on any one person for very long. Making her way through the crowd, Darkess tugged at Richard's robes.

"I just met this vampire, and she told me that she can walk on the ceiling, read my thoughts, and that Harlow sent her."

Angela laughed from deep in her belly at the look on Darkess' face.

"Jori has a thing for being very theatrical. She insists on a big entrance. She gets clothes from every country, every few years, and she uses them for costumes. You know she met our very own Virginia all those centuries ago. Never fear, she will help you. Not hurt you."

Richard asked Darkess. "Are you enjoying the party?"

"This is the best one ever!" She replied.

They all danced, and ate, and showed off their magical skills late into the night. Several rituals were performed in honor of the day that was coming. Then as the guests were clearing out, some leaving, while others found a room for the night, Darkess began to fall asleep in a large overstuffed chair. Daniel carried his drowsy daughter up to bed, while Jori, Richard, Angela, and Silver snuck into the small dining room to have a little chat. Before they had even made it to their chairs, Silver was grilling Jori.

"I saw you talking to Darkess…did you read her mind?"

The love of theatrics was shown again as Jori popped from the door to her chair before speaking.

"No, not really. I saw that she loves being a witch. She thinks that magic is serious, but…too much fun to be frightened of very many things. She's fearless and thinks that nothing can hurt her. Although she did get a much quicker heartbeat when I told her that I was a vampire. So, basically, what she is thinking and what she believes are a little different. She has courage and strength, and now, she has me."

"You saw nothing bothering her? No new power she may be practicing on her own?" Angela asked.

Daniel had arrived and was trying to get a better look at the vampire as he took a seat.

"I saw nothing else. She was so excited about her birthday, and the party, and then me…her thoughts were a scattered mess. She's only ten, and she's normal. Tomorrow I can link with the Oracle and see what she can get. She can sometimes see things so feint that no one else would even know they were there."

Everyone talked for a while about this and that after they returned to what was left of the party. Several people were saying their good-byes and leaving in various ways. There was only one thing left to do, clean up. Richard said all of his reversal spells, Roxy did a few cleaning ones, and Quinn yawned as he disappeared through a wall.

Slowly they all wandered off to bed. Joris' eyes glistened in the candlelight. She bid them a fond farewell and swept out the side window vanishing into the night. Richard chuckled as he closed the window behind her.

"That show off. Next time she comes, I believe that I will disappear on her."

☼

Somewhere in the Malachite Ocean between Asiattica and Aquatica, there is a small island. It is not discernable to the human eye and has been hidden for six hundred years. There are only a few living and even fewer non-living beings in the world that know of its existence or its location.

In the very center of the island, so it would not be easily stumbled upon should some one accidentally wreck there, is a castle. Jori had this castle built soon after she became a vampire. At the beginning, all of the people that worked on the castle lived on the island. Slowly one by one, they began to mysteriously vanish. By the time the castle was almost finished, hardly any workers were left. Fear gripped the remaining men and women, some even tried to escape the island. None ever made it, Jori made sure of that. However, this created a problem. She was out of food and was going to have to leave her sanctuary.

Money was never a problem, as she stole from her victims. She would buy some food; slaves were easy to acquire. She would also get a few inedible servants. During her travels, she came across a coven. Using lies and mind control, she told the witches that she was plagued by a demon and desperately needed their help. It worked, and the witches hid the entire island. Then she had another problem: What to do with the witches? Killing them would only stir up a hornet's nest that she didn't want to deal with. So she made them believe they had gone on a long journey, and when they returned home, all they would remember was a successful demon hunt. But the witches had a lasting effect on Jori, and she begun to study magic and even added to the protection of the island.

One night while Jori was out hunting on the ocean, she happened upon a small ship. It had only a skeleton crew, easy pickings for an accomplished vampire. It was Harlow's ship. He was trying to deal with his power, and that is how they met. It was purely accidental their meeting, but it was chemistry that Harlow survived. Jori watched Harlow every night, snacking on another member of the crew. She studied Harlow. Something about him was special – she just couldn't figure it out. After three nights, Harlow was alone on the deck looking at a star chart. He studied the skies, and with out a flinch he said,

"Hello there, Miss Nightly Visitor."

Jori stopped dead in her tracks, trying to read his mind. When she opened up her mind, Harlow's mind poured into hers, and they were locked together in his thoughts. Then they followed the wave of thoughts into her mind. Together the past memories mixed, and their present was combined. Their future plans seemed to become one. They blended their minds, melding together. A shiver crossed over both of them as their minds slowly retreated back into themselves.

"That was the most wondrous rush that I have ever felt." They said in unison, and smiled at each other.

This story of Harlow and Jori is a much different story. And it means little to the story of Darkess, save one thing. Harlow and Jori were meant to be together, wizard and vampire. But Harlow was aging, and didn't want to die, yet he didn't want to become a full vampire either. He wanted the powers he already had. Together, they made a tonic from Jori's' blood and a little magic to be taken once a month on the night of the full moon. It seems that they accomplished a great many things over the years, and this is where our stories collide. In the battle between good and evil, forces sometimes combine for one reason or another. Richard and Harlow became friends doing battle together. Richard, being a master potion maker, adapted Harlow's tonic into a serum. This was more potent, lasts longer, and need only be taken once a year.

Now back to the story at hand. When Jori left the Vallencourt castle and returned home, Harlow and Oracle were waiting. Landing on the roof of her own castle, Jori descended the stairs that led to the Oracle's tower chambers. Oracle was waiting for her on a large round pillow. She opened her eyes as Jori walked in, and said.

"Harlow will be here momentarily."

Jori made herself comfortable in a chair near Oracle as Harlow walked in. They had long since required the need for speech, Jori just opened her mind, and the two of them shared a long conversation in the time it takes for a few heartbeats. Harlow held his hand out towards the Oracle, and Jori knelt down in front of her. They grasped hands. They opened up their minds, and Oracle saw the very room in which Darkess had talked to Jori, even heard the conversation. After a few moments, she said.

"I need something of the child's."

"Do you think that Darkess is the great good, or the great evil from the prophecy?" Jori asked.

Shifting her weight slightly, Oracle said again.

"I need something of the child's."

Jori knew that she was fighting a losing battle, so she dug into her pocket; pulling out a ribbon Darkess had worn in her hair the night of the party. She held out her hand, lacing fingers with the Oracle.

"Close your eyes….hear Darkess' heartbeat. See the thought that you saw when you linked with her. Slowly sift through each image."

There was a jolt that slammed through both women. Oracle saw the child clearly. They both saw the party in their own minds. When the night of memories was concluded and Jori thought there was no more, a dog appeared. Jori's forehead wrinkled in a confused way as an enourmous blue wolf walked up next to the dog. Then a flurry of wings washed away the canines as hundreds of birds appeared. So many birds that everything went black. Jori's hands flew free, and she tumbled off the pillow onto the floor. It looked as if she had been punched in the chest, and she wheezed, out of breath. Jori shook her head. She was dazed, and the connection was lost. Oracle moaned as her head rolled around on her shoulders. Harlow reached for Jori's hand and hauled her up into a chair. Keeping silent, so they didn't disturb Oracle, their minds were abuzz with what had just happened. They were both anxious to know what Oracle was seeing now. Were the wolf and the birds something Darkess had seen, or was it a future event? Maybe it was a bad omen. Oracle's eyes opened again, and she took a deep breath.

"That...was interesting. I have no idea what it means. After our connection was lost, I saw all sorts of animals from all over the world, mortal and magical. They were lining up around her. She was sitting in the middle, cross-legged with her palms up. She had her eyes closed, but her lips were moving, though I could not hear what she was saying. Arranged in size from smallest to largest, so all could see her, the animals drew close to her. All were acting tame and shaking their heads as if listening to her. It looked like...a court session. She was communing with them, it seems."

Skepticism edged her voice at the end of her speech. Harlow sat down next to Jori. He put his thumbs under his chin and looked deep in thought.

"Figurative instead of literal?"

Inclining her head towards Harlow, Oracle spoke.

"My visions aren't always clear. You know very well it is probably figurative. How could all of those animals be in one place if magic weren't involved?"

Jori voiced her own opinion.

"I'm not sure of this, but couldn't the circle mean that she has power over animals? Or maybe she is being controlled by animals?"

"That's it. She either has or will have a power involving animals. Either that, or she violates some animal law and is getting sentenced by them. What else could it be?" Harlow chuckled at his own humor.

The amount of power used in the link with Jori had left Oracle severely drained and she spoke very softly.

"You very well could be right. Remember the tale you told about Darkess and that old mutt? He may detect the power in her. She...may not even know this herself. I will try again later. For now, some food and some rest. Come see me in the morning."

Without another word, Oracle rose from her pillow and headed towards her sleeping chamber. Harlow and Jori had other ideas.

The room was large and filled with the most exquisite furnishings. To the untrained eye, it looked rather like a library or office. And to a degree it was. There were tables and chairs placed around the room with a bar on one end -- an ordinary bar that swiveled into the wall and was replaced by a potions cabinet. One of the tables looked like a writing table, but its top flipped over to reveal a book of spells and potions. All of the magical items in the room were disguised to look like ordinary items.

Harlow always said that the best place to hide things is in plain site. He also said that centuries of magic teach one to be smart and secretive, even when in the middle of nowhere.

There was a sconce on the wall. Harlow tapped it three times. Sliding down the wall, the sconce revealed its secret contents. Stone communication birds. Harlow removed one, and the sconce slid silently back into place. Sitting at a desk, Harlow rapped his knuckles on its top. It popped open. Quills, ink, and parchment were inside, along with colored wax sticks and his signet stamp. One of the quills quivered in the drawer, one of his childhood creations. He called it "the scribe". It responded to only his voice. He had thought himself very clever in his youth.

"Alright, hop on the page." Harlow said.

Harlow pulled the cork from his ink, and the quill hopped in. It then hovered at the edge of the bottle, as to not drip on the parchment while waiting for dictation. Knowing that Richard would be excited, he planned his words carefully. Harlow cleared his throat, and the quill twitched with anticipation.

Richard, my friend, I have news for you. The link was a success. We believe she is manifesting a new power – speech with or power over animals, example the dog. Oracles vision was intense. Will look for more on this subject. Contact us if there is a change.
    Your faithful friend,
    Harlow

Harlow thanked the old quill for a job well done, and it hopped back into the drawer. Harlow closed the drawer and grabbed the stone bird. He rubbed its head gently, and it sprang to life. Tucking the letter into the silver tube, Harlow said,

"Go to Richard. He needs this information."

Standing near the window, Harlow opened up a special pane, and out the little bird flew. The sky was so black that only Jori's vision was good enough to see it, until it stopped, turned into one of the stars and was gone.

≈

Richard was snoring loudly when a tapping sound woke him. The sudden quietness of the room woke Angela.

"What is it?" she asked, lighting a candle.

"I thought it was a storm brewing, 'til I realized the tapping was constant."

Both of them got out of bed. Richard opened the drapes and saw the little bird. Cracking the window just enough to let the bird pass, he closes the window quickly. Angela was lighting more candles and a lantern.

"Tapping your fool head off, weren't you?" Richard asked the bird, annoyance dripping from his voice.

The bird landed on Angela's arm, so she unrolled the scroll and read aloud. When she finished, the bird began to twitter. Seeing the agitation of the bird, Richard thought that Harlow must want a reply. This required one of two things: stasis for the bird, which meant going to the tower, or sending him back with an immediate reply. Thankfully he was always prepared, and he had a small desk here full of supplies of all kinds. He pulled a scrap of parchment and scribbled out a response.

It's the middle of the night! Thanks for the news. Nothing new now. Use a strong potion on this bird, he's very excitable. Good night. Richard

The bird was guzzling water from a cup on the desk. Richard tucked the note and sent the bird on his way.

"Do you really think that you can go back to sleep?" Angela asked.

"No, but at least I can get some tea and wake up with out all of that twittering. This old mind takes a few minutes to wake up these days," Richard said in a crabby voice.

Angela held out her hand to her husband with a grin on her face.

"Would you care to join me in a hot cup and a little jaunt to the tower?"

≈

Digging through a large stack of books on a table in the tower, they were searching for people and powers that involved animals. Neither of them had known anyone with the power to speak to animals, Rufus, the stable hand not included. His power was not a magical one, but rather an animal one. He just understood them. He was like one of their own kind in an odd sort of way. He was from a magical family, but he has no real powers. So they searched. Talking to animals, turning into animals, anything that might help them. They found a few spells to control animals for a short period of time and two different abilities. One was the ability to reproduce the actual language of different animals. The other was telepathic, eliminating the need for growl, whinny, or hiss. They found a man that could only link with ocean animals, along with a blood family member that had two powers: conjuring things and animal control.

"It says here that his power to conjure was beyond compare, but his power over animals was his crowning achievement. Animals did what ever he thought them to do. Hmmm, makes you think. Will Darkess be like that?" Angela quipped.

"We'll see, I guess."

They continued the hunt, and further down the list they found an infant who had shown power over the castle's cats, but she had died young. Nothing else was written about her. Another one was a lady who could not only talk to birds – she could turn into one. She had no other power and lived to be quite old.

"That makes four so far…five if Darkess is one of them." Richard commented.

"Ok. That's enough for me. I need some sleep. Let us finish in the morning," Angela yawned "…or maybe the afternoon."

☼

Spring flowers were blooming around the courtyard, and the bees were busy visiting each one. Darkess was once again in her favorite tree. She was looking at a butterfly she had frozen on the end of her quill. Chakra was laying on a branch a little further up the tree. He was hanging over the edge, growling at the dog on the ground. Since Darkess was back, the dog was back, resulting in Chakra's attitude. There was one difference: The dog no longer chased the cat. Still, Chakra hated that dog.

"What's with you? You spoiled cat," Darkess demanded of the cat, throwing some old leaves at him.

Her action unfroze the butterfly, and it floated away on the breeze. Not expecting a response of any kind, she opened her book and began to read. Darkess heard a buzzing sound and waved at her ear, trying to shoo whatever it was away. The sound only increased in volume. She shook her head, continuing to read. The buzzing continued, and partial words seemed to be in the static. Darkess' eyes wandered from the pages as she started to listen to the sounds more closely. She could make out some of it now. The words were becoming clear.

'...pretty girl...so nice to me...play with...smell good...'

Confusion crossed Darkess' face, and she slammed her book shut. She looked around her, trying to find the voice.

"Who said that? Come out. Show yourself," Darkess demanded.

Just then she heard the voice again and realized it was coming from inside her own head.

'Ever since I was a small pup, I knew you were special. I could feel it when you looked at me.'

Darkess was peering over the edge of the tree, and all that she could see was the dog. His ears were perked up, his tail was wagging, and she heard the voice again.

'Nice to finally meet you. I've been tryin' to get you to hear me for a year. I just knew it would happen. My name's Tippy, by the way.'

Darkess simply stared at the dog and blinked a couple of times, her brow furrowed in disbelief.

'You're just a big bully. Now go away.' Darkess heard in a completely different voice behind her.

Darkess rolled over and saw her cat staring at the dog.

"You can talk?"

'Only to you,' the cat replied.

"Only to me? Then who called Tippy a bully? Can he hear you?" Darkess questioned her cat.

This is where being a magical being came in handy, and he took on an authoritative air. Chakra licked his paw and eyed his mistress as he projected his thought.

'Your ability to channel as well as your ability to speak to animals makes it possible for the animals nearest you to communicate. Basically, we can read each other's thoughts when we are in the same location. It is like projection with your thoughts. Right now, you are talking to me, and that mutt can't hear a thing. But, since I am a familiar, and made from magic, I hear whatever you project to him. He doesn't understand me anyway. I just think it's fun to torment him.'

Darkess' whole life was full of new and sometimes very shocking discoveries, so this wasn't too bad.

'What do you think of your new power?'

Her mind was in a flurry of thought. She just knew her grandfather was going to flip over this one. Looking back at the dog, she saw he was still waiting patiently. Then she looked back to her cat.

"I don't really know, I just found out."

Chakra commanded, 'Tell the dog to go home with your thoughts, and tell him you will see him tomorrow. See what happens.'

Darkess had a piece of jerky in her pocket and tossed it to the dog. Then she projected her thoughts to him.

'You're a pretty good old boy. Now run along...I'll see you tomorrow.'

Tippy snapped up the jerky and looked at her with his tail wagging.

'You know I will,' he thought, and off he went.

Darkess couldn't believe it. He had done just what she had said.

"Wow. I can't believe that worked." Darkess said.

'Of course it did. Talking to animals is a serious power. Add that to all of your other powers, and even the uneducated animal will feel your power and obey.' Chakra thought.

Darkess was dizzy with excitement over her new power.

Knowing that her grandfather checked on her periodically from the tower window, Darkess snuck around to the side of the castle. Checking to make sure no one was watching, she slipped around the corner and over to the chicken coop. She saw the big rooster, and he was headed directly at her. His wings were extended, beak open, ready to defend the eggs. However, once the rooster actually reached Darkess, he lowered his wings, closed his beak, and sat down in front of her. Darkess was dumbfounded. She looked around, almost nervously, and projected a thought.

'Can you hear me?'

The rooster blinked, cocked his head, and answered.

'Yes, miss.'

"Wow." Darkess whispered.

Chakra wound around Darkess' legs and sat at her feet. He yawned and twitched his tail as he thought.

'He feels your power and is afraid of me.'

"Amazing," Darkess giggled quietly.

There was a twinkle in her eye. She did like her new power. This will be an easy power to practice, she thought to herself, and no one will know. When I think the time is right, I will tell them…just not yet. Her mind was racing as she made her way back towards the castle for her afternoon lessons. Today, she was to learn a potion for making people fall asleep.

☼

Crystal City had autumn games every year. It was a time for buying, selling, and trading. There were contests for prizes, and thousands of people came from all over the country to watch and compete. There were animals of all kinds, and Darkess was floating on a cloud of happiness. There was almost an evil glint in her eyes as she thought, "Practice, practice, practice."

Darkess had learned long ago never to use her powers in public. Only in life threatening situations, and then only with extreme caution, combined with clean-up measures after the fact. But talking to animals was one of those things that can be done without the knowledge of anyone around you. Darkess had practiced on every animal on the castle grounds, and she had been doing quite well. Not a sole had noticed yet. She loved having a secret, even though she knew that it would come out soon enough.

Silver and Daniel walked Darkess all over the city's square. She projected thoughts to every animal she encountered, even the odd hairy beast that was spitting at its handler. Silver bought some dried herbs from an old cloaked woman who smiled at Darkess as if she knew her. Darkess returned the smile, but the woman had no animals, so she moved on to the next merchant. A loud cheer rang out across the square. Darkess followed the noise to a large corral with bleachers on both sides. This is where the contests for gold were held. Jousting was the event the crowd was cheering. The small family found a seat on the end to watch to show. Thundering hooves, cracking wood, and cheers from the crowd were the only things that could be heard. The next match was about to begin when Darkess noticed a small boy taking advantage of his distracted parents by slipping out of the bleachers for a better look. When the child hit the dirt, he fell to his knees unharmed. Darkess had a knot in her throat as she watched the boy headed for the horses. There was no time for explanations. She jumped to the lowest platform then vaulted the rail. The knights had begun their run, and one of them was lined up perfectly to smash the boy to bits. The knight was concentrating on his opponent, not what may be at the end of the arena. Darkess ran like she had never run before. Screams erupted from the crowd before the knights had even reached one another. Daniel saw what the commotion was about and screamed at his daughter.

"Darkess! What are you doing? Get back here!"

Somehow Darkess heard her father over the crowd. She threw up her hand, signaling that she had heard but couldn't stop just yet. She devised a quick plan as she ran towards the boy. Levitation and freezing were too visible. She was going to have to talk to the horse, reason with him. Splintering wood hit the knight, knocking him from his horse. The crowd screamed with excitement, anger, and terror as the horse with no rider raced towards the boy. Darkess was a just heartbeat away from him, who was now just realizing that he was in the path of danger. Fear gripped the boy as he stared at the on coming horse with terror in his eyes. The front of the boy's pants grew dark as his bladder let loose. Screaming came from the stands, and Darkess knew she was the only one who could save this child. Grabbing the boy, she shoved him behind her and locked eyes with the charging horse. In her mind, Darkess yelled at the horse,

'Go around me!'

The horse gave her the oddest look, but she heard 'huh' in her mind and knew that she had gotten through.

'I said, go around me, or else!' Darkess demanded.

In perfect unison, the horse pulled his stride to the outside right as Darkess spun around to pick up the boy. The horse thundered past, nearly careening with the stands, then trotted towards the end of the arena looking for a way out. Running to the stands, Darkess handed the boy up and hastily followed. The boy's frantic mother was shoving through the crowd, desperately trying to get to her child. Once Darkess and the boy were safe, a cheer went up through the stands. An amplified voice was heard over the crowd.

"Stop that girl! She's a hero!"

Darkess was nearly in a panic. She knew they would want to talk to her, and they would want to know what had happened. She wasn't willing to tell them. She couldn't lie it just wasn't in her. She would have to hide. Darkess ran through the crowd, ducking past anyone reaching for her. Her parents weren't very far away, and she knew they would be looking for her.

Silver had seen the entire act from where she was seated. She informed her husband to be ready to leave abruptly.

When Silver saw Darkess rushing down the row towards them, their eyes locked just as Silver pulled a handful of dust from her pocket. Darkess jumped into Daniel's arms, and Silver blew dust into the faces of the crowd nearest them. She produced a bottle of blue potion, gripped Daniel's arm tightly, and crushed the bottle at her feet. In a cloud of blue smoke, they departed from the stands. The combination of the befuddlement powder and smoke had perfectly disguised their swift retreat.

Rematerializing in the tower room of the castle, they startled Richard. The fuming cauldron tipped over, spilling its contents all down the front of him. His legs vanished.

"Well, will you look at that?" Daniel chuckled.

Richard smiled, looked at his legs, took a pace or two back and forth, and laughed out loud. Rubbing his chin in thought, he said,

"Make this magic go away, erase it now, it cannot stay."

As his legs began to reappear, he chuckled again.

"Can't believe that worked, actually. Thought I'd have to make a reversal potion, and who knows how long that would have taken. So, what brings you back in such a hurry? Everything alright?"

Silver was wiping dirt off of Darkess' clothes and searching for wounds. She thankfully found none.

"That was a little too close for my comfort. To answer your question, yes we are okay. Darkess saved a little boy who was nearly trampled by a horse from an unseated rider in the jousting event. We had to make a fast get away. And how, by the way, did you do that, young lady?" Silver asked.

Darkess had known this day would come. She fixed a few loose strands of hair, trying to stall for time. She just wanted a few more precious seconds alone with her secret. She knew it was futile, and she was going to have to tell them everything.

"Darkess, answer me. I know you didn't freeze anything or use levitation, but that horse veered away just before he hit you. What did you do?" Silver demanded.

Daniel knew his daughter was stalling for time. He could see her mind racing behind her eyes.

"Darkess honey, we just want to know what happened. You're not in any trouble. You could have been killed out there, so out with it."

Daniel sat down in a chair in front of Darkess and held her hand with a pleading look on his face. The towers door opened with a smack, and Angela bustled in with a flurry of robes. Quickly she knelt in front of Darkess and grabbed the girls' shoulders.

"Are you alright? What happened? You used the teleport potion! Will somebody tell me what is going on here?" Angela demanded.

Just when Angela was about to ramble on further, Richard grasped her elbow and pulled her to her feet.

"Calm yourself woman. We were about to get that answer when you burst in here rambling on. Every one is fine. Now, go ahead Darkess."

All eyes were upon her. Squaring her shoulders, Darkess looked at each member of her family in the eyes as she savored her last seconds of knowledge that only she held. One after another gave her 'the look', so she took a deep breath.

"About three months ago, the day I learned the sleeping potion, I had a little talk with Tippy. It was a one sided conversation, or so I thought. He answered me. It was Chakra's fault! He was hissing at the dog, because he used to chase him all the time. I got sick of the noise, so when I asked what his problem was, it was kind of fuzzy at first. Then I thought I was hearing voices, and we all know that isn't a good sign. I even looked for somebody, or something. Then all of the sudden it was clear. A perfect voice, inside my head."

Slowly all of Darkess' family took a seat, listening intently to her story. She continued in a very grown up manner.

"I practiced this power and checked it against every new animal I have come across. I just knew I was the only one who could save that boy. Freezing and levitation were completely out of the question. And I was almost certain that horse wasn't a magical creature. So I told him to go around, or else. That horse was as shocked to hear me, as I was when I first learned I could talk to animals. But, he went around, and I saved the boy."

Angela was horrified, and it showed in her face.

"You could have been killed. What were you thinking?"

"You are overreacting Grandmother. I could have frozen or moved him if I had to. I was fine," Darkess grinned.

Everyone was silent, each lost in their own thoughts. Then the grin began to slide off of Darkess' face. She was getting upset, thinking they thought she was foolish.

"But the man said I was a hero. No one saw me use magic. What did I do wrong?" Darkess implored.

Silver heard the anxiety in her daughter's voice, and then saw it on her face. The poor child thought they were reprimanding her. Silver slipped from her chair and went to her daughter.

"Darling, you did a very brave thing out there today. You are a very good little witch. And some day you will be a great witch. But you still have much to learn. You have a lot in your future, and we would all like to see you survive to be there for it. Despite all of your powers, we are your parents, and we must protect you. And no matter how old you get, we will always worry about you," Silver consoled.

Darkess leaned forward, a tear shining on the rim of her eye. She hugged her mother tightly.

"I love you," Silver whispered in her daughter's ear.

Standing up, Silver patted Darkess on the head and said. "Why don't you and your father go and find Roxy. Get us some food, hmm? I'll be down in a couple of minutes."

Silver eyed her husband, and they exchanged that parental look that meant, 'Later – now go!'

Darkess was quick to pick up the look. So as she went for the door, she said. "You just want to talk about me again. I can tell."

After the steps in the stairwell receded, Silver looked at her parents.

"Did you know she could do that?"

Richard's face turned a little pink.

"You did," Silver said, shocked.

Richard quickly defended himself, "Now wait. Harlow said when the Oracle looked at Darkess; she saw something that could be construed as animal control, or speech with them. But no, we did not know she could do that."

Silver sat back with a thud and thought, 'A new power, huh. What's next?'

"We think we should tell her on the day she turns twelve. And I believe we should start giving her more vigorous training. If she can stare down a charging horse, what else can she handle?"

Angela finally spoke her feelings.

"I think that we should start easy. Like fighting invisibility or fireballs. No actual demons or mind control. Nothing for the accomplished wizard. I don't care how many powers she has. Maybe one of us should turn into an animal to see how she deals with an animal she can't communicate with."

Angela eyed her husband and looked lovingly at her daughter.

"Let us think on it for a couple of days."

≈

Much later that night, the tower door opened. Richard was in his night robes and carrying an eight-inch glowing crystal he called his night-shine. His argument was that it was safer than oil or wax when wandering about late at night – quicker, too. Flicking a match, the chandelier burst into flame. He whispered 'dark', and the crystal in his hand went black. Pulling out the supplies he needed, he began writing to Harlow. Trying to find the proper words, Richard looked out the window at the stars. They were bright against the inky blackness of the sky tonight. One star in particular seemed to grow more intense for a heartbeat, then it went as black as the sky around it. Richard stared at that spot, wondering if it had been a star or not. He returned to his ink and quill when a knocking sound came from the window. Richard took up his crystal and went to the window.

"Illuminate," he said as he pointed the night-shine out the window. He saw a small bird desperately fluttering on the other side of the glass. Opening the pane, he allowed the bird in. He pulled out a small bowl and a pouch with seeds. Returning to the table, he took care of the bird and asked for its message. This bird was very serious about his job. Hopping on one leg, he presented the tube containing the note. Once the message had been retrieved, the bird began to fill itself. Richard unrolled the letter and read.

Richard,
Oracle bid me to warn you. A horse will charge down Darkess. She is in danger. Another vision revealed a fine woven basket with three very large eggs nestled in it. Does this mean anything to you? Are you still having a birthday party for her? Jori would like to see her again. Send a reply as soon as possible.
   In your service,
   Harlow

The bird began to preen itself as Richard read the letter a second time. Three large eggs, he wondered? What kind of eggs? There had to be hundreds of birds and other animals that laid eggs. Chicken large? Maybe goose large? Ostrich large? Richard was stumped. Opening the notebook where he kept all of his secret thoughts about Darkess, he thumbed to the section he had marked, 'Clues'. He added to the list numbers three and four.

#1 stone walls, cave?
#2 purple mist
#3 three large eggs
#4 fine woven basket

He closed his notebook and wrapped it in its leather bindings. He rubbed the bird's head and looked towards the stars once more. After several deep moments in thought, he began to write again.

Harlow-my friend,
No need to worry. Oracle must have seen the event in synchronized time, or maybe after the fact. She faced down the horse of her own accord. She saved an innocent child. Our idea was correct – she can talk to animals. Telepathy. Will check out the three eggs. The party is still on. You will receive an invite. We plan on teaching Darkess defensive and offensive tactics. And about her future. All of it. Keep in touch. Things are moving faster, magically speaking.
   Richard

Richard decided to return a different bird, letting this bird have a rest. Opening a drawer he pulled a fresh stone bird from his stockpile. He brushed its head to awaken it. Once the bird was fully alert, Richard whispered to it.

"Take this message to Harlow."

The bird promptly stuck out the leg with the silver tube attached. Slipping the message in place, Richard gently held the bird and took it to the window. Opening it up, he tossed the bird out into the night. Even after more than sixty years, he still watched every one of them. Even if all he could see was a point of light flickering out.

Richard was sure it would only take a day or two for a reply, but with Harlow, you never could be sure. He sat down and fed the bird a little more seed. He then started working on a contact list of magical people who could assist with his beloved granddaughter's training. She needed the very best. After about a dozen names, he decided to contact three at a time.

Letters had been sent, returned, and sent again. Richard took his time, considering the answers of each person as he waited for the next set of letters to be returned. After two weeks of correspondence, he had narrowed the list to three. And these three had good contacts of their own. That may help, too. Belthazor, Janine, and Brutus. He sent an invitation to each of them for the yearly celebration, along with some things he had planned for Darkess' training. The stone bird that had delivered that latest message was calmly waiting next to Richard's hand. He pulled out a special potion and poured it into a small bowl for the bird. Richard stroked the bird's back, gently pushing it towards the drink. The bird took a couple of sips, chirped once, and turned to stone.

The next morning, all of the Vallencourts and their staff were eating breakfast when a tapping came to the window. Darkess jumped from the table, anxiously opening it. The bird floated in and landed on Richard's goblet. Taking a drink and hopping to the table, the little bird presented its leg.

"Who's it from?" Darkess asked excitedly.

Pulling the scroll, Richard read to himself.

To Richard Vallencourt
Master potion maker
I thank ye very much for the invite. I will be comin alone. If you want I'll help teach Darkess.
We'll figure out what I cin do at the party.
Glad to help
    Brutus

Richard then read the letter aloud.

"Who is Brutus?" Darkess questioned.

Angela laughed out loud and said.

"Brutus is a very crafty wizard, best known for his ability to get in and out of tight places."

Angela and Richard had a good laugh while everyone stared at them in confusion.

"I'm sorry, I'm sorry. But once you meet him, you will understand what I mean. Do you see that crack under the door there? Brutus is quite possibly the largest man you will ever meet, and he can fit under that door…easily. His most prevalent power is, well, he can melt. He turns into a putty and oozes through tight spaces. Doors, crates, cabinets – you name it, he can usually get into it," Richard quipped.

Silver then asked, "Once again, who is he? And what does he have to do with teaching Darkess?"

Richard moved his silverware around his plate, forming his words before he spoke.

"Brutus is kind of, well, an off colored wizard. Some may call him shady. He gets paid to find things. Sometimes information, sometimes an item. Every now and again, a creature or person. He is a good man with a good heart, but his occupation makes some people look down on him. His gift creates fear, for everyone has secrets, and he can find them. Most people don't trust him. He has traveled far and wide, and seen more than most magical folk ever will. Because of his gift, he has found hidden tombs, previously undiscovered, and treasures that seemed impossible to find."

Daniel's eyes turned bright at the sound of hidden tombs.

"Will I get a chance to talk to him while he is here?" he asked with interest.

Richard was surprised at the attention Daniel was showing to magical training until Daniel said, "Will he tell us about the tombs, and what he saw in them?"

"I'm sure he would be happy to tell you about some of his exploits, but he will be here primarily to teach Darkess. He is a busy man, but I am sure that he will have plenty of time at the party."

Darkess wanted back in on the conversation and butted in. "What exactly will he be teaching me?"

Angela was the one to answer this with a motherly tone due to her granddaughter's rudeness.

"Let us worry about that young lady. It's months away. Can't you let anything be a surprise?"

"I didn't tell you I could talk to animals. That was a surprise." Darkess said through her smirk.

"Dark-esssss," Richard said, reprovingly.

The young girl's face dropped into a frown, so Richard decided to keep her mind off of it and give her a lesson now.

"Is every one done with breakfast?" Richard asked.

Nods circled the table.

"Lessons from your new curriculum will start today. How about a new version of a child's game? Count fifty heartbeats, then come into the kitchen and find me. Rules: Only you can find me by touching me," he explained.

Darkess had loved this game for years, and her face was beaming. Richard saw the look on his granddaughter's face and decided to add a challenge to the old game.

"New rules apply here. You can use all of your powers but one – no channeling."

"No channeling! That's not fair!" Darkess stated hotly.

"You didn't think I knew how you were finding me, did you? I could feel you pulling on my powers, trying to discover what I was. I shall know if you cheat."

Richard opened the door to leave and decided to add one more thought.

"Every magical being has a magical aura. Feel for it."

The door closed behind Richard, and Darkess' face tightened in concentration. She was determined not to channel her grandfather's powers, but how do you feel an aura? Darkess thought long and hard, almost forgetting that she was supposed to be counting.

Inside the kitchens, it was fairly dark when the large chandelier wasn't lit. Roxy did most of the cooking and cleaning for the family. She had stockpiled crates up to the ceilings and covering most of the windows. Richard raised his finger to his lips, winked at the small pink-haired witch, and turned himself into a crate. Roxy was used to the magical games commonly played here in the castle and returned to her work, shaking her head with a smile. Moments later, the entire family entered through the same door. Roxy was surprised they all were involved. Not wanting to give away any clues, she turned from them and chuckled as she walked toward another exit. On her way outside, she said.

"Good luck! I'll come back when you are finished."

Darkess' eyes roamed the room, doing a random inventory on the regular items. A large oven, shelf full of cauldrons, baking table, butcher table, table and chairs, stacks of crates, and burlap sacks. Odd utensils hung from a ceiling rack too small to be a human, so Darkess returned her eyes to larger items. Everything seemed normal, nothing out of place. Deciding to go about her search another way, she sat on the floor and crossed her legs. As she closed her eyes, she began to concentrate.

Angela was pleased at the way her granddaughter was trying to find Richard. Deciding to watch how this played out, Angela took a seat. Darkess rolled her head around on her neck and straightened her spine;

her breathing was deep and even. The oddest prickling feeling ran up her neck and crept over her head, causing her to shiver. Darkess knew it meant something, so she concentrated on it. She opened her eyes. Looking behind herself, she saw the door Roxy had left by. Darkess thought she was probably using her powers, that is what she does. Darkess turned in place, now facing that door. Blocking all she could feel from that direction, Darkess concentrated on the rest of the room. She felt five distinct presences in the room. A grin crossed her face, and with a devious voice she said,

"I feel you Grandfather. Now all I have to do is narrow it down."

Darkess looked at where each person was located in the room. Her father's presence was very weak. She mentally pinned the aura with the person. With her eyes closed she pointed and spoke.

"Grandmother is in the chair, Mother is across from her…Father is by the basin, and Tanner is next to the hall door. Roxy is outside that door, and Grandfather is right next to me."

Darkess had pointed directly at each person with her eyes closed. She opened her eyes, crept over to her grandfather, and sat upon him grinning. Richard transformed back into himself, and Darkess was sitting on his back. Richard groaned loudly in mock pain.

"Alright now, get off an old man and help him up."

Darkess jumped up quickly, grabbing his hand. Using her magic, she pulled him to his feet. Then she sat him gently down, as she had pulled him right off the floor in her excitement.

"Very impressive," Richard exclaimed. "It only took you a couple of minutes to find me, and…you never cheated. Very nice indeed. Why don't you go and find something to do until lunch? Then we will be learning about truth potions, who and what they will work on. What do you say?"

Darkess wasted no time running for the outside door. Roxy returned to the kitchen and said,

"That was a slick one. She is doing quite well."

Angela chimed in with a laugh.

"You're telling me! I thought he was that huge cauldron over there."

"Very funny," Richard said smiling.

Daniel was flabbergasted. He was almost never present for training sessions, and he was impressed with both his daughter's and Richard's powers. Silver added her feelings.

"Well I can't do that. I didn't feel anything except magic in the room."

Richard was smiling, thinking of Darkess' growing powers.

"She is going to be a very powerful witch. I hadn't expected her to find me the first time. I sure am glad she is on our side. Whatever she has to face on that far away day will be sorry it ever stepped into her path."

≈

Two days had passed, and Darkess was working on her own pot of truth potion. She checked her notes, reviewing what had to be done on the second day of brewing. Stir clockwise seven times, then counter clock once. Add a sprig of mint to counteract the bitter flavor, and steep for two weeks. Underneath was a smaller note (mint flavoring-add to tea for best results). Darkess covered her cauldron with a scrap of wet leather and levitated it to a high shelf out of the way.

Pulling out her candle chart, she studied it for a moment. Making a list of the supplies she needed, she devised her own spell. While her grandfather was away in his office, she collected the ingredients. She spoke as she placed each item.

"One black candle; to induce a deep meditative state. One gray candle; to neutralize any negative influence. One brown candle; to steady my concentration."

She lit each candle with the tip of her finger. Pulling three stones from her cloak, she laid them out in front of the candles.

"One amythest crystal; to induce meditation. One azurite stone; to stimulate visual images. One chunk of lapis; to penetrate subconscious blocks."

She sat down in front of the candles and stones and pulled out a small knife. Pricking her finger, Darkess dripped one drop of blood on each candle. Closing her eyes, she concentrated on her mother's power, trying to force a premonition. She wanted to know what they wouldn't tell her. She wanted to know now. Richard had taught her well. She had done her research and was using her knowledge. She kept her breathing deep and even. She wondered if her mother was too far away to channel her powers. Darkess recalled the story of Victoria, and how it had taken her time to learn to channel at a distance. She just wanted to channel through the floor. Her mother wasn't too far away, but far enough that she concentrated all the harder.

"Connect us by our blood, let me use her power for but a moment. Please give me a premonition with my mother's power," Darkess whispered.

Darkess swiped up the stones. Smearing them with blood, she clutched them to her chest and concentrated on her mother.

It was as if she had been slapped in the face. A vision hit her hard. She opened her eyes, and they were white, just like her mother's eyes when she received a premonition. She saw herself a few years into the future. She was in a cave, holding a crystal by a piece of leather, and it was spinning madly. When the crystal stopped spinning, she followed the direction it was pointing. The vision went dark. Suddenly she was standing in a long room she had never seen, and a lavender mist was surrounding her. She saw purple for a flash, then it was over. The vision was finished. Her eyes cleared, and Darkess realized that she had never moved from her seat. Her knuckles were white from clenching the stones. As she opened her hand, the stones rolled to the table. Her mind felt cloudy, stuffed with cotton as she looked about the room. All seemed normal. Seeing the magic mirror on the wall, she went to it.

"Show me, me."

The reflection remained unchanged.

"Show me my mother."

The mirror became liquid, and it showed Silver running up the stairwell towards this very room. Darkess knew she had been caught. Her mother must have felt the pull of her powers. Maybe she had seen the same vision. Slumping down in her chair, Darkess waited for her punishment.

Silver burst through the door with Richard hot on her heels. Darkess expected a good chewing and crossed her arms in defense. But to her surprise, her grandfather was grinning from ear to ear. Silver then explained that she had had a vision as a piggyback rider. Silver had a vision of Darkess having a vision, and they met somewhere in the cosmos. They caught her red handed with the spell ingredients in front of her.

"Well done, my dear, well done!" Richard took Darkess by the arm, and quickly asked,

"How did you do it?"

Darkess recited the words and told why she had picked the tools she had used. Silver's eyes began to sparkle as Darkess spoke. Silver was excited as she spoke to her daughter.

"Tell me what happened. What did you see?"

Darkess explained the lavender mist and the room she was in. Then there was the direction crystal. But what most excited her was what she had looked like, and she described herself in great detail.

"That is something. I saw the same thing, down to the last detail. Only you had that premonition, I didn't. It was as if I was floating above you, but I saw the vision through your eyes. It was thrilling. And different."

They all just sat there for a moment, letting it sink in. Silvers eyes were smiling as she thought now she could get a premonition whenever she wanted. Richard was not thinking quite the same thing, but that it was an amazing feat that Darkess had done. However, he could see his daughter, and knew she would want to use this but shouldn't.

"Magic happens for a reason Silver. While on one hand what Darkess did was splendid, but it should not have been done. She knows better than to borrow powers without asking in such non-necessary times. On the other hand, your power will progress with time, and forcing it will not help you. It will only end in disaster. Magic happens for a reason. Let it occur, as it will with your power. Don't force it, or sometimes, what you get is not what you want. And it may not be accurate, or to be worded better, before its time, not finished growing yet. Do you understand? Both of you?"

Both witches shook their heads, thinking on what he had said to them. Richard let it sink in before he changed gears and let his excitement take over.

"Did you see anything that may be familiar in the room where you were? Anything at all?"

The two witches looked at each other and shook their heads.

"No father, there was nothing else." Silver said with a crooked grin on her face.

"This is nothing to get snippy about. You know I'm right on both hands. And you know we should write down what you saw, whether it's real or not." Richard said, looking at both girls.

"The more clues we collect, the better off we will all be." Darkess said.

"Looks like Darkess is doing the teaching now," Silver winked at her daughter.

Richard retrieved their family's spell book, laying it in front of Darkess. Handing her an ink and quill set he said lovingly,

"I think it is time for you to make your first entry into the book. A first working spell of your very own. How to channel a premonition, or rather, how to force a vision. Very good my dear."

Taking the quill, Darkess smiled proudly and began to write.

≈

It was time for dinner once again at the Vallencourt Castle. Roxy had whipped up a feast in honor of Darkess' first spell. As the food floated around the table, a tapping came to the window. Richard read the letter after he had filled his plate.

Richard,
How are you? I'd be honored to help with Darkess. I will most definitely be at your party. Not sure if I will be alone or not. I'll be bringing something special. Thank you for thinking of me.
    Janine

Once again, Darkess threw questions at Richard, who put up a brick wall.

"It's for your birthday, and you are not allowed to know. You are just going to have to learn to have a little patience. Maybe we should make a potion for patience."

Richard winked at Darkess between the steaming bowls then said,

"Dig in everyone. Today was a good day. Praise that we have plenty of food."

☼

The next morning Darkess awoke to Chakra rubbing himself along her hand.

"I'm awake," she said.

Chakra walked around her purring. He ended his trip by sitting on her chest and looking at her closely.

'Your grandfather just got another bird delivery,' Chakra thought.

Darkess practically threw Chakra across the room as she vaulted from her bed. She dashed to the chest and grabbed her clothes, hastily dressing. Running out of her room and down the corridor, Darkess headed for the castle painting. As soon as the painting had cleared enough space for her, she squeezed through and pounded her way up the steps. She burst into the tower, finding Angela and Richard reading the letter together. They stared at her, waiting for her to catch her breath.

"And just where are you going in such a hurry?" Angela asked.

Darkess gulped from being out of breath and croaked,

"Chakra...told me...that you got a delivery."

"Oh, he did, did he?" Angela eyed the cat at Darkess' feet.

"Big mouth," Richard said to the cat.

Richard went back to his reading, and Angela pulled out a chair for Darkess. Just the thought that her grandfather might tell her who the letter was from made her sit up straight and still. She folded her arms on the table, doing her best to look like the perfect little angel. Richard finally sighed and said,

"Oh, alright. It's from a wizard named Belthazor. You'll know him from the annual festival party from years past. Remember the vampire that danced with Jori last year?"

Darkess' eyes got as big as saucers. She did remember.

"He is a wizard? Not a vampire?"

"Jori was the only actual vampire at the party last year. All of the rest were costumes or transfigurations," Richard explained.

"How do they know each other?" Darkess asked. "Because of you?"

"Belthazor has a fleet of ships. They met on the water. His ship was under attack, a pirate raid. The story goes that he had frozen some of the pirates with a spray of water. Then he fogged in both ships, using it for cover to escape. The amazing part of the story was that he escaped with his entire ship in tact, as well as his crew and the cargo. Jori had been flying over, looking for her dinner, and was so impressed that she landed to talk to him. In his haste to protect his ship, he sprayed Jori with water and froze her. What he didn't know was that such a small amount of ice can't contain a vampire. Her strength outmatched his, and she broke free, showering ice all over the deck. Shocked by the explosion, Belthazor covered his face, and within seconds, Jori had tied him up. To make a long story short, after a long talk, they are now friends. He helps magic folk and creatures move about the world unseen by mortals."

Darkess was absorbing everything her grandfather said like a sponge. She stared at her grandfather, waiting for more. Richard shifted in his seat, cleared his throat, and added,

"He will be one of your tutors. He has traveled the world's oceans and will be teaching you about the creatures that he has encountered – good, bad, and indifferent. He's seen more on the ocean than Brutus has on land. He has much he can teach you. Now, does that quench your neverending thirst for knowledge?"

Darkess decided that would be enough for now and raised one eyebrow as she said,

"I guess. But you know I will be back for more."

Darkess turned to leave, but her mind was wrestling with thoughts of enchanting something here in the tower so she could hear what was going on when she was elsewhere. Unknown to Darkess because she hadn't read far enough into the family's book, the tower was guarded against such things. No prying eyes, ears, or even teleportation was possible into the tower room. Only Vallencourt blood could come and go from the tower, but no one could break the charms hidden to defuse magic from prying. Many generations of magical protection made it impossible to snoop, so it would only frustrate Darkess to try until she becomes the Elder of the Castle. The Elder has the special family book containing all of the reversal spells and where all of the charms are hidden, along with some other choice family information on the castle and its secrets.

It was as if Angela could read her granddaughter's mind.

"Don't even think about it, young lady."

Darkess' shoulders slumped, and she shut the door on her way down the steps. Once the door latched, Richard finished the letter.

Richard,
It has been some time since I have heard from you. I am intrigued by your invitation and will be attending. Due to a prior engagement, I will be late, possible very late. Hope it is not a problem. We can discuss the child when I arrive.
Belthazor

Richard and Angela's eyes were aglow with excitement. The next phase of Darkess' training will begin in the middle of the autumn season, the beginning of a new year. Angela smiled at her husband as she whispered.

"Perfect."

Richard grinned back at her and said, "Indeed it is."

≈

The autumn season was in full swing with all of the party preparations underway. The yearly celebration was only days away, and Angela was looking through the garden. She was out checking on the last of the gourds and pumpkins in the fields. Tanner Silent Feet was out working with her. He was a loyal and most trusted friend to the family as well as a gardener and hunter for the castle. He comes from a long line of tribal medicine men and healers. Tanner grew the biggest and best of everything he touched. He also helped Angela with her herb and flower gardens. Between the two of them, they kept many of the locally grown potion plants in stock, because freshness can help considerably in potion making. Tanner also had very good connections with various traders that frequented the area with goods from other climates and countries. No matter the ingredient, Tanner could usually find it.

Angela was checking on the amounts of crops, trying to see if there was enough on hand to make it through the long winter ahead. Darkess picked at anything interesting, finding the last of this and that. Adding several small gourds to her basket, she dug deep into the weeds for another she had just spied. Tanner pulled up a dried old flower with a large root ball from the ground.

"Tell me, do you know what this is?" Tanner asked Darkess.

"It's a dried up old flower," Darkess giggled.

"Yes, but what kind was it? Why did we grow it?"

Darkess' body took on a more serious posture. Her face sobered to a grin as she answered,

"It was a purple flower with a yellow center called Echinacea. It is for infections and good health."

Tanner was mildly surprised. She had actually been listening to him when they were in the fields. Pulling a root from his pocket, he tested her again.

"What is this?"

Darkess took the root from Tanner, dug her nail into a small section and sniffed it.

"Goldenseal. Mostly used as a medicine. It cleanses the body and removes infection."

Tanner shook his head and smiled. He was again impressed.

"Do you see that bee over there?" Tanner pointed.

Darkess nodded her head, remembering the incident with her grandmother, and said,

"I don't like bees very much. But they did teach me to freeze. So I guess they aren't all bad."

"That bee is going back to its hive to make honey from what's left of the flowers."

"Ooooh, I love honey."

"Do you know what honey is?" Tanner asked.

"Of course I know what honey is," said Darkess as she smirked at Tanner.

Angela had edged her way closer, pretending to be busy but listening to the lesson.

Tanner shook his head.

"I don't think you do. You must look deeper."

Darkess stood there with her jaw slack. She had no idea what to say.

"The honey is food for the young and the hive. We eat it also. But did you know that it too is a medicine? It can save lives."

Angela was looking at Darkess and was sure that Tanner had her full attention. He had found something she did not know, and she was hooked.

"Battle wounds that get red and painful with infection, can be fixed with honey. It pulls the fever out of the wound, and the sickness gets better. We plant the best flowers next to the hives. It helps make powerful medicine," Tanner explained.

Darkess looked at her grandmother, then at the bees and said,

"I never knew that something so little could be so helpful."

Tanner handed another basket to Darkess to fill, saying,

"Every thing has a purpose. Some have more than one. The trick is to find it. Once you know what it is, it can be possible to save a life, maybe even your own. Your grandmother may not always be around to heal you. You must learn to protect yourself with knowledge about the world around you…from the herbs in the garden to the bugs in the fields and the animals in the woods and water."

Letting this sink in with Darkess, Tanner looked for more stragglers on the vines. Angela had all that she needed and was headed back to the castle.

"Darkess dear, bring up the rest of the tiny gourds when you are finished. But take your time."

Squatting down and squinting, Darkess searched for the last of the hidden gourds. Angela winked at Tanner as Darkess ducked behind the vines. Then Tanner went on with his lesson.

"Have you ever watched a storm blow in?" he asked.

Darkess mumbled "yep" from behind a clump of leaves.

"And what did you see, besides black clouds and things blowing around?"

Once again, Darkess looked clueless as to what the answer was.

"What do you mean?" she asked.

Making it easier to see Darkess and the last of the harvest, Tanner sat on the ground.

"Where do all of the animals go? They don't all live in the barn."

"I suppose they go and hide in the woods," she guessed.

"Some do," Tanner said. "And some go under ground, in caves or hollow logs, and some just hide under the thick brush. The thing is, they know it before we do."

Darkess looked at him confused and seemed to be waiting for an explanation.

"They feel the world moving around them. They feel the very changes in the air. If you pay attention, you can feel it also. It changes the pressure in your joints. Smell is another way to know rain is coming. However the animals seem to know first, so watching them is a good way to know when it will storm and how bad it will be."

Tanner moved to another area, and Darkess was quick to follow.

"The thickness of a wolf's coat can tell you how cold the winter will be. And when they lose their winter coat, you can tell that the warm weather is here to stay. The amount of food a squirrel hides for winter tells us if it will be a long or short winter. Wooly worms in large amounts can mean an early winter. The arrival of the migrating gross beaks means that summer is just around the bend. The world is full of signs to help you survive. All you have to do is learn and pay attention to them," Tanner said as he stood next to the fence pulling seedpods from a vine.

"These are the remains of a summer flower," he said. "Morning glories. Do you know why they are so named?"

Darkess shook her head no.

"They open when the sun starts to creep into the sky. Then when the sun gets to its appex, the flowers close until the next morning. We have them here for their beauty – and for a few potions. These are never to be eaten. It will give you bad dreams, and you will get very sick," he warned.

Darkess was making observations she had never made before. Tanner was much more than the quiet gardener and hunter; he knew lots of things. He knew magic more than he had ever let on before. She was seeing things in a new light, and she liked it. Tanner made learning fun. She loved her lessons in the castle, but outside had a special feel she enjoyed with Tanner. Darkess wanted to stay out here a little longer, but her basket was full, and she knew her grandmother was waiting. Tanner seemed more interesting now than he ever had before, and she smiled at him asking,

"Do you think I could come down here and visit you again sometime?"

Tanner gave her a full-toothed smile, one she had never seen before. They had connected in some special way, and it felt good.

"You are more than welcome here any time. I rarely sit still for long, and you may have to follow me around the grounds. Think you can handle that?" he asked.

Darkess nodded her head with excitement.

As she turned to leave, Tanner called out to her.

"By the way, if you ever find your little friend Chakra missing, he very well could be at my cabin. He visits me often."

"Thanks Tanner, see you later!"

As Darkess weaved her way around the remaining husks of plants, Tanner hollered, "Watch the world around you. Your powers are not the only magic in the world." He waved at her as she made her way toward the castle. He did so love to make her think.

☼

When Darkess rounded the corner of the castle courtyard, she saw her grandfather speaking to a rather mysterious man on the porch. She watched for a few moments, trying to figure out who he was, and why he was here. Trying to stay hidden, she thought that she could sneak up on them. However Richard turned toward her and looked her directly in the eye. Darkess was caught, and she knew it.

"How does he do that?" she whispered.

Walking boldly around the corner toward her grandfather, she acted as if nothing had happened. Adjusting a few of the gourds as she walked and still pretending to be innocent, she wandered toward the men. Richard knew otherwise, though. He glossed over the fact that his granddaughter had been rude and called out to her,

"Darkess, come over here for a moment."

Thinking that she was in for a good tongue-lashing, she dropped her shoulders and walked towards him.

"I would like you to meet someone. This is Philineas Nagel. And this is my granddaughter, Darkess."

Placing her basket on the ground, Darkess went up to the man and shook his hand.

"Pleased to meet you," she said.

Darkess looked into his eyes and realized they weren't human. Her cheek made the tiniest twitch, but she didn't want to get into any more trouble, so she pretended not to notice. Making a beeline to her basket, Darkess retreated inside.

Angela was digging through the basket she had brought in earlier. Darkess walked briskly across the room to her. Nearly out of breath, she asked,

"Did you see that man talking to Grandfather?"

Chuckling, Angela smiled at Darkess and said.

"Noticed his eyes, did you?"

Just then, Silver came down the steps into the room. She was carrying a basket full of potions and a small book.

"Noticed whose eyes?" Silver interjected.

Angela looked at Silver, then Darkess. Both had expectant looks on their faces.

"It is a very long story, but I will give you the short version. Philineas used to be a familiar."

Darkess' eyes got very large, and Silver sucked in a huge breath.

"Like Chakra?" they asked in unison.

Angela blinked, raising her eyebrows at their reaction and continued making centerpieces for the tables as she spoke.

"Yes…like Chakra. He helped quite a few young witches when they came into their powers. And he did it very well. He had done such a good job that he was given younger and younger children to protect each time. Once a witch or wizard accomplished their individual powers or was adopted into a clan if not born to a magical family, he would move on to a new child. Philineas' last child was a witch of extraordinary power, but she was young and inexperienced. A demon with the power of invisibility wanted to kill the girl and steal her powers. Not knowing how to find a demon she couldn't see, she was frightened. The demon had killed her parents but had made too much noise, waking the child and giving her time to hide. Philineas chewed open the sack of flour in the kitchen and spread it as far as he could. He then crouched behind the large sack, waiting for the demon to show himself. It didn't take long before tracks appeared on the floor. Philineas dug through the flour furiously spraying it in the air and giving the demon an outline. Philineas then tried to lure the demon. Not taking the bait, the demon merely threw something at Philineas. As he was looking for the little girl, the demon wiped at the flour, growing angrier by the moment. He walked past the little girl's hiding spot, so she snuck out to run away but was heard. The child had no choice now. She saw him clearly and her fear got the better of her. Screaming, she threw up her hands, and the demon exploded into a puddle of bits.

Philineas feared the demon wasn't alone, so he took the girl out through a window and escaped into the woods."

Darkess was intently listening to the story while Silver worked on the potion bottles. Angela's hands were flying over the ribbons she was weaving for the displays, and she continued.

"The next morning when Philineas lead the girl from the woods unscathed, the girl's grandfather was so pleased she was unharmed that he made Philineas human as payment for a job well done. He now lives out his life as a human. He has very little power, but his knowledge is vast, for he retained his memory as a familiar. And oh, yes…his eyes. I believe the old wizard didn't realize that he hadn't finished the transfiguration, and Philineas was too much of a gentleman to mention it."

Finishing up the piece she had in her hand, she laid it off to the side, and began a new one. Darkess was thrilled by this cat becoming a human story and had many questions.

"Will Chakra ever become human?"

"It is possible, I suppose. I am not sure where Harlow got Chakra…or how long he will be with you. He is not your average familiar. You were born into a magical family, and you had your powers in the womb. Plus, he was given to you when you were eight. He didn't appear to protect you out of nowhere. Not all magic is as measured as your potions, you know."

≈

Later that day, the three witches were deep into their project for the upcoming party when Chakra came bounding down the steps. It was as if he wanted to get their attention when he hopped up on the table.

"How long are you going to stay with me?" Darkess asked the cat.

Chakra licked his paw, rubbed his ear, and scratched his head. It was as if he were stalling for time. Chakra looked at Darkess with his bright green eyes, focusing on her shining blue ones, and thought.

'I will never leave you. But even if I did, you are not ready enough for me to leave yet.'

'Ready for what?' Darkess projected.

'I'm not exactly sure. But whatever it is, you still have much to learn. You should be as safe as you can, I do know that.'

Chakra's ears were swiveling around trying to locate something. His head swung around, and he focused opposite of the wall where Philineas and Richard were standing.

'Who is talking with your grandfather? I am getting an odd reading of this creature on the porch.'

Darkess burst into a peal of laughter, making both maters turn towards her. Darkess told them what Chakra had said then explained it all to her cat. Angela and Silver watched as the young witch talked to her familiar. As most magical folk can't speak this fluently with their familiars, it was an incredible site. Chakra ran to the large oaken door and clawed at it. Meowing loudly, he wanted out.

"Must be old friends," Darkess said as she closed the door.

Making wreathes for the door was one of the projects Darkess had requested. She dug through the baskets looking for just the perfect pieces. Silver watched Darkess then went fishing for ideas.

"What do you want for your birthday?"

"I really want a unicorn, but I will settle for my own horse. It is not for me to ask, though. What you give should be good enough for me. The party is what I really want."

Angela loved the fact that her grandchild was not a materialistic witch, but she knew Darkess was smart enough to try and finagle things into going her way, even birthday requests. Darkess taught her maters as much as they taught her. Sometimes it was amazing how much maturity resided in the little girl before her. She always saw everything different than anyone else in the castle. She often found pleasure in the simplest things and was amused by the smallest objects. Angela knew Darkess would be pleased with her gifts, but she would also check into a horse.

Just then, the door opened, and Richard could be heard talking to his guest. Chakra was right next to them as they entered the room.

"Then it is settled," Richard exclaimed. "You will be the entertainment for the party."

He clapped Philineas on the shoulder, and the two men chuckled as they walked further into the room.

"The entertainment? What do you do?" Darkess asked, intrigued.

Philineas bowed to the little witch. Replacing his hat on his head, he said,

"I have a set of bewitched instruments, and they play with me. I also have a few instruments for others to play, like you, should you want to join in."

Darkess smiled at the cat-man. She wanted to know more about him, and Richard could see it in her eyes.

"Why don't you two go over there and set up the stage the way you want it," he said. "If you need anything, I will be over here."

Silver picked up her spell book and flipped to a marked page. Pulling a couple of bottles from the basket, she recited from the book and threw the bottles at the floor, walls, and ceiling.

"Let this room be beautiful from ceiling to floor,
Bewitch this room for our party from window to door.
Spiders, bats, ghouls, and ghosts
Let this enchanted room dazzle even its hosts."

With those last words, a thick fog erupted from the potions as the room began to transform itself from normal to spooky. Giant spiders were spinning webs in the corners of the room while a horde of bats materialized and flew about and landed on what looked to be a cave ceiling. All of the furniture turned black and grew clawed feet. A moaning wail came from the wall periodically, as if it contained entombed spirits yearning to be free. Every crystal that hung in the room turned either black or silver to fit the theme. The entire room looked dark and sinister and was covered in cobwebs. Richard looked around with an expression of delight

"Splendid, my dear, absolutely splendid."

Across the room, the stage area stood empty, awaiting the magic that would transform it from bare walls and floors to a curtained stage suitable for entertainment. Digging through the potion basket, Richard took three bottles and headed for that area.

"Well, young lady, do you have any ideas about the performance area this year?"

"Blood red drapes…with silver star dust floating around," Darkess said with a smile.

"Hmph, I shall do my best."

Richard cleared his throat and recited a spell from memory.

"In this space we need a stage,
For magic acts with quite a range,
Trap doors and blood red curtains,
Smoke with silver star dust,
Make this the perfect place
For some to entertain us."

Richard tossed a bottle at the ceiling, wall, and floor. The bottles emitted a red and silver smoke that blanketed the entire end of the room.

Blood red curtains grew down from the ceiling, and a wooden riser came out of the floor. The sides became the wings of the stage, with a changing room and tables. Large silver structures erupted from the ceiling, emitting the perfect amount of light for the performance area. Smoke swirled about the floor, cascading off the stage where the curtains were parted. Silver dust hung in the air, giving a misty appearance. Darkess' eyes grew large, and her jaw hung open when two silver crystals as huge as pillars tore through the floor and soared all the way to the ceiling to make the front corners of the stage. Darkess clapped vigorously as the room came to a rest.

"It's wonderful, Grandfather!" Darkess exclaimed.

"What do you think Philineas? Will it suit your purpose?" Richard asked.

Without a second's thought, he answered.

"I would be honored to play on such a wonderful stage. Now, should we put everything in its place?"

Philineas grabbed the closest crate and heaved it up onto the stage. Darkess was more than happy to help with the heavy moving. When she reached the door, she peered out at the courtyard.

"Do you need all of those crates?" Darkess asked.

"Just the ones with the X on the side."

Darkess flipped the tarp off the wagon and revealed the crates beneath with a flick of her hand. She pointed to one at a time, wagged her finger, and watched it float through the air, inside the castle, and over to where Philineas was standing. When all of the properly marked crates were inside, Darkess recovered the wagon, closed the door, all with the flip of her hand. She smiled with pride as she returned to help set everything up.

"You are a right handy girl to have around, the perfect stagehand," Philineas said.

Darkess smiled at his words, for many people treat her with far more respect than she prefers. Chakra bounded up on the stack of crates, trying to get Philineas' attention. Darkess asked Chakra if he had known Philineas before he'd been turned human. Chakra replied in thought,

'He is a legend in the world of magic, especially for familiars of all kinds, not just cats.'

Before Chakra could say another word, Philineas turned and said.

"I'll be buggered. I can hear you."

Chakra gave a loud meow, and Richard said, "Hear who?"

Darkess was taken aback. She looked baffled at the cat-man and projected a thought to him.

'Can you hear me?'

"Of course I can hear you." The reply was said aloud.

It was now Richard's turn to look baffled, and he asked,

"To whom are you talking? Is there a spirit here?"

Darkess and Philineas smiled at Richard, and Chakra purred loudly, rubbing himself on the crates and marking them with his scent.

"Evidently, I still have enough cat in me to hear Darkess' thoughts when she projects them. I heard her talking to Chakra."

"Well, I'll be...did you hear that Ang? She can talk to Philineas!" Richard said excitedly.

"Uh-huh." She had heard the entire conversation. She smirked at her husband and continued working.

Darkess had never been able to communicate with a human before, and she was sure it would help the two of them become friends. How much fun this birthday was going to be, she thought.

"It does make sense. He was born a cat," Silver stated.

'What a wonderful present, being able to project to you,' Darkess said.

'Well, I believe that fate made me human, and destiny brought me to you. Magic happens for a reason. Sometimes we know why, while other times, it reveals itself over time. If magic has taught me anything at all, it is to follow my instincts and pay attention to the signs. I'm here for a special reason...that I know. And when you need me, we'll both know it.' Philineas winked at Darkess.

☼

The snow was blowing hard, feeling like ice chips on his face, as he trudged through knee-deep snow. He is searching for a hidden cave entrance, a cave in Asiattica that belonged to the Yen Coven of the Corundum Mountains. This particular cave looks just like any other cave high in the mountains, save one thing: a small engraving of a dragon's head. Ice coated everything, and the snow was deep, making travel difficult, and finding a small engraving nearly impossible. Guarded by an array of spells and charms meant to allow only members entrance, the cave itself looks like some large carnivore had recently abandoned it. With the amount of bones strewn around, it would discourage any human occupancy. However, this man knows that few people venture this high in the mountains, especially in a storm like this one. Fewer still know about the cave he is hunting. From nearly any vantage point, the cave's mouth looks like a fissure in the rock, easily missed by the untrained eye. He has been searching for this cave for nearly 50 years, and his patience is wearing thin from his near misses and the false information he had bought. He had killed several men trying to get better information, paying out hundreds of gold and silver pieces in his quest to find the Yen Coven and where they met.

Finally, a few weeks ago in a bathhouse near the edge of the Glass Desert, he finally caught a break. He overheard the cursing of a young drunken man. In slurred speech, he rambled on about his cursed family and how they always left him out of everything. The Corundum Mountains were big enough to hold them all, but he was always left to guard his family's home. As the man trudged through the snow, he relived that fateful night in the hot house. He had snuck around the bathing rooms, quietly slipping around the sliding doors to where he could hear the drunken fool better. He wanted to get a look at the man, and he listened and waited for his chance. The drunken man babbled on and on about the mark of the dragon, and how he was an important man and should be included, not left at home.

In the snow, the cloaked figure smiled beneath his hood. He could almost hear the fool's voice in the deep howling winds. He took solace in the bathhouse warmth all the way up the mountainside as his memory played on. He could hear the oils being poured into the water, followed by hot stones making a loud hiss. The attendant had finished her work and was intending to leave the room when the cloaked man stopped her. He handed the girl a gold coin and grinned as he whispered instructions in her ear. The girl returned to the room, poured another drink for the man, and began to rub his shoulders. The attendant took a sip of the liquor to help her deal with the customer and his ramblings.

"Really, I think your family is rude for not taking you along," she said as though she really cared.

This begun a stream of self-centered chatter that spewed from his mouth for nearly an hour. Our cloaked hidden man got more information than he had ever thought he could get from one person, at one time – especially without force. Among the many things mentioned were a tattooed mark, a cave in the Corundum Mountains, a big fall festival, and a great treasure with untold power. That was enough for the dark figure. He quickly dressed and left. That very night, he bought a horse and traveling supplies, and set on his journey up the Corundum Mountains.

For the next couple of weeks, the cloaked figure had traveled along the busiest trading routes, tracking the information he had received. Taverns were the best place to get what you needed, sometimes without paying for it. He had heard a few things about odd goings on in the area, even the mention of magic one time. He was sure the Yen Coven was near, and he was pointed in the right direction. He pushed on toward the top of the mountain. The wind changed, and he was temporarily blinded. The storm was building, making visibility only inches. It was as if the storm didn't want him here. His black cloak was turning grayer with every passing minute as the snow packed every crack and crevasse of him and the mountain. The sun no longer penetrated through the steely clouds overhead, and it seemed night was coming early today.

He clawed his way up the mountain at decreasing speed. This is pointless, he thought as he groped blindly along the rock face of the mountain. He was no longer in his memory, but in the present. As numbing cold chewed at his limbs, he felt around for some sort of shelter. Stumbling forward, he rammed his shin into a large boulder. Grasping the rock with one hand, and messaged his shin with the other, he decovered it was about thigh high. He found the boulder's top and ran his hand along it, finding a fissure on the other side. Stooping down he ran his hands along the outer edge of the crack. He discovered that it was reasonably deep. Making a fireball, he peered into the crevasse. Nothing appeared to be inside, and it looked large enough to hold him. He crawled into the hole with room to spare. Just being out of the wind made him feel warmer – but not warm enough. Removing his cloak, he secured it around the opening to keep the wind and snow out. Using a fireball for light, he searched his little haven. Finding some twigs and leaves; he brushed them into a pile. Using his asthema, he dug the cracks out to find more burnable material. He made two piles: one to burn and the rest to add later. As he stared into the flames, he remembered what his parents had told him. He could almost hear his mothers' voice.

"Search for the surviving members of the Draco Coven. They lived in Brumalia for three generations and were formed by three different magic families. In the old times, when magic was practiced in the open, and the world was a different place, two wizards and a witch believed that they were the last surviving keepers of white magic. The magic wars had been long and arduous, killing most of those using white magic. They knew that they were going to lose, and they believed they could protect the last surviving dragon eggs: the three sacred eggs of Galdore. Once the eggs were claimed by black magic, we would rule the world and all its powers.

"The founders of the Draco Coven were Vladimir of the House of Handorv, Zelena from the House of Copperstone, and Elijah from the House of Maplewood. Vladimir was the only living heir in his clan and sole possessor of the eggs and the knowledge of how they worked. He also knew that he alone stood no chance in protecting the eggs. Making a pact, the three of them moved to Brumalia with the hopes that they would remain hidden, thus the eggs would be safe. For years, they grew in numbers, passing down their knowledge, with one egg being protected by each family.

"Deep in Mount Colossus, they made a cave with magic. Their magic was hidden away for forty years before it was revealed to a fishing village resting on the edge of Brumalia. They were discovered when one of the younger wizards tried to marry a local girl. When she found out he had powers, she grew very afraid, and told her father she no longer wanted to marry the boy. The father had liked the boy, until he too heard that the boy had powers. Magic brought death and troubles they did not need. He remembered the magic wars. All of the humans who witnessed those wars remember, and thus they fear magic, white and black. Once the town folk heard about the magic near their quiet little village, they took up arms to rid their community of this problem. Little did they know, they were playing right into your father's hands.

"Yes, that's right, your father was then searching for the eggs. And the angry mob that intended to rid themselves of magic led your father directly to the only protection they had, the coven. That was long before he met me, of course. Takar, are you listening to me? This is important. You must know this in case anything would ever happen to us. Boy, now pay attention. We must get those eggs, and the books that control them. Now, as I was telling you, your father and a few of his partners used magic to stay one step ahead of the townsfolk and arrived quicker. Unfortunately, the entire clan was waiting for the townsfolk and ready for an attack. Four demons stood no chance against an entire coven that's ready and waiting for a fight. Two of your father's partners were killed quickly along with several clan members. Your father, one of his partners, and several of the clan sustained severe injuries. Your father escaped, having only glimpsed the cases that held the eggs. He was the only one that attacked the clan and lived to tell about it, that I know of.

"Before your father left Brumalia, he paid a man to watch out for unusual people moving about or moving away. Regrettably, the only information your father received was that some of the regular customers had stopped coming around. In fact, they had disappeared completely. The deduction was that the coven had split and gone in different directions under the cover of magic. Much later, the word came that there had been three ships hired for travel to unknown destinations. Memory charms must have been used on the crew, for once the ships returned, neither of the crews could remember where they had been or how long they had been gone. The surprising thing was, they had been paid, and handsomely. Only the white magic idiots would pay when they could have gone for free. Nevertheless, the trail had gone cold.

"For nearly 140 years, your father searched for some hint as to where they had gone. Had they reunited somewhere? Or had they gone their separate ways permanently? Then your father met me. I had heard a similar story about the three eggs in a fairy tale when I was a child. I was raised a white witch, dabbling in the dark arts in secret, and Jakara knew so much. Between the two of us, we knew much more, and we continued the search together. You must know what we know."

Takar could almost see the glint in his mother's eyes as he remembered their talks of power and knowledge. She had been the driving force that had begun this search for him. It was the memory of his mother that kept him searching for these three lost needles in an enormous haystack. Realizing that his small fire had burned down to nearly ashes, he added some more debris to it. Checking to see if the storm was letting up, he inched towards the opening. Pulling free a small corner of his cloak, he took a peek, and was bombarded by snow. Closing the crack between the cloak and the stone, he stared back into his fire and returned to his reverie. His mother's face begun to swim back into focus, and her voice filled his ears. This was a different memory, though, for his mother's hair was streaked with gray, and she had an anxious look in her eyes as she told him more about those fascinating eggs.

"Takar, we have found something. One of the eggs surfaced. We have found a peddler who has crossed the Corundum Mountains and claims to have seen the dragon's head signet. We are going there now to check on this. If he has lied, he will die for his insolence. But if he is correct, we may have the first egg. What a thrill, I can almost taste the power…"

"No, you stay here, no arguments. Await our word. We will send for you. No, your powers are still too unstable." She walked out of the room, leaving him home alone again. In a small way, he commiserated with that poor fool in the bathhouse, always getting left behind. He got angry thinking that his mother had just left him alone like that. The look he had seen in her eye was what he thought was desire, and maybe greed. But to anyone else, it was the distinct look of insanity. The search for power had driven her to the brink of madness. Takar saw the image of his parents holding hands and teleporting to the mountains. It was the last time he had seen either of them alive.

The fire was dwindling again, and the fuel source was getting low. Takar dug deeper into the cracks between the rocks around him, pulling out more dry leaves and twigs – anything to keep the fire going a little longer. The wind howled like a banshee, and his cloak rippled and bucked. Pulling his collar up around his small ears, he rolled over and tried to find a more comfortable position in the rough fissure he was huddled into. Situated once again, he brushed all of the debris he could find into a pile. He dug deep into his breast pocket for the letter had had carried for almost 50 years. The parchment was yellowed with age, and its corners were soft from being in his pocket on these trips. The fold lines were nearly worn through, but he loved it and always brought it with him on his searches. Since it was the last thing he had ever received from his parents, he considered it a will, with a last wish added in for good measure. It was a really small note with blood dripped on it. Whose blood he wasn't sure. Opening the letter for what was probably the thousandth time, he read.

My son
Sorry I have to write this. Your father was killed, trying to save me so I could warn you. The peddler was a set up. He works for Copperstone of the Yen Coven. They are still after me. I cannot return home yet. It's not safe. At the base of the stone archway is a hollow stone. Tap the faceplate three times. Inside you will find all we have on the eggs. Do not look for me. Be smart when acquiring information. Whatever you do, no matter what happens, think twice before you act. I will be home as soon as I can. I love you.
    Mother

The letter no longer brought tears to his eyes or a lump to his throat. What it did do was reinforce the anger he had toward this coven and its murderous ways. It made him want to kill them, every last one of them. The anger inside him was fresh when he read these words, and it helped to keep him warmer in this tiny tomb of a cave.

"I will avenge your deaths. I will make them pay. I will find the sacred eggs and live the life you dreamed. I will get the power and rule the world."

Takar swore this out loud, as if they were able to hear his every word. The glint that was in his mother's eyes when he was young was now mirrored in his own.

The madness was setting in. The more he searched, the more it progressed. It had taken him years to find the spot where his mother had died. He had used all of the magic at his disposal and a considerable amount of money in his search. When he had found her body, it seemed as though she had been hiding in a barn. It had been set ablaze to ensure she did not escape. Human bones were found buried under ash and rubble. As Takar dug through the debris, he found a necklace his mother had always worn. He had finally found her. Evidence showed that the walls had collapsed in, smashing his mother into the cellar and cooking her. Takar had wept in pain and anger. Clutching the bones to his chest in a pitiful show of human emotion that he now suppressed with every ounce of his demon half, he had cried himself out of tears. Moving passed pain and fully into anger, he had collected the bones and dug through the ashes until he found everything that had belonged to her. Wrapping the bones and jewelry in his cloak, he had climbed out of the mess that he was in to what was left of the floor above him.

Something had glinted in the crack of a splintered floorboard. Stooping down he retrieved it. Covered in black soot and slightly melted, he hadn't recognized it. He decided to shove it into his pocket for later inspection and slipped into the darkest shadows, worried that someone might see him. Running through the side of the burned out shell of the barn, he had hauled what was left of his dead mother on his back. With his cloak and pockets full and his clothes filthy, he snuck through the trees to a small shack hidden deep in the woods.

The shack was abandoned, unused in years. He laid his mother on the floor, and began to inspect the jewelry. It was all in pretty bad condition, so he cleaned everything up the best he could. He polished the necklace with extra care, as if it could make his wish come true and bring his mother back to him. He had forgotten the damaged ring in his pocket until now and quickly retrieved it. Caked with ash and soot, Takar rolled the ring in a rag to loosen the grime. Holding it up to the candle, he was shocked at what he found. Dropping the ring as if it were poisonous, he watched it rock in the candle light on the floor. It was theirs, he thought. It was from the Yen Coven, a dragon's head shone clearly on the face of the ring. It was his first piece of real proof that they truly did exist. He was on the right trail. The ring had had stone eyes, but the heat had collapsed the metal and the stones had dropped free; however, the shape was perfectly obvious. Inspecting it more closely, he picked it up and read the inscription inside the band. It was still too dirty, so using a twig; he dug at the letters, trying to clear them. Rubbing the band on the rough fabric of his pants, he polished the raised parts of the ring and revealed the words. Soot still caked the engraved letters, but the band was polished clean and shone brightly in the candlelight. Rotating the ring, he read three words: Passion, Strength, Courage.

"What's this?" Takar had asked himself as he placed the ring in his coin purse.

Takar can still remember that long arduous trip, with the bones of his mother in a special velvet bag he had made for her final rest. At the time, his only destination had been home. When he reached home, he buried his mother and immediately returned to the dungeon to consult more magic in hopes of finding something to bury of his father. Along the way, he could search for clues to the eggs. They were linked, these eggs and his father. Almost 50 years he had searched, and while he lay in this cold crevasse, he was seeing the most important parts in his mind all over again.

Mulling over everything in his search, he had never seen anything of his father's nor any physical evidence of the eggs, except maybe the ring. He could almost feel it burning in his coin purse against his leg. Rolling over to make his pocket more accessible, he pulled his purse out and dug for the ring. The misshapen dragon's head showed clearly on the polished metal, and Takar read the words inside once again. Passion, Strength, Courage. Was this the motto of the Copperstone Clan? He just knew he was getting close to some sort of answers. He could feel the magic in the air up here. He just had to be close to that cave. Replacing the ring back into the coin purse and back into his pocket, he rolled over to get more comfortable. He wondered how long this storm would last. Listening to the sound of the wind and the rippling of his cloak, he began to drift off to sleep.

≈

Takar woke with a start. Not sure where he was for a moment, he stayed stone still and waited for his eyes to adjust to the lack of light. He could smell the embers from a fire burning, but he could see no fire. Raising his hand, he scraped his knuckles on the roof of his tiny rock tomb and remembered where he was. Rolling over, he added the last of the debris to the embers and blew the fire to life. His stomach started to rumble when the smoke hit his face. Reaching for the bag he had stuffed into the crack, he pulled out some jerky and a travel muffin for his dinner. Laying his food next to the fire to warm it some, he pulled his cloak away from the stone enough to look out. He saw the legs of a mountain goat for a second, and then they were gone. But the goat's movement meant the storm had passed, at least for a while. Animals don't hunt or forage in the middle of a storm. Takar ripped down his cloak and slipped from the crack.

Outside the wind was brisk, so Takar wrapped his cloak tightly around him. Stooping back down, he retrieved his food and his bag. Shoving the food into his mouth, he kicked snow on his fire, extinguishing it. He checked to make sure he had not left anything behind and resumed his trip. The sun was starting to get low in the sky, although the climb up the mountain seemed to make the sun last longer than usual. It was as if he were climbing as fast as the sun was setting.

Takar scanned the mountain with fresh eyes. With the snowstorm moving on to hinder other travelers, he thought maybe he could find the cave within the next day. In two days time, the coven would be together celebrating. If he hurried, though, he may just beat them to the cave and steal their great treasure. Walking for almost an hour since he had left his small hide out, he thought he saw something in the rocks, but it must have been a trick of light on ice. He was just thinking that sometimes-bad luck can lead to good luck when he saw it – something shiny in a crack of the rocks. Pulling out his athame, he dug at the ice, imprisoning a brass object with a loop on it. Making a fireball, he held it near the object, trying to free it. The heat melted the ice, making a small waterfall with a rockslide that produced a button. It looked like an ordinary button, but upon closer inspection revealed the letter J upon its face.

Memories flashed before his eyes, and he saw his mother and father leaving him home as they came to this very mountain range. Takar gazed at his father in his memory. He saw the cloak his father wore, with the shiny brass buttons all emblazoned with the letter J. He had finally found a piece of his father. Then anger flared in his chest. A button? They must have annihilated him. Or, he could have lost it. No matter what happened, he wouldn't make the same mistake, and he would make the clan pay with treasure and their lives. His heart rate accelerated as he thought, I'm on the same path as my father and mother. I'm nearly there.

Are there any more clues? Takar searched the area slowly looking for any item out of the ordinary. Finding nothing, he continued his climb again. Takar put the button in his coin purse along with the ring and one of his mother's burnt broaches. He walked on with more urgency. Knowing that he had only an hour of daylight left, he begun looking for a new place to stay the night. Walking in the dark was too dangerous. He could miss clues, get injured, or worse – be seen by someone. Secrecy was needed at all costs.

He began to pick up pieces of wood, but kindling was few and far between in the deep snow. Takar spotted a black space in the rocks ahead. In his excitement, he dropped the wood and hobbled through the snow towards the opening. It was another small cave, but larger than the one he'd taken refuge in earlier. But it was not the clan's cave. He walked slowly into the cave with a fireball ready. He found that the cave was almost high enough to stand in. It was deep enough to sleep two comfortably with room for a fire. Sweeping up the debris in the cave, Takar dropped his fireball on it. The pile burst into flames, and Takar went on a search for more wood and maybe a fresh hare or ptarmigan for dinner.

≈

Returning to the cave, his cloak full of wood and a skinned hare hanging from his belt, Takar had a smile on his face. Setting up a sort of spit over the fire, he began to cook his dinner. He used his cloak as a door, leaving only the top couple inches uncovered to allow the smoke to escape. Now he was hidden from any prying eyes, creature or not. He knew someone might smell the smoke, but with the darkness and the wind, it would be hard to locate his position without magic. Takar spoke aloud.

"I need this cloak to seal this space,
Attach it here to close this place,
Guard me here while I rest,
Make this cave a safety nest."

As he said the spell, he traced the border of the cloak, pressing it to the rock with his finger. The cloak clung to the entrance just as it had before.

"Thanks, mom." Takar whispered as he looked at the new door he had made.

He talked frequently to his mother, and occasionally to his father, and he pulled out his trinkets as he lowered himself into a sitting position. Laying the ring, the broach and the button next to the fire, he ripped a leg from the hare and ate his dinner as he stared at each piece. When he had filled his belly, he lay down, still staring at the trinkets, and drifted off to sleep.

≈

Takar woke with a wicked smile on his lips. He had had a dream that he had found the coven. Using his powers he had scared them, and as they were caught off guard, he started throwing fireballs. Killing them one at a time, he screamed how he was doing it out of revenge for the murder of his parents. He was pretty sure they had no idea who he was, and they probably didn't even know who his parents had been since they had died before any of these pathetic humans were born. But as far as Takar was concerned, children and grandchildren could pay the price, as he, his parents' child, now carried on their burdens. As he killed the fifth clan member, the day came crashing in on him, and the dreamed evaporated. And though he hadn't gotten to the eggs in the dream, he had taken the dream as a good omen for the day about to begin.

Eating some more of the hare, he packed up his trinkets, wrapped the rest of the hare in a waxed paper and tucked it into his bag. He pulled his cloak away from the surface of the rock enough to see the beginning rays of sunlight streaking the sky with reds and purples. Ignoring the beauty of the morning, he scanned the area in front of him. Deciding to wait for a little more light, he let the cloak fall back into position. Sitting in front of his fire again, he picked at the carcass, nibbling on what little meat was left. He thought to himself, today I will find one of the eggs.

He stared into the fire, thinking about what his father had left him: drawings of a wooden box with intricate carvings of dragons on the sides and top. There were ancient symbols with writings about what they may mean and the possible size of this box. He had made all of the notes on where he had searched, and his contacts around the world. But Takar concentrated on the pictures on the box – a double pentagram, connected by two points, one in black and the other in white. There was a full dragon on the top, and the same head shape from the ring in his pocket was on one end. Hammered silver made the hinges, handle, and clasp. He stared at these images in the fire until he realized the sun was streaming into the cave through the vent he had left for smoke to escape.

Takar jumped to his feet, keeping to a crouch, and ripped his cloak from the entrance. Throwing the cloak around his shoulder, he scanned the mountainside from his hiding place. The only sounds were from the wind and the crackling of his fire. Stepping out into the full sun, he scanned the horizon for any movement. He saw nothing except the occasional dusting of snow in the breeze. Turning back to his cave, he kicked snow on his fire then started back up the mountain once more.

Takars' beady little eyes darted here and there as he looked for the cave entrance. He looked for signs of human life, a trail of some sort, anything that might point towards a coven. The mountain was almost completely barren land once you reached this altitude; only occasional scrub brushes dotted the terrain, which gave Takar a much wider range of sight. The weather had cleared, and he could see for miles. With his hopes high, he walked on for hours, searching every crack he came across. He would walk up and over a hill, then down and around it, making sure he hadn't missed a thing.

A rockslide above Takar made him jump from where he was to a large boulder. He stood completely still and listened closely, looking for what had caused the slide. Seconds clicked by, and he saw nothing. I'm very jumpy today, he thought to himself. Maybe it was melting ice. Slowly, he inched around the boulder to see if there was anything there when he came face to face with a snow leopard holding a young mountain goat in its jaws. Takar slowly raised his hand, and as the leopard began to growl in protection of its hard earned dinner, a fireball appeared. The fire scared the cat that instantly dropped his goat, and sent the leopard running off at full speed, and in an instant, it vanished over the next ridge. Closing his hand, the fireball was extinguished, and Takar decided it was time to fill his belly. Clearing the boulder of snow, he sat and ate. He could hear his mother's voice.

"It is better to eat a small amount of food when you are on the move. Too much will slow your reflexes and make you vulnerable."

Takar refilled his water bladder with melted snow, packed his things and moved on. After only a little while, he realized he was walking on a trail. He had been so intent on finding the cave he hadn't even seen the trail, and his pulse jumped a notch. Not sure if it was an animal or human trail, he decided to mark his location, and follow the trail for a bit. If necessary, he could return to where he was now and ascend the mountain further. Takar urinated on the rocks just as an animal would, leaving no signs of a human mark to give himself away, and followed the trail.

The snow was deep here, except for on the trail, and it seemed to broaden out the further he walked. This trail was deffinately not made by animals. He quickened his pace at the thought, and his body began to tingle with anticipation. Just a little further up the trail was a sharp bend that detoured the trail around an old rockslide. Reluctantly, Takar slowed his pace when he reached the outcropping of stones and peered around them carefully. With his acute senses, he believed he was alone and slowly walked around the pile. There was a large stone shelf above his head not twenty feet away. The years had brought down many slides around this shelf. The entrance to a possible cave could be seen in the middle of two piles of debris, and a few bleached out old bones were scattered about.

Takar could feel heat rising in him, his palms were sweating, and he could hear his heart slamming inside his chest and ears. Could this finally be it? There were no signs of humans, or animals. Not a sound could be heard here, except for the slight breeze. The mouth of this fissure was facing directly east. Edging ever closer to the fissure – looking, smelling, feeling for any other creature – Takar inched closer. The giant shelf above him bridged one side of this mountain to the next and made a walkway from one point to the next. But Takar was under it, searching for an opening. Looking overhead, Takar slipped quietly around and scanned the area around him. In the corner of the slides, he spotted crystals.

"Gotcha," he whispered.

Takar pulled out his slingshot, a childhood toy he'd learned proficiently enough to carry to this day, for hunting and other purposes, like knocking warning crystals out of place. He knew that he felt magic here. He had found the clan. It took him several minutes to locate and remove all of the crystals, six in all, and one talisman. That's when he saw it: the mark, the sign of the Coven of Draco. The engraving was on one of the fallen rocks and filled with ice, but the wind had scoured off all of the snow or he would have never seen it. His heart felt as if it would burst, and an evil glint filled his eyes, as he looked deeper into the slide of rocks. Feeling confident that he had found the outer protection charms, he stared at what he thought was the entrance only to find it was a solid wall. Scanning the rock piles, he spotted a fissure large enough for a man. It was jagged and sharp; but inside, the tunnel was smooth, bored by magic. Once he was inside, he found that light didn't penetrate very far. Worried that a fireball would give away his location, he pulled out a large crystal and concentrated on it. A dull red glow emanated from the crystal, showing him the tunnel led in two directions. Crouching down, he searched the floor for signs of use. Both ways looked well worn.

Deciding to use an old method, Takar pulled out his mother's broach and laid it on the floor.

"Show me the direction that this broach went."

Spinning madly on the floor, the pointed end where a bobble had once hung pointed to the left tunnel. He hadn't been sure that his mother had made it this far, but luck was with him. He slowly walked into the left tunnel and listened. He could hear running water somewhere but nothing else. Knowing the clan members could show up anytime for their festival, he was extremely cautious. He knew they could be coming from anywhere, by foot or by magic. But it had taken him two days from the town below, and it would take them less time because they knew where they were going. He had beaten them here, but by how much time? He had to hurry. Just then, the tunnel opened up into a small cave with a sitting room set up.

There were a couple of benches, a table, some torches, and a bunch of crates off to one side. Takar took a torch from the rack. It was full of oil, and he sparked it. Hide in plain sight, Takar thought as he pulled his cloak tight around his head. He walked further into the room and saw that there were two more choices if he wanted to proceed. Takar knew he was on his own. His mother had not made it this far, not if his father had sent her back. Which one to take? Walking to the tunnel on the left, he poked his head inside and listened. Nothing. The tunnel on the right had the sound of running water. That was what clenched it for him. He was taking the tunnel on the right.

Holding the torch high to keep the light out of his eyes, he proceeded down the tunnel, following the sounds of water. Anticipation building inside him, he had to tell himself to calm down.

"Focus," he whispered.

Be smart. Take it slow, he thought. The tunnel bent slowly to the right, and Takar followed the curve until he saw a light. He groped for his water bladder. Taking a drink, he swallowed hard and licked his lips, trying desperately to keep his mouth from drying out from his nervousness. Takar put out the torch, laid it aside, and inched his way towards the light. He clenched and unclenched his hands as he tiptoed closer to the entrance he could now see. As his eyes adjusted to the light, he peeked into the cave and spotted two people. This is too easy, he thought, and waited for a moment.

One older man was napping in a large padded chair down in the largest area of the cave. The man was snoring. He would be easy. Takar smiled. The other was a woman, a pretty woman, who was sitting at a desk writing in a book of some sort. Takar smiled again. Catch her off guard, and she will be the first, he thought. But something made him wait for a moment. Movement off to the side caught his peripheral vision. There was a third person in the cavern. A young wizard was levitating a book. When the woman spoke to him, the book dropped to the floor, causing the boy to turn towards the woman with a disappointed look on his face.

"Don't play with the book, read it," she said.

This was the distraction that Takar wanted. Stepping forward, he pulled a fireball out of the palm of his hand and heaved it at the woman. Before the boy had a chance to think, he too was slammed into the floor by a fireball. Both victims had been hit right in the center of their chests and were dead before they hit what was behind them. Two down – one to go, Takar thought. But the old man had vanished. When Takar had thrown his second fireball, the man had been there, startled and awake, but there. Where could he have gone? Takar scanned the room, his ears pricked for any sound.

"Damn," he whispered so softly that he hardly heard it.

Stuffing his hand deep into his pocket, he pulled out a handful of powder, and with a deep demon breath, he blew the powder around the room. If the man had teleported, he must act quickly. If the old man was merely invisible, he must find him, or the table would turn rather quickly against him. Takar was in luck. Not only did the powder make the man partially visible, he had blown the dust directly into his face. Coughing and rubbing his eyes, the old man seemed unsure if he could be seen or not. He stood frozen in place, trying desperately to clear his eyes while holding his breath. That was his downfall. He was the perfect target for Takar. A wicked smile spread across Takar's mouth. The corners of his eyes wrinkled with excitement that radiated throughout his entire body. With tingling going from his heart to his fingertips, Takar opened his hand and a fireball appeared.

With the sound of the fireball in his ears, the old man dropped to the floor, trying to focus on what the sound was through blurred eyes.

"Tell this to your ancestors when you see them. I have avenged my parents. And now…I have the egg."

It seemed there was venom dripping from every word and a split second later the fireball sailed into the old man's chest. Trying desperately to stay invisible, his powers and strength spent, the old man fell to his knees in flames, and then fell on his face. When the last breath of life finally left the man's body, the flames were extinguished.

There was a savage look of triumph on Takar's face as he stepped over the smoldering corpse. Deeply inhaling the smoke as he passed over, he said, "Ahh, the smell of victory."

Now for the crate, Takar thought. He turned in circles to ensure he was still alone and scanned for the crate he had seen in his dad's drawings. He began to walk through the cavern and saw many things he wanted to investigate. He did pocket a few small things, but time was of the essence. He had no idea how long he would be alone, or if the old man had sent out a warning before he had died. He turned his attention to the crates around the room. Unfortunately, there were several stacks of them, but the one he had in mind would not be stacked so carelessly. This was a very special crate. It had to be in a special place. Moving with the speed and stealth of a cat, he circled the room. Nothing resembled the drawings his father had made. He checked between two large tables and along the back wall of the room. The outer edge of the room held nothing for him, so he made his way into the center.

There was an altar and the desk where the woman had sat with something covered by a canvas.

"Oh yes," he whispered as he made his way past the dead woman to the stack of hidden items.

Pulling the canvas from its resting place, he found what he had been looking for. Checking for traps, Takar made a circle around the stack of crates. He looked closely for talismans or anything that may be dangerous. He checked the floor for trap doors and the ceiling for things that could fall and found nothing that looked dangerous. Holding his breath, he pulled the crate free of all the others. When nothing happened, he took it to the desk and lay it down.

Inspecting the box closely, Takar found no lock, but the clasp refused to budge. In his anger, his forehead flattened into something that looked less human and more like a ferret. His nose elongated, and he shook with rage. Then, almost as quickly as he had turned, he turned back.

"Damn," he whispered as though to calm himself.

Takar flipped the box up on end, looking for a release button but finding none. Gently laying the box back down, his attitude in check, he rubbed each of the engravings, feeling for anything that might trigger the clasp to open. He leaned over the box, checking each side. He felt a warm sensation coming from his pocket. Putting his hand to his pocket, he clutched what was inside. His face lit up like a light, and his breath quickened as a grin crossed over his face.

"The ring," he remembered.

Quickly he reached deep into his pocket, pulling out his change purse, and rummaged for the ring. When he found it, he held it up, slid it on his pinky and reached for the clasp once again. The clasp slid easily in his hand, and the lid opened smoothly. Takar's hands shook as he reached for the red velvet bag inside. The shell of a black egg with smatterings of red spots became visible, giving Takar a shiver. Reaching slowly for it, he touched it. Sucking in air quickly, his entire body twitched and his eyes fluttered. He was exhilarated to the point of sexual arousal. He groaned with excitement and with a ragged breath, he said, "I have finally found it."

The egg was warm to the touch and both smooth and rough at the same time. He could barely tear his eyes or his hands away from it. He seemed under a spell as he stared at it, breathing hard quick breaths. The tarp that had once covered the crate shifted, bringing Takar back to reality. Paranoia set in, and he covered the egg and closed the box. He must hurry, or he could loose his treasure. No body was going to steal his egg, he thought. He must get out of here alive, and with the crate intact. Fear and lust filled his eyes as he tenderly grabbed up the crate. His ears were intently listening, and his shifty eyes darted about.

Moving quickly and smoothly, Takar crossed the cavern and headed to where he had left the torch. Relighting the torch, he dumped his pack on the ground.

"Enlarge," he whispered.

The bag suddenly grew large enough to hold the crate and all of his belongings. Stuffing the crate into the bag and his things around it, he tied it shut. In one swift movement, he swung the bag onto his back, secured it firmly, and began his retreat from the cave's heart.

When the smaller room came into view, Takar stopped to listen. Not a sound emanated from it, so he slipped into the opening to have a look. Nothing had changed, and he was still alive. Heart racing, palms sweaty, his breath nearly catching in his throat, he crossed the room headed toward the exit and freedom. Flexing his hands, Takar readied himself for a fight. Blowing out the torch, he replaced it, trying to cover his tracks. Pulling out his crystal, he lit it with his mind and proceeded out the tunnel. He reached the bend in the tunnel, and behind him, he heard a blood-curdling scream. Someone had found the bodies, and he hadn't reached the opening yet. Fear heightened his senses and quickened his pace. His mind raced. Had there been another room with some one in it? Did someone teleport into the cavern? Takar decided to run for it. The tunnel seemed much longer now than it had earlier. Had he taken the wrong passage?

Just when panic was starting to squeeze at his insides, and long cold fingers of dread began to creep up his spine, Takar saw light up ahead. The entrance? His heart frozen with hope that it was indeed the way out, he darted for the opening fissure in the rock. Just before he was in the open, a scalding hot orb of energy slammed into his arm, causing him to duck. Two more orbs sailed passed his head in the time it took him to produce and throw a fireball in retaliation. His opponent had ducked himself and remained unharmed. Takar produced two fireballs, threw them in succession, and rolled out the entrance.

Once Takar was free of the cave, he threw an array of fireballs at the fissure, discouraging anyone from following too quickly and partially blocking the cave entrance. Smiling, Takar turned towards the path leading away, and the smile dropped off his face. An old wizard with a long gray beard and the hood of his white cloak pulled up to cover his face blocked Takar's path. A voice pulsed from the white hood.

"The egg is not meant for you."

Takar threw a fireball, ducked behind a rock, and yelled,

"I have it now!"

The fireball had missed the wizard by mere inches. The wizard had then returned fire, also missing. It seemed to be a momentary stand off.

"Power, I need more power," Takar whispered through gritted teeth.

He pulled at his strength with every ounce of his demon side, turning his head ferret-like again. He made a fireball that was double size and sent it hurling towards the wizard. Somehow the wizard had anticipated Takar's move, for he too had created a bigger orb, and when the two collided, the explosion sent an enormous shockwave that knocked both men to their knees. Anger sprung up in Takar's chest like a hot coil. He was going to outthink that old man. What did that old man want the most?

"That's it," Takar whispered, a foul grin spreading across his face.

Takar put both hands out in front of himself, extending his arms. He read the wizard's desires, and he had been correct in his assumption. Being almost certain that it was only the two of them in this battle, he lowered his arms, channeling his power of projection. A shimmering image of the egg appeared in front of him, along with an image of himself. The image was precisely formed so Takar looked around for his escape. Seeing a crack in the rock leading all the way to the shelf overhead, he began to climb. There were perfect foot holds along the way, making his escape quick. Once Takar reached the top, he dug for a few stones, and as he held them, he moved his image directly into harm's way. It took only a second before the image of Takar was nailed in its midsection with an orb. Takar quickly threw the stones he'd found down the side of the mountain, making his apparent death look more real as his astral body was thrown over the edge by the blast of the orb. The image of the egg lay on the ground, safe as the old wizard approached it. Swift as a mountain goat, Takar disappeared over the edge of the rocks with the real egg and made his escape. The shelf was long and sturdy, and Takar sprinted across it. When he reached the face of the opposing mountain, he knew he was safe. Out of the battle zone, Takar began his decent and let the image of the egg he had left behind vanish. There was only a heartbeat before he heard the pitiful cries of the old wizard.

"Noooo!"

The old wizard had found his heart's desire; however, when he tried to touch it, it had evaporated right before his eyes. The old wizard knew he had been fooled, and his painful sobbing was a testament to his heart. Takar could almost feel the desperation in the old man, and he quickened his pace. Picking the most difficult terrain, Takar walked through the deepest snow, on the side of the mountain where the wind was the weakest. He knew being younger and stronger wasn't necessarily an advantage in the world of magic, but he was using it for all it was worth. After a few minutes, Takar hadn't heard a thing behind him, and he almost began to worry. He had been sure that the old wizard wouldn't give up that easily. Reinforcements, Takar thought. How much time do I have? Scanning the mountainside, Takar was looking for the cave he had spent the previous night in. He knew he wasn't in the clear yet, and with knee-deep snow, slick icy rocks, and a heavy box on his back, he trudged on as quickly as possible.

The going was tough, and Takar slipped now and again, trying to keep his footing. He was beginning to think that he had taken the wrong path in his haste to get away when he smelled his urine marks. The very marks he had made earlier. He knew that he had a ways to go, but this time, the trip would be shorter, and more direct. The clan could show up at any time, so Takar stopped to get a breath and listen to what was around him. Silence. It seemed even the wind was trying to make sure he was heard in his escape. On he went, with fear as his fuel, looking for any cave he could climb into. That's when he found his cave. He couldn't believe that he had found it so quickly. When he reached its mouth, he stuck his head inside, and threw a fireball at the wood still lying there. Gently, he lay down the crate and pulled a piece of chalk from his pocket. He squatted down to write on the floor in a very childlike manner. He hobbled around on the balls of his feet, trying not to lose his balance as he drew out a pentagram on the floor. Once he had finished, he added several symbols around the edge, one between each point.

Takar took a velvet pouch from his cloak, opened it to check its contents then returned to the crate. He rubbed the crate with loving tenderness, picked it up, and placed it in the center of the pentagram. Stepping into the pentagram, he straddled the crate. The velvet pouch sat in the palm of his hand, and he dug down deep to get a large handful of the powder. He sprinkled the powder all around the points of the drawing on the floor, and smoke began to emanate from it. Takar smiled, and said, "Home."

The smoke began to swirl around him like an inverted tornado, completely obscuring the view of Takar and the crate. The smoke went up to the top of the cave and dissipated. Takar was gone, and so was the crate.

☼

A round table, taller than usual, sat in the center of a dungeon room. There was a huge iron chandelier above it, and it started to vibrate. The lamps flared to life as a swirl of wind blew in just next to the table. The vortex of air started at the ceiling, landed on the floor, and dissipated. Where there had been nothing before the wind, now stood Takar with the crate between his legs. Looking around the room, making sure he was alone, he picked up the pack and put it on the table. Carefully pulling the crate from within, and setting it in the center of the table, Takar circled the egg's crate, knowing there had to be hidden drawers, maybe with other treasures. He touched every carved area, feeling for a split or imperfection but found nothing.

Then Takar started feeling the top, the dragon's scales, claws, and teeth. He found the fire was in a kind of groove. Pulling out his money pouch, he laid the burnt broach, the ring, the newly acquired button, and a small knife on the table. He would use the knife if the ring failed to make it release. He put on the ring once again and passed it over the dragon's breath. Once again, nothing happened. Takar scooped up the knife and began to pry on the fire. The instant the fire was free of its carving, a red mist flowed from the wood bewitching the dragon. The carving came to life. Blowing a red mist-like fire, raising its head, and using a single claw, it pressed a button its head had been covering. A secret compartment popped out of the top. It contained a book. It was a leather bound book, containing all the instructions for hatching, use and control of the egg. Takar took the book out of its cradle and lay it down next to the crate. Opening the lid with a wave of the ring, Takar pulled open the draw string and stared lovingly at the egg. Touching it, a shock something like electricity went through him. His eyes glistened with excitement as he massaged it.

"It's mine…" he breathed in a greedy voice.

He could hardly take his hands or his eyes off of the egg. But he had to read that book. He had to know more. What do these eggs do? How do they work? Are there only three? Questions were flying through his mind. Questions that his parents had also had. He found there was a page missing. Wondering what had been on that page, he massaged the egg. He was finally getting a fix for his addiction. This addiction that his parents had instilled in him was now coursing through his veins like opium.

He finally forced his gaze from the beautiful red speckled egg to the book not wanting to leave the egg alone quite yet, he grabbed a travel cake and sat down for a nice long read, until he realized that he could not read the language that was printed. Oddly enough, instead of getting angry, he decided to rub the egg and imagine what the book said.

☼

Tomorrow just couldn't get here fast enough for Darkess. And her family insisted on a small family party before tomorrow's festivities began. They thought the amount of guests always took all the attention and spread it way too thin for a proper birthday for their little girl. And since today was the day she was born, whether she liked it or not, Roxy had made a cake for her. It had a tiny bewitched unicorn on the top that ran around every once in a while, magic dust streaming from its horn. Roxy had hidden the cake in a cauldron, away from prying eyes. Dinner was roasted chicken, sweet potatoes smothered in molasses, baked apples with pecans and brown sugar, summer squash and butter, and a heap of steaming biscuits. Darkess loved the food and the attention, but her thoughts were on tomorrow, not tonight. Even when they brought out the cake, it only held her attention for a moment, what with the prospects of the magic that will be performed tomorrow. Not to mention the guests.

The guest list was in Richard's pocket, and it was on Darkess' mind. She was waiting for him to get in just the right position for her to pull it out. Once everyone had stuffed themselves to near gluttony, and they were all leaning back in their chairs, Darkess asked for her presents. She knew they were waiting for the last moment to get her excitement up, so she just asked. Then her grandfather relaxed enough, and Darkess struck. The list went sailing through the air to her.

"Give that back!" Richard demanded in mock protest as he swiped the air trying to catch it.

Darkess caught the list and ran to the door before anyone could catch her. Her excitement grew when she saw that Harlows name was, for once, on the list. She also saw the arrival time was somewhere around midnight.

"That's all I needed," Darkess said with a syrupy smile, floating the list back to her grandfather while folding it in midair, just to show off.

Angela gave her granddaughter a sideways glance.

"That's all you needed, huh? Isn't there anything else?"

"Am I supposed to find my presents? Or what?" Darkess said with a crooked smile and one eyebrow cocked.

"Me first. I have a small gift from your mother and me. I acquired it at the King's museum. Come, sit here and open it," Daniel said.

Climbing back into her chair, Darkess opened the neatly tied little brown package. The brown paper revealed a small black velvet pouch. There was a smooth lump sliding around inside. Untying the satin ribbon, she dumped the contents into her hand, letting out a small gasp. Holding up the item for all to see, she said,

"Oh, it's wonderful. Will you put it on me?"

Darkess leapt from the chair, going to her mother. In her hand was a turquoise cabochon necklace.

"It was from an old witch who lived in Crystal City. She was said to have lived to be 299 years old. They say that this necklace is charmed to protect its wearer from falling from their horse. She said the freedom of her rides on horseback helped her to live to such a great age. Truth be told, we aren't sure that is true, but we thought you would like it," Silver said, kissing her daughter's head.

"Happy Birthday, sweetheart," Daniel said, hugging Darkess.

Richard stood saying,

"Ours is next. But for this gift, you have to follow me outside."

With a mysterious glint in his eyes, Richard proceeded out the door. Darkess looked at her parents, then her grandmother.

"Don't look at me, I'll tell you nothing," Angela said with a devious grin.

Daniel looked at Darkess and said,

"Better hurry…he could be going anywhere."

Darkess took off running, followed by her family. When she reached the porch, she saw her grandfather was headed at a good clip for the stables.

"A horse?" Darkess said, more to herself than anyone else, and took off to catch up.

"Where are we going?" Darkess prodded.

"Wait and see," Richard said and kept walking.

When they reached the stables, the door was shut. Darkess reached for the handle, but Richard's voice stopped her.

"Not until everyone gets here." He placed his hand on the door, letting Darkess' anticipation grow.

When they were all assembled in front of the door, Richard swung it open.

"For me!" Darkess was so excited, it came out in a whisper, and she dashed into the barn.

Several feet from the most magnificent black horse, Darkess skidded to a halt and extended her hand towards the beast. The horse shook its head up and down, as if to say yes, and snorted at her.

"Not only is he for you, he's no ordinary horse. He was bred in the Glass Desert of Imhotepus. A very special breed made for magical beings. They have a much longer life span, and have power. He can communicate with any horse or horse-like creature, and he teleports, anywhere his owner wants to go," Richard said.

"With permission," Silver added.

"And he can sense you. If you are stranded somewhere, all you have to do is concentrate on him, and he will come for you. He is yours Darkess, and you get to name him," Angela said as she finished Richards' speech and patted the great beast on the head.

Darkess seemed dumb struck as she inspected the horse more closely. Tanner saw the family clustered in the barn as he returned from the woods to get a better look at this extraordinary gift. He had heard but not seen this animal, and he was intrigued.

"What shall I name you?" Darkess said, looking at and touching the horse gingerly.

"His mane and tail are beautiful," Silver said.

"What do you think Tanner?" Daniel asked, turning towards the Medicine Man.

In his own quiet way, Tanner inspected the horse as if he were going to buy him, lifting his feet up, and checking his teeth, pulling up the long forelock to check if there was anything hiding beneath. Then he scratched the horse's neck and looked him in the eye. Everyone waited for a response from Tanner.

"White coronets on the front legs, as if he's wearing his finest shoes. A white hoof shape on the forehead, connecting his ears in an arc…that is good medicine. Nice long feathering along the cannon bone and fetlock. He's a young horse, maybe three or four years. He is very healthy and intelligent. He is very special. You must think hard on his name."

Tanner patted Darkess on the shoulder, smiling at her. Darkess thought hard, looking at the horse. She rubbed his nose and looked in his eyes, projecting her thoughts to him for the first time.

'What do they call you?' she asked him.

Not knowing that his new master could project her thoughts, he was surprised, and snorted. He lowered his head, looked her in the eyes, and told her:

'My mother called me Zaphod. The wizard who trained me called me Nightlinger.'

"Than I shall call you Zaphod," Darkess smiled, rubbing her new friend's nose.

"Zaphod, that is interesting, why did you pick that?" Richard asked.

"He said that his mother did. The man who trained him called him Nightlinger, not very original," Darkess commented.

"It looks like you two have a lot to talk about. Tanner, would you stay with Darkess while we go inside? We have something else to do," Angela said.

"Of course, ma'am. If you don't mind, the two of us will take that magnificent beast for a little trip," Tanner replied.

Silver knelt down to talk to Darkess.

"Now you listen to Tanner. And don't go too far. When it gets dark, please come up to the tower room. Your last gift will be waiting."

Darkess looked at her mother, a surprised look on her face. Silver hugged her daughter, and then Darkess went to her father and grandparents, and hugged each of them, thanking them for her wonderful gifts. As the family began to return back to the castle, Tanner climbed upon Zaphod and pulled Darkess up in front of him. As they trotted past the family, Richard called out, "Have a good time!"

☼

As the elder members of Darkess' family made their way back inside, Tanner gave Darkess a most mischievous look and said,

"Ask Zaphod if he is ready for a good run."

Before Darkess could relay the message to Zaphod, the horse took off at a good clip towards the gardens. After he had followed the path out of the garden to the other side, he poured on the speed, shooting off through the fields, jumping the four-foot fences like they were downed saplings. Zaphod ran towards the forest, and it was a smooth and invigorating ride. The bushes were but a blur as they ran on with ever more speed. The feeling was like flying, the air whipping their hair, and Darkess never wanted it to end. She had never felt so free. The forest was closing in fast, and Tanner thought it would be a good idea to return to the castle, so he reined in the horse. They came to a stop next to a tree emblazoned with autumn shades of red and pink, and a small amount of white had also began to appear.

Jumping to the ground, they walked Zaphod for a few moments until his breathing had calmed, then they stopped, facing the breeze. They watched as the sun began to slip behind the mountains. Darkess played with her new horse's mane, and Tanner sat on a nearby stump. He watched the girl with her horse. He knew they were getting better acquainted and didn't want to interrupt. He knew he was merely a chaperon on this courtship. The chemistry between Darkess and Zaphod was better than he had expected, and quicker too. It seemed they were made to be friends. They both love adventure, neither has much fear, and they are both magical beings whose special powers complement each other. If this horse were a boy, they might very well be in love, Tanner thought as he chuckled to himself.

"What is so funny?" Darkess asked Tanner.

"Oh, nothing. Just thinking out loud, I guess. What are you thinking? I can see that look on your face, even in the fading light."

"You know exactly what I am thinking." Darkess said sarcastically.

"Yes. I do."

"Come on Tanner, you and me, just once, from here to the castle yard. We aren't beyond Vallencourt borders...and you know they know that I have to try. Come on..." Darkess whined.

After a couple of seconds, she added.

"They wouldn't have told me his power, and they wouldn't have given him to me if they didn't think that I could handle it. They would have bought me a regular horse," Darkess pleaded.

Tanner gave her the, 'I'm not sure about this' look and said,

"What am I doing?"

Tanner climbed back upon the horse, pulled Darkess up, and asked,

"Do you know what you are doing?"

The glint in Darkess' eyes was almost dangerous as she said,

"No, but he does. And the best part is I don't have to say the destination out loud. He can hear me, so it will always be a secret."

And with that, Darkess thought, 'To the barn,' and everything seemed to get tight, like the world was shrinking. The feeling was almost stifling. There was no air, and the pressure was enormous. But as soon as she started to think, 'This can't be right,' and right before she thought, 'This will kill me,' the pressure was released, and everything started to feel normal again. She hadn't even realized that she had closed her eyes until she opened them. They were back where they had started.

"In all my years, I never thought that I would do that...without the help of a potion." Tanner said with an invigorated look on his face.

"Zaphod, you were brilliant!" Darkess said as she began toweling him down.

The other horses in the barn shuffled in their stalls at the abrupt appearance of a new horse out of thin air. A few of them kicked at the walls, and one whinnied loudly in a protest of jealousy. Tanner taught Darkess all of the things to check on a horse after a journey, down to the hidden treat box in the tack room.

"Sugar cubes?" Darkess questioned.

"Only for special occasions," Tanner warned.

Counting out the cubes, Tanner took one for the horses next to Zaphod, and two for him.

"Shouldn't we give them dinner first?" Darkess asked.

Tanner laughed deep in his belly as he said,

"Rufus will feed them in a little while. It is not good to feed a horse if he's too hot, it could make him very sick. Magic or not, Zaphod is still a horse and must be cared for properly. This stall down here looks to be his." Tanner pointed to the brand new wood carved sign on the door.

Darkess was surprised they had already made a sign, but she was proud and walked Zaphod into his new home. Fresh straw was on the floor, and Zaphod snickered contently. Closing the bottom half of the stall door, Darkess giggled.

"This is kind of silly, don't you think?"

"Guess I never thought of it that way," Rufus said

Kissing Zaphod's nose while scratching under his chin, Darkess didn't want to leave the barn quite yet. But she knew everyone was expecting her at the party, so reluctantly she said goodnight to Tanner and Zaphod. Making her way to the porch entrance and taking the shortest route to the tower room without the use of magic, Darkess thought of her new horse the entire way. Chakra showed up along the way, his cocky attitude visible in his walk.

'So, who's your new friend?'

Scooping Chakra up in her arms, Darkess told her cat the story of the day. The gifts that she had received, the cake, and her evening ride. Chakra's reply came as a surprise to Darkess. She almost thought he was lying in jealousy, until she got to the tower room.

'If you think Zaphod is your greatest gift, you are sorely mistaken. I've been listening in on them, and you have a lot ahead of you. I'll be in your room when you are done. I heard a mouse in the kitchen earlier, and I mean to have him for a snack.'

With that, Chakra leapt from Darkess' arms and scampered to the kitchen. Darkess continued to climb ever higher in the castle, wondering what in the world could they be doing that was better than the magic horse? But the entire way, the reason eluded her. The door leading to the tower was only a few steps away, but Darkess was apprehensive and did not touch the knob. She hated not knowing what was going on. Something seemed different here. A gift in the tower, what could it be? The doorknob turned easily in her hand, but there was a knot in her throat, and her palms began to sweat. Why she was nervous, she wasn't sure, but she felt a twitch in her stomach as she entered the room.

The tower room had its usual warm glow, but the room had been rearranged. Walking to the large table, her family all had smiling faces for her, which eased the tension a little. Richard being the elder, and bookkeeper, asked Darkess to sit in the chair he pointed to. He leaned over the table pushing a small ivory box towards her. The box had an intricately carved woman on the lid. The sides were smooth with a slight curve, making the bottom larger than the top. There were tiny-clawed feet carved on the bottoms of the legs that held onto tiny onyx balls that kept the box about an inch off the table. There wasn't a scratch or chip on it from her view, and Darkess wanted to examine it more closely.

"It's a little chilly in here. Would you stoke the fire, dear?" Angela asked Darkess. Darkess waved her hand without looking, and a large log landed on the fire and engulfed in flames. Richard eyed his granddaughter, took a deep breath, and said,

"This gift is not from us. This box contains the verbal prophecy made by a Vallencourt wizard more than four centuries ago."

Darkess' eyes became huge in her thin face as she listened to her grandfathers words.

"But before we give it to you, before you can hear it for yourself, you must know…you will be entering the world anew. Many things will change. For you are more than just a witch…just as Chakra is more than just a cat, and Zaphod is more than just a horse."

Darkess was more confused than ever. Can't they ever just tell me anything, she thought? I want to know what is going on. I think. She wisely kept her thoughts to herself, listening to her grandfather.

"Alright. Go ahead. Open the box. It will do the rest," Richard said.

He sat down, and Darkess looked around apprehensively as she pulled her chair closer to the table. With trembling hands, she opened the box. A shimmering white mist filled the air over the box, and there was the sound of an old man's scratchy voice.

"A babe born with extraordinary powers that will grow infinitely throughout her life, a babe with hair a flame…with curiosity and wisdom beyond her years…a babe with a heart of love and strength will be born to our line. She will be a powerful woman in many ways. She will be the greatest force against evil to be born in more than 500 years. Her burden will be great, and she will be tested. However she chooses to act, the results will be fantastic. Her destiny will be revealed on the night of the blood moon, soon after the passing of a loved one. Train your daughters well, for they will be the key to the chosen girl's salvation."

With the prophecy concluded, the mist swirled and retreated into the box, awaiting the next listener. Sitting in stunned silence, trying to absorb what the man in the box said, Darkess looked from one mater to the next around the table then back to Richard.

"Who is that man?" Darkess asked.

Richard's reply was simple.

"Wolfbane Vallencourt, a wizard of our line, from many years ago. He was a great seer. He told many prophecies and saw much in his time. He saw hundreds of years into the future, and much of it has come to pass. He saw you and carved this box from what he saw of you."

Rubbing the woman's face with a thumb, Darkess said,

"That's not me."

The denial and misunderstanding were both in her quivering voice. Angela heard fear and was up and around the table. Putting her hands on her granddaughter's shoulders and giving her a little squeeze, she kissed the top of her head. She then pulled up a chair and sat next to Darkess.

"My dearest, you need not be afraid," she promised.

Silver was on the other side of Darkess, and placing her hand on her daughters' shoulders, she said,

"It is you. You, in a handful of years. Darkess, you are the witch from the prophecy."

Shaking her head no, Darkess got to her feet, walked towards the door, and said in a very firm voice,

"It is NOT me!"

Flinging the door open, Darkess jumped through it and slammed it behind her with her mind. As she ran down to the barn, with each set of stairs, she concentrated on the door to the tower, keeping it shut so no one could follow. And it was working. Once she was crossing the courtyard, she forgot about the tower door and concentrated on the barn in front of her. The doors on the barn opened just enough to let Darkess through, and then they closed behind her. Opening the door to Zaphod's stall, Darkess scaled the wall next to her horse and climbed upon his back. Clenching her knees, she thought,

'Pumpkin patch.'

In a few squeezing heartbeats, they were gone.

Appearing in the pumpkin patch not far from Tanner's little house, she prodded Zaphod into a trot down the orchard looking for the hunter. Spotting a fire down by last year's pumpkin patch, Darkess swung Zaphod towards it and headed over. Throwing old vines and debris from the fields onto the fire, Tanner was sweating and covered in ashes. Darkess always heard him say that the ashes from dead things helped to bring life to the soil for the next year's crops. As she rode closer to the fire, Tanner continued to work. Not even looking at her, he said,

"Out kind of late, aren't you?"

Darkess didn't respond to his question, but countered with one of her own.

"Did you know what they had planned for me tonight?"

Darkess flipped her leg over Zaphod's back, rolled to her belly, and slid off the horse as Tanner answered.

"I have known you were special from the night you were born. And no, I wasn't sure they would tell you tonight. But you are growing up and need more from your studies. Knowledge is power, you know."

Darkess began throwing sticks on the fire, and the two of them stood quietly, thinking and throwing.

"So what's so different about me that makes everyone think that I will be able to fight evil and win? Why me?"

The silence descended, except for the crackling of the fire. Tanner collected his thoughts.

"Life is a path. Sometimes the path is even and clear, and we can walk it with ease. Other times, the path is rocky, thorny and uphill. Some would return to the cleared path. But the ones with strength, wisdom and bravery stick to the rough path, knowing it will lead to the proper place for them. You have strength, and it will grow as you grow. You are brave, and young bravery shows us that in the future, you will be steadfast in your quest, facing your fears instead of running from them as you just did."

Darkess got angry with Tanner and said in a bitter frustrated voice,

"I didn't run from my fears..."

Her voice trailed off. There was another silence, uneasy, like the lie was hanging in the air between them.

"Okay," Darkess said. "I didn't run from it, I just needed time to think."

Tanner broke a large limb and thrust half of it into the fire. A shower of coals blew up on impact, making ashy sparks hang in the air.

"Now you are showing signs of wisdom. Some wisdom can be taught, but most wisdom comes with experience. Sometimes the harder road must be taken, and hard lessons will be learned, but it will lead you to a better place."

The fire crackled on, snapping as they threw on more sticks, each lost in thought.

"You know you will have to return to the castle and face your family sooner or later. And they are going to teach you what you need to know to fight your own battles and follow your path through life. No two paths are ever the same, but each has something to show you that could make your path easier without leaving it."

Tanner let that last thought sink into Darkess' sometimes-thick skull and threw another limb on the fire. Darkess picked up the cold ends of the longer burnt limbs and threw them in, making a circle on the fire.

"For hundreds of years, your family has accumulated knowledge in their battle with evil. Now they are trying to use it to help you. You are not alone. Your ancestors are behind you, the dead and the living. Besides, you will not have to fight anything just yet. You are safe here."

Tanner poked at the fire with a long stick, spreading the coals and making the fire roar with the next gust of wind.

"Do you really think that I am this powerful witch?" Darkess asked again.

"You have more power now than most mastered elders. You have never met anyone as gifted as yourself, have you?"

Darkess shook her head no.

"You know that your family would never lie to you."

Again Darkess nodded her head. They may not tell her the whole story, but they wouldn't lie to her, and she knew it.

"Some day you will fulfill your destiny and save the world from a great peril. But for now, I suggest that you not worry about the future. It will get here when it gets here. And I think you should stop your parents' worry and return to the castle."

Unknown to either of them, Richard had used the mirror on the wall in the tower room, and knew that Darkess was with Tanner and just fine. However, Tanner was right, and Darkess knew it. Tossing one last stick on the fire, Darkess smiled at Tanner and said,

"Oh...alright. Will you give me a leg up?"

Tanner grabbed Darkess by the rib cage, heaving her upon her horse. She settled herself on Zaphod, and looked into Tanner's eyes.

"Thank you for talking to me. Will you be at the party tomorrow?"

"I will," Tanner replied.

Turning Zaphod around, Darkess began trotting back towards the barn. Over her shoulder, she called out, "See you tomorrow!"

☼

There were two torches lit by the door when Darkess arrived back in the courtyard, and the barn doors were open. Rufus stood holding a lantern, waiting for Zaphod to return.

"Yer mother is waitin' fer ya, miss." That was all Rufus said as he took his new charge and led him to his stall.

Making her way up the steps and looking for her mother, Darkess followed the torches up to the bedrooms. She heard her mother moving around in her room and knocked on the door.

"Mother?"

Darkess poked her head around the door.

"Have a nice long walk?" Silver questioned.

Silver grabbed her daughter's hand and ushered her out the door and down the halls to her own room.

"I was doing some thinking," Darkess said, rather grown up like.

"Where did you take Zaphod?"

After a step or two, Darkess looked up at her mother.

"I went to Tanner's, then to the old pumpkin patch. Do you really believe what you told me is true?"

Entering Darkess' bedroom, Silver lit the candles off the one she had carried with her.

"Darling, I understand you are shaken with this news. Believe me when I say that it was quite a shock on me. I was nearly twice your age when I found out. But the thing is, if we teach you…show you how to learn on your own, you will have a much greater chance in the future."

Darkess changed into her nightdress and was climbing into bed when Angela stuck her head in the door.

"Oh good, you're home. Well, do have sweet dreams." With that said, she swept down the hall.

"Why did you tell me?" Darkess quietly asked as she pulled up her covers.

Smoothing the wrinkles out in the fold over her daughter's chest, Silver patted gently.

"Because…you're ready."

Darkess didn't say anything for a moment. She stared at the oil lamp by her bed wondering, "Am I ready?" Silver blew out all of the lamps, save the one next to the bed, and said,

"Do you think you can sleep?"

"Yeah, I'm kind of tired. I guess."

"You know where I am if you need me. Things will look better in the morning. After the party, things will all fall into place. I think you will be happy. It will take a little adjustment, but it will all work out. Good night, darling," Silver said as she kissed her daughter's cheek. She blew out the bedside lamp and went to the door.

"Good night," Darkess whispered to her mom.

When the door closed, she relit the candle with her fingertip then stared at it for a few moments. Before too long, Darkess' eyes were sliding shut, and she was fast asleep.

☼

There was a loud howling coming from the wall behind the stairs as Darkess came walking up to the top. She looked out at the guests who had finally started to arrive. There were some odd looking creatures in the crowd she noticed as her eyes scanned the room, looking for people she knew. A morphin was standing by the door, changing its look with each new person who entered. The crowd laughed as the morphin did its best to shock or surprise each guest.

"Wow, what a power that would be to have. You could go anywhere," Darkess said more to herself than anyone else, not realizing that she wasn't alone.

Chakra had walked up. Jumping on the railing, he said,

"Looks aren't everything."

Spinning around too quickly, Darkess knocked the cat off the rail. She immediately froze him in mid-fall, raised him back up, and gently placed him on squarely on the rail.

"See what I mean? I'll bet he can't do that," Chakra said.

"What? I nearly killed one of my best friends!" Darkess spat in her own defense with a little embarrassment.

"No, you silly girl. You may have knocked me off, but you saved me from possible injury as well as the poor person I would have landed on," Chakra said while looking over the edge at the room filling up with people and other things.

"You do have a small point. Still, that power would be loads of fun," Darkess said as she swept off the landing onto the steps.

Dressed as a swordsman from the magic wars, Darkess held tight to her sword as she descended, letting her cape swirl around her with each step. She made an impressive warrior, and once she called for Zaphod for her little show later on, her costume would be perfect. Knowing her mother wouldn't let Zaphod stay inside for very long, she decided to let the room fill up before she pulled her little stunt. Grabbing a sugar spider before it could escape the bowl and eating the legs first, she skirted the room looking at the unique costumes. She played a game with herself: Exactly who was in each outfit? Philineas had his band in full swing, and Chakra was flipping his tail as he watched the crowd. Richard and Angela were greeting more guests, but she still hadn't seen either of her parents. Then she heard her mothers distinctive laugh and saw her standing with a large hairy beast. Her father?

Making her way through the ever-thickening crowd, Darkess pushed towards her parents. Silver was dressed as a fairy princess with shimmering wings extending from her back. The big hairy beast was indeed her father. She was sure of it once he spoke.

"Your mother made me a potion to simulate a werewolf. What do you think?" Daniel asked his daughter.

"You look like you forgot to shave for about a year," Darkess giggled.

Growling loudly, Daniel chased after his daughter in a manner that couldn't have been more human. The nearby guests laughed as Darkess yelled,

"Somebody get a silver blade!"

It seemed that Darkess was accepting the news of last night…at least on the outside, anyway.

☼

Since the Magic Wars of long ago, good magic has struggled to keep the balance of powers even. Their covens have grown in numbers and size over the centuries, but without the dragons, they have had a tough time keeping the demons at bay. Having kept the eggs under the influence of good for so long helped more than anyone of them could have possibly imagined. Crops had grown well since evil was no longer in control, and living hadn't been near the struggle it once was. However, Takar had one of those precious eggs now, and the balance was starting to shift ever so slightly into the hands of evil. At first not even the magic folk knew what was happening, and the humans noticed nothing. But the air seemed heavier, the sun not as bright, and the night seemed to last just a little longer each time. It wouldn't take long for the animals to realize something was amiss, but the farmers would have to wait a whole season to take notice that there was a problem.

Sometime this year, stories will start to circulate in the far regions of the world. People will become afraid and not know why. A seed of fear is growing in the world that has not yet reached Xyloidonia. Demons and the like will begin to surface again to wreak havoc anyway they can. Spirits will be first to notice the change that is coming. Ghosts in particular. Some of the world's leading kings will be covertly invaded by demons that are slowly trying to take back the world. Darkness slowly grows.

☼

The party is in full swing back at Vallencourt Castle, and Darkess has spotted her grandparents. Weaving through the crowd towards them, Darkess spots the ghost they were speaking with. Darkess' mind was stuck on the new horse she wanted to show off, but something about this ghost intrigued her. He seemed to be a woodsman or trader, and he had died a most painful death by the look of it. There was the hilt of a short sword sticking out of his shoulder blade, and by the size of the hilt, the blade had surely pierced his heart. There were other small wounds on him, but the sword was most definitely the killing blow. Darkess was surprised by the way the three of them were laughing, as most ghosts aren't funny at all. It took a moment for them to notice Darkess, but when they did, the ghost spoke first.

"Well, hello there missy. How are you on this fine sacrosanct day?"

Darkess smiled. Holding her sword, she bowed to the ghost and said with an air of elegance,

"I am having a wonderful evening. My name is Darkess, sir, and yours?"

Bowing back, the ghost replied,

"My name is Quinnlen, but you may call me Quinn."

Smiling again at the ghost, Darkess was still intent on getting her time on stage with her new horse, so she turned to her grandfather. In her most syrupy voice, she asked.

"Please, can I show off Zaphod now, Grandfather?"

Before Richard could answer, Quinn floated a little closer to Darkess and asked,

"What is a Zaphod?"

Darkess giggled at his ignorance and the look on his face.

"Zaphod is the name of my horse. But he's not just an ordinary horse, he can teleport. And he is so pretty. I just have to show everyone. Please, Grandfather, please?"

"And just how do you propose that you do that in the middle of all of these people?" It was only then that she realized she hadn't planned what to do. Darkess froze for a moment, thinking on her new predicament. Quinn spoke up quickly.

"I have an idea."

Darkess' eyes squinted with skepticism, but she said,

"Okay, let's hear it."

Quinn floated close and whispered in her ear.

≈

A loud scream came from the back of the room furthest from the stage. The band stopped playing and everyone turned towards the disturbance. Darkess came tearing through the crowd with Quinn floating behind close enough to nearly grab her. They parted the crowd all the way to the stage. Darkess reached the stage, levitated herself upon it, spun around to face her pursuer, and drawing her sword, yelled,

"Zaphod, save me!"

Quinn drew his sword, and in his meanest voice, said,

"You can't get away from me!"

Just as the last words fell from the ghost's lips, a magnificent black stallion appeared on the stage next to Darkess. Oohs and aahs escaped the crowd when Zaphod shook his head and whinnied as Darkess floated up on his back. Just as they had planned, Darkess thought to her horse,

'See the empty space by the back? Go there now.'

Quinn swooped at Darkess, and the instant before she was touched by his cold presence, horse and rider disappeared. They reappeared in the back of the room, and Zaphod whinnied loudly as he reared up. The crowd turned again, looking for Darkess. She held her hand up to her hat. Waving at Quinn, she exclaimed,

"Maybe next time!"

Darkess nudged Zaphod in the ribs, and they bolted through the door. Clapping and cheers went up through the large room, the band began to play again, and the chatter that had previously filled the room started up again. Everyone who knew Darkess well was surprised at how quickly her powers were growing. And Zaphod had been a hit with the magic folk, as his breed is few and far between.

Brutus walked out of the crowd, smiling largely at Angela with his arms extended toward her.

"Angie, how are ya?"

Scooping her up in a bear hug, Brutus squeezed the air out of her as he spun her around then placed her back on her feet.

"Oh…my. Brutus dear, I'm fine, and you?" Angela asked as she straightened her hair and dress.

After regaining her composure, she made introductions.

"Brutus, this is my daughter, Silver, and her husband, Daniel."

The large man shook hands with both of them.

"How do ya do sir? Nice to meet ya ma'am. So whar is Richard, that ole rascal?"

Looking around the room Angela spotted Richard talking to an elderly couple dressed as a crone and a hermit. She pointed.

"There he is."

Turning towards Richard, Brutus said.

"I will be talkin to ya again later. If 'n ya'll cood excuse me." Off through the crowd he went.

Brutus was a huge hulk of a man. Towering over even the tallest of guests, he did not get lost in the crowd. After he apologized to half of the room for his size, he finally reached Richard, who burst out laughing at the sight of him.

"Well if it isn't the god of the ocean as I live and breathe. How are you?"

The two men shook hands heartily.

"I knew this'd be a great party, but ya have outdone yurself. This place is impressive, and whut a hoity toidy guest list. I'm amazed that they'd even let me in the door."

"Now Brutus, you know if I cared what everybody thought, I would not have thrown a costume ball. We'd have the rituals and be done with it. But, as you see, I prefer to be my own person. Be damned the rumors, or whatever hogwash circulates. It's all a bunch of mule fritters, and you know it. I do what I want, when I want, and with whom I want to do it. And you are right – this place does look good, so thank you! We all had our hands in it this year."

Richard looked around the room for Darkess, who should have come back in by now.

"Have you seen any of the family yet?"

With a lopsided grin, Brutus said,

"I think I may've let the air out of Angie. An I met your daughter an her husband."

"I wonder where that girl has gotten off to," Richard said as he headed towards the door to check out in the courtyard. Skirting the edge of the crowd, looking around between the clusters of party guests, Richard and Brutus made their way towards the deck area.

"More room to breath and less noise," Richard said loudly, pointing towards the open door.

Outside the air was much cooler, and there were benches for them to sit and talk. Nodding to a couple of guests as they passed, Richard was taking a seat when Zaphod appeared.

"There you are, young lady. Did you enjoy your little show?" Richard asked.

Brutus took a seat on a stone bench as Quinn soared down from the roof. Darkess jumped off Zaphod and was beaming with pride.

"It was brilliant. Quinn, you were perfect."

"Glad to be at your service, Miss," Quinn said with a bow.

"Quinn, Darkess, I would like you to meet a friend of mine. Brutus, this is my granddaughter, and the specter is Quinn."

Darkess shook Brutus' hand and looked at it funny when he opened his hand again. Her hand looked like a doll hand in his. Quinn bowed, saying,

"Nice to meet you. And I am sorry, but my time here is almost over, and I have a few things that I would like to do before I go…"

An odd look came over Quinn's translucent face, and he floated a few feet further up in the air and hung there looking sick. The color of the ghost's body turned to a more black color, loosing its silvery appearance.

"Whoa," Quinn said as his color began to return to its former blue-silver.

"What was that?" Richard asked the ghost.

"That's a good question. Something is wrong. But what I am not sure."

The two men exchanged glances, leaving Darkess to wonder what she may.

"Now I really must go. See you next year," Quinn said, and in a cold wind of silvery mist, he vanished.

"Where did he go, Grandfather?" Darkess asked with a perturbed look on her face.

Brutus butted in quickly.

"Can I answer that one, Richard?"

With a nod of his head, a slight bow, and a wave of his hand, Richard said, "Be my guest."

"On this special day, when the veil between realms is at its thinnest, we cun connect with the other side. On this day, demons, an ghosts locked on the other side find it much easier to pass over. And spirits locked on this side cin finally pass over to the other side. Some wait for this day to seek revenge, an others come back ta visit with loved ones, and some – like poor Quinn there – well, they are stuck here cause they was wronged in life an are lost, haunting the place where they was murdered. That's why we wear masks ta disguise our dentities, ta protect ourselves from the evil that knows how ta cross over. Ya see, demons walk amongst us on this day, an our protection from them is vital. Some of those that cross over on this day cin only do so on this day, an only this day. Quinn cin only be seen on this day, but he is always here. He is stuck here."

Darkess' question wasn't exactly answered, but she understood now that there were other places that can't be seen or touched by human hands. She knew there was a place only the dead could go, and since they were all still alive, she would have to ask Quinn herself next year.

Realizing that he had begun to delve deeper into the subject than he needed, Brutus lightened his speech. Smiling at Darkess, he said,

"With all o this power around us, we is safe here. No worries tonight."

"Well done there, professor. I think that will do," Richard said to Brutus with a smirk on his face.

"So what do you think? Does he sound like he could teach you anything?"

Standing on her tip toes and trying to get eye level with the sitting giant, Darkess succeeding only in making herself look silly.

"Yeah, I think that he'll do," she said. "So is Quinn here to haunt or visit us?"

"He said that he was drawn here by the massive pull of good magic at the castle," Richard responded "and when he saw that we were having a party, he decided to stay. He has learned much about magic since his death and prefers our company to that of demons and other ghosts. It seems he just can't let go of his life."

"How sad for him," Darkess said. "I do hope he returns next year. He was loads of fun."

A tray of decorated sugar cookies floated past them. Each of them took one and munched delightedly when Angela reached the three of them.

"There you are. I've been looking everywhere for you."

Behind Angela stood a severe looking woman with her hair pulled tightly into a bun.

"Janine is here to see you," Angela urged.

Introducing them all around, Angela took a seat by her granddaughter on the bench across from Brutus and invited Janine to sit next to her.

Richard explained,

"We were just discussing the value of knowledge and the power of this day. But now since we have sweets and a new guest, maybe she should pick our next topic."

"Why, thank you Richard, but I haven't any special topic to discuss, other than the fact that I wanted to finally meet this extraordinary young lady. Oh, and I brought her a gift."

Janine's severe appearance was the opposite of her attitude entirely. She was sweet and gentle, even a little silly. She begun to dig through a large, brightly colored woven bag she had slung over her shoulder. Her severely pointed nose and chin along with her tightly secured hair made her look hardly able to blink. Her clothes were dark and unassuming, and the only hint of a costume was the silken mask she wore. Pulling a small cloth from her bag, Janine unrolled it and revealed a silver object, which she rubbed gently and handed to Darkess. It was a silver coil with tiny claws and a small head. There were folded wings about a third of the way down the coil, and some scales could be seen in the light. Realizing it was a dragon; Darkess' eyes glistened as she looked at the fine detail in the claws, horns, and scales. The face was exquisite, looking real enough to open its mouth and blow out a flame.

"It's amazing," Darkess breathed as she slipped her hand through the bangle and pushed it up her forearm.

"It was meant to be worn like this," Janine instructed and pushed the bangle further up Darkess' slender arm, past her elbow.

Seeing that it was much too large for the girl at this time, Janine manipulated the metal. The dragon stretched out its long body. Coiling one more time, it gripped Darkess' arm and laid its head on her as it finally settled into place.

"Wow, how did you do that?" Darkess questioned.

"That is my gift. I can control metal, every kind that I have come across so far. But in the world, I am a silversmith and a jeweler by trade, making both regular and magical jewelry."

"You will love to talk to my mother then. She is a jewelry person, too. She studies old items looking for magical properties, and the jewelry is always her favorite."

"Oh, how interesting," Janine twittered before asking, "But do you know why I made you that particular piece of jewelry?"

Looking at the bangle, Darkess had no idea and shook her head no.

"When I heard from Richard that you were in need of more diverse schooling, I went to my seer and asked her about you. I asked her specifically what symbol of strength matched you. What metal or stones should be used that would match you for years to come, and the seer searched the cosmos for you. What the seer found was mysterious. The crystal ball showed a dragon surrounded by purple mist. That was all. Nothing else. So I thought about it and used amethyst for the eyes along with the purest of silver. There must be a dragon in your future somewhere."

Richard's brain was compiling all of the evidence so far that was leading to Darkess' future. Purple mist has come up twice, eggs, stones, fine baskets, and now a dragon. Angela saw the look on her husband's face and knew what he was thinking; but the party was in full swing, and there were more guests arriving all the time.

"Richard," she said, "we must see that the rest of the food gets out, and there are a few other people inside looking for you."

They locked eyes for a moment, and Richard realized there was no time for list making now. He smiled at his wife.

"Oh, yes, well you are right, dear. We can talk about all of this tomorrow when all of the other guests have gone. I guess for now, we should enjoy the party, meet new people, and pay our respects for the day. Darkess, will you show Janine and Brutus to their rooms? I'll be in the main room somewhere if I am needed. Enjoy, everyone, enjoy."

☼

A few hours later, the bonfire in the courtyard was burning low, and many of the guests had begun to clear out. It was coming on midnight, and some of the guests had far to travel home. Richard was seeing an elderly couple to their carriage. He was wishing them a safe journey and closing the door when a bluish smoke appeared. As it dissipated, a man appeared inside it. The large man was holding a canvas bag over his shoulder, and he was dressed in a long woolen coat that smelled of sea salt. Richard shook his head and walked towards the man.

"I see you've been using my recipes again."

Waving away the remaining smoke, Richard chuckled and said, "I'd recognize my potions anywhere. You old scoundrel, how are you?"

Richard shook hands vigorously.

"I'm tired, but doing alright. An yourself? An Angie?" the man asked.

Motioning towards the castle door, Richard said,

"We're great, wonderful in fact. We haven't had too much demon activity lately, which I'm assuming is good, and we have found more clues to the prophecy. The party has had a wonderful turnout. As a matter of fact, the only ones left to arrive are Jori and Harlow, and I'm sure they will be along soon."

Richard opened the door to the castle, and they walked into the last of the party crowd.

"Hungry after your long trip?" Richard asked.

With a longing in his eyes, the man scanned the table.

"Famished," he said.

"You go ahead and eat while I look up the family."

Richard pointed to where the man should put his bag then wondered off in search of his wife. Just as the man had filled his plate and was headed for a seat, Darkess appeared next to him.

"My grandfather told me to keep an eye on you. Said you might need some help with your bags."

"Oh he did, did he? He's older'n me, the old coot. I'll show him about carrying bags,"the man said with a surly kind of chuckle.

"You must be Darkess," he proposed.

"Yes, I am, and you, sir, are Belthazor," Darkess said as she turned and levitated the bag to eye level and started to walk towards the steps.

"Hey, where d'ya think yer a goin' with that?" Belthazor grunted.

"Grandfather said that you needed help with your bags. I will be right back."

Up the stairs she went, bag floating in front of her as she disappeared towards the guest rooms.

≈

Moments later, Darkess returned, sat next to Belthazor, and said,

"It is nice to meet you. Are you going to help teach me?"

"Yes, I believe that I am. Belthazor at your service, Miss."

Belthazor offered his hand; Darkess took it with a huge, jaw-locking yawn.

"It seems ta me that it is well past someone's bed time."

Belthazor winked or blinked, Darkess wasn't sure, and she said,

"I've been waiting a long time to meet Harlow and see Jori again. I think I can wait a little longer."

Sinking down into a large overstuffed chair, Darkess took off her boots and leaned back to talk with Belthazor. Chakra jumped onto the chair next to Darkess and rubbed against her, craving some attention. Petting her cat, Darkess sunk a little deeper into the chair and asked,

"What sort of things will you teach me?"

Stuffing his mouth full just as she asked the question, he had to chew for a moment before he could answer.

"I'm not really a teacher in the normal sense of the werd. But I suppose that I do know a thing or two that I could teach ya from all a my travels. I expect that yer family wants me to broaden your horizons, so ta speak, and introduce ya to the sea an all a her wonders. Your grandfather an I'll talk…sort it out. Don't worry your purdy little head."

Stuffing the last bit from his plate into his mouth, he stood and returned to the table to fill it again.

Darkess heard Belthazor mumble but only caught a few words.

"…home-cookin'…"

Upon refilling his plate, Belthazor returned to where he had been seated earlier, only to find his hostess had fallen fast asleep. Chakra was lying in her lap, wide-awake, flipping his tail, and watching the crowd move about. Filling his belly, Belthazor joined the cat in watching the crowd dissipate, neither paying much attention to the other. Then just after midnight, a large family was leaving by way of teleport potion when the door blew open. In came the icy wind, strewn with leaves, followed by Jori and Harlow. The wind died down, and Harlow pointed to the door, which promptly closed. Jori stood grinning with her arm around Harlow's.

"Even though it is past midnight, and most of the guests are gone, you still can't resist making an entrance, can you?" Richard asked as he walked towards his new guests, giving Jori a hug.

Jori sniffed at his neck and smiled as she returned the hug. Turning towards Harlow, Richard grabbed his hand and shook it vigorously, saying,

"It has been a while, old friend. It is good to see you."

A mumble came from the chair behind Richard, and everyone nearby turned to see what it was. Darkess was talking in her sleep. She seemed angry at something and was tossing in her chair. At this point, Chakra was sitting on the back of the chair, watching Darkess intently. Silver moved over towards the chair, but Harlow stopped her.

"No. Wait. I see what she sees."

Stepping closer, stopping only a foot away from the sleeping girl, Harlow closed his eyes and held out his hands, absorbing the mind waves she was throwing off. It was a vibrant dream, filled with exploding colors, swirls of light, and curved and blurry edges. She was running, throwing fireballs at an unseen enemy. Constantly moving, around corners, in every direction, she looked ready for anything. In her hand she clutched a tiny golden egg. After making sure that she was still alone, she looked at the egg for a moment. The lines on it were changing direction, and Darkess looked in the direction that they indicated. The way was clear. She listened closely, heard nothing, and then proceeded. She was looking for a sign, something to point her in the right direction. A crunching sound came from behind her, and as she spun around to check it out, she put her foot down in empty space. She fell. Harlow jerked rather hard at the fall, and Darkess' eyes snapped open.

With burry, sleep-filled eyes, Darkess looked around the room. She saw everyone staring at her, including Harlow and Jori. Rubbing one eye and licking her lips, she asked,

"Wh-what happened? Why are you all staring at me?"

Then awareness seemed to enter her eyes, clearing the sleep further from them.

"Oh, my dream. You were there. Well no, you weren't there, but well… you know what I mean," she asked Harlow.

"I believe what you mean to say is, we were psychically linked. I saw your dream. I was there. Just not in a conventional sort of way. I saw exactly what you saw. Have you had this dream before?" Harlow answered.

Darkess thought for a moment, sitting up more straight in her chair, her brow furrowed in concentration.

"You know, I don't know. It kind of felt like I'd been there before, but why was I lost if I had been there before? And fireballs I didn't know I could do that."

Everyone at the party looked around at each other.

"It very well could have been a cross between a dream and a premonition. Your subconscience could have tapped into you mother's power and contaminated a normal dream with magic," Harlow said as he turned towards Silver.

"Have you had any premonitions of Darkess in the future? Or any premonitions at all recently?"

"A party premonition," Silver said nonchalantly. "Saved some child's silliness from becoming a seriously damaging accident. Nothing else. Why?"

"Did you feel her channeling your power?" Harlow questioned.

Darkess butted in quickly, defending herself.

"I haven't done that since I forced a premonition on mother that one time."

Harlow rubbed his bristly chin in thought and slapped his thigh in frustration.

"You know, magic is not an exact science, but it does happen for a reason. I've learned that over the many years of practice and study, and practical use," Harlow added.

Stepping forward, Richard took control of the conversation, saying in a tired voice,

"For now, let us introduce everyone, and add that to the list of mysterious things. Shouldn't we all settle in for the night? I need to sit these tired old bones down for a while."

After all the introductions were finished, each of them looked a little more tired, except for Jori. They all began to climb the stairs and headed for their perspective rooms, when Jori said teasingly,

"I'm really not that tired. I think that I'll just snoop around your castle while you sleep. I'll see you all tomorrow evening."

Jori led Harlow off to his room, and the rest of the group departed for theirs.

☼

The next evening, the entire family and its employ, and all of the guests minus Jori, sat around the dinner table talking. All of the food had been removed from the table, leaving only the drinking goblets and the half-burnt candles in the middle of the table. With the discussion about Darkess' training close at hand, everyone was keeping the subject easy, telling jokes, stories, and laughing. Just a few minutes past the setting of the sun, there came a rattling of the doors as Jori finally came down to join in on the planning.

"Miss me?" Jori said silkily as she seemed to glide over to the sideboard.

Reaching inside her cloak, Jori pulled a flask, grabbed a goblet, and poured whatever was inside, and drank a large draught. Again she seemed to glide across the floor to the empty chair next to Harlow left open for her. The seriousness of what was to come seemed to sober them all, and Richard stood to be better seen by everyone. He took a deep breath and said,

"I have asked you all here tonight to discuss the future of my granddaughter."

Darkess quickly straightened up in her seat when a couple of guests looked towards her. She was as interested in what he had to say as the rest of the table and grinned a little self-consciously as Richard continued.

"As you know, we believe whole-heartedly that Darkess is the witch from the prophecy. We have decided that to better prepare her for what is to come, she will need more than we, as her family, can provide. This will be a great test to all of us. Each person will have a part. Some will play a larger role than others. But there will be danger at every turn. It is essential that you know the risks involved here. We know not how many we are up against, or who, for that matter. I am certain that there are those both good and evil who know of Darkess' coming and for that, our lives could be in jeopardy at any time."

Richard looked at everyone around his table and began again.

"We don't know how long we have until the actual battle takes place, or what it may entail. If we need the expertise of someone other than this group, we will talk it out. The amount of information given to outsiders must be limited. We must be a unified team. Now, before I go on, I would like to know if anyone here would like to back out. There will be no hard feelings towards you, and you will be free to go. I need to know if you are fully in this, for the lives of my family are at stake if you are not."

All present at the table craned their necks looking to see if any one was getting up from their chairs. But some shifting in seats was the only movement, and they all settled back and looked at Richard. After a good long moment, Richard finally said,

"Good. You all need to sign here. It is a binding oath, making the signer unable to speak to anyone about this, other than another signer, of course. Your tongue will cease to work if you try. If you attempt to write someone about this, your hand will be paralyzed. Should your life become in jeopardy while you are working on our mission, your name will glow upon this sheet and show me or whoever is in the tower. We can then send help. It works to help us all. Please use this ink and quill."

Richard handed the parchment to Jori. She signed it, and passed it to Harlow, who in turn passed it to Roxy, then Philineas, Tanner, and Brutus. Brutus' signature was nearly as large as his hand, causing Janine to squeeze her name onto the side of the parchment. Silver and Daniel signed on the opposite side of the page. Darkess signed her name with a flourish, trying to look older, leaving just enough room for Richard and Angela to sign. With all of the names now dry on the page, Richard held it up for all to see.

"Repeat after me: With this signature, we seal this pact."

In unison, they all took the oath. The names on the pact burst into flames and quickly scorched into the parchment, leaving each swirl and swoosh ashen black and binding each one to his word.

≈

After using Richard's famous teleport potion, the thirteen members of the newly formed group arrived at Vallencourt tower in a huge plume of blue smoke.

"Everyone pick a spot where you can see this board, and we'll get started."

The tower had never had this many people in it, and it felt good to have so much help at a time like this. Richard smiled as he looked around the room.

"This should help all of us see what we have in our arsenal. I know we have all introduced ourselves, but now I believe specialties, powers, and weaknesses should be shared. Shall we all tell a quick story of who we are and what we can do? Let's go around the room. Roxy, how 'bout you?"

"Um, well, yes, I am Roxy. Cooking and cleaning are my specialties, and I dabble in potions. Been with the family for more'n twenty years, and I will do any thing to help Miss Darkess," she giggled and sat down.

"I am Jori, a Vampire. But you have nothing to fear, at my age, I rarely need human blood, and I prefer to hunt those who deserve to die. If I concentrate on you, I can usually read minds. I can defy gravity. And I have contacts all over the world – some good, some not so good. I will be teaching Darkess hand to hand fighting with swords and knives."

Harlow stood next. Pulling his brown cloak up tight around his neck so the only skin showing was his hands and part of his face, he said,

"I am Harlow, a very old wizard, schooled by many years of life. My power is telepathic. I hear thoughts. I know what you are going to say before you say it. It can be rather maddening at times. However, over the years, I have learned to turn the volume down. I will not be teaching Darkess very much, but I will use my contacts and my oracle to help in any way I can."

Bowing his head to Richard, then Darkess, Harlow took his seat.

Brutus was next, but he remained seated as he spoke.

"I'm Brutus of the family Montague. I've a very uncommon power. I cin melt an reform. My color helps me hide in the dark, an I cin squeeze through spaces small enough fer only a bug. I don't have a very good reputation, but I'll help you 'til the end."

It was obvious to the elders at the table that Brutus had had shady dealings in the past but Darkess saw only the good in him, and she smiled largely when he bowed his head to her.

Daniel raised his shoulders at Darkess, as if to say that he too had not understood what Brutus had said about his reputation. Then he stood and said,

"I am Daniel, Darkess' father. I am essentially non-magical, but I do know about ancient artifacts, some dating back as far as the magic wars. I know a lot of influential families around the world along with some collectors of odd things, some magical. I will do anything to help my daughter and will kill anything or anyone that tries to stop or hurt her."

Daniel looked around a little nervously. He sounded threatening to himself, but he knew in his heart that almost anyone at the table could kill him in an instant. When he looked for reassurance from his wife, Silver patted his hand under the table then stood to say her peace.

"I am Silver, mother to Darkess. I am well versed in magical talismans, jewelry, and spell working. I am a master weaver, and my power is that of premonitions. I have read nearly every book in this room, and I hope that between all of us, we have the knowledge to help Darkess in her quest. I would give my life to save white magic, even more so to save my daughter. May we stand strong together in this fight."

Silver sat down, patting Tanner on the shoulder. It was his turn. He stood tall and straight as any great medicine man would, and even though he had a slight accent, he spoke with a clear voice.

"I am Tanner Silent Feet. I am the seventh son of a seventh son, both medicine men of the BaKunata Tribe in the northwest territories."

All shifted in their seats to get a good look at Tanner as he spoke. Even Harlow took notice, for being a medicine man had helped Tanner to close his mind from invasion, although not entirely. Richard had not even known all that his good friend was saying and listened intently as Tanner shared his secrets.

"I took a spirit journey long ago. It told me the path to get here unscathed, and I followed that path. It was supposed to lead me to the Great White Witch with the flaming hair. My journey and yours are connected."

Tanner looked only at Darkess as he talked. It was as if he were meeting her for the first time. He had his hair pulled back, and his tattoo was much easier to see. There was a line through his eye, extending from his forehead all the way to his jaw, and an odd crystal like structure on his cheek. The crystal had three forks at the bottom, and one at the top.

"It took me ten years to make it here, learning as I went. I followed the signs. I prayed. I fasted. I worked hard to find you, and with a little blood, a lot of sweat, and a few tears, I made it. Only then did I learn that you were not even born yet. I have spent my whole life training to protect you and teach you all that I can to help you along your journey. My ways are not magic but more like spiritual guidance and knowledge of the world around us, nature. I may die along this journey, but I will do it in service of you."

Tanner knelt down in front of Darkess and took her hand. There was a look of awe on the faces of everyone seated around the table when he spoke again.

"My life is yours."

Waiting a few seconds to see if Darkess would say anything, Tanner looked at her feet then up into her eyes.

"I have put up every totem of protection that I know. They encircle the entire grounds. I have brought every thing good and pure here and removed as much of the bad as I can. I will be teaching you to survive alone with no food or shelter. I will teach you to hunt and protect yourself without the means of magic."

As Tanner stood back up, Darkess said to him,

"Thank you very much." It was all she could think of.

Richard stood as Tanner took his seat.

"Well, that was, mmmm, unexpected. Thank you, Tanner. I believe it is Janine's turn."

Richard smiled at Janine as he tried to wipe the amazed look off of his face. Janine stood and cleared her throat, trying to make sure that she had everyone's attention.

"I am Janine of the Fipps line, the owner of the finest shop in Crystal City. I make items to match the person. And I use my powers to make the piece. I control metal. Any metal. All that I have come across, anyway. I believe that I will be teaching Darkess about enchanted items along with the components and uses of metal. And I know the most prominent people in the city. I believe she will accompany me to meet some of them. Information moves quickly through the mouths of the wealthy upper class, and she will learn more about the ways of non-magical society. And I do know some upper class wizards; however, like us, no one knows they are powerful people. Darkess will be meeting some of them, too. Oh, we will have a grand time doing your studies," Janine giggled.

Smiling at them all, Janine took her seat, and Philineas stood up. He waved at them as he stood out of slight embarrassment and humility.

"I am Philineas, adopted to the family Nagel. I used to be a familiar, but now I am human. I have extensive knowledge of the magical world, but unfortunately I don't have any real magical powers. I've been told I am handy to have around, because I still have the senses of a cat. My very nature is that of protection, and through the world of familiars, I will do my best to help Darkess and protect her. I believe someday, Darkess will be a strong force against an evil that is coming. I think I am here to help her know when that evil arrives."

Sitting down swiftly without a sound, Philineas winked at Darkess. Belthazor slowly got to his feet and looked around the room.

"I am Belthazor of the Family Thomlinson. I'm the owner of a fleet a ships, all operated by witch or wizard. We take cargo o every kind whereever it may need to go. I deal with anyone who cin pay, which means I know both sides a the fence. I try ta deal with doers of white magic only, because they are true to their werd. But when it comes down to money... well, if they behave, pay up front, an agree to stay below deck; I have been known to allow more'n I should. An when it comes to the creatures, well, they aren't always black or white, if ya know whut I mean. My power is o'r water. I cin move it, freeze or boil it, even make fog. That's how I made me start. I personally've never lost a ship to any other ship, nor to a squall. The most precious of cargos sails with me. That is what I guarantee. If it's with me, it's safe on the water, safer than on land. I'm here to show Darkess the realm of magic beyond the land, show her the creatures from beyond Xyloidonia. I think that 'bout covers it." He grunted in a gravely voice and sat down.

Everyone then turned and looked towards Darkess. She felt the weight of all the eyes upon her, and her mouth suddenly went dry. Swallowing hard, she forced her tongue to work. She didn't know that she was to talk. If so, she would have thought about her presentation before now. The wheels were turning in her mind quickly as she thought of what she should say without making herself look like a stupid child. She was talking herself into what she knew she had to do. She swallowed again and pulled her swollen tongue off the roof of her mouth. Smiling a weak and nervous grin, she began.

"I'm sure that you all know me better than I know you. I seem to be the reason you are here. I have a bunch of powers. I can levitate myself, and pretty much anything I want, at close range. I can start and put out fires. I can freeze things, talk to animals, and channel."

Darkess stopped for a moment to think. She was trying to make sure she hadn't forgotten something. Her forehead furrowed in concentration then smoothed as she spoke.

"I brought this to show you."

Swiftly she pulled out the small box that contained her prophecy.

"Do you want to hear it?" Darkess looked around the table at her guests, then to her grandfather for his approval. He nodded his head towards her, and she opened the tiny latch on the side. The lid opened silently and once again the air was filled with silvery vapor. A scratchy voice repeated the prophecy once more.

Once the vapor was sucked back into the box, and all had heard for themselves, Darkess put the box back into her cloak and slipped back into her seat. Richard winked at his granddaughter, and she gave him a nervous grin.

Angela got to her feet. Smiling, she chuckled,

"Well, you all know me. Most of you call me Angie. I am Darkess' grandmother, as you well know, and I am a healer by trade, so to speak, and it is my power. I specialize in medicinal plants and potions, and I do spend a lot of time with Roxy in the kitchens. I am here as a grandmother and as a witch. I want to make sure that Darkess has everything she could need at her fingertips when the time comes. And I'll be close by should training get a little rough."

Angela took her seat and nudged her husband as she smiled at her granddaughter.

"I believe you're next," she whispered to Richard.

Richard laid a few items on the table then stood up to face the group.

"I, am Richard. You all know me. I'm a chameleon, a master potion maker, and keeper of the Vallencourt secrets of magic. I have decided that you are all worthy of the secrets we will be sharing here. I also believe we can all work together to save the future; not only that of white magic, but quite possibly the entire planet."

"We know the magic wars from five centuries ago caused the world to spin out of balance. We know that since the death of the last dragon, things have not gone well for white magic or the world, but we have a fragile hold on it – for now. Evil is no longer in power, but it is coming close to returning in force, and we must be ready to stop it. Now that you have all heard the prophecy for yourselves, and it is no longer just a myth, there are several more things I have been working on over the years that I would like you all to hear. A response is not needed but would surely be appreciated if you can help me out here."

Richard picked up a long slender crystal, turned towards the window and tapped one of the stones next to it. Out of the ceiling dropped a large piece of ecru canvas. It covered the entire window and a couple feet around it.

"Project," he commanded.

The crystal emitted a beam of red light, that when exposed to the canvas, left a mark. Richard scrawled quickly on the canvas, the group watching intently as images were left behind for them to read. It was a list of clues that he had collected. When he finished, he whispered,

"Diminish."

Instantly the intensity of the light grew much dimmer. Turning halfway towards the group, Richard pointed at the list.

Purple mist	Oracle
Stone walls, cave?	Oracle
Eggs-unknown type	Oracle
Fine woven basket	Oracle
Dragon	Janine
Tiny golden egg	Darkess' dream

Richards explained his list to the group.

"These are the pieces to the puzzle that Darkess must solve. These first two items are from a few years ago. Oracle had them in a vision. Years later, another vision from her gave us the third and forth items. Janine arrived and gave Darkess the dragon with amythest eyes. Again, the color purple was seen by a specialist as well as the dragon. And the last piece, which may or may not fit our particular puzzle, was in Darkess' own dream witnessed by Harlow. It is the tiny golden egg. This egg seems bewitched to give the user directions to something – what, we still have no clue. So, if you add up the clues and the prophecy, what do you get? Anyone? Ideas?"

Janine, being so small, leaned forward in her chair to speak.

"Mmm, not to make you sound like a fool sir, but it seems we have dragon eggs, or maybe even a dragon with an egg hidden away, maybe a place with stone walls, a cave? The basket sounds like a carrying case for the eggs. Maybe they are getting ready to leave where they are hiding, which means that a human or magical being is involved, because I don't think dragons can weave. Oh, maybe Darkess has to find it and protect it, either from who has it, or who is trying to get it. But aren't all dragons dead. I thought they were killed off during the magic wars by money grubbing dragon slayers who were duped by black magic into destroying the very magic that helped to keep the world in balance."

Before anyone could say another word, Harlow jumped in.

"I have heard of dragon worshipers through the years – even clans that supposedly had an egg in their protection. But rumors run rampant in any world, magic and mortal alike"

Richard's shoulders drooped. He was disappointed. He had hoped to get more ideas, but he did have fresh new minds working on the problem now, and that felt good.

"Any other ideas on any of the pieces of this puzzle?"

Richard scanned the room hoping for something, but the room stayed silent. Turning towards the wall, Richard tapped the long crystal on the same stone as before and the canvas retreated back into the ceiling. Putting the long crystal back down on the table, he said.

"Extinguish."

And what was left of the light in the crystal died out.

"Is there anything that anyone wants to add or ask?"

Jori spoke up quickly.

"While I was exploring your home last night, I happened upon a door that refused to open. When I went outside to try and to look inside the windows, I discovered that the entire tower is impenetrable. May I ask what you have hidden inside?"

The look on her face was one of mischievous excitement. The rest of the group looked on with bewilderment, each moving just enough to get a good look at Richard. Placing the tips of his fingers together, he took a deep breath and said,

"I was wondering when that question would come up."

Silver, Daniel, and Darkess knew nothing of the locked tower, and neither did the rest of the group, except Angela. As far as they knew, that side of the castle was unused due to the smallness of the family at this point. In years past, those rooms had been used frequently, but were now blocked off to preserve the furniture and prevent general wear and tear on the rooms.

"The story goes like this. The closed off rooms are that way because they are not in use. The family is much too small to need all of those rooms; nevertheless, the tower has been locked for centuries. It was Wolfbane's private quarters. According to the family's book from that time, upon Wolfbane's death, the entire tower – doors, windows and all – locked themselves. Even the glass is enchanted. If you actually manage to break it by some lucky strike, it will grow back almost instantly and bar your path. Potions, teleporting, spells – nothing seems to work. Everyone with the curiosity bug in our family has tried to get inside to no avail. My guess is…either he has something in there that he didn't want anyone to lay their hands on, or…he's protecting us from something he has locked up. And a possible third reason: I suppose he could have left it locked up for a special time, or person, perhaps," Richard said then continued.

"Maybe the next great seer of our line will be able to get in. Wolfbane was an extraordinary seer, obviously. Darkess is here, and so far, many of his prophecies involving her have come to pass. I wonder…"

Richard's voice trailed off in thought. Tapping his fingers on the table next to him, he stared at the floor for a long moment.

"Silver? Have you ever tried to get into the tower?" he asked.

"Who me?" Silver said with incredulity. "No, I have never been in that part of the castle. It always gave me the creeps."

Swinging his head around quickly, Richard zeroed in on Brutus.

"What about you? Ever been to our tower?"

A purely mischievous grin spread across the large man's face as he said,

"No ser, but I cin tanight, you permitten o'course."

The excitement of new discovery sparked in the eyes of everyone around the room. The looks on their faces were definitely unanimous when Richard said rather than asked,

"Anyone up for a little walk?"

≈

Filing down the tight stairwell used to come and go from the tower, the assemblage of wizards talked in groups of two, some walking separately lost in thought. Darkess was right up front with her grandfather, igniting the torches ahead of them and extinguishing the ones they no longer needed. The old castle was drafty tonight as a near winter storm began to blow in. The nearer to the locked tower they got, the more fierce the storm became. Lightning and thunder threatened to split the sky apart and throw the pieces down on them.

"I think something is trying to warn us away from that door," Silver said with a wary voice.

"Nonsense. I could feel all day in my bones that this storm was coming," Angela waved at her daughter.

Finally reaching the door to the tower, Richard tested the door once more. The knob turned only a fraction before lodging in place. It was still locked solid.

"Silver, try the door please," Richard said, moving to let her pass.

Hesitating for but a second, afraid the lightning might strike her dead for trying, Silver squeezed her eyes shut and grabbed the knob. Nothing happened. So she opened her eyes and tried turning the knob either way. Nothing. The knob didn't even budge.

"Sorry, Father," she said and backed away from the door towards Daniel.

"No need for that Silver…Darkess, why don't you try," Richard said.

With a confidence not shown by her mother, Darkess marched boldly up to the door and grabbed the knob. She gave it a good torque, but again – nothing. Her shoulders slumped. She thought she could open it. Richard patted her shoulder then turned to Brutus.

"Okay big guy, how about giving it a try?"

Everyone had to move to let Brutus have access to the door. He eyed the door, every crack right down to the floor. A flat metal plate took the place of a keyhole. Brutus grunted, intrigued by the locked door without a lock. Then Brutus held up his hand, and it became flat as a thin coin. He tried to shove it through the jam of the door, but the opening was blocked.

Getting to his knees was a cumbersome act, so he stretched his arm down long and skinny and tried to run his hand across the threshold from where he stood. His hand did slip beneath the door, but he was barred any further entry. Running his hand over to a corner and feeling for even the tiniest crack, he found nothing. Not even a hair could be pushed through. Pulling his arm back, he remolded it into to its former shape and said,

"No go Richard. Sorry ser."

Patting Brutus on the elbow, Richard said.

"It was worth a try."

≈

As they returned to the dining hall, the group discussed the times they would be available for training sessions when Darkess got an idea.

"We need a name," she said.

Since everyone else seemed to be talking to someone else, the conversation had drifted off in several directions. No one heard what she said, so she repeated herself a little louder this time.

"I think that we need a name."

Angela seemed to have noticed the tone in her granddaughte'rs voice and said,

"What's that, dear?"

"I said, I think we need a name," Darkess repeated for the third time, a little peeved.

"What do you mean dear?" Angela queried.

"You know, every group or clan has a family name, a code name, a title of some kind. We're like a secret society. We need a name."

Harlow liked the idea and said so.

"Good idea, young lady. Do you have a name picked out?"

"Not exactly. I just thought it would be a good idea."

Daniel was quick to chime in.

"How about the Dragon's Order?"

Without making Daniel feel like a fool, Janine jumped in quickly.

"Maybe the Society of the Purple Mist?"

Jori had an idea of her own.

"The Coven of Fire…. for the dragon's breath?"

Everyone walked on in silence, trying to think of a name for the group. Upon reaching the ground floor, Richard said,

"Dessert first, then we name this group of daft wizards."

After seating themselves around the table, it took only a few moments for Angela and Roxy to prepare a sweet delight. The cored apple was filled with butter, brown sugar, and cinnamon, covered with a crumb topping, and baked to perfection. As they all dug into their desserts, Jori pulled out a flask and drank right from it this time. They scheduled sessions for Darkess as they ate, all complimenting Roxy on a fine job with the food. Richard had just finished writing down the last date they were sure about when Darkess yelled.

"I've got it!"

They all turned as one to look at her. Harlow peered down his long nose and asked as if he didn't know,

"Exactly just what have you got?"

"The name – I've figured out our name!" She exclaimed.

"Well?" Silver asked.

"Since we don't know exactly what we are doing – or why – and we are trying to save the future from some unknown evil, how about the Order of the New Horizon. Get it, new horizon?"

With a small chuckle, Richard said,

"Yes, we get it. And that's very good. All in favor of the name raise a hand."

Scanning the table, everybody had raised a hand and had a smile on their faces.

"It is now official. We are the Order of the New Horizon."

☼

And so it came to be. The secret society known as the Order of the New Horizon began their worldwide search for dragons, their eggs, and other groups associated with them. The rigorous training of young Darkess had begun. In an average day, Darkess spent two hours roaming the grounds with Tanner, learning all the plants that grew in the region and their qualities; such as poisonous, edible, medicinal, or magical. Tanner also had Indian rituals of purity planned and rites of passage to teach her both endurance and ingenuity. Darkess loved his classes. Tanner nearly had to shove her back to the castle for her other lessons.

There was always an hour with either of her parents when she learned about talismans, weapons of all sorts, and how to spot and defend against common bewitched items. Daniel's knowledge of myths, legends, and artifacts helped well in this case and seemed to bring him closer to his daughter, as well as his sword sparring capabilities. And considering his non-magical status, he had little to teach her but did all he could to be around her, trying his best to help. Lunch usually followed. Sometimes she ate with the family, and sometimes she ate in her favorite tree. But when she knew she had plenty of time, she wolfed down her food and sprinted to the barn for a good tear across the grounds on her good friend, Zaphod. It seemed a good release during the long hours of learning.

The hour after lunch was reserved for either Roxy or Angela when she learned general cooking, cleaning, and healing potions, the things that could be taken for granted but were essential in the every day life of a wizard, especially if they were on their own. These were not the most fun lessons, but Darkess knew they were important and put as much into each one as she could muster. After all, she knew when she was finished; she would have the most challenging lessons to learn next – in the tower with her grandfather.

Richard was a master potion maker, and he made sure that Darkess knew her potions well. What could and could not be mixed and how to experiment as safely as possible with new potions. He also taught Darkess how to create spells; even old stand-bys from the family book, not to mention everything found in that family book she had to know by heart.

After about three months of her new training, winter was almost halfway through when a letter arrived from Janine in the usual way. The letter was requesting the company of Darkess for a week's stay. In the letter, there was a description of the clothes that Darkess would need during her stay and an excellent drawing of the front of her shop in the city. The drawing was sent to help Darkess tell Zaphod where to go. There were instructions about coming after dark and using the alley beside the shop so no one would see her arrival. Darkess was to attend the birthday party of a very influential friend of Janine's in Crystal City. Some of the King's own consorts would be there, possibly giving Darkess her first chance at meeting royalty. But the party itself was for a lady with a hidden fetish for dragons. Richard had met her just once, long ago when he had a secret meeting with the king. He often consulted the king on many things, usually late at night when the rest of the castle's inhabitants were asleep. The woman had been scurrying down one corridor, nearly colliding with Richard on his way around a corner. Since they each had their own private business with the king, they went on their ways quickly. The secret here is that the woman, Alieria, and Richard are magical beings, neither known to each other. The two consorts would eventually meet sometime later, both with a shared destiny.

When Darkess heard the news about visiting Janine, she could hardly wait the few days until she was to leave. Packing all of the required items from the list into a magic duffle her grandfather had provided, Darkess' anticipation grew with each item. Once something was placed into the bag, it shrunk down to make room for the next. Marking her list as she packed, she realized that she would be doing more than attending a party. There were work clothes on the list, too. Wondering what kind of work Janine would have her doing, she finished up by adding her favorite writing supplies and a couple of personal items, including her Turquoise necklace and a stone bird.

Climbing up into bed, Darkess knew she wouldn't sleep well, so she pulled the duffle up close to her, and removed the turquoise necklace – anything to help her get through one more night before her first trip away from the castle alone. Her excitement was nearly palpable as she fluffed her pillow for what seemed the hundredth time. Just when she thought that she would never fall asleep, she opened her eyes to sunlight streaming across the foot of her bed.

"Today's the day," she whispered with a glimmer in her eye.

She jumped from her bed and went to the window. Tanner and Richard were talking in the courtyard, and Rufus had the barn open wide to let in sunlight and air. It was such a wonderful day, she thought, and a perfect day to travel, even if it only takes a second or two. Throwing clothes around the room while looking for her outdoor clothes, she dressed hurriedly and ran down to breakfast.

Darkess' belly was full, and her warm clothes buttoned up tight as she went outside to find Tanner and her grandfather. By now they were in the barn with Zaphod and Rufus. Half out of breath from running to the barn and in a big hurry to get this long day started, Darkess stopped next to her grandfather and leaned on the wall, panting. She was waiting for her day's instructions to begin when Richard informed her that she could do with the day as she pleased. Darkess turned on her heals and hightailed back to the castle's kitchens. Roxy had already packed her a lunch of chicken and biscuits along with apples and carrots, which she handed to Darkess with a wink.

≈

Later that day, the sun was getting low in the sky, and the fire was beginning to burn low as Darkess kicked dirt on the remaining flames. Climbing on Zaphod, she took one last look at the setting sun then nudged her horse into a good clip back to the castle. When they cleared the orchard, they slowed to a walk as Darkess thought about the future. The entire afternoon had been spent looking into the flames and contemplating what she was in for. Her entire life had changed over the last few months. Some of it was great, but it all made her feel so different. Different wasn't necessarily bad, she thought, some of it was good, but the scrutiny of everything she did was getting extremely annoying. Maybe this little outing was just the freedom she needed. A fact-finding mission would definitely break up the monotony of the daily routine she seemed to be stuck in.

I'll be somewhere without the prophecy hanging over my head. I can just be Darkess again, if only for a little while. Her thoughts occupied her all the way to the barn where Rufus was milling around talking to the horses. Zaphod snickered as they entered the barn doors. Rufus turned to them and said,

"Hello there, Miss. Did you have a nice ride?"

Darkess jumped down off Zaphod, and replied,

"I had a thinking day. I guess it was a good day, and the ride was great, as usual."

Darkess scratched her horse's head and kissed him on the nose.

"I kept busy with the fire. My mind went on a long journey while I tended the flames."

"So you didn't overwork Zaphod before your long journey?"

"You taught me better than that Rufus. He munched on treats from Roxy and brush around the woods, and we walked until he was cool on the way back."

"Very good. He has a lot to do tonight, so I'll clean him up and get him ready. I'll have him all set in an hour or so," Rufus smiled and bowed his head slightly at Darkess and led Zaphod to his stall.

Darkess returned to the castle to eat dinner with her family if her stomach would let her. It seemed to be filled with butterflies now that she was headed into say goodbye before leaving for a week. What was wrong with her, she wondered. Just a few minutes ago, she had been excited to leave. Now she was getting apprehensive. I can't let them see, she thought as she smoothed her clothes and tucked stray hairs behind her ears. They can probably smell my fear. She took a deep breath, and whispered to herself,

"You can do this. Just say goodbye and enjoy the trip. There is a lot beyond the Vallencourt borders that I can see and learn from. There... that feels better."

Darkess pushed open the door to the kitchens and found Roxy alone finishing up dinner. A spoon was stirring a large pot of gravy as Roxy was carving a large chunk of venison into strips.

"Where is everyone?" Darkess asked.

"They'll be down from the tower in a few minutes. Why don't you set the table?"

Going through the swinging door to the small dining room and pointing her finger at the stacks of dishes, she put each one into place followed by silverware and drinking goblets. As she was finishing up, Roxy brought in a cart full of food, and, as if on cue, her family and Tanner entered the room.

"Perfect timing," Roxy said as she served a steaming bowl of redskin potatoes, a tray of venison smothered in scallions and gravy, a fresh loaf of bread, and a bowl of snap beans. Everyone ate and enjoyed themselves, and when the meal was complete, Richard looked at the clock standing along the wall.

"It seems that it is time to go. I have brought your duffle down. It's by the door. I am sure Rufus has Zaphod ready to go."

As Richard spoke, Roxy slipped off to the kitchens and returned with two bags.

"This one is for you, and give this to Rufus for his dinner."

Roxy gave her a hug followed by all the members of her family. Tanner squeezed her shoulders, and then she was on her way out the door with Silver as her escort. As predicted, Rufus had Zaphod all ready for the trip. Rufus took Darkess' duffle and secured it to the saddle. Pulling Janine's drawing from her cloak, Darkess handed it to her mother. Climbing on her horse, she said,

"Okay mother, I'm ready."

To her horse, she projected her thoughts.

'Boy, are you ready?'

Zaphod shook his head and snorted his approval.

'Mother is going to show you where we are going. I've never been there, so it's all up to you.'

Turning to look at his rider, Zaphod replied,

'You're safe with me. I'll find it.'

Turning back towards Silver, the horse looked at the drawing and pawed his foot. Snorting a goodbye, horse and rider disappeared in an instant.

≈

The squeezing feeling of the teleport was normal to Darkess now, and before she knew it, she and her horse were in the alley of a store with bars over the glass.

"We're here," Darkess whispered into the darkness.

They had rematerialized on the wrong side of the store and had to walk out into the open street to reach the opposite side. There was no one around. They had not been seen, so they continued the slow walk around the storefront.

Zaphod pulled his own head around and walked into the alley. It was dark, and quiet. There was a strange looking black cat with orange spots on its face and paws sitting on a stack of empty crates. It stared at the alley's two newest occupants as if he owned it and was questioning their very presence. Darkess focused on the cat and asked,

'Do you live here?'

No response came from the animal, but it did jump one crate closer to Darkess, sat down, and stared at her again. Darkess decided to take a different approach this time.

'Excuse me? Do you know the shop owner Janine?' Darkess projected as she pointed at the building.

This time the cat decided to reply.

'Are you the young witch coming to visit?'

Darkess was getting mildly irritated by this cat, so she answered a little gruffly.

'Just how many non-magic folk do you know who can speak through telepathy to animals?'

Jumping down from the crates, flipping its tail high in the air to show its irritation, the cat replied,

'You have a point, follow me please.'

Zaphod followed the cat down the alley towards a small stable well hidden behind the shop, his ears twitching as he listened to every sound. Darkess was a little on edge as they continued down the dark path, deeper into the night of the city. Their guide was a strange cat with an attitude problem, so she kept her guard on high and her hands free in case she needed them. A little further down the alley, a voice came to them from the deepest shadows. Zaphod and Darkess froze as one, and the cat continued to walk towards the voice.

"Who goes there?"

The voice was elderly, probably male, although Darkess wasn't sure, so she said boldly with her hands half open in front of her,

"Darkess Goodspeed. Who are you?"

Stepping away from the darkest shadows and into the starlight came a bent form in a black cloak pulled up to hide the identity of the wearer. Knobby old hands clutched a wooden staff as a voice emanated from deep within the cloak and said,

"Prove it."

Still unsure if this person was friend or foe, Darkess pointed at the hood of the cloak and pushed it back to reveal the wrinkled face of a man that looked very similar to Janine, only balding with small tufts of white hair around his ears and several hard years older. The man raised his staff. Darkess took it as a threat and pulled the staff away from the man.

"Ouch. Bold moves for someone so young. You must be Darkess. Kindly give me my staff, and bring Zaphod into his stall."

The old man turned and walked slowly into the barn. Upon hearing his name, Zaphod followed.

"Janine will be here soon. She had to deliver a piece of jewelry for the party tomorrow. I'm her father. Ardimas is the name. Sorry I scared you out there. You never know just who may be creeping around at night in the city. Put Zaphod in here, and I'll be through that door. When you are finished, bring your things and come inside."

≈

The tack was all hung up, her horse was brushed and munching on some grain, and that rude cat from the alley was sitting in the stall watching when Darkess pulled her duffle from the floor and headed towards the door. Once inside, she saw a glow coming from down a short corridor. Assuming Ardimas was there, she followed the glow. Her assumption was correct, and she found a cozy little room with a fire ablaze and chairs in a half circle around it. The old man was pouring a steaming pot into a cup when she appeared.

"Want a cup a tea, dear?"

"Please."

Pouring a second cup, Ardimas pointed towards a chair.

"Sorry for the odd greeting before, but…you can never be too careful. Cookie? Yes, well, then, you are the miraculous witch I've been hearing all about then."

Darkess swallowed some cookie and said,

"I don't know about miraculous, but I'm a witch alright. Your cat seemed to know who we were."

"A bit snippy, isn't he?" Ardimas chuckled.

Darkess saw the glint in the old man's eyes as he laughed. He's a good man, she thought. She pulled back her cloak and settled into her chair. A poof of green smoke blew in from the doorway. Darkess looked to see what had happened as Janine stepped into the room.

"A variation of your grandfather's potion." she giggled as she waved her hands to rid the room of smoke. "Good to see you again. I'm sorry I'm late. Society witches are so picky, you know."

Removing her cloak, Janine tossed it towards a door that promptly opened, snatched the cloak, pulled it inside, and slammed shut again. Smiling at Darkess, Janine said,

"I see you've met my father. Did he make you pass a test to get in here, too?"

Before Darkess had a chance to answer, Ardimas quickly jumped in,

"Of course I made her pass a test. Do you think that I would let just any witch into the house? What kind of an old fool do you take me for?"

"Now dad, no one called you a fool," Janine said reassuringly.

"You think my tests are foolish, what's the difference?"

There was a look of challenge on his old face as he stared at his daughter and waited for her to answer.

"Oh, Dad. Do you really think there's anyone else with flaming red hair on a big black horse with special markings that can teleport here exactly as we planned?"

Stirring his now cooling tea, Ardimas mumbled.

"People can be mistaken for other people, demons can impersonate, even posses – you know that."

He was angry, because they were both right, and they both knew it.

"We have a lot to show dad, don't we Darkess?"

Janine smiled at her guest. Having a family argument in front of company was embarrassing, and she pursed her lips and wrinkled her nose at her father. She pulled the pin from her hair, and it spilled onto her shoulders, relieving the severity of her looks.

"Darkess is a very skilled young witch," she said, "and you will be amazed at all that she can do."

"I've already seen her use telekinesis, and she must talk to animals, because she followed that uppity cat of yours. And that in itself is impressive, my dear."

Ardimas smiled at Darkess and offered her another cookie. Darkess was rather enjoying herself. Someone else was arguing about who can do what, or was old enough to protect themselves, or what was or wasn't correct procedure for something. Smiling back at Ardimas, Darkess kept her mouth full and stayed out of the conversation. She liked these two and preferred not to take sides in the matter. She was, after all, the student here.

"Impressive. Wait until you see what she can really do. Maybe a little demonstration is in order. Darkess, what do you think? Are you up for it?" Janine asked.

Darkess chewed slowly, looking from Janine to Ardimas and back again. Darkess could tell by their looks that they both wanted to see her powers, so she said,

"What do you want me to do?"

Janine thought for a moment and instructed,

"Light this piece of wood."

Janine stooped down, picked up a piece of kindling, and held it up.

"Freeze the fire, levitate the kindling to that pot, and then unfreeze the fire."

In the time it takes to take a breath, there was a small flaming stick in the pot on the counter in the kitchen.

Ardimas' eyes were protruding, and his jaw was hanging slack. Janine was clapping and said,

"Well done. What did I tell you! Now that was impressive."

"In all my years," Ardimas admitted, "I have never seen such power or speed in someone so young. You are without a doubt an astonishing young witch. I am glad I didn't test you any harder than I did."

Ardimas winked at Darkess and offered her another cookie, which she refused with thanks and asked him, "What is your power?"

"I'll show you," Ardimas said and promptly disappeared, then reappeared.

"Wow! I've never seen anyone do that before."

"I didn't even know I could do it until one day, my father almost caught me snooping around in his study...and let me tell you, I was afraid for my life. He had experiments going in the room and forbade me to be in there without him. When he opened the door, he looked right at me. He hadn't seen me, or his wrath would have exploded upon me. He went on about his business as if he were alone. I snuck out before the door closed behind him when I realized he hadn't seen me. I snuck down to my parents' room and stood before my mother's mirror. I was clear looking. I was becoming visible again, but I had been completely gone for a while there. Took a bit of practice becoming invisible at will, fear response, you see. I was in my fourteenth year, I believe. How old are you?"

"Twelve winters this year," Darkess replied.

"Well, I'll be," Ardimas said.

"You have one more power that you haven't shown dad. Want to try it now? One more surprise will make him sleep well tonight."

Smiling at Darkess, Janine looked over her shoulder at her father and pointed with her thumb at him.

"Fear response, you say?" Darkess questioned.

"Fear response," Janine confirmed.

It was like they were reading each other's minds. Janine wanted Darkess to channel her father's power. Darkess concentrated on being scared, taking larger and quicker breaths. For a moment, nothing seemed to be happening. She concentrated on using the same feeling she used to freeze as she stared into the flames. Slowly, she began to fade out, the color bleaching out of her entire body, clothes and all. Then all at once, she was gone.

"By George, she can channel!" Ardimas said, slapping his knee.

Darkess reappeared laughing at the old man's excitement.

"I knew you two would get along. She is just skillful enough to keep you occupied for a while and out of trouble. We should have a good week together. Oh, and Darkess, while you are here, I would like you to make the acquaintance of a few people. We will do some research into those dragons of yours, too. Tomorrow morning, we'll go through my shop, and I can show you what I do. And then tomorrow night, we will be going to the party…in full wizard style."

Janine said all of this with great animation, and her eyebrows wiggled there at the end. Darkess was surprised by all of this. Janine's hair was down, and the severe business persona seemed to have vanished, leaving behind an overly excited witch. She was going to be more fun than the stuffy lady she seemed to be in the public eye.

"But for now, lets get you all settled in. Your room is across from mine."

≈

The following morning dawned gray and dreary, nothing like the day before. But that seemed to have no bearing on the mood of the house. When Darkess awoke, she tore off her covers and ran to look down the hall to see just who was awake. She heard noise coming from the kitchen and smelled a rich brew. Making her way around the corner and into the great room, she saw Ardimas and Janine milling around.

"Morning!" they both said in unison.

"Morning," Darkess replied as she yawned and rubbed the sleep from her eyes.

Climbing on a tall stool, she leaned on the butcher block as Janine put a steaming cup in front of her. Darkess breathed in the aroma and blew on it.

"Ready for some food, or do you want to wait a bit?" Janine asked.

"I could eat," Darkess said as her stomach growled from the smells wafting through the air.

Cracking an egg into the skillet, Ardimas said,

"Good, I'm starved, too. Bread, jam and eggs, whaddya think?"

≈

After breakfast, Darkess dressed for work and met Janine at the back door of her shop. Upon opening the door, torches flared up. There were glass cases, wooden crates, an enormous workbench, and piles of stones and hunks of metal. Standing in the middle of the room was a dusty forge, which was workable, but almost never used. There were crates with bones, glass, wire, and small pouches all labeled. On the other side of the workbench was another door. Janine opened it and stepped through. This was her shop, the area where the customer placed the order or bought something already made. There were display cases, wood trays lined with felt, and finished pieces laid about. A lot of items were on display. Some were not for sale but meant to show the skill in Janine's workmanship. There were the hidden cases, meant for only magical sales, and Janine could fit any style, for man or beast, or the occasional cross-breed.

Janine let Darkess look around, and then she showed her the process that each piece went through. It started with the interview, requests for design, metals, stones, and the like. A seer was sometimes consulted for both magical and non-magical customers, depending on the purpose of the piece. Then the most important part: making the item.

There were a couple of small boxes lying on the workbench, and Janine reached for one of them, spreading its contents out on the surface. There was a small nugget of gold, five stones of different colors, a piece of parchment with a name, a description of what was wanted, and the specific item to be made – in this case, a necklace pendant.

"I need you to just sit quietly for a moment, and watch while I work on this," Janine explained. "It takes a little concentration then we can talk."

Rolling the stones around on the surface of the table with her finger, and then looking at the piece of gold, Janine began to get the feel for what she was going to make. Picking up the chunk of gold, she rolled it between her palms, and it began to change shape. It began to look more flat. It smoothed out, becoming a tube. Then in one hand Janine held the piece, staring at it, it began to elongate. It curled up on itself looking very snakelike. She took a stone from the table and laid it on one end of the piece. It immediately sunk to the perfect depth and froze into place. Janine repeated that step with the next four stones, arranging them along the length of the shape.

Once all five stones were properly placed, Janine pinched one end of the piece and stared at it until a small hole appeared in one end. The end piece was a curved golden tube, very snakelike, but not a snake.

"There. What do you think?" Janine asked.

"That was amazing. You have such control over the metal. Do you do that with all the pieces?"

"Magic saves time and material, so yes, I do this even on pieces for mortals. However, for this, it's a chakra necklace. It is meant for balance of energy, and we will be putting a spell on it."

"A spell? For what?"

"Well, this particular witch seems to believe she's cursed, and she has bad luck because of this curse. So, in order to help her help herself, we're going to try and give her a little boost in morale. No one has been able to find any source of a curse. Her family and a seer both believe her bad luck to be from lack of believing in herself. We are going to try and change that. Can you give me the silver flecked candles from that cupboard? There should be three of them."

Darkess retrieved the candles and placed them on the table in front of Janine. Darkess lit each one as Janine pulled out the spell that she had written for this piece. Janine spoke as she went through the process.

"Silver candles, which help stability, leech the negativity from this poor girl. An adventurine stone will help remove unhealthy thoughts and help the healing process. One green tourmaline to help balance and add strength to sooth the nerves. One moonstone to help even out the emotions, give a sense of peace, and help with hormonal issues. One sodalite to help the mind think clearer. It elicits deep thought and can calm those who normally overreact to a given situation. And last, but certainly not least, a tiger's eye. This is for protection, and it's a personal courage stimulant.

"Now Darkess, if you'll hold my hand and recite this spell with me, it will give it more strength."

Janine took Darkess' hand and together, they read,

"Damaged spirit with unbalanced chi, take these stones unto thee. Use their strength to guard completely. Give the wearer of this piece a sense of tranquility."

For a moment each stone had a glow, like a tiny fire burning within. Then their colors returned to normal.

"That was incredible," Darkess whispered with a sparkle in her eyes.

Janine looked at Darkess with surprise, and said,

"Yes, I've never seen that happen before. Your magic is strong. You were the incredible part."

"Who me?" Darkess said with a wrinkled forehead. "What did I do? You wrote the spell."

"That I may, but you gave it a kick that I have never witnessed. I hope this woman is happy. That spell should help quite a lot."

Cleaning off any fingerprints, Janine put the necklace in a small silk bag with a tiny mother of pearl button and replaced it in the project box. Janine's mind was racing as she looked from Darkess to the silk bag. You could almost see the plan taking shape in her mind. What could Darkess do with metal if she had the chance? Her powers were unbelievable. There's no telling the depths of this child's power, Janine thought. She could be the most powerful witch alive.

"Want to try making something from metal?"

The look on Darkess' face said it all, but she said,

"Oh, would you?"

"I'll let you have one on me. If you do anything else, it goes on sale in the shop. Unfortunately, I don't have the resources that you do," Janine laughed, patting Darkess on the back.

"You go ahead and look around at the materials. I'll fetch us something to drink and a snack. And check on dad. Err...would you mind an audience while you work? I know he would love to watch."

"Sure," Darkess said over her shoulder as she was digging for her supplies. Janine slipped out the door as Darkess reached for another bowl with leftover bits and pieces of this and that.

≈

Opening the door Janine held a tray with a steaming pot, three different cups, and a small plate of dehydrated fruit. Darkess was involved in her work and continued to scribble furiously on a scrap of parchment, saying nothing when they entered. Ardimas was directly behind Janine with a smile and a flush look on his face. Janine walked over to the workbench and set down her load quietly. She watched Darkess work as Ardimas circled the table to get a better vantage point.

"A spell?" Janine asked.

"Do you remember on the Holiday when I had that dream? The one Harlow shared with me?" Darkess asked.

"Yes..." Janine nodded her head. "What about it?"

Smiling big and wickedly, Darkess said,

"The egg. I'm going to make the egg."

Darkess' mind drifted off to her dream, and she just knew the egg was real. The dream was a sign, and she was going to make it...with Janine's help, of course. After a moment of silence and thought, Janine looked at Darkess and said,

"Alright there Missy, let's see what you've got."

Pulling a small, leather-lined tray towards her, Janine saw that it contained a small chunk of silver, a much smaller chunk of gold, and a smooth piece of moonstone. The parchment that Darkess had been working on had both the spell and a drawing on it. Janine smiled and said,

"It seems rather advanced for a first try. But if you'd like, we will try. But please don't be discouraged if it doesn't work out as you've expected. Okay?"

"You'll let me do it myself, alright? No help. Umm, I mean, I'll channel your power, but I really want to make this myself," Darkess said in her enthusiasm.

Janine waved her hands and backed up a step, saying with her hand over her heart,

"I will only help if you ask."

Darkess looked relieved as Janine pulled up a bench for her. Ardimas quietly watched.

"Alright, you have your idea and your materials, now all you need is focus. Concentrate on the metal. Any metal will melt. Some just take more time than others until you get a handle on the power, anyway. Which metal is first?"

"The silver," Darkess answered.

"Hold the silver in your dominate hand, and hold mine," Janine instructed. "To get a feel for the melt, as I call it, concentrate."

Darkess picked up the silver, and cradled it in her hand. She stared at it, concentrating on the core shape of the heart of the egg. The bottom of the egg needed to have two arrows with points on both ends for the four directions. And it needed to be flat so it could sit on a hard surface, or in the palm of her hand. The top center would hold the moonstone. The gold would be the skin of the egg that held in the stone and would shift open around the silver arrows to show direction.

For what seemed like an eternity, the silver did nothing but tremble slightly in her hand. Nearly frustrated, Darkess wrinkled her brow in concentration. Janine spoke softly,

"You're seeing the shape of what you want? Now try seeing the metal for what it is – a solid. Now turn it into a liquid. Concentrate on the liquid, then the form."

Janine was fighting herself by not showing Darkess exactly what to do, but it was difficult. Seconds later, the metal became gelatinous then a liquid, and suddenly began to ooze across the palm of her hand. It began to drip off her hand and onto the work surface.

"Nice try," Janine said as she pulled all of the metal into one lump again, hardening it. "Now try again."

Darkess took a deep breath and exhaled quickly in mild frustration, then she evened her breathing and stared at the lump once more. The metal became gelatinous again but only enough to start moving where Darkess directed it to go. The silver turned into a tube about three inches in length. Slowly, it began to shrink, getting fatter and more rounded until it was a perfect egg shape. A small dimple appeared at the apex of the egg.

Watching Darkess work, Ardimas realized that she no longer had a hold of Janine's hand but was holding both hands out over the work surface as she manipulated the metal. Both he and Janine were amazed at how quickly she had picked up the power. "Prodigy," Ardimas mouthed to Janine when they exchanged glances of awe. Janine shook her head yes, then quickly looked back to see what Darkess would do next.

Darkess had the egg standing on the table and was placing the moonstone in its dimpled top. Without missing a beat, Darkess took the gold chunk and began to manipulate it in her hand. It began to melt instantly, turning thinner and more like a sheet of parchment. She placed one edge of the golden sheet on the side of the silver egg, and it began to bond, encasing it and holding the moonstone in place with a small circular lip. Darkess picked up the egg and watched as the arrows in the silver were now traced in gold but still perfectly visible. The gold now encased almost the entire egg. It was finished, and Darkess looked at it from every angle, studying it closely for any flaws. When she seemed satisfied with her work, it was time for the spell.

The silver candles that had been on the workbench earlier had been replaced by white pillars, which Darkess lit by pointing at them. She pulled the spell closer to her, and read aloud the words that she had only written a few minutes before.

"Take this gold, shiny but lifeless, and give it a sense of direction. Give it the knowledge of north, south, east, and west, and give it to me at my request."

The egg shined so brightly for a moment that it was difficult to see. Then it returned to its original luster.

"Whew," Ardimas said as he passed out the tea and fruit. "Try to see if it works."

Placing the egg in the palm of her hand, Darkess said, "Show me north."

The egg spun around wildly on its moonstone top. When the egg stopped, the arrows on the bottom pointed to their perspective direction. Immediately, the two arrows pointing east and west wrapped themselves around the egg and pointed to the same direction as one of the arrows still on the base of the egg, which was now its top. It was pointing north. The smile on Darkess' face could only be matched by the one on Janine's, for the twelve-year-old girl had mastered her power in only ten minutes and had written a powerful spell in the process. Janine spoke quickly,

"Try again. Only this time, ask it for a place, like Vallencourt Castle."

Before Darkess could say even one word, the egg began to spin wildly again. The egg stopped in place as it had before, only this time, it was pointing in a different direction. The north and west arrows remained in place, and the south and east arrows were waving towards the center of the stationary arrows, northwest. Darkess sucked air in quickly and said.

"Look. It knows where to go. Where is Crystal City's Palace?"

The egg repeated the process it had before, again pointing northwest.

"Wow," Darkess breathed. "Did you see that, Ardimas?"

His face was more puzzled than anything else as he asked,

"Why did the egg respond to Janine's voice? Your spell said: Give it to me at my request. I'm not trying to overshadow the delight of your success, but who else will the egg respond to, I wonder?"

"Well…why don't you try," Janine suggested.

Ardimas moved closer to Darkess and said,

"Show me where Splunkits Market is?"

All three of them stared at the egg and waited for its wild dance, but the egg remained motionless. Darkess looked from Ardimas to Janine as she spoke.

"I used her power to make the egg. That must be it. What else could it be?"

"It does make sense. My power, used by you, and your spell. Plus, we were holding hands while you were making the core of your egg. It recognizes both of us. Extraordinary," Janine said.

"Extraordinary indeed," Ardimas said.

≈

Studying and questioning the egg extensively over lunch, meeting customers in the shop with Janine, and readying themselves for the party that evening made the day full. By the time they were in the carriage and on their way to the party, Darkess was yawning every minute or two. Janine finally said,

"You can take a nap. It'll be a little while before we get there."

It wasn't long before Darkess had drifted off to sleep and was dreaming of riding Zaphod through the fields at home. Just as she was tearing through the woods, throwing fireballs at targets, a voice came to her in the fogginess of sleep.

"Darkess…we're here. Wake up."

Rubbing her eyes, her focus was blurry for a moment. Then she saw the carriages, rows and rows of them. There was an odd rack with brooms and what looked like rolled up carpets on it. Clouds of blue, red, green and gray smoke erupted here and there around the courtyard as wizards appeared from afar. The most beautiful Pegasus was standing in a secluded area behind the carriages, mostly hidden from view; however, it extended its wings, shook its head and snorted, as if to say hello. As the carriage came to a stop at the furthest end of the row, Darkess saw it. They were so rare that she had only ever seen a drawing of one. It seemed to have been made of different creatures: part lion and part golden eagle. She pointed to it with a look of wonder on her face.

"Yes. It is a gryphon. Her name is Sugar, and she belongs to Alieria. She always dreamed of having a dragon for a pet and riding it from place to place. But since none have been seen in hundreds of years, she got Sugar. Just wait 'til we get inside," Janine said with enthusiasm and raised her eyebrows nearly up to her hairline.

The gryphon crossed her legs and quietly watched the guests arrive as she lay in the shadows of the hedges at the corner to the front of the castle.

The sleepiness that Darkess had felt only moments ago had vanished as she got down from the carriage. She and Janine walked towards the castle, their steps muffled by the hard packed earth beneath them. Excitement registered on both their faces as they reached the main entrance. Just inside the door, there was the most different person Darkess had ever seen. He seemed to be wearing a snug suit of burlap bags that were dyed black. He asked each person for their names and announced them as they arrived. He was a large man with an oddly misshapen head and a deep gruff voice. Before he asked Darkess who she was, he announced loudly.

"All welcome Janine of the family Fipps and Miss Darkess of the family Goodspeed from the Vallencourt Clan."

He nodded to them, and they proceeded down the steps towards the crowd.

"He knew our names," Darkess whispered to Janine.

"Yes dear, we have met before. And he was probably told by that sprite next to him who you are. Prak is a half-breed, Ogre and human. That's the reason for his odd appearance. He's a good man and very trustworthy. The little sprite there has a guest list, and I am sure it knew who you are, especially since you are somewhat of a celebrity here in the magic world," Janine smiled at Darkess.

A loud cackling laugh erupted off to the side of the steps and both witches turned to see the source of the noise. Janine realized it was Alieria squealing with delight that they had arrived. Alieria was practically shoving her way through the crowd to greet them, and in a thick Muscovatan accent, she said,

"Oh, my darlings, I am so glad you have finally arrived. I have been so looking forward to our meeting, Miss Darkess. I was told that you are fond of the dragon."

Alieria draped her arm around Darkess, leading her over to a padded bench seat near the fireplace. Ordering a servant nearby, Alieria barked,

"Drinks for my friends…ladies, anything you want, just ask."

≈

After being introduced to as many people as Alieria could shove past her, Darkess began to wish she had not come at all. Everyone seemed to be gawking at her, and it seemed as if they had all either met her, or knew of her, and Darkess was feeling uneasy. She had only come here to learn about dragons, not to be the center of attention for someone else's social climb. She did not intend to be the shiny new toy for some witch wannabe socialite. Why does the only dragon expert in the country have to be a social butterfly with more hot air than any real dragon could ever produce?

Darkess took a deep breath to steady herself and grabbed an hors d'oeuvre as the tray floated past. She removed her cloak, chewing with a fake smile spread across her face as Alierias' mouth kept pace with the king's fastest runner. Finished with the mouthful she had, Darkess scanned the room for another tray of food when Alieria noticed the bangle on her arm, which had been previously hidden by her cloak.

"Exquisite. Darkess, dear, that bangle is just exquisite. Is it Janine's work?"

Surprised that Alieria was talking to her instead of about her, Darkess nearly choked as she squeaked out a response,

"Yes. Birthday present."

Having lost all train of thought, Alieria ogled the bangle, taking in every detail.

"You didn't order it?"

Wetting her mouth, and clearing her throat, Darkess answered,

"No, it was all her idea."

"How fascinating," Alieria breathed.

"What's so fascinating?" Darkess asked.

Taking Darkess' arm and walking towards her own private seating, Alieria's entire attitude changed.

"You're not just some child with a craving for dragons, are you?"

There was a moment of silence. Darkess wasn't sure what to say or how much to tell Alieria, so she looked around for Janine, who was cutting quickly through the crowd towards them. Alieria prodded more.

"Come, come child, did you hear me? What exactly are you here for?"

Janine arrived just in time.

"You know exactly what she is here for and who she is. She is of the Vallencourt Clan," Janine said rather hotly.

"That's not what I meant, and you know it. That bangle looks similar to drawings I've seen in some ancient dragon manuscripts from the old country. These drawings are so old that few living eyes have seen them. Neither of you I am sure. What are you two after?" Alieria demanded.

Darkess butted in, defending the two of them.

"I am here to hear the legends you know about dragons – all you can tell me. I want to know how they lived, their powers, if there are any left in hiding, and are there any eggs around? Whatever you can remember, no matter how odd or obscure would be helpful. I need to know more."

"Why?" Alieria asked with caution in her voice.

Darkess looked at Janine and knew that she couldn't tell Alieria what she wanted to know. So going against what she believed in, and to stop an argument, she lied.

"I can't stop dreaming about them. They almost seem to haunt me. I must know more."

Alieria's attitude was slowly defrosting, and she said,

"But the bangle?"

Janine pulled out a lie of her own.

"The seer described the dreams of Darkess in great detail. She could see glimpses of them, and she said that the dragon was the girl's totem. The seer drew a picture of a statue from one of Darkess' dreams, and this was very similar to that drawing. She is not here to steal from you, but to learn from you."

Janine lightly touched Alieria's arm, trying to convince her that they were not here under a veil of deceit – even though they were.

"You're sure you are only here to learn and not steal my most precious things?" Alieria cocked her head to the side and eyed Darkess viscously.

Darkess smiled the best smile she could muster under the circumstances and bowed deeply, never breaking eye contact with Alieria as she said.

"On my honor as a white witch from the Clan of Vallencourt, I beg you. I am here to learn as much about dragon lore as I can. I swear on my honor that I am not a thief. I do not wish to steal anything, and I find it rather rude that you would think it of me. I have openly come here to be your friend and student, but if you are so guarded against friendship deeper than public status, then I shall take my leave and be done with you."

Darkess' highhanded manner and blunt tone provided the perfect combination to open Alierias' eyes to the fact that Darkess was indeed here to learn. Logic overruled Alieria's guarded behavior, and she returned a guilty smile, saying,

"I am sorry for my reaction. I just protect my treasures well, and that bangle looks like an ancient clan symbol. Anyone wearing it would most likely be here to rummage through my collection without the best intentions."

Leading Janine and Darkess from the room by way of a hidden door under the stairs, Alieria whispered,

"Follow me."

One by one they passed through an archway that led deeper under the castle. When they had all passed the archway, Alieria turned to them both and said,

"You have just passed through a gateway that determines, shall we say, if you are good or evil. To me, that is. Your entry would have been barred should you intend to do harm to me or my household."

Walking further down the tunnel, they could see a light at the other end, beckoning to them. Janine and Darkess looked at each other with questioning looks.

"You have passed the test. Between that and the bangle, I will grant you the use of my private library."

They walked briskly down the rest of the tunnel to the brightly lit room. Before they entered, Alieria said one more thing in a voice with warning behind it.

"The only thing that can leave this room is knowledge. The exits are blocked with a spell that prohibits any item from leaving…another of my protection spells."

Alieria stopped just inside the door and turned to get the reaction from their faces when they saw the collection stored in the hidden room. Both witches looked like they had been slapped. Neither of them had had any idea about the mass of this collection until they stood looking at it. A huge bolder lay on the floor all the way across the room, and on top of it stood a real dragon, expertly preserved. It was an infant with immature wings flexed out, talons gripping the stone, and rubies where eyes had once been. Knowing it would be the first thing they noticed, Alieria said,

"Yes, it is real. It was killed generations ago, and my ancestors believed, as I do, that the dragon was a sacred creature to be loved and protected. So, they stole it and had it preserved. It has been perched on that stone ever since. This entire collection has been amassed over centuries by my family and close friends who believe in the same cause."

Darkess approached the dragon and looked into its ruby eyes. She felt like she was on the right path. Somewhere in this room, she thought, is another key to this mystery that is my life. Her eyes floated slowly away from the infant dragon and drifted around the room at the shelves of books. Hundreds of spines faced the room, some with names printed on them others were plain. There were stacks of scrolls from before there were books. Some were so old they were turning to dust. There were jars of powder and some with liquid. Darkess also saw bowls filled with horns, scales, and things she could not identify.

Alieria made herself comfortable on a padded seat as the two witches made their way around the room. They were lost in their thoughts, hands trailing over objects and searching through all the amazing things this room contained. She waited patiently for the questions to begin. Janine opened a large armoire and found an unbelievable collection of athames, swords, and a few other assorted weapons. Everything was marked with a dragon or took the shape of one.

"Such wonderous artworks of death," Janine said, more to herself than anyone else as she picked up one knife to inspect it more closely.

Darkess had found a map of the world painted on the wall, from the floor to eight feet up the granite. Closer inspection of it proved to be very informative. Flag pins marked tiny dragon shapes all over it identifying areas where dragons had been in legend, seen alive, and where bones and skeletons and eggs had been found. She walked from pin to pin, reading what each said. Some of the flags referred to books, others to things found in the room, such as the nearly perfectly preserved baby dragon, the skull hanging from the ceiling, and the broken eggshell resting on a blanket on a near by shelf. There were even references to different magic clans, and Native tribes that had the dragon as their center of worship or guardianship. Items from all over the world were marked. Most had a date or dates connected to some now extinct tribes, while others were recent enough to be marked with modern city names.

"You could stay in this room for years and never see it all," Darkess said as she looked up at the ceiling and all that was suspended there.

There was a paper mache dragon from an ancient festival in the old world and some amazing tile work depicting a knight in full armor fighting a fire-breathing dragon with a woman clutched in its claws. There were the words of the knights' code written around the picture as its border.

"You can say that again. I've spent a large portion of my life in this room...or searching for the truth to the legends. I've even found a few items on my own, but I own this, and I'll die not knowing all that is here. Unless I find a dragon who will grant me the gift of a longer life," Alieria said, gesturing about the room.

Then Alieria went silent, her eyes went out of focus, and she drifted off to another place. Darkess went back to sifting through all of the different sections in this large room. Along another wall, she found a desk sitting between two large bookshelves. On it were several pieces of parchment and a painting of a splendid red dragon that caught Darkess' eye. Pulling out the chair, she took a seat and pulled the painting close. She was delighted with the amount of detail in the picture, down to the shading of the scales and claws and the odd cross pattern in the scales on the dragon's chest. Darkess was looking intensely at the painting when she heard Alieria say,

"I see you've discovered the secret of the Hercules Dragon."

"The Hercules Dragon?" Janine inquired, joining the other witches at the desk.

"That is what I have been working on over the last few months. 'The legend of the Hercules Dragon.' I've been hunting for actual proof of this dragon's life. The story goes that this particular dragon saw the slaying of an innocent traveling monk. It was said that he refused to hand over his purse, which contained gold coins that he had collected for a family that had fallen on hard times. The monk died trying to help the weak and the sick of his parish, and this enraged the dragon. He wept a river of tears that flowed down his face and neck. It is said that when the tears dried, his scales had changed their shape and formed the shape of a cross. The dragon vowed to protect all those pure of heart...monks, fryers, and priests on their travels through the lands where he lived. Supposedly, he protected the good monks so they could better serve their flocks. And, he has an extra sense. He can smell rot and evil, and any man of the cloth who was a charlatan would be swiftly dispatched, just as any thief or killer would be," Alieria said and continued. "I haven't heard of any sightings in my lifetime of him, and my grandmother was the first to hear of this tale, or at least the first to write of it. Unfortunately for us, these stories are all second hand. There have been no eye witnesses, and no one knows the name of the monk who died, or when or where he was killed."

Raising her shoulders and arms up to show how confused she felt, Alieria finally said,

"Tis a hopeless fairytale. But isn't the story touching…and such a work of art, even if it is from the imagination."

Alieria touched the page lovingly as if she needed to feel the texture in the painting to feel something of this legend, trying somehow to make it real. Darkess connected with Alieria in that moment and touched her hand, which ripped Alieria from her reverie back to reality.

"I know the feeling, the hunt for the proverbial ghost. I know, believe me, when I say I understand your search, and maybe, just maybe, one of these dragon tales will be more than just a cracked egg, a bone, or a story someone heard," Darkess said with a smile.

"Are you sure that you are only twelve winters?" Alieria asked, squeezing Darkess' hand with a tear glistening at the corner of her eye.

"Foolish me, crying over a beast that has long since died out. Go back to your search ladies. I'll get us some refreshments. I shall return in a snap." Alieria sniffed and turned to leave by way of another tunnel, dabbing her eyes as she went.

"Poor Alieria. I wish that we could tell her what we are after. I wish that she was a member of the Order," Darkess said as she thumbed through the parchment pieces below the painting, finding that they were various stories about the Hercules dragon.

"We shouldn't speak of the Order. Just keep looking. Maybe we will find something helpful. She won't be gone for long," Janine said quickly in a whisper as she went to another cabinet and begun to gently rummage through its contents.

Darkess stood up and looked about the room with the hopes that something would call out to her. She saw an odd scale laying on a piece of white fur. The scale was black with a hint of blue around the edges, and the fur lay on a pile of parchment connected with leather straps. Darkess gently removed the straps and took the stack back to the desk. The first page was titled, 'How to Kill the Hellfire Dragon.' The second page had a potion that had to brew for a month along with instructions on how to use it and the spell to combine with it. The power of three strong wizards from Alieria's family line or another Dragon clan was required to make it work. The next page was the most interesting. It contained the legend of the

Hellfire Dragon. This dragon had been the portal to hell used by the Dark One himself and was in slumber, buried deep in a mountain somewhere. The legend also stated that if ever found and properly controlled by potion or magic, the dragon would permit the portal to hell to be reopened, thus allowing the darkest of evil creatures to return to the surface of the planet and bring about the end of times. This scale was supposed to be from this dragon of lore. The sword, of some ancient wizard trying to use the dragon's scale to make a potion to control it, knocked it off. The dragon, according to legend, killed the wizard with his black flame, which is said to capture the soul upon death, and pulled the body into its cave. Once inside, the dragon blew down the stones covering the entrance and enclosed himself with them, taking one last meal before his long slumber. Some other wizard hunting for his fallen comrade found the scale, and that is all that he found. This story was written nearly one thousand years ago with not even a whisper of a clue to his whereabouts since.

Darkess closed the book, put the fur and scale back in its place, and said,

"Well, that was interesting but of no use to me."

"Nothing of any use here either," Janine, said without stopping her search.

Alieria returned with a tray of food and drinks floating in front of her.

"Find anything interesting dears?" she asked.

"Interesting describes everything in this room. So what exactly do you want us to say? I've been in awe since I caught the first glimpse of this room" Janine admitted.

"I'm sorry. I tend to take this room for granted since I grew up here," Alieria said. "Food is served dears. Take a break, and enjoy some of the party you are missing."

The three witches got themselves a plate of food and chatted for a while. After a plate of food and a lot of conversation, Darkess had a pang of selfishness and said,

"Are we keeping you from your guests?"

Alieria let out a loud laugh and said,

"They are all so into the who's who. They probably don't even know that I'm not floating around the room. Besides, I said hello to quite a few of the newcomers at the food table. They all seem fine. Prak will come find me or send someone if there are any problems. I'm enjoying this. I allow so few in here, though I have had requests from several overzealous dragon fanatics. I still refuse most people entrance. Theft is all they have in mind, so I have several guests who are here to help with security. You know, the crazies can sometimes slip into the party. But they'll never get down here."

Feasting on some marvelous food, Darkess was now truly enjoying herself when a thought hit her

"Alieria," she asked, "do you know any stories about baby dragons?"

Alieria cleared her throat, thinking.

"No. Well, just him," she said pointing at the preserved dragon.

"Any odd dragon stories?" Darkess queried.

"I believe the oddest legend I have heard of is one that starts with a genie. Well no, it actually starts with an evil witch who found the genie's lamp. The witch was destitute, dirty, and a little on the loony side. She was a hermit who studied dark magic. When she found the lamp, she couldn't help but wish for beauty, which she promptly received. She would stare into her mirror for hours at a time, until she finally noticed her clothes. They were dirty, old and worn, so she wished for wealth. The next day, a man came to her small hut to tell her that she was the bastard child of a wealthy land baron. He had died and left her a huge house, a large cash roll, and a vast amount of land.

"Even as crazy as she was, she decided to save her last wish, trying to make the last wish the best one. In the meantime, with her newly acquired wealth and beauty, she had a great many suitors once they found out she was unwed. But in comparing her old life with her new life, she truly missed the solitude that came with her old way of living. So she began to want her wealth and beauty without the responsibility that came with it. There were always too many people around for her to work on magic, and when her father died, he had left her a job to continue the money's flow into the house. She hated the job and began thinking about her last wish. After much thought, she wished for control over the entire countryside and for all of the people to leave her alone to do whatever she pleased. But the genie refused, because she was a selfish being who also wanted wealth, beauty, and suitors for herself. She no longer wanted to be a servant of other people's whims. She hated her lamp and wanted the freedom her masters had to come and go as they pleased. She couldn't stand the idea of being corked away ever again, so she plotted against her current master, the evil witch.

"The genie finally granted the witch's final wish, convincing the witch that the two of them should look identical to pull it off. The witch could have wealth and beauty, and the genie would take on the role for the public eye. The genie performed her magic, with a little twist the witch knew nothing about, and the final wish was complete. For a week or so, the genie played her role as the public side of the witch, all the while plotting her revenge for being corked away for so many centuries. One day, the witch decided to leave her home to get more supplies for her stores. The day went as she planned until her return home, when the guards stopped her for being an imposter. She was thrown from her own grounds by her own guards with a threat that she should never return or she would be killed on sight. That was the genie's first big mistake.

"She should have killed the witch or locked her up, for she had spent her entire life in the wild hills and had no fear of being alone. She was a strong witch who knew her craft well. So the witch went to her old shack, which the genie had kindly left unguarded, and she waited. She brewed up two potions. One was to turn a human into a dragon. The other was to temporarily alter the appearance. It would take two weeks to brew the first potion and a month for the second, so she plotted and waited patiently for her plan to evolve. One lunar cycle and one day later, she was ready.

"Wearing the garb of a local church and carrying a basket full of baked goods, the witch made her way back to her new home, disguised from head to toe. In executing her plan, she made a cake for the guards with a sleeping draught in it and a plate of cookies for her secretary and other consorts tainted with befuddlement potion to keep them distracted but awake should they be needed. She also had a bottle of potion for reversing the appearance as well as the genie's favorite: one apple tart laced with the dragon potion.

"The witch walked directly to the guards, presented her sweets, and requested visitation with the young baroness. Being unaccustomed to such generosity, they wolfed down the cakes as they showed the witch inside. They promptly fell asleep and hit the ground hard. When the witch arrived at the door to the home, the secretary allowed her entrance when he realized the guards were not protesting. The witch smiled and played her little game with the workers in the home, giving them treats mixed with befuddlement potion. When everyone was off in his or her own little worlds, the witch made her move on the genie.

"Announcing herself as the good Sister Margurite, she asked if she could borrow some of the baroness' time. Knowing full well that food and flattery work well on this particular genie, the witch pried herself in the door. As she spun her fake tale of woe, the unsuspecting genie gobbled the tart. When the potion started to take affect, the witch knew her plan was working.

"The genie's face began to contort, and she looked at the disguised woman in pain. A smile spread across the face of the witch as she pulled a piece of parchment from her sleeve and unfolded it. The physical appearance of the genie began to change. Her eyes began to bulge as she clenched her stomach and whimpered in pain. She began to back away from the witch, but the witch was on her in a flash, shoving the genie out an open window. Laughing as she watched the genie tumble down the roof and off the edge, she jumped to the roof herself to find her victim writhing on the ground. She floated down to her and read the spell aloud.

"Take this trickster in disguise,
Give her a set of beady eyes,
Make the greed that's in her heart,
Consume her from horn to dart,
Have her skin erupt in scales,
And make her a dragon right down to her nails."

"A gray smoke filled the air around the spasming genie. The witch drank her potion, reversing her appearance and making the genie scream in anger and pain as the two of them changed into something different together. The smoke became so thick that neither could see the other. When it began to clear, a growl erupted from it. The witch had stopped her laughing and started to back away from the larger cloud. What lay beneath it was no longer a genie but a gray dragon, twitching and growing in size. Backing away from the beast she had created, she watched as the spell took full effect. The dragon rolled over, got to its feet shakily, and stared at the witch. The eyes of the dragon were human, but for a moment, and the witch gasped as she watched them change shape and color to a brilliant red. It had worked."

"Quickly the witch ran screaming around the front of her home, breaking the befuddlement potion's grip on her aids and secretary and waking the guards from their induced sleep. The dragon followed, whether there was anything human left at all is uncertain, but she followed the witch in a roaring huff until the guards jumped out of their shelter with swords drawn. The witch feared being discovered as a witch more than she feared the dragon; so instead of using any form of magic, she ran to the house and let the guards do their job. Once inside, the witch ran down to her hidden study where all of her magical supplies were kept. Then she heard it: screaming and a splintering crash. In all of her planning of how to regain her wealth and remove the genie from power, she didn't even think of consequences. She had forgotten to put a control element in her spell, and now the dragon was after blood. The witch had made it to her study and was flipping through a book looking wildly for a spell to control the beast or a protection bubble she could use on the room until the dragon left. She was looking for anything that would get her out of this mess with her life still intact."

"She flipped through the pages, whimpering as she heard the crashing above her. The screams had ceased, though. Either everyone was gone or dead. Panic gripped the witch's chest as she tried desperately to find something, anything to help her. Then the door exploded open, showering her with wood chunks and imbedding a large sliver in her neck. Clutching the wood in her throat, she gurgled and started to slump, when a burst of flame came pouring into the room, burning the last breathe out of her. The dragon had won. But the magic did not reverse. Whether out of frustration or anger, the dragon rampaged through the house, flinging horn darts, bursts of flame, and every muscle into destroying the house. In the end, the dragon was seen flying away with something gold clutched in its claws."

"Though no one has seen this dragon for more than four hundred years, the legend tells that the dragon is still alive and hording gold today. So...the search goes on. Oh, and one small tidbit of gossip: She is rumored to have laid three golden eggs those she hordes deep in a cave. This is an unsubstantiated footnote added by some obscure relative to the story of the genie-dragon."

Finishing her tale, Alieria took a drink, grabbed a bite, and walked over to a bench. She opened the seat and pulled out a small hidden scroll. Darkess and Janine exchanged a small knowing look. Alieria said,

"Here's a story you two might like. There have been rumors about these eggs off and on through history, but no one knows the whole story. Luckily for me, about six months ago, my cousin heard about the theft of a very special dragon egg – an ancient egg somehow associated with two others, which were hidden elsewhere."

Alieria brought the scroll to Darkess and Janine. She didn't notice their furrowed brows as she dove back into her plate and said with her mouth full,

"Here...read this."

It was a letter from Alieria's cousin. The writing was a fancy script, and some of the words were difficult to read, but Janine stumbled through the letter, her face full of astonishment.

My dearest cousin,
I have fallen in with a dismal band of leaches here in this foreign land, but they are good for information. Just two nights ago, there was an attack on a coven deep in the Corundum Mountains. Three were killed, and the demon that did it escaped with the clan's treasured dragon egg. They are devastated and have been searching for the demon, caring not that they are showing once again that wizards are real and what they can do. They have hit every seedy spot in the area during their search. Cousin, it is bad here. The townspeople don't like witchcraft and are up in arms. And the wizards are rampaging back. Demons are showing their faces after a great many years. It's all out war here. Even the weather seems to be reacting, as the seasons are changing early this year. I have been careful to hide my true identity, because it is unsafe here. Rumor has it the egg was one of the Eggs of Galdore from the old myth. Supposedly, there are two more like it, although no one seems to know what the Eggs of Galdore really are – or what they are for. It seems that the demon attacker was quick and smart, but no body knows who he was, where he came from, or where he went. I will keep you abreast of the situation. Guard the castle well, for he could attack at any time. If he is a dragon hunter, he'll be after us. He may even think we are connected to these alleged eggs. You could be in great danger. I'll be in touch.
    Ever vigilant,
    Tasha

"Has she sent you any other letters?" Janine asked.

"Yes," Alieria said, "but there was nothing new. She is still traveling, and she has her ears open, so who knows. Isn't it so exciting? It is the most recent, shall we call it, dragon sighting I have been involved with."

Darkess cleared her throat, eyeing Janine over Alieria's head.

"Do you know anything more about these ancient eggs?"

"Only the silly things that humans say when they really have no idea what they are talking about. Such as: they will give you great wealth, power to rule the world, or they have the power over eternal life...the usual nonsense."

All three witches were lost in their own thoughts. Alieria was munching away on something and staring off into space, Darkess was looking at the map on the wall with a furrow in her forehead, and Janine had her lips pursed tightly as she dug through a stack of books.

"This is so exciting. I have dreamed of dragons for so long. This place is just what I needed," Darkess said in a whisper. "Thank you so much for allowing us into your most private room."

Alieria smiled a devious smile at her guests and said,

"You are welcome to return any time. Just make sure I know that you are coming," she winked.

"If you would like to see my favorite legends," she continued, "this desk is mine, and it contains the very best ones, according to me anyway."

Alieria pointed to the desk and the bench where she had pulled the scrolls earlier. Janine saw that Darkess was headed in that direction, so she continued to dig in the spot where she was currently standing. The room had the sound of rushing air and the occasional flip of a page or opening and closing of a cabinet. Together with the crackle of the fire, the atmosphere seemed to induce deep thought.

Alieria had finished her food and was cleaning up when the flow of air in the room seemed to change direction. Darkess felt the hair on the back of her neck stand up. Sensing danger, she stood up with her hands extended in a defensive pose. Alieria noticed this odd behavior and asked,

"What is the matter dear?"

Janine spun around just in time to see Darkess and hear an explosion coming from the tunnel. The room shook, which caused the ceiling items to sway and a few items to topple from their shelves. Then several explosions happened in succession as the three witches ran to the doorway to see what happened.

"Stay here," Alieria said.

"No, I'm going with you," Darkess said immediately.

"There's no time to argue. Stay here."

Alieria swept off down the tunnel with Darkess silently on her heals. Janine didn't want to be left behind, so she followed Darkess until she scuffed her shoe on the floor. Alieria immediately spun on her heels, put her finger to her lips to indicate silence, and pointed to Janine's feet. Pointing to the wall, Alieria continued down the tunnel. Janine removed her shoes and quickly followed. Small explosions sounded off a few more times, and then the tunnel went silent. Alieria held out both arms, intending to stop the witches behind her. She then crept slowly around the corner looking for what had made the explosions when she was hit in the chest by a fireball.

Instinct kicked in when Darkess saw Alieria had been hit. Figuring that she was dead or dying, Darkess jumped forward to protect her. With a fireball of her own, Darkess heaved it into the black of the tunnel with all her might. She then grabbed Alieria and pulled her aside just as two more fireballs came sailing past them.

"I'm fine," Alieria protested and pulled away from Darkess.

Janine grabbed Alieria and inspected her charred dress, looking for a wound. The dress was trash, but her skin beneath was perfectly pink and healthy. Janine gasped as Darkess said,

"But…you took a direct hit."

Both Darkess and Janine stared at her as if she weren't normal, when she said,

"I told you I could handle this on my own. My entire family, except for a very few, are fireproof. It comes along with the dragon clan of old. We protect them, but they don't all accept it, hence the fireproof skin. Now, stay here!" Alieria demanded.

She walked around the corner again with her hands up to deflect any oncoming attack and saw a man squatting and drawing something on the tunnel floor. He obviously hadn't made it through the enchanted doorway and had been trying firepower on it. Alieria had no real defensive power other than mild telekinesis, so she tried to knock him against the wall with her power by shoving her hands at him. He was slapped by the power, but unharmed. It only angered him, and he threw a barrage of fireballs at her. Alieria deflected them but was not strong enough to send them back to their maker.

Another fireball flew at her before she knew it, and it slammed into her shoulder. The flame burnt bright red into her arm then quickly began to burn out until it was gone in a puff of smoke, leaving charred clothing but no wound. The man continued to draw on the floor between throwing his fireballs. He was trying his best to keep the witches at bay, which only made them want to know what he was doing. When he stood up, the witches took cover around the corner. They peeked around the edge to see him pulling a bag from his pocket. He sailed a fireball at the witches, who ducked behind the corner once more. Then Darkess peeked around again and threw the fireball back at the man. The light from his own fireball revealed his face for Darkess for a second as he sprinkled a powder around himself, and said,

"Home."

A vortex of smoke enveloped the man, and he was gone. The three witches rushed the smoke, Darkess throwing fireballs the entire way. When they arrived at the spot where the man had been standing, they looked at the floor where the intruder had been drawing, and there were symbols on the floor that burned away as they watched. Darkess threw out her hand, freezing the spot on the floor. She was attempting to get a good look at the symbols before they completely disappeared. Janine quickly took off a couple of her silver bracelets and threw them on the floor. She began to melt the metal before the bracelets had even come to rest, pooling the metal and running it over each shape to make a literal replica. Janine checked all of the shapes to make certain she had copied all that remained of the design. She then retrieved each piece in a clockwise direction so she would know how the shapes laid out later. Then she said,

"Okay Darkess, let it go."

Darkess waved her hand and the fire came back to life and burnt itself out.

"Quick thinking. You two are quite handy to have around," Alieria said. "Did either of you get a good look at the man?"

Janine shook her head, but Darkess spoke up.

"I saw him. He was an odd looking man. Well, I'm not sure he was a man at all, or at least only half human. He looked normal, but when he used his magic, he seemed, um…well, he seemed like a rodent of some sort. Maybe a weasel. What I'm trying to say is, his head changed when he drew on his powers."

Darkess became quiet and stared at the wall. Janine became mildly worried about her young friend and asked,

"Darkess, what's wrong dear?"

"He changed, like human then weasel, just like that. I can't explain it any better."

"You must have only seen him for a second or so between fireballs. Maybe you only think he changed. It could have been the shadows and smoke," Janine suggested.

"No, I'm sure I saw him change. Brown hair and eyes, long pointed nose, and his head…it seemed too small. Like it fit a smaller man's body. Do you know him?" Darkess asked.

"I think that he's the one that tried to get in here once before. I assume it was him anyway. About a year ago, I was asleep and a bunch of explosions woke me with a start. By the time I got down here, there was no one here. There was nothing gone. That won't be his last attempt, I'm afraid. He'll be back again. Until they die or get what they want, they always come back."

☼

Screaming at himself in a fit of fury, Takar picked up the chair he had just materialized next to and threw it at the wall. But breaking the chair wasn't enough. He began to throw fireballs at the pieces lying on the floor. He was trying to calm himself after his second failed attempt to enter the witches' dungeon.

"Stupid witches!" he screamed as he threw one last fireball at the already disintegrated chair.

He had been expecting one witch, not three of them. One was only a child, and what was a child doing down there, anyway? A child with no fear and advanced powers, he thought, where did she come from? His head hurt, and he rubbed his temples, trying to relieve some of the pressure. Exhausted from his trip, he went to his pantry and pulled out a hunk of meat, what was left of a loaf of bread, and begun cramming his mouth full and chewing heartily. Once his belly was full, he felt a little better, and he stumbled back to the room where he hidden his egg.

He was determined to find the other two eggs, and he just knew that that castle had dragon lore in it, and possibly the information he needed to find the second two eggs. He knew that witch was connected to the protectorates of dragons from centuries past. He had watched her and knew she never let anyone in that room. How did those two witches get inside? Pacing all around the room, he thought about all his parents had taught him. They had pinpointed several clans with deep dragon ties, and he just knew that castle had the information he needed. Rubbing his eyes, he said,

"Think, think, think, dammit."

"P-p-pardon me sir," a small soft voice said, "but you really should follow the witches for a while. Watch the castle for a week or two. I am sorry sir, but I think you should know more before you go there again. Next time, you may not be so lucky, and you need to know what you are up against."

Staying hidden from view in fear of retribution, Tuma cringed while waiting for a reply from Takar.

"And just how would you know what I've been doing? Show yourself and answer me," Takar demanded.

Slowly, two yellow eyes with vertical slits appeared in the air about three feet off the floor.

"Well?" Takar asked harshly.

Scales began to fill in the rest of the mostly tan colored reptilian face. It had no ears, slits for a nose, and flat narrow lips in a darker brown tone. He was the size and shape of a small boy but completely covered in scales. He wore a small tunic, old but clean, and he trembled as he appeared in front of his master.

"Takar, I have served your family for hundreds of years. I have known many witch hunters in that time, and I know you are angry. You are angry at yourself for not being better prepared, and you know it. It is obvious by your flaring temper," Tuma said as he looked at the smoking remains of the chair.

Takar wrinkled his lips and sneered at Tuma, but neither flinched. Takar knew Tuma was right, and he hated Tuma for taking the upper hand. His hand clenched and unclenched. As bad as Takar wanted to kill the servant, he knew it would not serve his purpose very well, and he pulled in his urges.

"Get me a spook. I don't care where, and bring it to me. Now!" Takar roared at Tuma, who promptly disappeared.

≈

Pouring over the book that had been with the egg he had stolen months before, Takar found that one of the dragons on the case was detachable and useful in finding its egg mates. The only catch was the locator had to be within a mile of the other egg for it to work – really only good if you already knew the location of the other eggs. It was made for hiding the eggs by burial and finding them later. Pulling the piece from its perch, Takar inspected it closely. It was made of a metal he had never seen before. It was like silver but much harder. The eyes were made of a black stone that was made to glow when near another one of the eggs. It was intricately made, down to the scales. Even the claws were sharp enough to draw blood.

This gave Takar a spark of new hope, for since he could not read the words, at least some of the illustrations made sense to him. His demon eyes began to glow in the semi darkness of his study. He rubbed the tiny dragon under his thumb, thinking deeply about his next move. A shuffle sound came from behind Takar, and he turned to see what had made the noise.

"Beggin' your pardon sir, I have your spook," Tuma said from the shadows.

Tuma laid a small black bottle on the table next to Takar and backed away.

"Good. Now go prepare a meal,' Takar demanded. "I will be hungry when I return. Leave me. I have much to do."

Tuma padded quietly from the room, and Takar went back to his new book. It had only been a couple of hours since the witches had forced him to make a swift retreat, and he was sure by the amount of people at the castle that the party was still in full swing. Returning to his pentagram, Takar changed one of the symbols, refilled his velvet pouch from a bucket near the portal, sprinkled some around himself, and said,

"Dragon ladies castle, topiary garden."

In a vortex of smoke, Takar was transported to a large garden out side of the castle. Luckily for him, the party had been uninterrupted, and there were people everywhere. Staying hidden, Taker sat on a large rock, between two hedges. From this vantage point he could see the small castle's front entrance and the side area where some of the guests were accumulating. Talking filled the garden, and Takar thought that maybe they were talking about him, and this made him smile. Pulling out an athame and the small black bottle, he placed them on the ground in front of him.

Clearing his thoughts, he picked up the asthema. Looking at the black bottle, he wondered if this could help him, or if it was just another waste of time. Drawing the blade across his thumb, fat drops of nearly black blood soaked the end of it, filling the small trough that ran down the middle of the blade. When the trough was nearly full, Takar took the tip of the blade and flicked it over the cork on the bottle, nearly covering the entire cork with blood. Using his bloody thumb and forefinger, Takar pulled the cork free, ensuring blood was the first thing to enter the bottle. This made the spook feel who its new master was. When the spook floated free of its bottle, it settled on the ground in its master's shadow.

"I am your new master. You will answer only to me," Takar explained. "Inside that castle is a child. She is maybe ten or twelve years in age. She has flaming hair, and I think she was the only child present. Her powers are strong. Find out what you can – who she is, why she's here, anything. And the witch with the blond plated hair, watch for her. They should be together. But should the two part ways, follow the child. Report back to me one hour after the sun reaches its zenith every day, or anytime the information is immediate. Now go."

The spook slithered into the deepest of shadows and was gone.

≈

Alieria had returned to her party, intent on finding out if anyone had seen the mysterious intruder. Had he been alone or was there an accomplice? How had he gotten into the party? Was he a guest in disguise? Darkess and Janine had a few questions of their own. Their search for information had been an interesting one, and they still weren't sure if it had been profitable or not, especially since it had been cut short by a demon attack. The three witches made their way through the crowd, looking for suspicious persons who were still amongst them. As she followed Darkess and Alieria, Janine clutched the symbols in her hand, which were slightly hidden by her voluminous sleeves.

Janine wasn't sure why she felt compelled to keep copies of these symbols, but she did. When Alieria stopped to talk with Prak, she pulled a large buckle from her belt and made duplicates and hid them in her cloak. None of the guests has seen a thing inside the main room next to the entrance to Alieria's secret passage or anywhere else. The explosions had been muffled and only seemed to cause a few to wonder what had happened. Alieria was incensed that someone had gotten as far as they had without being noticed, especially with so many in attendance. Leaving Janine and Darkess, Alieria made a sweep of her castle, looking for evidence of an intruder. This gave Darkess time to talk to Janine. Together, they decided the demon had come in the same way he had left, and the two of them would tell Alieria then take their leave of the party.

When Alieria returned, she looked harried and annoyed and spoke quickly in her thick accent.

"Can you believe it? No one heard a thing, except for a few sitting against that wall. No one has seen a single man wearing all black fitting the description you gave me. Can you believe all that racket and not a soul knew what was going on? Just the three of us. Well, at least we have the symbols from his portal. Maybe they can help us out, or help me out, anyway. Are you sure you are alright?"

"We're just fine. But we must thank you for the party, the entertainment of my fetish in your library, and…" Darkess whispered the last few words, "the demon fighting."

"Oh, well, yes, then, tell your grandfather I hope to see him again some time, and you two as well. It was an experience. Prak will walk you to your carriage if you like. Safe journey," Alieria said, slightly distracted by the demon attack. She squeezed the two witches' hands then turned to leave, but stopped.

"Oh, the symbols, can I keep them or copy them?" Alieria asked.

Still holding the originals in her hand, Janine handed them over, and said,

"They are yours. I hope they do you some good in finding out who that demon is."

☼

The sky was black as oil, and the clouds were thick and rolling swiftly across the sky as the two witches, led by Prak, walked across the front courtyard. Their carriage was waiting for them in the deep shadows of a night with a storm ready to break loose at any moment. The horse was munching on the weeds growing up next to the hitching post when the clouds parted, shining moonlight down on them and causing them to cast a slight shadow for but a moment. The horse's ears perked upon their approach, and Darkess stopped in her tracks. Instinctively she raised her hands as she looked into the deep shadows of the hedge, seemingly ready for a fight.

"What's wrong, miss?" Prak asked in his deep gruff voice.

After a second or two, Darkess lowered her hands and said,

"Nothing. Just jumpy, I guess."

Janine had seen the look on Darkess' face and knew there had been something. But in present company, she was unwilling to talk. Janine acted as though it were nothing until moments later when they were leaving Alieria's grounds.

"Spill the beans," Janine said.

Darkess knew exactly what she meant.

"The shadows moved," she responded. "There is no wind yet, and I know the clouds were drifting across the moon, but I'm telling you the shadows moved. There was something in those hedges, and it wasn't human. I could feel it watching us."

Janine clicked her tongue, prodding the horse to move faster while she thought for a moment.

"Maybe it was that demon. Maybe he was waiting for us to leave so he could try again. Oh, we should warn Alieria."

Darkess pulled her trusted pack out from under the seat and dug deep inside, feeling around for a stone bird. She ripped a piece of parchment, found a special quill that didn't require ink, and wrote a quick note to Alieria.

I know that we just left, but take heed to my warning.
In your courtyard, I received an intense feeling of being watched.
I also saw something in the hedges – what, I am not sure.
Beware, the demon may be watching you.
Send for me if you need me.
    Darkess

Rolling the scrap tightly, Darkess awoke the bird, inserted the scroll and whispered,

"Take this to Alieria, the dragon lady."

The little bird took flight, and Darkess watched it fly high, turn to a pinpoint of light, and disappear. She exhaled, not realizing that she had been holding her breath.

"Well, that's that," she sighed. "I'm sure she'll be okay."

"Yes, yes, I'm sure you're right," Janine said. But in the dark, you could still hear the waver in her voice. When the moonlight appeared again, she had to force the wrinkles out of her forehead and pushed forth a smile for Darkess, who didn't believe her for a second. Janine was scared. She knew Darkess was by far a stronger witch than her, and if she had sensed something in those hedges, something had been there. Thinking deep on the subject, Janine felt the hairs stand up on the back of her neck, and goose bumps broke out down her legs and arms and raced down her spine. What if the shadow dweller had been watching them and not Alieria? She had to try and calm herself. She tried to convince herself that Darkess had no enemies, and neither did she.

"Nerves, it's just nerves," she said to herself, "from the earlier attack. When we get home, I'll feel much better. It has been a long day." Too long, she thought.

Under the carriage, the spook clung to the shadows. Even if they had looked, they wouldn't have seen it, for it had become the actual shadows shape, maybe a little darker than usual but not discernable from the actual shadow.

≈

The next morning, Janine let Darkess sleep as long as she wanted and took time to write Richard. She wrote about the attack at Alieria's and described the amount of power and keen senses Darkess had shown. She assured him that Darkess would be on her way home as soon as she was awake and ready to go, and she would be bringing the shapes Janine had described in the encounter with the demon. The plan was to let Zaphod jump from inside the barn directly to the Vallencourt grounds. It was daylight, and there was something watching – what and who, they weren't sure. Janine told Richard to keep in touch and to be on the lookout, and then she sent the letter.

Putting on a pot of water for tea, Janine pulled out a couple of biscuits when she heard a rustling sound from down the hall. Ardimas had been asleep when they had arrived last night, and she was sure he would be interested in the events of the previous evening. Down the hall came Darkess, yawning and rubbing her eyes, with Ardimas right behind her. Janine looked at the girl in a new light, and thought about what power comes from such a youthful package.

"Sleep well?" Janine asked.

"I had a dream about that demon from last night, and I woke up with a fireball in my hand," Darkess answered between yawns, "but I put it out before it could do any damage."

Ardimas was quick to respond. "What, what? Demon? Fireballs? Seems that I missed out on all the fun. Do tell."

After they ate breakfast and shared the events from last night, Darkess packed and prepared to leave. Ardimas gave her a big hug and extended a small vile wrapped in brown paper and tied with twine. With a confused look on her face, Darkess asked,

"What's this?"

"There is much more to you than meets the eye. What's more important is that there's much more going on here than meets my ears…" Ardimas winked at Darkess, arching his eyebrow at his daughter.

"That," he said, pointing at the vial, "is for an emergency. It's good for only one use. It is my blood, and with your power to channel, you can hold the vial and use my gift. My guess is that it should last for several minutes, but I am not sure. But you must remember…you will only be invisible, not invincible. Several demons detect heat, and your body is still as vulnerable as when you can be seen. Please use it with extreme care. And, if you ever need my help, just ask. Maybe someday, you will tell me just exactly what is going on here."

Giving Darkess another hug, Ardimas ruffled her hair, and said, "Safe journey."

Janine gave Darkess a hug, and squeezed both of her shoulders.

"Make sure you give these to your grandfather as soon as you see him," she instructed. "I know he is already anxious to get you home. I'll be in touch, and we'll see each other soon."

Darkess climbed upon Zaphod, and she smiled at them.

"Thank you both. For everything," she said.

Without another word, Darkess waved, and then she and her horse vanished.

≈

Takar sat on the floor of his study with his legs crossed, thinking on what he should do next, when the spook slipped across the floor and entered his shadow. Takar opened his eyes, sensing the presence, and looked at the floor.

"Well…report?" he demanded.

Leaving the sanctity of the shadows, the spook stood up and washed over Takar. Taking a deep breath, Takar's eyes clouded over for a blink or so. He saw what the spook had seen through his inky form and said,

"What do you mean you have nothing? You've been watching them for a week without report, and you tell me you have seen nothing of the child? Why didn't you go inside the house?"

Once again, the spook slipped over Takar's head.

"I see. Then there must be something special about these witches. Why else would they magically seal the entire premises?"

The spook again slipped back into the shadow of his master and awaited further instruction. Takar spoke in a stern voice on the edge of anger.

"Go back to the house for another week, then report back to me, unless you see something of importance. Now go."

The spook slithered up the stone steps and was gone.

Takar looked at the world map he had hung on the wall. There were twenty black pins on the map and one red one. Off to the side of the map were one hundred more black pins and two more red ones. Takar had marked the spots on the map where he had been searching, and with each new spot, he tried the locator in desperate hopes that it would find one of its mates. So far, he had found nothing, so the red pins would have to stay where they were for the time being. Takar picked out another spot on the map. Going to his portal, he drew the required symbols around its edge. Sprinkling powder around the pentagram, he was on his way.

☼

The day was sunny, and humidity hung in the stagnant air as Darkess sat in her favorite tree, reviewing the notes she had made about the attack at Alieria's earlier in the year. She had looked through all sorts of books in the attic as she searched for the symbols. She had found a few of them but was still no closer to unlocking the code left behind by the demon. Her journal lay open on her lap as Darkess scanned the skyline around her. She was more alert now than she had ever been. A tiny wisp of a breeze blew through her hair, giving her a miniscule of relief. It was just enough air to turn the page in her journal. The page showed the list of dragon stories and details from Alieria's secret room. She had long ago committed all of this to memory, but it sometimes helped to look at the details. Sometimes she saw new links on the page when she examined it with fresh eyes.

Unfortunately, nothing new clicked today, so she closed the journal and headed down to talk to Tanner. When she arrived at his little hut, he was nowhere to be found. She scanned the horizon. She saw movement in the old wheat field, so Darkess walked towards it. When she neared the field, she saw Tanner walking back and forth across the field with two pieces of bent metal. He was so intent on his work that he didn't notice how close Darkess was until he turned towards her in his walking pattern. He waved her over. Tanner continued to walk his pattern until the two pieces of metal crossed. He stopped walking, pulled a long wooden stake from his bag, and shoved it in the ground at his feet. Unsure what Tanner was doing, Darkess didn't want to yell and possibly break his concentration, so she waited until she was in range before she said,

"What are you doing?"

Tanner motioned for Darkess to follow as he continued with his work.

"The creeks have moved again," he explained, "and I am trying to find them."

Darkess looked around and raised an eyebrow as she said,

"Tanner, I'm not sure that you and I are in the same place. It seems to me that we are walking around in an old dried up wheat field. It's as dry as an old bone out here."

Tanner chuckled as he continued to walk, the thin metal strips still crossed in his hands, wiggling slightly. He stooped down and put another stake in the ground every twenty paces or so. Quietly, the two of them walked until they reached the tree line at the back of the property. Darkess was used to not getting immediate answers to the questions she asked, so she waited patiently. She occasionally glanced back at the line of stakes behind them and found that it wound its way across the field, definitely not in a straight line. Tanner placed one more stake in the ground and turned to see his path with Darkess standing beside him.

"Connect all the stakes and what do you see?" he asked,

"A squiggly line," Darkess answered.

Tanner looked at her in the eyes. With all seriousness, he said,

"Look again. Look deeper than the surface."

Darkess looked back at the stakes. Starting with the furthest one, she followed the flow with her eyes and ended with the one at Tanner's feet.

"Does water run under ground?" she asked.

"That's my girl. Now you're thinking."

Tanner sat down on the ground and explained.

"The water is always there, even if you cannot see it. These are called divining rods. Holding them gently so they can move easily, I walk about. And when they cross, water is present. We have found water, and if the season is worse than last year, I will know where to dig to get some. They have one flaw: They do not tell you how deep you will have to dig to find it."

≈

Darkess was so busy with her training that the summer seemed to fly by. Fall was even busier with the harvest, the party, and the onset of a horrific winter. She was so busy she hardly had time between her lessons and the family business to do anything for herself. Finally one night, Richard declared,

"Do what you will for the night."

Darkess didn't need to be told twice. She darted for the hidden passage and headed for the tower. Once she arrived, she made a beeline to her private bureau, pulled out her store of leather, the special thread that Tanner had given her, and a drawing she had made. Sitting at the largest table in the room, Darkess' fingers flew over the piece as she cut, stitched, and braided away the hours. Admiring her work, she decided that it needed one more thing. Pulling out the dragon bangle Janine had made for her, she placed the head and front arms against the face of the pack. Producing a fireball, Darkess levitated it towards the perfect spot then pushed the flame against the surface of the leather, quickly extinguishing it. Pulling away the bangle, she saw that no serious damage was done to the pack, but the shape was perfectly burnt into the leather.

"Perfect," Darkess whispered to herself with an excited grin on her face.

Adding a few beads and baubles she had collected over the years, she lay her handiwork down on the table to examine it. While testing the straps, rummaging in the large compartment, and opening and closing the small ones, she realized she had forgotten one small part. She added a tiny pouch on one of the straps to hold her navigation egg.

Darkess pulled out several items she thought were important enough to put in her pack, such as her journal and the blood potion from Ardimas. Even the divining rods Tanner had given her had their own little slots. There was also a pouch for her turquoise necklace. At the bottom of the pack was a hidden compartment filled with the box that contained her prophecy. It was nestled in the cutout of a lightweight wood made to disguise and protect it. The golden egg fit nicely in its pouch, and a knuckle knife disappeared behind it on the strap.

Next, she headed to the potion cabinet. She filled one-time use potion bottles with the various potions she thought would be handy, including the teleport potion and the truth potion. She also included dried potion sachets, such as the befuddlement powder and Tanner's growth booster with some of her grandmother's added touch. Darkess knew she wasn't to use this powder yet but thought it could be useful in her future. She never knew when she would have to make something grow extra quickly. She also grabbed a small bottle of the healing salve her grandmother made, which was used for demon battles when she wasn't close. She also gave it to the peasants with affliction and wounds.

Darkess decided what other items she would want in her stores. She added sage for meditation, a stone bird and a second one just in case along with the potions for them. Then she added three white candles, which are the balance of all colors and used for cleansing, clairvoyance, and even healing and enlightenment. Darkess then added one magenta candle for immediate action and levels of power higher than normal. She grabbed a small amethyst crystal, because one can never be too careful, and tossed it into the bag with the candles. Finally, she sat down to admire her handiwork. A scuffing sound came from the stairwell, and a few steps later, the door opened. Richard poked his head through the door and asked,

"Can I come in? Or is this a private work session?"

"Oh, Grandfather. This will never be a place where you are not welcome. Come in, see what I made."

Darkess handed her newly made pack to her grandfather for his inspection.

"Well, what do you think?" she inquired.

After opening the various pouches and pockets and turning the pack over a couple of times, he finally answered.

"You made all of this?" he said looking over his spectacles at her.

Darkess nodded her head vigorously.

"How did you get the dragon on the flap?"

Darkess explained the entire process, including why she picked each item for her pack.

"Very impressive," he winked at his beloved granddaughter. "You know you get this talent from your mother, pack making and such. I believe it is the way of the only child to entertain herself. Oh, and by the way, this came for you."

Darkess hadn't even noticed the oddly shaped package lying just behind the white candles on the table. She reached for it and opened it quickly. Inside was a large green crystal and nothing else. Darkess inspected the package, looking for an explanation, when Richard said,

"It's a pictocrystal."

"Pictocrystal?" Darkess asked excitedly. "What does it do...who sent it?"

Richard loved it when she got like this. With a chuckle, he answered,

"Well, it has a password that makes it project pictures on whatever. Belthazor sent it to you. Let's see what's on it, shall we?"

Retrieving his projector crystal, Richard tapped the stones and down dropped the ecru canvas. Stacking the two crystals and aiming them properly, he stated clearly,

"New Horizon."

A beam of light emitted from the tip of the emerald looking crystal and landed on the ecru canvas with perfect clarity. The first picture was a handwritten letter.

Darkess,
I've captured many photos for ya this year.
These are the best ones, each with a side note.
I hope ya'll are well and learnin much.

This year, ya may be able ta join us on a lil trip.
I'll discuss it with Richard.
I've found nothin new in the way of eggs.

> Ever vigilant,
> Belthazor

Once the letter had been read, Richard commanded the crystal, "Next."

The crystal went dark for a moment then relit, and the first photo appeared on the screen. It was the most beautiful unicorn Darkess had ever seen. The caption read: This is a young male, lavender as a youth, bought for a young witch learning magical animal husbandry and transported here by me.

"He's beautiful," Darkess smiled at her grandfather.

"Next," Richard said.

The second photo appeared, and Darkess leaned back slightly at the sight of it. A reinforced cage held the biggest snake she had ever seen. Its caption read: This is a giant asp brought here from Imhotepus. This snake is bred for guarding things and is highly dangerous. Its venom kills quickly, and once it reaches maturity, one look directly in its eyes will turn you to dust. Believe it or not, this one is an infant and its hide is prized as a depressant and for shields and other protective devices as it is nearly impenetrable.

"Next," Darkess said, and a third photo appeared.

A brilliant red bird was shown, perched on a large gilded stand. Its caption read: The Phoenix, one of the rarest of birds with the power to heal wounds, even the most grievous ones. The feathers are prized for wands, staffs, and spells concerning flight or levitation.

"Next," Darkess repeated.

A foul ugly creature appeared in the next photo. It was all grays and greens with odd scales and horns and an almost human build. It had tiny useless wings and webbed fingers and toes that ended in large claws. Its eyes were large and black with no lids. The description read: The Chupacabra. This mythical creature is real, and it kills with a powerful swiftness if disturbed. It normally feeds upon animal flesh but will eat a human if it gets in the way. There is no known method to kill this one, short of dropping a mountain on it, but they are easily enough contained with magically reinforced metal. This is the only one in captivity, possibly the only one ever recorded by photo.

Richard scowled over Darkess' shoulder as she read the caption, knowing full well that Belthazor would only have a creature like this for dark reasons. No respectable wizard would use such a creature to guard something precious or dangerous. He would make a mental note concerning the razor's edge on which Belthazor seemed to be walking. Maybe he was more of a pirate than I thought, Richard's mind tabulated.

The next photo was an animal Darkess had seen before: a Gryphon, the great flying beast with the body of a lion, the head and wings of an eagle, and huge talon-like claws on its massive cat feet. The caption below the photo read: Mostly used for travel, and protection. Fiercely protective of their masters. Their claws are very special as they change colors if they detect poisons; which comes in handy for the paranoid or stalked wizard.

"Next," Darkess chimed again.

The next photo flashed upon the canvas with a blast of white so intense that they both shielded their eyes for a moment. When their eyes had adjusted, the focus of the photo was an albino looking, nearly human female. She had large pointed teeth, clear blue eyes, and long white talons on each finger. She seemed to be staring directly at them with her mouth agape, seemingly in pain. The caption beside this photo read: The banshee is a demon that feeds on human pain and suffering, a mindless creature that screams at its victims until the blood boils, killing them. She used to be a witch. Now on her way to exile for preying on innocent victims, she will be entombed in a rock for the rest of her days. Beware: Any witch in miserable pain that is detected by a banshee will be hunted ruthlessly. And, any witch who hears her cry will be turned into a banshee and join her in her search for more pain. There is no known way to revert back to human form. It is permanent.

"That's terrible. How could he get a photo of her? Won't he turn too?" Darkess queried.

"Do you see the shine on the photo? Richard asked. "She is in a sound proof box, specially designed for these types of problems. Next photo please," Richard said.

The next photo was of a small stocky fellow with bright red hair and matching beard and mustache. His eyebrows were so thick that he almost looked like a small bear cub in the face. He wore a long black coat, a derby like hat, and was waving in the photo. It read: This is a Leprechaun out on holidays. He told me to tell you that his kind has heard of the great witch from the prophecy, and they believe in you. He is the keeper of luck, both good and bad, whichever is best for the person at that time. Good luck all the time would be bad for anyone, and bad luck helps you learn and grow. He calls himself the equalizer, helping to balance out your life.

"Next," Darkess repeated.

The flash of light changed to that of a straw bed with a three-headed pup. Its caption read: The Cerberus, or guardian of the underworld, is a very rare find. Only three have ever been recorded in history. A collector had acquired this one and intends to tame it. These beasts are strong with only one weakness, which is a secret. Only their masters know what calms them. His master caged him for the trip, or you would not have this photo.

"Next," Darkess and Richard said in unison.

The canvas showed a photo of an odd creature, fat and fleshy it was, and very much like a lizard. Its tail was more like a giant flat flipper, and it had four stumpy legs connected to its massive body. It barely had a head, more like a face on the end of its bulbous neck. Its eyes were large and watery, and its nose was mashed in, with two slits for air. It had rough skin but no scales, and wrinkles only where the different sections of its body met. The caption below the photo read: This may look like a rare find, but in fact, these are extremely plentiful in the Isles of Ardor. They are called Obsidian Diggers. They live mostly in the depths of a volcano where they swim in the lava and eat glasslike stones produced by the heat. They are prized for their fireproof, exceedingly thick hides and their uncanny ability to find precious stones, which they consider a delicacy. They are fast diggers and can disappear under the lava for long periods of time without air. Their weakness includes anything cold. They prefer boiling water to sleep in and drink. This one is rather tame and stays to the boiler room of his own accord.

A beautiful fairy was in the next photo. She had long blondish hair that shone lightly sea green in the sunlight. She wore a tiny crown of plants and shells over diminutive pointed ears and a short dress that seemed to be made of sea plants and hung to her knees in points of seaweed. The caption beside this photo read: She is a Sea Fairy and rides my ship frequently, trying to understand life on land. She has only set foot on a small island where her tribe has its counsel meetings and such. Her station in life is to help the creatures of the sea. She has a mild kind of magic over water and its plant life, and when she becomes of age, she will be crowned Queen of the Sea Society. Then she will return to the lagoon on their island and reign as High Priestess of the Ocean's Court. There is always a possibility of meeting her on my ship if you get to visit. Her name is Oceanna.

"Next," Darkess commanded excitedly.

The next photo that appeared was a small bundle of fur, entirely white with small pink eyes and a tiny pink nose. It looked very much like a rabbit but had short ears, more like small bumps with furry holes. It sat in a pile of ice. The caption read: It's a Snow Puffer. Native only to Brumalia, it can survive in any snowy region. It eats snow algae and burrows through the snow so quickly that it is nearly impossible to catch. However, if caught, this creature is easily enough tamed. They have no magical properties but are prized for their ability to find anything lost in the snow. Snow Puffers are loving creatures and make good pets, because they respond to commands much like a dog would.

"Next," Richard said.

The pictocrystal clicked over to one last photo. Instead of a caption, a letter was attached.

To the Order of the New Horizon
When Oceanna visits with me, she is always alone, but she has told me some stories from her world. It seems that some kinds of dragons lived in the ocean. As a matter of fact, the tribe of Sea Fairies believes there are still some hidin in deep caves waitin for a safer time to emerge. However, they have seen none for more'n two generations. (They live much longer than we do.) She knows nothin of any eggs or actual living dragons anywhere. Sorry. Will be in touch. –B

"Done," Richard said, and the pictocrystal went dark.

☼

Three months of unending snowstorms and unrelenting cold left everyone with pent up frustration from being stuck inside with nowhere to go and nothing new as far as mail or guests. Information was as frozen as the landscape. They became crankier when the steely gray clouds came floating over the sun that had rarely shown itself the whole winter. The fact that they had the teleport potion only seemed to make the cabin fever worse, because they could not use it for fear of being caught. The entire Vallencourt family, staff, and even the animals, were distressed. In the interest of saving lives and household belongings, Richard decided to distract them with the story about how the castle came to be at its current location. So at the dinner table, he asked them all a couple of questions.

"Are you all as miserable of this wretched weather as I am?"

A variety of yeses came from around the table along with a mumble from Rufus, who would have rather been in his barn with the livestock. Then they saw the look on Richard's face and realized he was up to something. Smiles began to creep upon the faces of everyone around the dinner table.

"What are you up to, you old coot?" Angela asked in mock anger.

Darkess had straightened up in her chair as far as she could and stared at her grandfather. Everyone's posture had changed. Even Rufus seemed curious.

"I have planned a little storytelling for this evening, and you all are invited," Richard said.

Everyone was even more curious, and they shifted in their seats to look at each other, trying to see if anyone else was in cahoots with Richard.

"But first, I must go do some preparation. If you would, please meet me in the library in an hour. Please find your seats, and the story will begin," Richard said with an air of mystery. He then swept his robes away from his feet and left, leaving all remaining in the room with questioning looks.

≈

It was dark in the library except for the roaring firelight when they all arrived. Silver and Daniel was arm and arm just a couple of steps behind Angela. Darkess was walking beside Rufus with Tanner and Roxy brining up the rear. It seemed that none of them had been here before as they searched the room looking for their patriarch. As they took their seats, Richard appeared in a puff of blue smoke, startling them and making them laugh. It seemed the castle fever was slowly dissipating from its inhabitants.

Richard was wearing a long emerald colored cloak with a silver stitched pattern around the edge made to look like interlocking Vs. At his side was a large scabbard engraved in the same V pattern. His hand held the sword that went inside this scabbard. The blade was inscribed with a fancy script, and the hilt was intricately patterned. Richard wore a chainmail suit under his cloak, and a hood of chainmail covered his head. The look was both regal and warlike, causing everyone in the room to be spellbound by him.

"This armor was worn a little over five hundred years ago by the warring wizard Tobias Vallencourt," he explained. "Tobias was the sole surviving male heir to the Vallencourt line, and the magic wars between Asiattica and Muscovata had spread further and further from the borders of the two countries. Imhotepus had been pulled into the battles now, and peace seemed gone forever. Bloody battles raged between white and dark magic, pulling in civilians and destroying villages along the way towards the cities."

Richard moved slowly across the fireplace as he talked, laid his sword on the mantle with a clang for effect, then continued his story.

"Tobias knew he had to survive, or the Vallencourt blood would be lost forever. He also knew that if he stayed in his beloved family's castle, they would all surely die or become slaves. And if he ran, all the family would be lost. He had a hard time deciding what his next move would be. He thought for days, and then one night, one of his friends, Malachi, came to ask for his help. With his house burnt and his family dead, would Tobias put him up for a while? Tobias would never turn down a friend in need, and so the two came to talk about both of their predicaments."

"Deep into the ale, and with tears of sadness dropping occasionally from one or the other, they stumbled upon an idea. Get together enough power, and they could move the castle out of harm's way."

Richard sat down on a tall stool he'd placed next to the fire, drank from his goblet, and continued.

"They laughed and cried in their silly drunkenness, until Tobias realized that he'd seen a spell about how to move something large when he was trying to figure out what to save and what to leave if he decided to go. Tobias stopped laughing, and seemed almost sober. His friend laughed for another minute or so until he realized he was laughing alone. He stopped and said, 'I'm sorry, did I miss something?' Tobias wiped his mouth and said, 'No, just thinking. Enough power might just move this castle.' Malachi said to Tobias. Standing up, Tobias grabbed his friend by the arm and hauled him to his feet. 'Come, my drunken friend, your idea may have just saved us both.'"

Richard continued the story.

"Away they both stumbled, up the stairs to the tower. Together, they searched for the spell and found it once again. Tobias pulled the scroll down and unrolled it, tacking it to the table with candles and such. The examples used for the spell were large trees and hut sized boulders, but these items only required the power of one wizard and one potion bottle.

They sat and did the calculations, and after many hours of working, they had the potions ready. They had made twelve times the amount listed. Now all they needed were ten other wizards or witches to pull it all off. Tobias had a sister and a senile old aunt. That made the number four, still leaving eight, and during this awfully fearful time, many people had gone into hiding or simply left. Some had gone to fight, but that still left them with the uneasy search for eight willing participants."

"The sun had finally peeked over the hills, and the sounds of battle had begun again. It seemed they were only a few miles down the road, and Tobias knew the chances of them finding eight more magical people were dwindling, but they had to try. The two men decided to separate, both in search of dependable magical folk with a desire to relocate, quickly. At sundown, both men returned to the castle. Tobias had four people in tow, and Malachi returned with three. They were one power source short. Most of them had met at one time or another, so they all began to talk, and they came to the conclusion: They had only one chance left – the old crone who lived just outside the castle walls. She had lots of power, but she hated people. Loved her solitude. This was going to take a lot of work, and it needed to be done quickly for the war seemed closer now than it had just hours before. Tobias' chance to save his castle and all of his family's work was narrowing, and he took off running for the crones hut."

"Tobias saw a faint glow through the filthy windows of the crone's hut. He knocked on the door and received an immediate response. 'Who's there?' the crone bellowed at him with her gravely voice. Tobias said, 'I need your help.' The crone answered with, 'Ha! You came to the wrong place for that! Go away!' Tobias braced himself and knocked again, saying, 'I'll pay for your services with gold. Let us strike a deal.' This time, there was no response. Not a sound came from the hut. Tobias held his breath and was ready to give it one last shot when the screeching sound of rusty hinges told him the door was opening. Finally exhaling, he stretched out his hand toward the shrouded figure standing behind the door. 'I am Tobias Vallencourt,' he said, 'and I will give you food, shelter, and gold if you will lend me the use of your powers. Let us come to an agreement.'"

"The crone did not shake his hand but responded gruffly, saying, 'I know who you are boy, now get inside before you are seen, and hold your voice down.' Tobias looked into the shadows where the old woman's face should have been and stooped over the threshold with a questioning look on his face. Before Tobias had time to adjust to the lack of light and the dank smell, the crone had closed the door and was hovering near him. She said, 'Yes boy, I knew who you were before you were born, and I knew that you would come here tonight to ask for my help.' The crone offered him a stool as she took her own and said, 'Now, exactly what do you want? Then I can decide on what it is worth to me to do it.' Tobias described the potion and the power needed to accomplish his dire task and he added that he would take care of her for the rest of her life should they actually get away with the plan. Then he added the ultimatum: All of this had to happen tonight, for tomorrow would be too late. Tonight the dark wizards and their drones would be sleeping, but by tomorrow, they would surely storm the Vallencourt castle. Time was of the essence."

"The old crone pulled a worn leather bag from one of the many folds in her seemingly endless cloak and threw the contents out on the table next to her. Before she looked at what she had cast, she told Tobias that she must consult the bones. But when she saw them, she gasped. Tobias quickly leaned forward to get a good look at what the crone was seeing. 'Calm yourself boy,' she said. 'I see success in our future.' She looked from one bone to the next then mumbled gruffly. 'Go home, and ready your group. I will pack my things and be there before the moon is at its highest in the sky. Worry not. I accept your deal for food and shelter for these old bones before they turn to dust.' They shook hands, and the crone shoved Tobias from her hut."

"Tobias' heart felt lifted but not completely relieved. He was unsure of the crone and her odd behavior, but he convinced himself the cause was old age and loneliness. The arrival home brought him a surprise. The families had arrived at the castle in his absence. Most of the seven people they had found had requested the group save a relative or two in exchange for their service, all except for one. However, occupancy had risen more than double since Tobias had left. He was glad to see everyone was quick and efficient about their business, and he shuttled them all into one room and told them his plan. The castle was to be home to every one present at the time that they left, instead of payment for helping out. However, they must do all that he instructed until the castle was safe from destruction."

"Tobias had left Malachi on look out for the crone and any late night movement from the troops. His sister had helped by passing out loaves of bread while everyone waited. Many hadn't eaten in a while, and were quite dirty from hiding, but they were grateful to be involved in the scheme. News had come earlier that all of the castles along the mountain ridge had been sacked, and every village in between had been burned to the ground – its inhabitants killed or taken prisoner. No one had seen a dragon in months, and there seemed no protection from the black magic as it rolled its way across mountains and plains, building in strength from the fear it brought. Tobias wondered if he was a coward for running. No, he thought. Not when every one else had died for this cause. Someone must bring back the planet to its rightful position. Someone must build forces and stop this war. They weren't going very far, just a few days out of the war's range where they could try and devise a plan to bring white magic back into control."

"All the while Tobias was thinking on his plan, Malachi watched as the moon grew higher in the sky. Before too long, the shadows below the look out tower moved, and a silhouette made its way along the path to the gates. The crone had arrived. The one castle guard that still stood his post at the gate pointed the crone to the correct staircase. Tobias reached her halfway up and helped her the rest of the way with her heavy bundle. 'We must make haste, boy,' the crone whispered. 'I heard the clanking of metal when I was approaching the gates. They must be planning an attack at dawn. Are you ready?' Tobias answered the crone. 'We have the required twelve magical beings, the corresponding potions, and a spell to move us several miles to the north. Just far enough to be safe, but close enough to still fight later in the battle,' he answered.

"The crone scratched absently at her head and looked around the room. It was filled with refugees from the battles, and she snorted at Tobias. 'These are your magical beings? They don't look like much.' Tobias looked at the wretched-looking, half-starved people and then back at the crone. 'It's the only chance we have,' he said. 'We must try.' The crone breathed harshly, 'Very well then. Let's get them into position,' she sneered. 'Oh, and I will need to read the spell. I am sure that I have the most power of any of the rabble here.' Reluctantly, Tobias handed the spell to the crone, and the hairs on the back of his neck stood up for a moment. Tobias once again dismissed it as excitement and began to place each person where they would need to be."

"There were ten placed outside the castle – one wizard on each corner, one on each end, and two on the longer front and back sides of the castle. Tobias himself took the dungeon and centered himself as well as he could. The crone, however, had the spot of power. She was on the roof, standing in the center of the top of the castle. They had set up a signal. When the loud boom sounded, they would each throw their potions while touching the castle and thinking of greener pastures while the crone read the spell. If all went as planned, and there was enough power, the castle would momentarily disappear then reappear where the spell had sent them. Tobias' power was that of telekinesis, and he took a cooking pot and sent it flying up through the chimney from the dungeon's fire pit. When it reached the mouth of the chimney, it let out a huge pop. The sound began the process. As each person threw their potion, the crone threw hers with a greedy smile pasted on her pale lips and let the spell fly into the wind. Then, she pulled a gnarled piece of parchment from her cloak and read the spell she had written instead.

"This castle is in danger, from war and strife,
We must move it now, to save our very lives,
Move this castle, from spire to foundation,
Make the new land Xyloidonia, our destination,
Take the magic from we twelve,
Into a new nation we will dwell,
Move this castle, through time and space,
Make it inhabit a brand new place."

"The night was deep. Each wizard and witch stood in the dark with hands pressed to the cold stone of the castle. They closed their eyes and waited for the spell to work. Unknown to the others, the crone had finished the spell, and as expected, the castle vanished. The feeling of weightlessness came over the wizards on the outside of the castle, and they had to fight to stay where they were, attached to the castle by the skin of their hands. Seconds later, the feeling of gravity overtook them as they reappeared under a different sky. For a few moments, none of them realized what had happened. There was a mutual feeling of happiness as they all made their way back to the common room where their journey had begun. The families inside the castle were fine, although some of them complained of mild nausea and dizziness."

"Tobias had made his way from the dungeon to the roof to help the crone only to find her dancing on the roof with an energy that was unexpected from one of such age. Tobias thought the amount of spent energy must have taken the old woman over the edge. But when the crone saw Tobias, she grabbed his hand and pulled him into the dance with her. She seemed to have dropped more than twenty years in age, and she exclaimed, 'We've done it, boy! We've saved the castle and our own skins to boot! The war will never reach us here!' Tobias looked a little confused by her last words, but he dismissed them as folly from the old crone, and they went down to be with the others."

"There was a party in progress when they returned. Tobias' crazy aunt had broken out a small wine cask and was passing out tankards full. 'Everyone will be drunk by sunrise, and we have much to do,' Tobias said, more to himself, than to anyone. He took a tankard and a chunk of bread and made his way to a window to get a good look at the sunrise on this special morning – the morning the tables were turned on black magic and white magic made a comeback. Devouring his bread and sipping the wine, Tobias watched out the window. He turned at the clapping behind him as a man pulled a small wooden flute from his pocket and began to play. This was the first happiness any of them had shared in many months, and it was wonderful. Given that they hadn't slept in some time, they were more rambunctious than expected."

"When the flutist had finished his second song, Tobias returned his gaze to the sunrise, only to see that there wasn't one. He furrowed his brow and searched the sky. He moved to another window, then another on the opposite wall. The sky was black there as well, not even a star or the moon to guide him. Surely the sun must be nearing the horizon by now. Malachi noticed Tobias was no longer enjoying himself. As a matter of fact, he looked down right frantic, going from window to window. Malachi decided to follow Tobias to see what was happening. When he was close enough to hear Tobias' muttering, he heard, 'Where the hell are we?' Malachi cleared his throat to let Tobias know he wasn't alone and asked, 'What's wrong?' All Tobias could say was, 'I knew it.' He scanned the room looking for something. When his eyes landed on the crone, he made a beeline for her, clenching and unclenching his fists and growling as he walked, trying desperately to control his seething anger."

"Alone in a corner nibbling on a crust of bread, the crone was consulting the bones, unaware that her treachery had been discovered. Malachi asked Tobias what was wrong, but Tobias was intent on talking to the crone and ignored him. Malachi continued to pursue Tobias. He grabbed him by the arm a few feet from the crone and spun his friend around. Malachi's voice was firm, as he demanded to know what was going on. Tobias looked at his arm where his friend had hold of it and said in a quiet but perfectly clear voice, 'The old witch betrayed us. We are not in our own country any longer. We are in a foreign land."

"Tobias turned, pulled his friends hand off his arm, and growled at the crone, 'I want to know where and why.' He was tense with rage as he awaited a response. The entire room went deathly silent, all eyes were tuned into what was happening in the corner."

"Removing her hood, the crone looked at Tobias with her one clear brown eye. Her other eye was milky white, and its color seemed to pulse and shift every now and again. She whispered, 'I fear you not child. Now sit and listen before you attack and lose.'"

"Though Tobias was filled with a rage he hadn't felt in some time, he pulled a stool closer to the crone and plopped down, waiting for some explanation. Pointing her knobby finger at Tobias then herself, she reminded him, 'You came to me. You saw me read the bones. Was I supposed to go against destiny and not do as they said?'"

"There were mumblings from the crowd but not a soul moved. There was no music, and none of them felt like dancing any longer. It was an uneasy rest waiting to find out why Tobias was so angry. Malachi also pulled up a chair to listen. Just as Tobias leaned forward, there was an intense look of agony on his face when he asked, 'Where are we?' For a moment the crone simply stared at the bones. She took a deep ragged breath and began her lengthy response.

"'When you were in the womb of your mother, she came to me for sickness remedies. You were making her violently ill, and whilst we talked, we consulted the bones. They said you would be a powerful man.' The crone paused for but a moment, and Tobias jumped in and said, 'But I was a powerful man where I was. Now I don't know where I am or who lives here. My family doesn't know where I am. How can they find us here – wherever this is? I have nothing but what is in this castle. All of your plans...' The crone shot him a look that froze his tongue, and Tobias stopped before he could drone on any further. 'Shut up boy and listen,' she commanded. 'You were to be a powerful man in a foreign world.' This perked Tobias and Malachi's attention, and they leaned in a little further to hear more about this foreign land."

"The old crone continued. 'I saw you with silver hair and a large family. Again, there was food and wealth, not like when the dragons lived, but better than now. You were at a celebration of some kind, and you were talking to a red skinned man with an odd bonnet of feathers.'

In the middle of his story, Richard stood up and looked at Tanner. He took a deep drink because he'd been talking for quite some time. Then he looked at Darkess.

"They had never seen natives from this country, and their skin color was one they had never seen anywhere before. They hadn't even heard of red skin, so you can imagine how Tobias felt as the crone described people like Tanner. Okay, on with the story…"

"The crone had Tobias and Malachi completely confused. So Malachi asked, 'Red skin and a feather bonnet? Is this man burnt and crazed? Maybe he is painted for war.' The crone took a labored breath and said, 'So young and naïve. Do you really think that white and yellow are the only skin colors out there? This world is much larger than you think. There are at least three more skin colors out there you haven't seen. One of them is red, another is black.' Right then, the whole room burst into laughter, for who had ever seen black or a red man? But the crone would not be silenced by their naivety. Louder than she had ever spoken, she said to them all, 'I have brought you across the great waters to the land called Xyloidonia. This is where your destiny is. Here is where your families belong.'"

"Tobias sat stunned at her revelation. But where is here? He begged for more, saying, 'How did you pick this spot?' The crone's face softened as she realized he really didn't understand his family's powers and their castle, as he should. She said, 'I only pointed the motion in the proper direction. The castle brought you here, because your family line was dying in the old world. The next part of your family will flourish here in this place. With my help, of course,' the old crone said with a wink of her good eye. The entire room was thinking the same thing. At this point, there was no going back, and anyone alive in the old country would be left there to never know what had happened. Tobias was deep in thought, and Malachi had leaned all the way back in his chair in stunned silence. 'Who else knew of this…just my mother?' Tobias demanded. The crone answered him with a softness that was completely unexpected. 'When your mother came to me, we talked of this day in great depth. She made me promise never to tell a soul. When she died, I was the only one who knew. You were the one to make the plan to move. I had no idea at the time, but over the last year, I came to know that the time must have been drawing near. The only real part I played in this plan of yours is the final power you needed, so I directed the castle to where it knew it should be. Nothing more.'"

"Leaning forward, Tobias knelt next to the crone and asked her to read him. Returning the bones to the bag, she shook them for a moment. 'Blow into the bag, boy,' she said. Tobias blew into the bag, and the crone massaged the bones between both hands then tossed them on the table once more. The closest people in the room tried to see what had landed on the table. Malachi craned his neck to see over Tobias' shoulder as the crone placed her hand on Tobias' head, and said, 'Power, such amazing power.'

She kept her eyes closed tightly for a moment then looked at the bones. 'I see a child, a powerful young witch. She is your granddaughter many, many years down the line. You and your wife will bring about one of the most powerful and influential families in all of Xyloidonia.' Tobias looked at the crone and asked, 'My wife?' The crone laughed gruffly and replied, 'You will meet her here. She is a native. She will help guide you through your new life here. She too is a witch, a witch of a different kind, and her family will meld into yours.'"

"Too intent on what the crone was saying, Tobias had not realized that the rest of the occupants in the room had crept closer to hear what was being said. Once he did realize it, he asked one last question. 'Where exactly are we?' The crone was a wise old woman and painted the perfect picture to calm the mass that stared at her, waiting for her answer. 'You are at the base of a mountain,' she explained. 'A day's ride by horse to the nearest village, which will someday become a thriving city. Don't fret. We are all in this together. We are much better off here, and together we will all find a way to deal with our new surroundings.'"

"Then Tobias stood up and gave the first of many orders to his new found family. 'Everyone must get some rest,' he announced, 'for tomorrow we begin our new lives. We will prepare for the future. We will fight back in a way that dark magic won't see coming.'"

Richard sat down next to Darkess and took a large gulp from his cup. Then he looked at her over his spectacles and said,

"You are the reason this castle was moved to this site. It's true. I read his journals. I did embellish a little, but you can read them yourself if you like. They are very well preserved."

It was an impressive story, and it had served Richard's purpose: It gave them all a well deserved night of relaxation by way of imagination. For a while, they had forgotten about being stuck inside the castle by the raging snowstorms outside. More importantly, it had given Darkess a little more insight into history and their family's impact on it.

☼

The summer sun was baking through the windows the morning that Darkess was to take another trip to Jori and Harlow's castle for another lesson. Darkess felt relief at the sight of it, because the anticipation had been making her jittery. Now that she was on her way to the barn with her bags in tow, Rufus decided to meet her in the blinding sunlight with Zaphod only a step behind him. Her horse was freshly cleaned and trimmed, even his hooves were shined, and he was walking proudly with his head held high. Darkess had come to love him very much, and she beamed a smile at him and said,

"Hey there, handsome! How about you and I go for a ride?"

Rufus cocked his head to one side, scratched it, and replied,

"A mite young for that kinda talk, don't ya think?"

Darkess' face blushed a dark shade of pink. She quickly jumped on her horse to hide her face for a moment then said,

"See ya' later, Rufus."

With a squeeze of her thighs, Zaphod leapt into a run. When they reached the end of the courtyard, they vanished.

≈

When Zaphod reappeared with Darkess, grinning from ear to ear on his back, they were running on the beach of a hidden island somewhere along the Malachite Ocean. Jori's castle was a huge towering hulk set on top of a sheer cliff. There was only one-way there: a single path leading the visitor steeply up to the gates. Darkess loved the ride, so they took the long way up for a change of scenery. There were flowers and birds here she had never seen before, and there was always something new to spy.

The castle gates were opening when they came into site. Harlow knew they had arrived, of course. Darkess looked up at the highest tower where the Oracle kept her chambers, and a faint gold glow came from the windows. She must be up there watching, Darkess thought. She had so wanted to meet her the last time she had come here, but as it turned out, she was even more of a recluse than Harlow was. Then her mind leapt to a different thought. If this castle was built for one originally, what could possibly be locked up in all of those rooms? An odd thumping sound came from the Oracle's tower just as Darkess entered the gates and could no longer see it. Jori had told her the last time she had visited to just ignore the sounds, but Darkess couldn't stop thinking about them. The sounds and the Oracle had her wondering. This piqued her curiosity once again, and she knew she would do just about anything to catch a glimpse of that woman.

Once Darkess was inside the castle and the doors began to shut, a sweet smell wafted from the kitchens. As before, there was no one to greet her, so she followed her nose. Tying Zaphod loosely, she made her way towards the smell. When she arrived in the doorway of the kitchens, Darkess began to laugh. There stood Harlow at a wooden table, covered in flour and looking unamused at Darkess' laughter. Then he caught a glimpse of himself in a pot of water on the counter and realized what the laughter was about. It looked as if he had bathed in flour. It was everywhere, even his backside, where he had evidently wiped his hands at one point. Harlow began to laugh with her now and invited her inside.

"Come in. Try some cookies. I was trying to surprise you with a little human contact and domesticity, and it seems I've made a mess of it."

Darkess took a bite of one of the cookies and smiled a rather fake smile.

"They are delicious," she mumbled through the over-baked cookie in her mouth.

"Maybe not so long next time," Harlow said as he jumped up and pulled another pan from the oven.

"Here, try one of these," Harlow said, dumping the tray out onto the table with out any finesse.

Darkess scooped up a hot cookie and nibbled the edge carefully.

"Better," she said, continuing to eat the entire cookie.

"Jori said that I act less human than she does, and I should try to do something with you. And, I do have a weakness for baked goods. Something we have little of around here. So, I tried…"

Darkess scooped up another cookie and began to nibble a little quicker this time, saying,

"One of my favorites. I'm sure you'll do better next time."

"I'm not sure there will be another time," Harlow said with a doubtful look on his face as he began to clean himself up with a damp rag.

"This place is a mess, and so am I. Remove the flour, and make it shine."

As soon as Harlow finished the spell, a swirl of air was floating around him, then the bowls and table, and when it disappeared, every thing was clean and tidy.

"There. That is much better. Follow me, please." It seemed that Harlow's stuffy old attitude was back, but he grabbed a few cookies from the second batch and wrapped them in his handkerchief, stuffing them in his cloak as he began his walk through the castle.

When they arrived at the weapons room, Harlow unlocked the door with a very large key, and they went inside. It was very dark in the room with no windows, so Darkess lit the torches. There weren't many torches, but there were enough to find the proper cabinet. Harlow opened a large wall unit with swinging doors and pulled out a small set of black knives, five in all. Upon closer inspection, Darkess found that they were each a slightly different shape, but all fit perfectly in the palm of her hand. She liked this, which seemed odd, because there was nothing magical about them at all. They were completely human tools.

"Jori asked me to have you work with these for a while this afternoon in the sunlight. With no powers," Harlow said.

"Huh, No powers?" Darkess said with a disheartened tone in her voice. "Why not?"

"I believe she wants you to learn something new." Harlow answered. "Must you always question everything?"

Without waiting for any response, Harlow continued in his gruff manor and pointed at the other end of the room. A large plank of wood was standing there with circles painted on it and a torch on either side to light the targets.

"Every one knows you have a handle on your current powers. Now get a handle on these," Harlow instructed. "Aim for the circles. Oh, and when you hear the bell, come down for dinner."

Without another word, he shut the door behind him, leaving her alone in the room to practice.

"He tried, I guess, and for a while it worked. But he has to put in a lot more work to be human, considering he is one." Darkess said to no one at all as she spun around and threw her first knife.

"I heard that," came muffled from down the hall as Harlow walked away.

Darkess was smiling at Harlow's words as the knife hit the board. Her smile quickly dissipated, because she hit the board but completely missed all of the circles.

"Ohhhh," she groaned. "This may be a little harder than I thought."

Throwing each knife in succession, she realized that each one flew a little differently. She only cheated when retrieving the blades. Using her magic to pull them free was much easier than walking over to the board to get them. She practiced with each knife until she had hit at least three circles in a row before switching to the next and practicing with it. Unbeknownst to Darkess, the sun had crossed the sky while she was deep in practice. And as if on cue with the setting sun, the torches blazed higher for a moment.

Darkess was now to the point with the blades where she was beginning to enjoy herself. Now she took all five of the knives and threw them, hitting five different circles on target, dead center.

"Take that!" she hollered with glee just as the towers bell ran out.

Darkess pulled the blades from the target and replaced them in the scabbard. Laying them on the table, she ran for the kitchens. She hadn't realized how hungry she was until that moment, and it quickened her pace. She had her hopes set on a big dinner.

There was a steam cloud billowing out of a pot on the cast iron stove, and Harlow was sitting on a stool at the table watching it.

"I see you have impressed yourself and are ready for dinner," Harlow rumbled.

His ability was disconcerting, but she was getting used to it. Sometimes it was nice to have your thoughts read, other times it was awful, and it could change in the blink of an eye – or the sighting of your dinner.

"Don't tell me you have never seen a crab. Well, I will give you that. They are different. But I love them, and I think that you should try them at the very least," Harlow said as he scooped out a crab and flopped it out on the table between them.

"That is one of the most plentiful of food sources around here with the ocean and its many inhabitants."

Grabbing the giant water spider with gloved hands, he ripped into its body, tearing each leg off and throwing a few towards Darkess, who looked repulsed by it. Harlow ignored her and began to crush the knobby legs, pulling the meat from inside, and devouring it. Darkess watched in fascination for a moment, then crushed one of the legs on her plate, dipped the meat into a bowl of melted butter, and took a bite. Before she could swallow to talk, Harlow said,

"Yes, I know."

The two of them ate in silence until there was nothing left but scraps of shell and drips of butter on the table.

"Funny how using all your thoughts to concentrate can make you so hungry. By the way, Jori is on her way up. She will want to see what you can do. Are you up for it?" Harlow asked. Without waiting for a response, he got up and walked towards the weapon room.

Darkess never said a word. She just wiped her hands and mouth on a rag and followed him.

≈

Jori was waiting for them when they arrived at the weapons room.

"Harlow tells me that you have already accomplished your task. Now I want to see it. And just to make sure you aren't using your powers, even subconsciously, I've brought this out."

Darkess' head swung towards Harlow with a scowl on her face. She had wanted to tell Jori herself, until she heard Jori's last words. In Jori's hand was a carved stone amulet. It looked very old, and there was an ancient language carved into it. One that Darkess had never seen before. The center had a carving of an odd lizard-like creature, and it was hanging on a long leather cord.

"Ohhhh, what is that?" Darkess asked as she reached for it.

"This…" Jori said, "is a Kubar Amulet. Depending on its use, it blocks or removes powers."

Darkess' hand recoiled in fear. Jori ignored her reaction and continued to speak.

"Most honest people wouldn't think of having one of these. But what would a demon care? They do have some good uses. For instance, you know what I am doing to you. Can you imagine receiving this as a gift? You could get killed before you realized it was the amulet that was blocking your ability to protect yourself or someone else. Imagine giving this to the bodyguard of the King…or someone in need of protection, such as yourself. The battle would be much easier to win."

Darkess' face was deep in thought, wondering about Jori, and she was having a hard time keeping her mind blank when Jori finally made her feel better.

"We…are going to use it as a training tool. Your powers will be fine when you remove the amulet," Jori assured Darkess as she handed her the amulet.

"We use it to guard things," Harlow added. "Most criminals, demonic and magical alike, use their powers to steal. This makes it harder for them if they actually get close enough to our treasures for it to work."

"One more thing," Jori warned, "if you wear it for an extended amount of time, perhaps more than one hour, it will drain your powers, maybe even make you lose them for a period of time. But for our purposes, we will only be using it for a few minutes. Did you know the subconscious can use your powers, too?"

Jori handed Darkess the set of knives she had practiced with earlier, then went to get comfortable for the show. Harlow was seated and lighting a carved bone pipe.

"Go ahead. Show us what you can do," Jori said.

Darkess was feeling a little self-conscious about the fact that maybe she had used her powers and hadn't realized it. She felt a tremor in her hands, so she took a deep breath and steadied herself. She got ready to throw the first knife. Harlow cleared his throat, and this made Darkess blush. Firmly, she gripped the blade and narrowed her eyes. She concentrated on the target, and with one swift move, she flung the blade at it. It seemed like an eternity before it slammed home, but when it did, it hit perfect center on the smallest circle of the plank. Darkess smiled, her shoulders slumped, and the shake left her hands, so she threw another knife. It hit its target, and so did the next three. Then, just to prove she could really do it, she threw all five of them again, each hitting the target nearly perfectly. She was so excited that she tore off the amulet, and tossed it to Jori. Darkess spun around and faced away from the plank. She tossed all five knives into the air and sent them sailing towards the plank. All five hit the plank simultaneously, and of course, they all hit their targets. She had not used her powers, and they had not weakened from use of the amulet either.

☼

The fall season had rolled around once more, and with it came an Indian summer. Darkess found herself wandering the woods with Zaphod. She was thinking about her second cancelled trip to visit Belthazor, and she kicked a clump of leaves into the air, showering Zaphod and herself with debris. Zaphod gave her a snort of disgust for the mess that was now in his mane.

"Sorry boy," Darkess said, beginning to pick the debris away.

"What I don't understand is, if I'm this great witch, why do they baby me? What's the big deal if there is a prisoner on the ship? He'd be guarded and locked up, right? So what is the big problem? Besides, I am pretty good at defense. That is what they keep teaching me, all of them. Try this, and try that. Can you do that without your powers? How about from memory? What's this? What's that? It's all so aggravating!" Darkess nagged.

She hadn't really expected an answer, but one came anyway.

"You're simply not ready yet."

Darkess spun around and found Chakra sitting on a tree limb staring down at her.

"What do you mean, I'm not ready yet? I'm working hard all the time, and I'm better at everything than they thought I'd be. So? What is it?" Darkess practically screamed at Chakra.

Chakra licked his paw and rubbed it over his face before he said,

"Screaming at your familiar is one of the big deals. I'm not what you are mad at. You want to be grown now, and it takes time to grow, not lessons. Experience makes up for at least as much as practice, and one demon fight doesn't make you experienced."

"How am I supposed to get any experience if no one will let me go anywhere?" Darkess asked, kicking a pile of leaves again.

Zaphod nudged Darkess in the back, knocking her forward, and she retaliated.

"What was that for?"

"Finish cleaning my mane, or I will go home and have Rufus do it. You are in such a mood today."

Darkess began to pick more debris out of Zaphods' mane again, grumbling as she worked. She was so upset that she was crushing the leaves, making the job more tedious than it should have been – which only aggravated the situation even more.

"You know, I never asked for this," she yelled. "And now that I am willing to stare directly into danger's face, they all hold me back. The big party is almost here, and I don't even care. I want to see new things, and Belthazors' ship holds many new things. And it's not locked up here!" Darkess yelled.

Then she turned and walked towards the castle. Her shoulders were slumped as she walked, and her gaze was at her feet. Chakra looked at Zaphod. Neither knew what to say, so they just caught up to her, and the three walked silently back to the castle.

≈

Over the next couple of weeks, everyone's excitement continued to grow, except for Darkess'. Chakra was constantly with her, acting more like a cat than a familiar, trying to give her comfort, which was having no effect. Richard had noticed the way that Darkess seemed to be moping her way around the castle. He hadn't seen a real smile on her face in days. Finally, he asked her to meet him in his study after dinner to discuss any new alterations to the festive decorations, but he had other motives.

When Darkess arrived at the study, Richard was reading from one of his old books. Lowering his spectacles, he said,

"Sit dear, please."

He indicated a chair with an outstretched hand and noticed that her pattern of downturned eyes did not waver. Richard cleared his throat, which got no reaction, so he said,

"I called you here under false pretences."

This finally got her attention. Her gaze went directly into his. Darkess gently shifted in her seat but said nothing, and her eyes never left his.

"I think everyone else has been fooled by your little act, I am not. What is going on in that red head of yours?" Richard asked his granddaughter.

"I don't want to throw a party. I just don't feel like it," she mumbled, lowering her eyes once again to the floor.

Richard pursed his lips, as he knew this was going to be a long talk, and he asked,

"You are not happy that your birthday is almost here?"

Darkess shifted uneasily in her chair.

"No," was all she said, but she switched her gaze to her fingers, which were making knots of themselves in her lap.

"Why not?" Richard asked quietly.

"Oh Grandfather, it's just that…" her voice trailed off, and a tear glistened at the corner of her eye.

Richard stood and walked around his desk, sitting in a chair next to her. He reached for her, and the tear that had only been on the verge of falling turned into a silent river streaking down her cheek.

"It can't be all that bad, can it?" he asked lovingly as she collapsed into his arms.

"There now, tell me what is wrong, dear," he whispered into her hair.

Darkess sniffed a couple of times, lifted her head from her grandfather's chest, and looked into his eyes. The sadness in her eyes overwhelmed him, and he wiped the tear off the end of her nose and kissed her forehead.

"We've never had secrets between each other. Now I insist. Tell me what is wrong? I can't help you if I don't know what the problem is."

Darkess sniffed a couple of times, wiping her face on a handkerchief Richard had handed her. Through trembling lips she told him,

"I'm scared…and I'm mad. Oh, I'm so confused. I don't know what to do."

Then she broke down in a full-blown attack of tears and shivers. Richard hugged her for a moment and rubbed the long hair down her back, trying to comfort her.

"There; there now, feeling a little better?" Richard said as she sat up, trying to compose herself.

"Y-yes," Darkess stuttered, as she wiped her nose.

"For starters, what are you scared of?" Richard asked.

Darkess pulled the hair away from her face and tucked it behind her ears.

"I think…they are combined. Oh, what I mean is, well, if I'm so good at what I do, why are you all holding me back? If there is something to be afraid of then I must not be as good as you all say I am. How can I become this great witch if no one will let me go anywhere? Without a guard. Experience is what I need, but I can't get it…and now I'm scared, well, that I'll be afraid when I need to be strong. If you all need to protect me, oh, it's just a big mess!" Darkess said with pain in her voice as she flopped back into the chair and began to cry quietly again.

"I see…" Richard said as he rose from his seat and made his way back around his desk. Digging deep in a drawer, he pulled out something small enough to conceal inside his closed fist, then he made his way back around to sit by Darkess again.

"First I will say one thing. Then you and I are going on a little trip."

Darkess once again tried to dry up her face, and Richard took a deep breath, saying,

"I am truly sorry for the burden that has been placed upon you. I see your misery, and it cuts through me like a blade. However, this burden would not have been placed upon your shoulders if you were not worthy of it. There have been two major premonitions depicting your place in this world. The crone did the first; remember the prophecy she gave to Tobias about his future? In the story about how the castle came to be here? She told him of you, only vaguely. Then, almost a hundred years later, Wolfbane predicted you again, in much greater detail as proven by the box you now have."

Darkess' tears were now dry, and she was sitting up, leaning forward in her chair and studying her grandfather as he spoke.

"You must learn that the battle between good and evil is never easy, even with age and experience. And it won't get any easier. Not for any of us, even with age or experience. Add to that the fact that we all love you. Sometimes emotions can get in the way. You were foretold many centuries ago. That is a rare and special thing, and you are our only beloved grandchild, which is one of a kind, and very special."

Richard readjusted his robes and smiled at his granddaughter.

"Prophecy and grandchild…both are special and must be protected. But you are not to the age where all the knowledge that you seek should be divuldged. If something happens to you, even by odd accident, the world would suffer in ways it has never suffered before. We will always try to protect you. And sometimes that includes keeping you in the dark on a few things. At your age, ignorance can save your life."

Darkess looked into space for a moment or two, deep in thought. The small twitching of the tiniest muscles and the dilation of her eyes made it seem that she was actually realizing what he had said on a deep level, more than she ever had before. She looked at her grandfather, then at her hands, then at the large book on the podium, and then back at her grandfather again.

"Are you going to say anything?" Richard gently prodded with one eyebrow raised, amazed at her silence.

"Yes. Where are we going?" Darkess asked, raising the same eyebrow.

This made Richard raise both eyebrows and his head slightly.

"Nothing else?" Richard asked her.

"Nope," Darkess stated.

"Are you still upset?"

"Depends on where you are taking me," Darkess said, raising both eyebrows and staring back at her grandfather.

Darkess kept this look frozen on her face, and Richard did the same for a moment. Then he shook his head and chuckled as he said,

"Very well then. Promise me that you will come to me when you decide that you are ready to talk."

"Promise," was all Darkess said, but the light that had gone out of her eyes began to spark again.

This made Richard smile. The normalcy seemed to be returning to her attitude. He opened his hand and showed Darkess the item that he had earlier retrieved.

"Have you ever seen anything like this?" Richard asked, knowing very well she hadn't.

The object in his hand was a silvery-black, and it seemed to pulsate with life. As the color changed from silver to black, then to silver again, Darkess wanted to touch it. As she reached out, she was sure it would be soft, maybe even liquid to the touch. But she was surprised to feel that it was hard and smooth on the surface.

"Oooh, what kind of stone is it?" she asked.

"It's a mistake. But I find it useful at times," Richard said, staring into the object.

"A mistake? What was it supposed to be?"

"It was supposed to be the elixir of life, a youth potion that went completely awry. And I've never been able to produce it again. Plus, it only works for me. I can, however, take a companion along. I've done experiments with it for years. Combine the stone with one drop of my blood and our teleport potion. When we arrive at our destination, everything is frozen, in a way. We are on another plain, where time nearly stands still. I have spent an entire day away, and when I returned, it had been only an hour here. I call it my Zivits, because it is a silly, scatterbrained object. And though the name sounds fun, it can be wrought with danger. There are demons that use those other planes to move about, but together, we should be able to avoid or fend off any we come across. What do you say? Up for a little jaunt to another dimension?"

Darkess was so excited she could hardly contain herself, and with a gleam in her eyes, she said,

"Yes."

"Then grab your bag, and I'll get us some provisions. Meet me in the attic in one half hour. Tell no one. Your grandmother would have my hide."

☼

Darkess arrived back long before Richard, so she looked out the window to see what Tanner was doing when she heard a sliding sound. She turned, thinking her grandfather had arrived, but she was still alone. The smile slid off her face and was replaced by a smirk. She stood still, waiting to hear the sound again. After a minute or so, she turned back towards the window, dismissing the sound and returning to her nosiness. She heard the sound again. This time, she realized where the sound was coming from, and she noticed that the old chessboard seemed to be playing itself. Positioning herself beside the table on a small stool, she watched as the white's bishop slid down the board to take black's knight. Darkess had seen the game played before, but it had always looked so slow that she had never taken much interest. Believing that her grandfather would be a few more minutes, she settled in to watch. It was fun wondering which piece would move next.

The next move wasn't long in the waiting. In retaliation for losing its knight, the black side took white's rook with his surviving knight just as Richard opened the door to the attic.

"Playing chess, are we?" Richard asked with a surprised sound to his voice.

"No, the board is playing itself. Must have gotten lonely. I was merely watching," Darkess replied, turning her gaze back to the board.

Richard closed the door, walked to the table, sat down his bundles, and said,

"That board has never played itself in all the years I have been around. And you didn't do anything to it?"

Darkess shook her head no and watched to see the next move on the board.

"Hmmm. Lets see…oh yes. Specter here in our midst, show yourself for but a moment."

The ghost Quinn appeared, sitting next to Darkess, reaching for a black pawn. Darkess gasped, then smiled as she exclaimed,

"Quinn! What are you doing here?"

"You can see me then?" Quinn asked in a very faint voice. Darkess shook her head yes.

"I'm here for the party," Quinn explained. "Your family always throws the very best ones. I arrived early to watch you prepare. It can be dreadfully lonely, this between life and afterlife."

The color of Quinn's face turned a darker shade of silver, as if he were blushing. Then he said,

"I sometimes come and watch you train. You are becoming quite good, young Miss."

Just then, Quinn started to fade away.

"See you soon…" came from the air as thin as a whisper, and then he disappeared.

The black pawn moved two spaces forward. Darkess smiled at her grandfather and said,

"Thanks."

Richard reached for his bag, and responded,

"Don't mention it. Only benign spirits can get into the castle, or I would have been more on the alert for who it may have been. Ready to go? Collect your things and let us be on our way."

Richard pointed to a spot on the floor with plenty of room to move about, situated his bag, checked his pockets, and handed a bottle of potion to Darkess. In his hand was a small knife. He used it to prick his finger and then said,

"Now, when you throw that bottle, think of me, and I will guide us."

He placed the bloody hole in his thumb on the Zivits.

Darkess held Richard's hand as tightly as she could and threw the potion at their feet. Together, they closed their eyes and felt the pull of magical travel.

≈

Takar had been sneaking around Alieria's castle every now and again, trying to catch another glimpse of that powerful child. He was now obsessed with two things, and they seemed to be tearing him apart. He was still searching for the eggs, but an odd feeling made him believe that the little girl was involved. He had no proof, it was more of a hunch, and he continued to look for the connection. The map on his wall had nearly fifty pins in it now, and Takar was trying to figure out where he should travel to next. Tuma's eyes appeared in front of Takar's face. Being in such deep thought, Takar jumped back into his chair.

"What news do you bring?" he demanded.

Tuma's face and body appeared, and he stammered out a response.

"O-our source says there will be a ship coming in tonight at these coordinates. It has been out to sea for three months and has traveled to many countries along its journey. It may carry something you seek."

Takar leaned forward in his chair and narrowed his eyes at his servant, then hissed,

"What, that I seek, is on that ship?"

Tuma's eyes stayed visible, but his head became transparent, and his body completely disappeared as he took a step away from his master.

"Source says 'tis a magic ship, sir," Tuma squeaked

"Magic ship? What do you mean by magic ship?" Takar pressed.

"Beggin' your pardon sir, 'tis run by magic folk. Caters to the magical world. It's said that there is a prisoner on board. Has to be influential people around with a prisoner on board, specially a magical prisoner. I was thinking that maybe you should have yourself a look."

"Who asked you to think?" Takar said as he ripped the paper out of Tuma's hand.

On the paper was written the name of the ship, its dock number and city of destination, along with a few other tidbits about the kind of ship. Takar thought for a moment then spewed orders at Tuma.

"Pack me food for a week. Get my black cloak, and be quick about it."

Tuma disappeared, but you could hear his shuffling steps as he left the room. Takar crossed the room to his map and shoved a pin into the ocean. He would be going to the ship, not the dock.

≈

Takar stood inside his pentagram, sprinkled the edges with powder, and vanished in a tornadic wind. When he reappeared, he was on the deck of the ship Tuma had told him about. It was cloudy and damp, so it was not out of the ordinary to have a hood pulled down around the face. Takar blended in nicely as he wandered about the ship, seeing what seemed like ordinary people everywhere. However, the deeper he went, the fewer humans he saw. He may have found something interesting, but so far, nothing that added to his obsession with the eggs. He hadn't seen a child yet, and at this rate, he doubted that he would see one at all. This was a rough cargo ship, nothing that would haul around families. These people all looked rather desperate, a few even eyed him with suspicion, but fortunately, they all seemed to want their privacy as much as he did.

Rounding a corner, he found the stairwell that led down to the bowels of the ship. It was devoid of movement for the moment, so he decided to go down further. The next level's passage was empty, and he contined his search deeper into the ship. He had been quiet, trying not to draw any attention to himself, but now that he was so far into the ship undetected, he feared that his time here was running short, so he pulled out his egg detector. Checking both directions again and making sure he was alone, he held out the small golden dragon. It showed no signs of life. There were no dragon eggs aboard this ship.

"Damn," Takar whispered in defeat.

Continuing his walk down the corridor, Takar was nearing a corner when a large black dog stepped out. The beast's eyes glowed in the dim lighting from the porthole, and it stared directly at Takar – frozen, waiting. Takar stopped. Something seemed ominous about the dog with no master insight. Baring its teeth, the dog let out a growl that came from deep in its throat but lasted only a second or so. Takar did not want his mission here to end quite yet, but it seemed that this standoff could give him away.

"Good boy," Takar whispered, holding his hand out towards the dog in a calming gesture. He was ready to throw a fireball if needed.

The beast transformed into a large hulking man with long greasy hair, filthy clothing, and a sneer to match.

"Yer not sposeda be here on thisn' here level," the man-beast snarled.

Not wanting to blow his cover, Takar decided to play stupid. He tried to back out slowly without having to leave just yet.

"Curiosity sir, sorry. I will just be on my way," Takar said, lowering his hand slightly and backing towards the stairs.

A second set of eyes appeared next to the man-beast's thigh. Backup had arrived and was watching to make sure nothing was going to happen. Takar saw the second dog and slipped up the stairs without setting off any major alarms.

"Curiosity can get ya kilt mister. I suggest ya don't ferget that fer the rest a the trip!" the man-beast called after Takar had left his sight.

"That's what you think, guard-dog. Hmph," Takar whispered in a snarl.

Returning to the deck of the ship, Takar wondered what Tuma's source had meant by something I seek would be here. Then he dismissed it as he had finally found a spot on the deck where he could draw out his pentagram and leave this wild goose chase behind him. Takar sprinkled his home symbols with the potion and was on his way.

"Wasted trip," he grumbled as the smoke enveloped him.

☼

Arriving at their destination, Richard and Darkess opened their eyes and could see nothing but ocean. There were no sounds. It was as if the entire ship was padded with cotton, and the ocean was frozen. Time seemed to stand still.

"Where are we?" Darkess asked in a voice that sounded strange, muffled and distant.

"We are on Belthazor's ship, the one with the prisoner who wrecked your trip. Now move carefully, for we can move through walls and floors. We will be able to see any spirits and dimensional travelers. So we must watch closely the things around us. Shall we take a tour?" Richard said nonchalantly.

Darkess has never been on a ship. It was quite exciting, especially without the possibility of seasickness. She was happy to be exploring something completely foreign to her. There was a man standing a few yards away who was hauling a massive rope over his shoulder. She tried to touch the rope, and her hand went completely through it. Gasping, she pulled her hand out of the man, and his rope and turned quickly to her grandfather.

"We are in another dimension. I said that you could pass through walls. What did you think would happen?" Richard asked as Darkess' face turned a shade of pink.

Should have paid closer attention, Darkess chastised herself. They continued to walk around the deck of the ship, and Darkess was intrigued with some of the things she saw. Her hands passed through everything she touched, so she stuck her head through the wall and looked inside the ship. Richard smiled at her, nearly laughing at the sight of her half through the wall. So far she had seen many new things, but they were all nautical, not magical. Even though this was interesting, it wasn't exactly like she had expected a magical ship to be. As a matter of fact, it was nothing like she thought it would be.

Almost halfway around the deck of the large cargo ship, Darkess saw a frozen vortex of smoke. This had the look of magic to it, she thought. Not only was it in a place were there should be no smoke; it seemed to be enveloping a man.

"Grandfather, look," Darkess pointed at the vortex behind the small cabin at the tail end of the ship.

"I wonder what that is?" Richard asked, eying the cloud suspiciously.

Together they walked towards it. Richard led the way, holding Darkess behind him. Once they got close enough to see what was happening, Darkess held her hand over her mouth and gasped.

"I know that man. He was the demon at Alieria's party."

Frown lines creased Richard's forehead, and his cheeks drooped as he tried to get a closer look at the demon behind the smoke. A feint portal was opening at the demon's feet, and Richard noticed the pentagram. Dropping wearily to his knees, Richard took a closer look at the symbols drawn on the deck. He had seen these symbols before. They were the same ones Janine had reproduced from the same party Darkess had been talking about, and he had seen some of them in the book of black magic they had stored away at the castle.

"This can't be good," Darkess said.

The longer Richard and Darkess studied the demon and his portal, the more smoke surrounded him, obscuring not only him, but his portal also.

"I thought you said things were frozen here?" Darkess questioned her grandfather.

"Time is still moving, it is just at a much slower rate than the dimension we are on. If we had been on our own dimension when he had initiated his portal, it would have taken only a blink or two of the eye, and he would have been gone, giving us no time to see him this closely without any danger."

Just then, the demon disappeared, and his smoke screen began to dissipate. When Darkess looked at her grandfather, her shoulders slumped with disappointment, but only for a second.

"Ooh, I know, I know, let's go!" Darkess said excitedly, swiftly grabbing her grandfather's hand.

"Sometimes it can be downright disappointing to realize you are growing up, but you seem to be taking it better," Richard smiled at his granddaughter.

Darkess hugged her grandfather. When she pulled away, she tugged at her cloak, trying to find the potion to send them home. Smashing the bottle on the deck at their feet, a large blue cloud erupted, and they were on their way back home. Mission accomplished, Richard thought to himself. Darkess feels better, and we have a new clue.

☼

Richard sent correspondence to everyone in the Order, starting with Belthazor. After all, it was his ship. He added a special note to Janine, asking her to speak to Alieria about her special visitor, and if he'd come around recently. Richard then set about the task of writing everything down, from Darkess and how upset she had been, to the demon on the ship. Who was he? What did he want? Or get? How was he associated with Darkess? Then the only thing left to do was tell the family. Richard had let Darkess do as she pleased for a while, so he could take the heat from the family about the forbidden trip and tell them about the demon.

Darkess had made herself scarce while Richard was working, but when he headed down to tell the family, she decided to listen in on the little talk. That was, until she heard her grandmother yelling. She could not make out all that was said, but when she heard the words "idiotic, irresponsible, and foolhardy," she decided she had heard enough and didn't stick around to hear the rest. The furthest place from the family would be the safest, so she returned to the tower to see if the chessboard was playing again.

☼

With her fourteenth birthday over, and the holiday just a memory, Darkess sat on her bed looking at her new things. She had stopped wearing dresses entirely and had taken to breeches. This had allowed her unhampered flow in her fighting movements, and enabled her to fill her pockets instead of always carrying her pack. Dresses had plenty of room, her mother had told this to her over and over. But Darkess insisted that they could easily trip her up – a huge embarrassment if she actually did trip. And even if dresses held plenty of items, it was hard to get to them swiftly.

Darkess was devoting all of her time to preparation, for what she wasn't exactly sure, but she wanted to be ready. There was a brand new knife on the bed. She had pulled it out of a brand new boot sheath and wasn't at all happy with its blade. Deep in her pack was a wet-stone, and Darkess pulled it out and set to sharpening the knife. Once she was finished, she inspected her work then slid the knife into its sheath and tucked it securely into her boot. Taking a lap around the room, she looked into her mirror and smiled to herself.

"Can't see it. Feels good. Perfect," she said to her reflection.

Turning back to the bed, she picked through all of her gifts until she found them a proper home. Chakra lay on the pillow, purring and gently flipping the tip of his tail. There was one gift still on the bed. It was a belt with two small knuckle knives hidden in the decoration and small loops in the back for potion bottles. Harlow and Jori had it specially made with hammered silver and thin strong leather. It was one of a kind. Slipping it into place, she again looked at herself in the mirror. Smiling at what she saw, she spun around and flung both knives at her practice board. They slammed home, side by side.

☼

Darkess held tightly to Brutus' hand as they both melted and seeped down through the cracks in the wall in front of them. Once they reached the other side of the wall, they slowly reformed inside a completely black room. They had to leave all of their tools behind, which made Darkess a little unnerved, but she had her magical powers. With their location, they should be completely alone and totally safe, but that didn't seem to calm Darkess at all. The air was stale and thick. Brutus reminded her that her potions and knives were only back up, but she felt naked without them. Her precious pack and dragon bangle were still outside, and for some reason, she felt like she was leaving herself open for attack.

"Wer in the middle a nowhere, prably a hunred miles from anyone," Brutus said. "Calm yerself, trust yerself. Have a lil faith," he whispered as he squeezed her hand for reassurance, then let go. "How's about a lil light?" he requested.

A fireball erupted in Darkess' hand. She levitated the ball high enough to see about the room.

"Here," Brutus said, handing Darkess an ancient piece of wood covered in some sort of oil.

The torch burned brightly, and they walked down the length of the room.

"Look," Darkess said, pointing to a wall painted from top to bottom with hundreds of tiny pictures.

"It's hieroglyphs, a ancient piture language. They tell a story wit pitures instead a words," Brutus said as they continued down the wall.

"Wow. Look here...and here," Darkess pointed to a painting of a creature that resembled a dragon.

"An here," Brutus had found another of the same painting, but this one had three ovals with it.

Darkess' breath started to come quicker as they searched further. The entire wall was a story about dragons, and their powers. There were pictures of fire and water, fields of crops, and every phase of the moon. Some of the paintings were repeated, and that made them seem very important.

"I wish I could read this. It must be how they lived with the dragons back then. How they coexisted," Darkess said with a twinkle in her eyes.

Brutus was glad he had found something new and exciting to show Darkess.

"I believe we are the first ta enter this tomb since it was sealed many hunreds a years ago. An you are the only person I culd bring here ta see it without damaging it. It's too bad we cin't bring a interpreter down here."

They were so enthralled with the paintings that they hadn't noticed the small doorway at the end of the chamber. Brutus had to nearly bend in half to fit through the entrance, but Darkess made it through with a couple inches to spare. Once the light reached the center of the room, they found a sarcophagus, several urns, and a few tables with the deceased's possessions. But what caught Darkess' eye was the golden statue of the dragon that stood at the foot of the sarcophagus.

"Will ya look at that?" Brutus said more than asked when he realized what had stopped Darkess.

Darkess nearly melted at the sight of it, and she knelt down to get a better look.

"A most wonderous artist made this. Just look at the detail. It looks alive…it looks sad." Darkess said, looking deep into the dragon's eyes.

"Uhh," Darkess sucked in air and jumped to her feet.

"Did you see that?" she asked in an unbelieving voice.

Brutus jerked at her reaction and pulled her back, saying,

"See what? Are ya ok?"

Darkess held her hands out defensively and said apprehensively,

"I'm sorry. Yes, I'm fine, but I could swear I saw that statue blink."

Brutus patted her shoulder with his big paw, knocking her around a little.

"Must'a been the firelight. Plays wit the eyes sometimes," Brutus said in a slightly worried tone.

Together they stared at the dragon, but it was only unmoving gold with exquisite detail. Darkess raised her shoulders and said,

"Jumpy I guess. Sorry 'bout that."

However, she squinted at the statue one more time before continuing on to the other items in the tomb. The sarcophagus had a dragon carved into the chest, and there were pictures carved all the way around the sides. Once Darkess reached the head, she noticed that the flattened part of the base also had symbols carved into it. The symbols on the head and shoulders of the base matched the symbols on the wall of the outer chamber.

"Whoever this person was, they were very important," Darkess observed. "Maybe a link to the dragons? But what kind? Was this a magical person or a worshipper of dragons? Maybe a dragon hunter? One of the protectors of the dragons during the magic wars, or was this one of the people who ruined our world? You can see by the pictures around the room that this place was lush and green then. Now look at it. Brutus, if I need to come back here again, can you find it?"

"Yes Miss, sure cin."

"Good," she said. "What I think we need most from here at this point are these three symbols. I want you to see what your local contacts think of them, your interpreter as you say. But remember, we must keep the location of this tomb a secret. No one must know of it. Tell anyone that you saw the symbols on an old crate or something. I have a feeling this is a very important place, whether it was for good or evil, and we don't want evil to find it."

Brutus had continued to search the walls as Darkess was talking, and his eyes suddenly bulged from his face, and his mouth dropped open when he pointed at the wall.

"Miss, look," he whispered in awe.

"Oh, wow," Darkess breathed heavily when she saw what he had found.

Stepping closer, she held up her hand to touch it. There was a painting of a woman on the wall. Darkess traced the bangle that was painted on her arm. It was an exact duplicate of the one now tucked away in her pack outside the tomb.

"How can this be?" Darkess asked Brutus.

"The seer...the one that Janine talked ta...must've used the power a the dragon, a creature that was said to be around fer thousands a years to make that bangle. Maybe this woman had the same job as you, an the spirits know ya are the next great protector. So, they showed that bangle to the seer who channeled it ta Janine. Ooh, or maybe you are her reincarnated," Brutus said enthusiastically, using his thumb to point at the sarcophagus.

Darkess raised her eyebrows over his comment, but she didn't dismiss it.

"Hmph," she snorted and continued to look the tomb over.

The three dragons were repeated on the walls, but here next to the body, they were in brilliant color. They were all mostly black, but they each had a different color of detail: one red, one blue, and one lavender. Darkess had a shiver race down her spine, and all the tiny hairs on her stood up when she touched the paintings of them.

"Ohhh." Darkess shivered at the sensation that covered her. "This is very important. How did you find this tomb?"

"By accodent. I's hired ta find the tomb of a high priest who's rumored ta be buried with a magical book a the dead. But I never found it. I lied an told'em there was no tombs here an directed them ta nother hunter who'd take'em to another area a the desert. A place where hunreds a tombs, raided tombs, wit notin' a magical value. Searched'em maself. Told'em I's too afeared a the magic a the dead. Gave'em their money back an tole yer grandfather about it." Brutus answered, his eyes twinkling in the firelight. "You're more important than a little money an a lot a trouble."

"You really should get a higher class of clientele," Darkess grinned.

A little later as they were melting down to retreat through the cracks they had come through, the small dragon statue blinked its eyes and let a small puff of smoke escape from its nostrils as he watched them leave.

≈

Nothing had been found or missing on Belthazor's ship. Alieria had not seen the demon since her birthday, and none of the members of the Order had found out anything new. It seemed that the world was sleeping, for the demon front had been quiet for a while now. Richard had sent Darkess on a trip with Brutus, and they should be arriving home any day. Richard was hoping they had found something of value in that tomb to help their cause. Thumbing through his notes on this mysterious demon, the symbols were bothering him. He knew they were ancient and dealt with black magic, but they had a familiar feel to them. He just couldn't put his finger on it. He slammed his fist down onto the table.

"Damn it all," he swore.

His frustration was intense.

"What am I missing?" he demanded of himself.

"There has to be something I am overlooking."

Putting all of his notes away, Richard went over to the window. There were a few birds flying overhead, and he watched them as they swooped and chased each other. Just then, movement down below caught his eye. Darkess was trotting towards the barn on Zaphod. The frustration of the previous hour was replaced with a sprinkling of excitement.

"What has she found, I wonder," Richard whispered to himself.

≈

Darkess came ripping through the door as if she were on fire and screamed,

"Grandfather! Come quick!"

Of course, everyone with a set of ears in the castle heard and came to see what the commotion was all about. Even Tanner, who had been coming in from his cabin, had heard and quickened his step. Darkess ran to the nearest table in the small dining hall and quickly began pulling scrolls from her pack. Every one gathered around the table, waiting for some explanation for the outburst.

"Look. You'll never believe what Brutus found."

Spreading the scrolls out, laying candles and such on the corners of each, she pointed to each one as she spoke about them.

"The sarcophagus of someone special. Drew it from memory, so it may be a little sketchy. It had this carved into its chest. The chamber walls had three different types of dragons painted about: one red, one blue and one lavender. There were absolutely hundreds of drawings in the two chambers. Everything from the changing of the seasons and the phases of the moon to these three dragons...and fields full of food that were burnt to ash. It was wonderful, and awful. This language is so old, there are very few who understand it. It seems to ask more questions than it answered. Oh, and the statue, he was at the foot of the sarcophagus, and the most amazing item in the entire chamber. The detail would make Janine weep. Here's a rough outline of his form. There were urns, four on a shelf, and baskets full of food, and all sorts of odd stuff in there. It seemed that the dead woman lived there before she died."

"Woman? What makes you believe that the body was a woman's without seeing it?" Richard asked.

"That brings me to the last drawing. Crude, but you get the idea. She looked like me, down to the last detail. She wore a bangle, just like me. Her hair, the blades strapped to her – they were the same. Only the clothing was different. Oh, I wish you could see it. We can use the teleport potion..."

"No, no. We believe you," Richard said. "Go on."

"I think that tomb has been undisturbed since she was buried there. There were some empty shelves that had me wondering. But other than that, it seemed the entire tomb was intact. I wonder if she was the keeper of the eggs in her time."

"Or the maker of these mysterious eggs," Richard stated.

"Either way, I sent Brutus on a mission to translate some of the symbols if possible. And see if the symbols were her name or something else entirely. So, what do you think?" Darkess asked, aiming the question at her grandfather.

Darkess' voice was a higher pitch with the excitement, and she had been speaking so fast that everyone was staring at her in shock. Shock from her attitude of authority, the speed of her speech, not to mention the information she had spread all over the table. Angela was the first to break the silence.

"My dear, you are in such a tizzy. Sit, calm yourself, and tell us more."

Roxy came into the room with a tray of bread and cheese. They ate and discussed the tomb for quite a while. Darkess described everything in as much detail as she could muster and answered all of their questions. And when the food was gone and the story told, Darkess had come to a decision. She said,

"I want to visit Alieria again. I want her to become a member of the Order."

Silver leaned forward in her chair with an intensely serious look on her face and asked her daughter a question.

"You hardly know the woman. What makes you think you can trust her? Whatever gave you such an idea?"

Darkess stood up and walked around the end of the table, chewing absently on a hangnail as she thought of an answer.

"I think her private room may be holding something we need. More information than we found. And I think she is the best link to the dragon world that we know. We'll have to be smart about it. There must be a magical contract, just like the rest of us. However..." Darkess stopped talking but continued to pace around the table.

Placing both hands down on the end of the table, she looked at her family and said,

"We tell her nothing. Until she signs the contract – in blood. Then and only then can she hear the entire story. What do you think?"

Darkess looked about the table at all of the people she considered her family, and they all showed expressions of being impressed. Daniel stood up and hugged his daughter, saying,

"You are growing up so fast...and it seems that you are really taking control of your destiny. I am glad you are home safe."

Behind Daniel, Richard smiled at Darkess and gave her a thumb's up.

≈

Late that same night, Richard was drawing up a contract similar to the one they had all signed the night the Order of the New Horizon was born. He had sent letters to all current members asking them for a yea or nay on adding a new member to the group, and, of course, the reason for the addition of this member. He also added a long list of notes, copies of all of Darkess' drawings, and her new change in attitude. Her new freedom to travel has had a huge impact on her confidence. The time could be near, he thought, as he put all of his notes away. He looked at the stars in the sky, turned towards the door, and headed for bed. He blew out the candle.

☼

The next afternoon was cold and rainy, which kept everyone inside. Daniel and Richard were playing chess. Silver was polishing up an old box she had bought at the market. Darkess was writing in her journal when a flock of birds started pecking at the door. Darkess knew that it could only be one thing. She pointed at the door and with a twitch of her finger, the door swung open. A flood of tiny birds twittered into the room and landed all around Richard. Darkess then held her palm out, and the door gently closed. She didn't stop writing, and she never looked up.

Richard read all of the letters and was pleasantly surprised that they had all said yes to inviting the new member. Janine had gone as far as setting up a meeting time for the initiation of Alieria and was awaiting a return bird with an answer. Deciding that all of the letters needed a reply, Richard postponed the game of chess and headed for the tower. Darkess looked up as her grandfather walked by, then returned to her journal. Daniel sometimes hated the fact that he had no power and was always sitting on the side watching. He looked at his daughter, then the chessboard, and with a smirk he headed off towards the kitchens. Silver put down the box that she was working on and moved closer to her daughter.

"What are you working on?" Silver asked.

Darkess had a far away look on her face as she mumbled,

"A spell."

Silver realized that her daughter was more like Richard than she had previously thought. She decided to leave Darkess engrossed in her work and followed her husband to the kitchens.

☼

The winter weather was getting worse with each new year. This year was proving the rule. Winds howled like a hundred banshees surrounding the castle, and the cold seeped through bones like it was threatening to freeze your soul. The initiation was set for noon that day, and all of the members had arrived at Vallencourt Castle, except for Janine, who was bringing the new inductee. Darkess was a little nervous, and she paced back and forth in her room. She couldn't figure out why she was nervous, and she wondered if something was wrong. But what, she thought. Finally she grabbed her pack and headed down to the great room to see the rest of the members when the broom by the fireplace fell to the floor.

"Someone's here," she said as she closed the door to her room.

Sure enough, when Darkess arrived at the great room, all the members had arrived, and her nerves began to calm. Everyone seemed quite at home, munching on food and chatting, when they realized that Darkess was with them. Alieria smiled, saying,

"You are a very special girl, and I have some news that may be of interest to you. I have received a letter from my cousin, Tasha."

Darkess stared at Alieria, searching for the name Tasha in her memory. Recollection registered on her face, and she asked with excitement.

"What did she say?"

Only Janine had any idea what the two witches were talking about, but they all listened intently to what was being said. Alieria sat down on the chair nearest to Darkess and pulled out a leather case with a small stack of letters.

"Maybe you should just read the letters," Alieria said, handing the stack to Darkess.

"Excuse me while I read these," Darkess said, as if she were now running the meeting.

Darkess settled into her chair and read the correspondence. For several long moments, the only sounds in the room were the crackling of the fire, the shift of pages, and an occasional rustle of clothing as each person finally found a place to sit. Everyone waited patiently to see what would happen next. Everyone except Harlow. He had his eyes closed and was reading right along with Darkess, who in turn was channeling them to Jori. Richard had sat down next to Darkess, intending to read the letters next, if permitted.

When Darkess finally finished reading the letters, she looked at Alieria, then Janine, and lastly her grandfather. The look on her face was complete astonishment, making everyone wonder just what those letters said. At last, Darkess said with a quiver in her voice,

"I think we've found it."

"Let me read those," Richard stated, snatching the pages from her hands.

"What is all of this about?" Angela demanded.

"Yes, I thought that we were here to add a new member to the group," Silver added.

Richard being Richard, he merely waved his hand slightly as his eyes dove into the words, his mouth unable to speak for the moment. So Darkess took it upon herself to explain the situation, and as she spoke, Richard read the letters, followed by Janine.

"According to Tasha, there have been two sacred dragon eggs stolen from two separate covens. The first coven was in the Corundum Mountains of northern Asiattica. They were brutally attacked, and the demon disappeared off the map with the egg. Only one wizard survived the attack, and it seems that he leads a hunt for the demon still. The second egg was stolen from a castle at the opposite end of the Corundum Mountains in the southern region of Muscovata. The entire coven was decimated. Everyone at the castle was killed. The only surviving members are two small children and an old man who is not well enough to remember any thing. So, the only thing we could get from the children was their family stories, relation and such. But, it was the sacred day, and it was in the same sort of box as the other egg that was stolen. The rumor in the wizarding world is that there is a third egg that belongs to this collection, and that it is hidden well. Some place far from the first two eggs, though they were indeed many weeks journey apart. Over in that part of the world, they believe that it is hidden in the new land. Here, somewhere in Xyloidonia. There are a few who believe that the Isles of Ardor hold the key to the eggs, but at this point, it is all just speculation."

"There were few clues. Several burn marks at the second coven's holdout matched the ones found at the cave of the first coven. Tasha believes the same demon is involved, and that he now has two of the three eggs. She is on her way back to where the first egg was taken. She is trying to get a meeting with the wizard who actually saw this demon and somehow survived to tell the tale. She wants to ask him for more details about these eggs."

Darkess shifted in her chair towards Alieria with an odd look on her face and asked her a direct question.

"Exactly how did she find out about the second egg?"

"Her power is that of persuasion. Her voice has a sound to it that will make you tell your darkest secret to her without the ability to stop. She had questioned the children from the coven, and she found them by some sort of cosmic influence. Tasha was lucky. She happened to be eating at an inn where the children and old man were brought when they were found wandering alone. She fed them, questioned them, and helped to board them until some distant relative could come and collect them," Alieria explained.

"Sounds like karma, not an accident, that she stumbled across them," Richard added.

"It is a shame they had no more information on the eggs, though. But if I know my Tasha, she will send us more, and it will be good," Alieria said.

"Darkess, do you think this is what you are looking for?" Silver asked.

Darkess looked around the room at all the faces that meant so much to her, and finally said,

"This is my destiny. I do believe that, but we still don't have what we need."

Janine spoke up quickly.

"And what is that?"

Darkess rubbed her knuckles and licked her lips.

"Well, where the third egg is, what magic they perform, and the demon – who is he and how to fight him…"

Her voice trailed off, and she looked at her hands as they tied themselves in knots.

"…and…someone has to die."

Everyone froze and looked at her. The pain she felt was circulating around the room. Except for Alieria, who would find out soon enough, they all knew that one of them was not going to be around when the last egg was found. One of them was going to die before the final clues to this mystery would be revealed. Angela saw that the mood was turning towards the macabre, and she stood up and said,

"Let us tend to the business at hand, and add our new member. Then we can hash the facts all day and night."

☼

After the group inducted its newest member and made introductions about the rest of the members, the sun was setting and evening had begun. Alieria was upset that she didn't know more about these eggs to help in the cause. Darkess felt she was wrong in her feelings and told her so.

"So far, you have been a great source about dragons in general. You obviously hold more of the keys to this mystery than you realize. You will be a valued member to our Order. Now that you know why I couldn't tell you why I came, and I had no idea what I was looking for at the time, you should understand me a little better."

Darkess pulled out her notes, and everyone fell into talking, except for Harlow. Knowing it was going to be a long night, Roxy slipped out the door and returned with a tray of steaming tea. Daniel decided to slip out with Roxy and help prepare dinner. And Jori finally put in an appearance, immediately saying,

"Harlow had our minds linked during your entire discussion, and I think Darkess is correct. This feels like the warmest path we've been down so far. Let us not forget the tomb that Brutus found. Speaking of which, dear Brutus, have you anything new?"

Even sitting on the low bench, Brutus towered over them all. But his smile and low gravely voice put Alieria at ease.

"I've n old witch from Imhotepus workin on the drawings," he said. "These things take time. It's only been a month. I'll be returnin to see her tomorra with the help of a few potions from Richard, an I won't be returnin here until they are translated or considered unreadable. Will that work fer ya?"

Brutus looked at Jori, and she smiled her evilest smile as she cooed, "That works for me."

Immediately the room erupted into conversation. It was truly going to be a long night.

☼

Richard was already reading the letter that had just arrived by bird when Darkess ran up the stairs to the tower. She was panting, completely out of breath from her jaunt up the stairs, when she stammered,

"Well, what does it say?"

"It seems the old witch is having to use spells to invoke the dead language written on the wall. Evidently, it's a pretty serious undertaking. Sorry, but I believe it is going to take some more time, if they can crack it at all," Richard said.

Darkess was not happy, and she sat at the table next to Richard and said,

"Well, I guess I'll just have to occupy my time trying to replicate my powers with spells."

"With spells?" Richard quipped.

"Don't sound so cynical. I know you believe that the potions work better, but not always. And besides, Jori has this amulet that disables my powers, and I'm trying to write some spells to help me out. It's my next assignment for Jori. She wants me to be as strong without my powers as with them."

Richard shook his head back and forth and said sarcastically,

217

"Should have known Jori would have a Kubar Amulet. Smart teaching method, even if they are immoral. That amulet is dark magic. Use it sparingly…and be careful. I really would rather that you don't use it at all, but if Harlow thinks you will be safe then just be careful."

☼

The middle of winter was just as awful as the beginning, showing no sign of a reprieve. The sheer amounts of snow was by far the biggest story. The only way in or out of the castle was by way of magic. Even Daniel was using the teleport potion just to go out and visit Tanner or get out for a moment. Every tap or bang had Darkess checking for messenger birds to no avail.

"The wait is the worst part," Darkess said as she slumped back down into a stuffed chair.

Angela was reading from an old book, and without lifting her eyes, she said,

"Patience child, patience."

Darkess wrinkled up her nose as if the word patience had an awful smell. Pulling a potion bottle from her pocket, Darkess dropped it at her feet, and in a ball of blue smoke, she was gone.

"You best stay on the grounds, or your grandfather will have our hides!" Angela warned, then turned the page and continued reading.

When Darkess materialized, she was in a small warm room with a fire blazing. There was a large hide pulled down tightly over the only window. Tanner had been digging out the center of a round piece of wood and jumped at Darkess' appearance.

"You could have knocked, you know."

"That would have gotten me completely covered in snow," Darkess pleaded.

"Courtesy, common courtesy," he said and returned to his carving.

Darkess pulled up her cloak and squatted down to the floor to make herself comfortable. She watched Tanner work on his project for several quiet moments. Tanner could tell she had something on her mind, but he let her come to speak of it in her own time. And finally, when Darkess had figured out the proper wording, she spoke.

"What do you do when you are overly anxious about something?"

Tanner scraped the wood a couple more times then looked her directly in the eye.

"That rarely happens at my age."

Tanner saw the look Darkess was giving him and added, "However, you can teach yourself to be more relaxed."

"I can't turn off my thoughts Tanner, I've tried."

"I didn't say one word about turning your thoughts off," Tanner assured her. "But I may be able to teach you how to turn your anxiousness into something else."

Tanner dumped the shavings from his carving into the kindling bucket and turned to Darkess.

"Have you ever seen me wear out the floor with this anxiousness?" he asked.

Darkess shook her head no.

"That is because I turn it into good energy. When I'm disturbed about something, as you seem to be now..." Tanner eyed her intensely then continued cleaning. "...I, depending on the degree of agitation, either sit and breathe deeply to calm myself through meditation..."

Tanner could see the look on Darkess' face from his peripheral vision, and he changed directions.

"...or, work until I am completely exhausted. Either way, I end up more calm. I can actually sleep, which helps mental anxiety. And sometimes, I can see the entire picture, all the details, once I change my mind's direction. I am sure I have told you all of this before."

Darkess looked at Tanner, closed her eyes, took three deep breaths, and opened her eyes again.

"I think maybe I just have a case of cabin fever," she said. "I haven't seen you for a while either."

"You know how the weather affects the animals, and the food stores. I have so much to handle right now I really have not had the time to visit in the castle lately. You'll just have to pop over now and again and check on me. Or calm yourself – whatever the case may be. Now, breathe deep, close your eyes and meditate. I will return in a moment."

Tanner left the room through a small opening covered in leather, and all Darkess could hear was the sound of the fire crackling and the wind howling outside. She closed her eyes, putting her palms on her knees, but she soon began to fidget on the floor. Darkess opened one eye and found herself still alone. Crawling nearer to the fire, she sat facing it. Assuming the same position she had before, she closed her eyes and straightened her spine, rolling her head around on her neck. Her breathing became deep, and her thoughts raced through all of the drawings on the cave walls. Then she saw the letters she had read from Tasha, and from there, she jumped to some of the notes she had compiled in her book.

She was so deep in her thoughts that she didn't realize that Tanner had returned. The sound of the log he had put on the fire brought her back to the present. Darkess smiled at Tanner, and he spoke.

"I see you have calmed yourself," he said. "Did you find a solution to your troubles?"

"I knew you would ask that," she answered. "And I'm not sure I want to tell you."

Darkess wrinkled up her nose, gave Tanner a guilty look like a puppy that piddled on the floor, lifted her shoulders and said,

"They'll kill me if they know beforehand, but afterwards, they'll just have to deal with it."

Darkess looked at Tanner with near fear in her eyes, and he returned the look with one of concern.

"What are you going to do?"

"Tanner...come on," Darkess bargained. "Don't drop the wrong ingredient into my potion. Oh, all right. I should have lied to you."

"You know you couldn't have done that either."

"Are you going to stop me?" she pleaded.

"That depends on what exactly you plan on doing."

Darkess' shoulders slumped. She might just lose this battle, but she told on herself anyway.

"I'm going to steal mom's power and try to force a premonition."

Tanner said nothing but reached for his small leather pouch. He pulled out a smaller leather pouch and a long wooden pipe. Stuffing a dried herbal substance into the carved bowl, he pulled a burning twig from the fire and inhaled while lighting the pipe. The room smelled sweet and inviting as Tanner puffed away. Darkess waited impatiently for Tanner to say something. Finally, after several longs moments, Tanner blew a smoke ring that slowly grew larger in size as it floated to the fireplace and slipped up the flue.

"At this time, I can see no reason to thwart your plan. I see no way for an injury, but...you have been warned about borrowing powers without true need of them. And you know how your family feels about getting permission. You know the consequences, so weigh the positives and the negatives, and go from there. I feel confident you will make the proper decision."

"So you're not going to stop me? Or warn them?" Darkess asked.

Tanner winked ever so slightly, or did he? His face is very blank, so it could have been a twitch, Darkess thought.

"I'm too busy to check on you all the time. And by the feel of it..."

Tanner rubbed his shoulder and rolled it in its socket, gently in a circle.

"This storm is getting worse, and I have much to do," he said, abandoning his previous thought. "It would probably be best if you were on your way back to the castle. I'm sure your grandfather will be looking for you soon."

Tanner puffed away on his pipe, sending more rings into the flue. Darkess smiled her most devious smile, pulled a bottle from her pocket, and said quickly,

"I will visit you again. Soon. Oh, and thank you."

"For what?" Tanner responded. "I did nothing."

Darkess smashed the bottle at her feet, filling the small room with blue smoke, and leaving Tanner grinning in her wake. He was shaking his head as smoke rolled out of his nose.

☼

Darkess had rummaged here and there around the castle, getting all the items she needed. She made her presence known and acted as if she was deep into her notebook as usual, but she was not. When Darkess had collected all the items on her list, she returned to her bedroom and locked the door. Chakra lay on the mantle above the fireplace and watched Darkess intently. In front of her on the bed was a dining tray. On top of it were three candles and three stones. She lit the candles and began to breath deeply. Calming herself, she tried to feel for her mother's essence. Darkess held a small pile of sand from the entrance of the tomb from Imhotepus.

After several deep breaths, she could feel her mind relax, and she pictured her mother. Suddenly, she felt as if she were floating. Her head rolled slightly on her shoulders. Then, like lightning, it hit her. Her body went rigid, flashes of light crossed before her eyes, and they went white – just as her mother's did when she had a vision. The tomb she had visited before appeared before her. Only this time, it was new, and there were workers chiseling on the door to the room where the sarcophagus was to be held. There were no paintings on the wall yet, and the men working were speaking in an unfamiliar tongue. There was an old woman being helped down into the tomb through the entrance that was now sealed. The woman was dripping in gold and jewels, and a dragon was stitched into the breast of her dress. She walked with a staff, which had a dragon's head on the top with emerald eyes. She seemed to be directing the workers as she went, pointing and speaking quickly.

The old woman pulled out a piece of parchment with a drawing of three crates that would be holding the eggs. The old woman pointed to the drawing and then at the wall. She took her staff and drew a large rectangle in the dust on the floor. This was where the empty shelves had been in Darkess' present. The old woman was telling them to build them. Then there was a flash of bright light, and the tomb was different. This time, there were brilliant paintings, and the three crates that the old woman had shown were now sitting on the shelves that had been made for them. The tomb, at least this room, was finished. The old woman was reading from a scroll when an unseen assailant crushed an earthen pot over her head, killing her instantly. Two men entered the tomb. Their faces were cloaked in black as well as the rest of their bodies. They swiftly snatched up the three crates and exited the tomb.

Another bright flash of light cleared Darkess' eyes, and she was seeing her room again as before.

"Whoa," she breathed.

This wasn't exactly what she was trying to see, but new information was better than no information. Chakra was still staring at her from the mantle, but now he was licking his paw and twitching his tail in what looked like agitation. Then Darkess heard it: yelling from somewhere in the castle.

"Here we go again," she said to herself in the mirror.

Quickly she crossed to the door and unlocked it. That would make things so much worse, Darkess thought. She just knew her mother would be here any second demanding an explanation for such an intrusion on her powers. This is going to take some explaining, Darkess thought.

"Sorry, Tanner," she whispered to her friend. "You were right."

Darkess opened the door to accept her punishment…and try to explain what she had been trying to do.

☼

Several weeks of cold blowing snow and one disappointment after another had the entire family in cranky moods. Tasha had acquired no new information, because she had not been able to find the wizard who had survived the first attack of the demon. He had gone into hiding and was proving difficult to find. Brutus too was having trouble getting through all of the text they had drawn up. His contact was an ancient woman who was wearing thin at his insistence to hurry. She was doing all that she could, which wasn't nearly enough. The Order had not been back together for months, and Darkess was getting more temperamental by the day. Chakra was circling her legs as she looked out the window one day into the blinding light that reflected off the snow. She smiled a weak smile and whispered,

"Looks like the start of a vision."

Chakra jumped into the window to take a look. He pawed at the window.

"What's out there?" Darkess asked her cat as she squinted into the daylight, trying to see what held her cat's attention.

'Delivery bird,' Chakra told Darkess as he jumped from the windowsill down to the table.

Darkess opened the window, and a small bird twittered his arrival. Darkess was immediately excited when she saw the large parchment tied to the bird's leg. Not waiting to tell anyone of its arrival, Darkess pulled the letter loose and began to read it. Her eyes grew large as she read, and her breathing grew quicker. Finally, her hands began to shake.

"Enlarge," Darkess said to the letter, and it swelled up to full size and thickened.

Behind the first page were several others. Darkess flipped through the other pages quickly. As she looked at each new page, her excitement doubled. Hardly able to contain herself, Darkess tore open the potions cabinet and pulled out several small blue bottles. Tossing one at her feet, she said,

"Grandfather."

☼

Deep asleep in his bed, Richard murmured.

"Take that..." he snored slightly and rolled over.

When he found a more comfortable position, his snoring increased. He was truly enjoying his afternoon nap, until a cloud of smoke erupted around his bed and instantly woke him.

"Who's there?" he snorted through the smoke.

His crystal showed that there were no evil intruders, and as he crawled out of bed, he saw a figure coming for him. Darkess scrambled out of the smoke, extremely apologetic.

"I'm sorry, Grandfather. I didn't realize you were napping. I just had to get this to you right away. You must read it."

Darkess handed the stack of parchment to her grandfather. He straightened his clothes, while Darkess lit the oil lamp. Sitting down at his dressing bench, Richard began to read the letters from Brutus. The translations of the symbols were believed to be finished. The eggs are believed to be around one thousand years old. And the tomb of the old woman was to be hidden by magic, never to be found. It seems that the murder of the woman and the theft of the eggs had broken the magic before it had been completely installed. The dead woman was the third protectorate of the eggs and had no apprentice. So the eggs were to be buried with her upon her death and sealed in with her for all eternity. It says that the eggs were turned to dark magic and were feared. They must be turned from their evil before being hatched, or the world would be in more danger than it was without the help of the dragons. It seems the dragons had burnt one field a year for their own consumption, and sustained themselves on the ash. This would keep the ground properly seasoned for future growth of crops. Each year, the crops were rotated, and each year, one was donated to the dragon that lived in that area. In return, the dragon protected the fields and crops grew much better and larger fruits. Without the dragons, food growth was suffering more with every year.

There was also a detailed description of each egg, and the powers attributed to it. The first egg listed was black with red speckles. It is believed to be a three-toed wingless red dragon that breathes mist and has the powers of passion, strength, and courage. The second egg was deep blue with black blotches and was said to hold a four-toed blue dragon with large leathery wings that breathes fire with the powers of wisdom, harmony and peace. The third egg was black with odd lavender spots. It housed a five-toed black dragon with lavender horns, claws, and small gauzy lavender wings that breaths fire. It is said to have power over power, success, and idealism. Apart, these dragons were a definite force, but yoke their strength, turn their hearts evil, and they are unstoppable.

The walls of the tomb had many unsolvable symbols, and time had erased some, so there were only partial details on how to use the eggs. There was something about a potion and a spell that were separated into three books, one accompanying each egg. These books also had the instructions on how to hatch and control each egg. Temperature control and making the sex of the baby either male or female was described in great detail, along with feeding youths and dealing with dragon puberty, which evidently was a very dangerous time. These were ordinary dragon eggs stolen by a black wizard whilst the mothers were out. How he concealed their scent from the mothers is not known. But he hatched and raised three females, performing the darkest of magic upon them and making their eggs evil. He intended to rule the world with them, but a large male dragon that was intent upon mating with the wizard's females had killed him.

It is written that a seer had a vision of the wizard's death and went to save the eggs. Upon doing so, the seer became the protectorate of the eggs. This woman was an Imhotepus high priestess who passed the eggs to her apprentice, who then passed them to hers. At the end of the last page was a note that read: There is no record as to the eggs' whereabouts after they were stolen – not in the tomb and not in the records hidden in archives under the Castle Imhotepus, which has long been abandoned, and buried under the sands of time. The last thing written said that if someone wanted more information about these eggs, this person would have to acquire them, or find someone who had had possession of them.

Richard looked at his granddaughter. He was shaking with excitement when Darkess said,

"This is a thousand-year-old mystery, and we are going to solve it."

Darkess yanked her grandfather up into the standing position.

"What do we do next?" Richard asked.

Darkess stopped dead in her tracks and looked up at her grandfather with a completely confused look on her face.

"Tell the Order?" she asked.

"So you don't quite know every thing yet, huh?" Richard said with a grin on his face.

Darkess' face turned an elaborate red all the way to the tips of her ears, nearly matching the intensity of her hair.

"Sorry," she grinned at Richard.

"Oh, don't be. You are doing very well. And soon, you will be in control of your life. You'll know what to do when the time comes. But you're only half correct: Tell the Order, but then start looking for any surviving clan members, and maybe even that demon that seems to keep popping up in unexpected places." Richard said with one eyebrow raised. He had a very serious look on his face and a far off look in his eyes.

☼

Unknown to Darkess, Richard had been leaving the castle frequently in search of the demon presently linked to the eggs. Talking to some of the more shady characters he knew had turned up very little, but Richard pressed on in his search. He knew the more he could help Darkess, the better off she would be. Sitting in his chair in the tower with the rest of the castles inhabitants fast asleep, Richard concentrated all of his power on the spell for the power of clairvoyance. Feeling the edge of his mind go slightly foggy, he knew the spell was working.

"Red-Eye Tavern," he whispered, and a place he knew well appeared in his mind.

The main room of the tavern came into focus. Each detail was perfect, as if he were actually in the tavern. The only thing missing was the smell. And depending on the clientele, the smell being absent wasn't necessarily a bad thing. Richard looked around the room he was visiting in his mind and searched for a familiar face. He recognized a few patrons and the workers, but he was looking for a couple of people who traveled in rougher circles, not the regulars. He continued to search the large tavern when he heard a tinkling bell behind him. Turning back towards the door, he was pleasantly surprised at who came in. It was just the man he was looking for. The cloud around Richard's vision closed in, becoming increasingly darker until it was black. When he opened his eyes, he was sitting in his darkened tower with only the faintest flicker from the lone candle. With a smile, Richard dug deep in his pocket and removed a blue bottle. Smashing it at his feet, he whispered again,

"The alley behind the Red Eye Tavern."

Behind a billow of smoke, he vanished.

☼

Reappearing behind the tavern, Richard hugged the wall as he surveyed the street ahead of him. It was late, and there were few sounds let alone people. Darkness clung to every shape, making Richard move slowly towards the front of the tavern. When he reached the door, he opened it to see only the barkeep and the hooded figure he had seen from the castle. As shady characters do, the cloaked figure turned slightly to see who had come in and grunted his approval. Richard made his way through the tavern, and when he reached the cloaked figure, he took the stool next to him. Richard asked for ale, and the two men sat quietly sipping for a few moments. A raspy voice floated from the hood of the cloaked figure.

"Another."

The barkeep filled a second stone cup with smoking liquid. The cloaked figure took a drink of the fetid looking liquid, smacked his lips, and gruffly whispered,

"I say Richard…what brings you out so late? Slumming are we?"

A morbid laugh rumbled from under the hood of the cloak as he took another drink.

"What a foul mood you're in," Richard replied, sipping his ale.

"Bad business," the figure grumbled.

Richard pulled out a large gold coin, and standing it on its side, rolled it to the cloaked figure. The coin caught his attention immediately, and his hand shot out to grab it.

"Who do I have to kill to earn this?" said the voice from the cloak.

"No one needs to die. I just need some information," Richard said.

The barkeep had also seen the flash of the gold coin and inched a bit closer to listen in on what was conspiring. The cloaked man rolled the coins over his fingers, and a grin appeared in the dark hood of the cloak, his crooked stained teeth flashing in the lantern light. Then the cloaked head snapped towards the barkeep, eyeing him intensely. The barkeep knew not to annoy whoever was under that cloak, and he quickly backed away, wiping the counter profusely. Slowly, the cloaked figure turned back towards Richard, and his voice issued from the blackness inside.

"Just what exactly do you want to know?"

"For starters, this is only half…" Richard pointed at the coin rotating across the hairy knuckles.

"I'll give you the other half when you return with what I want. Second, have you ever heard of…" Richard's voice dropped down to the smallest of whispers, "the Dragon Eggs of Galdore?"

The cloaked figure cocked his head back and to the side, showing a nasty frown peeking from the shadows.

"No, what are they?" grumbled from the cloak.

Richard's shoulders slumped in disappointment. He was sure there were people out there who knew of this, demons, he was posotive. They were valuable. This man just had to know something about them.

"That is what I need to know. Rumor has it that there are still dragon eggs, three we believe, and two of them have been stolen by what seems to be a very powerful demon. My granddaughter is somehow linked to them, and I need to know how. I need to find this damned demon before it's too late."

Richard's aggravation was clearly coming to the surface. The shrouded man saw the anxiousness in him, pocketed the coin, and said,

"For you, I'll look into it."

Sitting back in his stool, Richard's posture changed just slightly, showing some relief from his burden. They both took a drink, the cloaked man finishing his.

"Another?" he invited.

Another steaming mug was placed in front of the dark man. Richard tossed a silver coin at the barkeep, who nodded as he caught it.

"Take care of my friend here," Richard requested.

The barkeep ambled away.

"In one week, meet me here, same as usual," Richard said finishing his ale. "When I see you, I'll get here."

Turning to leave, Richard stood up and said quietly to the cloaked man, eyeing him very seriously,

"Good luck. You are going to need it."

Not another word was said, and Richard went out the door into the night.

☼

Somewhere hidden away, deep under his home in the catacombs, Takar was sitting between the two eggs. He was right in the middle of a large table made from a wood plank and two giant boulders. With one hand on each egg, he looked from one to the next. There was a maniacal look on his face, and he began to laugh.

"The fools! The second egg was even easier to steal than the first. White magic is so simple to defeat. They care too much. Now all I have to do is find the last egg. Mother, Father, I am on my way."

Takar laughed until he was crying, all the while massaging the eggs as if they were his lovers. Off in the corner, two glowing eyes watched in fear as his master sunk deeper into madness. The eggs were so beguiling that Takar couldn't leave them. He had taken to sleeping on the table between them and jerked awake at every sound. He feared that someone would find his hideaway. He had all of his meals delivered down here by Tuma. He also had Tuma roaming his grounds, doing guard duty, even though the entire property said go away, what with its over grown plants and high stone walls, not to mention the spells hiding the place. Tuma worried that Takar would never leave the castle again, causing him constant terror and grief. Then again, he feared that if he did leave and find the third egg, his life would become considerably worse. But, he had done, as he was told, and as swiftly as possible, avoided all confrontations in any way he could.

Takar had sold the spook. It hadn't turned up enough information for him. Tuma wondered if being sold might not be such a bad idea. Maybe he could get himself sold or more likely, killed. He quickly discarded that idea. Jakara had been great to work for; even his witch was somewhat acceptable. But the child was unbearable. Even as a grown man, the child was terrible at best. What am I going to do? Tuma thought.

"Get me some food!" Takar yelled.

Tuma disappeared as ordered.

☼

A week later, spring arrived, and warmer weather came with it. The snows finally began to melt after months of piling up. Richard had been antsy all week, waiting for his cloaked accomplice to return and wondering what he may have found in his search. Nothing particularly exciting had happened for a while, and Richard knew something was bound to materialize soon. In the wizard world, quiet meant a storm was brewing on the horizon, and none of them wanted the peace to end, which usually meant that it would. Great power always meant a lot of work and responsibility. They all worked diligently in their search to eradicate evil, right down to the youngest participant. Darkess was doing all that she could to learn every thing that was thrown at her, and Richard was proud. He sat in his chair concentrating on her and how well she was doing, especially considering her age. He shook his head as if trying to change his thoughts physically and started his deep breathing.

"Red-Eye Tavern," he said once again, and in his mind, it began to appear.

When the tavern was in full focus, Richard began to look around. He saw the regulars, but his cloaked friend was nowhere to be seen. Shaking his head again, Richard opened his eyes to see his notes in front of him on the table.

"Too early," he said and ran his fingers through his hair.

He hadn't been able to sleep for the last couple of nights, and he knew if the cloaked man didn't show, he was going to be a mess trying to get through another night of wondering. Richard checked his herb supplies then, dug through another drawer looking at the things that didn't really have a place, anything to burn off some time. Finally, Richard crossed over and looked at the stars out the window. The night was clear. From this window, he could see for miles, especially with the leftover snow for a backdrop. The landscape was beautiful under the full moon with dew sparkling on all the new buds on the trees below. It was almost breathtaking tonight, and it helped to burn a few more minutes, but that was all he could take.

Richard returned to his chair and closed his eyes. His hands rested on the wooden arms of the chair, and his breathing was deep and even. He was concentrating deeply on a specific place then he whispered,

"Red-Eye Tavern."

Again, he saw the darkened tavern and the dwindling number of patrons, but this time there was a cloaked figure at the bar. Richard changed his perspective of the room and saw the chin of the cloaked man just as a steaming stone mug reached it. He was there. Richard's heart leapt in his chest, and he jumped to his feet. But he had not cleared his mind of the tavern and knocked his knee on the table leg, spilling tea and covering some of his notes.

"Blast!" he cursed as he cleared his mind and saw the mess in front of him on the table.

Wiping his hand over the notes and nearly touching them, the tea dried instantly, leaving only a slight blur of writing. Then he remembered why he had been in such a hurry, and his face brightened again.

"Oh yes, yes," he said as he plucked the tipped over bottle of potion from the table and smashed it at his feet.

☼

Inside the tavern, most of the candles had burned out, and the oil lamps were turned down low. Richard entered and made a beeline toward the cloaked figure. Flipping a silver coin to the barkeep, Richard smiled.

"A tankard please, and another for my friend."

Pulling up a stool, Richard sat down and took a large swig as he looked towards the cloaked face. The hidden man sipped on his drink then whispered,

"What you seek will be extremely hard to find. I have heard about these eggs. They are highly prized in the demon and wizard worlds alike. The list of peoples looking for these treasures is getting longer as we speak. The stories have varied greatly, especially on the location of the last egg. But it is agreed that there are three. It is believed that the location has been narrowed to a few desolate places. But these are vast and uncharted regions of the world."

The cloaked man took another drink, either for effect, or because he had much more to say. Richard wasn't sure, so he took another large gulp from his tankard then looked around the room, making sure they were still alone before returning his gaze towards the cloak.

"One is an island inhabited by lizards and birds, where the rivers burn, running in thick streams and destroying all in their path. It is a dangerous place, this burning island. Another is a desert place, where the stones reach up from the ground like jagged teeth and are painted many colors. It is an arid, nasty place, where no food grows, no animals trod, and the water is poisonous. Still another is the frozen lands up north, across the ocean in a far away and inhospitable place. The winds never cease to howl, and the snows are deep and full of dangers we have never seen. It is said there are huge ghostly bears and enormous swimming creatures that flop upon the ice to eat their bloody kills. There were several other places mentioned, each just as unlikely as the next, and each sounded more deadly, save one. One old hag told of a green meadow that leads to the base of a mountain that contains many caves. It seems getting there would be easy, but the search would take a lifetime for a human. It is said there are thousands of caves in that mountain, some miles deep, but it seems to me if you used the proper magic, it would take considerably less time, making it too easy, and definitely not the place to hide a magic egg."

The two sat there quietly sipping their drinks for a moment.

"What of the demon?" Richard asked.

The cloaked man cleared his throat, as if stalling, then whispered,

"On that, you will have to wait a while. He is a slippery one. But I'll find him, don't you worry. Give me some more time. Maybe a month or so? I have to go abroad for some, shall we say, business. Maybe I can do more than find out who he is. What would that be worth to you?"

Richard dug down deep into his cloak and pulled out one gold and two silver coins.

"This is for what you have found so far."

Richard handed over the gold coin.

"And this is to help in your search."

Richard passed the silver coins. They drank quietly for a while, each ordering another. Richard again dug into his pockets and pulled out a small bronze coin. He rubbed his thumb across its surface and handed it to the man.

"I thought you might need more time, so I made these. They are identical, and I have the other. Carry it with you on your travels. If you need me or have urgent news, place one drop of your blood on the side with the sun. The coin will turn warm in my pocket to alert me, and I will come to the location of the coin. If you should be compromised or you need to warn me of danger, use the side with the moon. It will freeze in my pocket and warn me to protect my family. The same applies to you: Warm, come here. Cold, stay away."

The cloaked figure turned his head towards Richard.

"This is extremely important to you, I see. How did you get mixed up in such a predicament?"

Richard took a large gulp from his tankard and grimaced towards his cloaked friend.

"Such is the life of a white wizard with a family to protect. But you know life wouldn't be quite as interesting if I were a normal human."

☼

Five months all passed as quietly as possible. Angela kept up on her regular visits to the city to help the sick and diseased as much as she could without detection. Richard continued his usual weekly visits to the King for consults, and Daniel and Silver resumed their search of the city's arts and treasures. Darkess moved forward with her training. Tanner used the summer to grow everything possible while teaching all that he could to Darkess along the way. Tasha was no closer to finding the wizard than she had been five months ago. The Order had found no news on the eggs or the demon collecting them. No one had found anything. It seemed that they were still playing the waiting game. Now the rumors were getting more plentiful, but that was all they were – rumors.

Darkess was being kept as busy as possible, and Angela decided to take her and her mother on a shopping outing to the city. Spreading the wealth just before the season changed for the worse was always one of the ways the Vallencourts helped the poor and sickly humans that they protected. Besides giving them food and medicine, they handed out money. And Angela always passed along a little of her special brand of healing. Roxy had loaded the women down with food parcels and special tiny bundles for the children.

"Just because they aren't wizards doesn't mean they can't celebrate our holiday," Roxy said as she handed them another bag full.

The party was getting near, and they needed supplies for the coming winter anyway, so it was a trip for many reasons. Richard watched them as they took the large wagon and went without magical transport to the city for the day. He was mildly irritated that his cloaked contact hadn't sent him any messages. He wondered what was going on.

≈

Takar had taken to leaving his tunnels only once a month to look for the third egg. And it seemed to take him a full month to recover from each exhausting trip away from his precious eggs. Tuma had thought of fleeing his current job despite the rules of his kind, but he feared Takar's retribution so much that he just couldn't leave. But he did love the times when his master left the grounds. Even when Takar returned, Tuma wasn't afraid again until his master had slept for two days and eaten like a wild animal upon awaking. That was when the lunacy returned along with the energy to scream orders of insanity. Tuma was glad that the search had slowed considerably, but for how long? The pull of these eggs was immense, even he felt drawn to their power. But he refused to go within ten feet of the table where they laid unless he was ordered to for some terrible reason. Still, he caught himself staring at the eggs for minutes, sometimes hours at a time. Once he had thought of stealing the eggs for himself to buy his freedom. It was ludicrous to consider such a thought, so he kept himself busy to avoid being near the eggs. Then the thought crossed his mind and made a shiver run down his spine: Would Takar go completely insane if he got the third egg? Would he destroy the world or himself with the power of the eggs? Looking on through the entrance of the room that Takar was in, Tuma saw the steady rise and fall of his master's chest as he slept deeply. He had to do something, or everything would be lost. He closed his eyes, and a tear rolled down his invisible face. As he turned from the room, he whispered in a miserable voice,

"What am I going to do now?"

Then he disappeared. The only thing that could be heard was the soft pad of his footsteps as he walked away.

☼

The wagon was completely loaded down, almost to overflowing when Rufus pulled it up to the kitchens door. The women smiled as they got off the bench, and Richard laughed at them.

"Did you buy out every vendor in the city?"

Richard reached up to help his wife down, and she slapped him in the shoulder for his effort and replied playfully,

"Your words to us were, make this the grandest party to date. So we are."

"Yah, the hardest part was loading all of this stuff. But unloading it will be a snap," Darkess grinned in her deviousness.

She point at the door, and it swung open. Then she held her palm out, and the complete load hovered in the air, formed a line, and floated inside the castle. Darkess followed it, grinning broadly.

"Show off," Silver said, tossling her hair as she went by.

≈

Once all of the barrels, burlap sacks and crates were stored away, and all of the décor were in their correct places, everyone set out to make the food, potions, and spells for the party. Darkess' birthday was the following day, and the yearly celebration was the day after that. This year, the excitement of the parties overruled the anxiety of waiting and wondering, which was good for all of them. Absently grabbing his pocket, Richard checked his coin occasionally but was doing it less frequently with all of the party obligations. Roxy and Angela had quite a show going on in the kitchens with spells, potions, and food flying about everywhere. Daniel had occupied himself with some book he'd found but hung around just incase he was needed. He found that the ladies were more interesting than the book and was merely holding it while he watched them work. He chuckled now and again as something nearly missed its assigned location or whizzed past his head. In general, though, he was pretty quiet so as not to incur the wrath of the working witches. Silver was in the tower brewing up a new batch of teleport potion and a couple of defensive potions just in case a demon, rogue beast, or displaced spirit showed up and tried to spoil all of the fun.

Darkess was writing in her book. There had been a series of stories circulating that the third egg would soon be found. And there had been an insurgence of evil trying to find anything they could by any means possible. There had been people coming up missing, mostly hunters and outland gatherers, but it had started. She felt it in her heart. Nothing had been able to penetrate the Vallencourt grounds so far. However, it was possible to hear and feel the intruders trying to make entry in the deep of the night every once in a while. Obviously nothing truly strong had tried to get in…yet.

Tanner had nearly doubled the talismans around the border of the grounds and was currently checking on them. Richard and Darkess had placed protection spells on them, and Tanner had done some of his own. Working together, they kept the grounds free of all but animal and plant life, which meant there were a few special shape shifter talismans just in case someone figured out a loophole in the plan. Tanner rarely rode upon Zaphod, but he seemed to like the ride around the grounds, at least until he came across something in the bushes. Not used to Zaphods' behavior, Tanner wasn't sure why the horse was pawing the ground and snorting.

"What's wrong big boy?" Tanner said as he patted the horse's tense neck.

The horse whinnied softly and pawed the ground a couple more times while shaking his head up and down. Tanner jumped down, took a look deeper into the shrubbery, and found nothing. But Zaphod was insistent that there was something in those bushes, and used his nose to shove Tanner deeper into the greenery. Tanner stumbled forward, quickly steadied himself, and stood back up.

"What was that for?" he asked Zaphod. "There is nothing in there. Look for yourself."

Tanner stepped back, allowing Zaphod a good look. The horse took a deep sniff then snorted loudly at the odd smell. Tanner was right there, but didn't detect anything. Zaphod shook his head in confusion as Tanner climbed back upon him.

"Shall we finish our rounds?" Tanner asked his ride.

Zaphod looked at Tanner then swung his head around and continued to walk along the border.

☼

Belthazor and Janine arrived a day early to spend Darkess' birthday with her. The dinner table was full of Roxy's finest specialties, and the conversation was loud and boisterous. There was a pile of gifts on the table for Darkess, and her eyes strayed to them now and again in her excitement to open them. Even at fifteen, she still had the anticipation of a small child coupled with the maturity of a person much older, and she hid the quivering inside of her quite well. She held herself in check until the last person was done eating, then she could contain herself no more. From the time that she ripped open the first package until she laid down the gift from the last package, it took nearly twenty minutes. An odd assortment of things was lying on the table. A beautiful leather belt with a sterling dragon on the buckle that Janine had made was lovingly tucked into her pants. Belthazor had given her a book called, <u>Magical Creatures of the Earth</u>, <u>Sky and Water</u>. And Roxy had given her a small spell book written in her own hand on how to make all sorts of food and drinks from peculiar items. Then came the gift from her grandparents: It was a family heirloom bound in leather and silver with all of the family line extending back as for as the records could be searched. It also had a blank section in the back where Darkess could add her family to it. Tanner had bought her a marble mortar and pestle of her very own, which is the best material for keeping the products pure of other ingredients. And her parents had given her an outfit, and not just any outfit. It was tailor-made. The shirt had no sleeves, and a dragon painted across the chest and running over the shoulder. There was a small pocket at the nape of her neck suitable for holding a single blade. And two pockets at the waist could warm her hands or hold something small. The breeches were leather also and had pockets down the legs for different items, two in the front and two on the rear, and two on the side of each thigh. Then there were the boots – almost knee high with dragons cut out and stamped into the front and a blade sheath in each. They were a tad too big, but as her mother pointed out, she wasn't finished growing yet. Darkess grabbed the pile of clothing and dashed from the room.

Moments later, Darkess returned to the room completely dressed for battle. She was wearing her new clothes and boots, belt and all. Each hidden pocket had been filled with a knife or some special item, and her pack was strapped to her back with her cloak tied beneath it behind her. Her dragon bangle was tight on her arm, and her favorite necklace was dangling from her throat. They all gasped as she returned to the room. She seemed to have aged a few years in just a couple of minutes. There was a confidant air to her as she stepped into the room. It was as if she had just popped from the pages of a storybook.

≈

Late that night while everyone was fast asleep, Darkess slipped silently from her room and made her way along the long corridor. Her destination was the locked tower. She used a small crystal to shine a path up the stairs to the locked door on the upper floor. In the near dark, she stared at the door until she heard someone clear his throat behind her only a few feet away. Spinning quickly, she held her hands up in defense.

"Whoa there, missy," Richard said from the dark as he lit up his crystal.

"Grandfather!" Darkess hissed with a touch of annoyance. "You scared me! I could have hurt you!"

Chuckling softly he replied,

"I knew you would come up here tonight. I have already tried. Now it's your turn."

Darkess turned back towards the door. She clenched her eyes closed tightly and thought to herself,

'Please let me in. I want to see your secrets.'

Opening her eyes, she reached for the knob and clasped it firmly. As she turned it ever so slowly, it stopped solid after only a quarter turn. Darkess exhaled. She let go of the knob and said in a disheartened tone,

"Well, I guess it's just not the right time yet."

☼

Music was floating off the stage as people and creatures danced on the crowded dance floor. The smells of the food made everyone's mouths water with anticipation. Most of the guests had arrived, and the family was mingling from one side of the room to the other. Tanner had entered the main room with a very serious look on his face. He was searching for someone. Once he spotted his target, he cut through the crowd and whispered something into Richard's ear. The two men turned in unison and retreated out the door. Thankfully, the crowd did not notice what was happening between Richard and Tanner, and the party continued as usual.

Outside behind the barn, Tanner and Richard were talking in haste about an odd creature Tanner had caught in the bushes by the gates. Neither man had ever seen one before. It was a truly unique creature. Tanner had placed it in a wire cage used for catching foxes and such. Six crystals were placed all around it to keep magical creatures from escaping. It was covered with burlap bags to ensure that the prying eyes saw nothing. Richard instructed Tanner to talk to Rufus about it then interrogate it. He was to tell no one else except Rufus, who should also tell no one. They were to make sure that Darkess wasn't on their trail. She had enough on her plate without adding this. Besides, she had much more important, although not as exciting, things to do.

Tanner went about his business, making sure to cover his tracks, and Richard returned to the party. It seemed that the family had been so absorbed in their conversations that they had entirely missed what had transpired. Richard was sure they were none the wiser and smiled as he greeted a late guest.

≈

At the end of the night when everyone was teleporting or leaving by whatever means of transportation they had, Richard slipped out and left the rest of the family to do the good byes. Each member of the Order had talked to him at some point in the night, and they were all in agreement that they needed to find out more about the third egg before evil had a chance to get a hold of it. Time was short, and despite the circumstances, he had hired an investigator, and had kept this mans' identity a secret from the group. He had also shared this with everyone. All in all, the night was a success, even if they had nothing new to share with each other. And Richard was somewhat annoyed with this fact.

Quinn was still hovering around and watching everyone go when he saw Richard go from the shadows around the side of the barn. Hastily, he shot across the yard to check on his old friend. When he turned the corner, he caught Tanner covering a cage.

"What have you caught?" Quinn asked, startling the two men.

"Damn it, Quinn! Wear a chain will you? You're too quiet. You scared five years out of me, and I can't afford to lose them," Richard said.

"Beggin' your pardon sir, I was just tryin' to make sure you were alright. This is a very powerful night. Nearly anything can happen."

Richard looked at Tanner, then the cage, then back to Tanner.

"What do you think?" he asked Tanner softly.

"I can't see how it could hurt. He'll be gone in an hour or so for another year. Ask him."

Quinn put his hands on his hips and stood up a little more straight, as if he were speaking to children and asked,

"Ask me what?"

Tanner uncovered the cage.

"Do you know what this is?" Richard asked.

Quinn had a surprised look on his face as he slipped closer to get a better look.

"It's not exactly evil, but they usually serve evil, demons and wizards alike. Where did you get it?"

"Caught it trying to get through the gates," Tanner answered.

"Has it said anything?" Quinn asked.

"He says that he needs our help. Says he's trying to keep the world from ending," Richard replied.

Quinn stared at Richard for a moment, then at Tanner, then to the creature sitting silently in the center of the cage floor.

"I don't know that I would believe him. They are intensely loyal, usually born into servitude, and rarely sold, because they have too many secrets from being close to their masters. Don't forget, his master will torture and kill him if he thinks that he has done some wrong to him. My guess is…it's a trap," Quinn said.

Richard looked at Tanner seriously and said,

"You know what to do."

Richard turned to Quinn, and ghost and wizard walked around the barn and headed towards the courtyard. Just before they turned the corner, Quinn took a quick look back at the cage. Tanner was covering it. Richard could be heard in a dwindling voice as he led the ghost away,

"Thank you very much for your help."

☼

Exactly two weeks to the day after the big party, the day dawned bright and sunny. The frost on the grass was brilliant. Richard was sitting at the table in the tower drinking hot tea with honey. He seemed to be doing his best to wake up for the day. He could hear Angela's shuffling feet on the stairs just outside the door. She opened it and said,

"I think these stairs get taller every year."

Richard smiled at his wife, raised one eyebrow, and asked,

"Are you ready to step down and let the younger generation take over?"

With a devious grin similar to Darkess', Angela replied with a twinkle in her eye,

"Are you kidding me? They don't know near enough yet. And I'm not that old."

Richard laughed heartily at his wife as he stood up and kissed her forehead.

"That's what I thought," he said as a pecking sound came from the window behind him.

"Well, well, let's hope this is good news. Um, yes, well then, we should let it in shouldn't we," Richard said as he went towards the window.

The small bird fluttered in and landed on Richard's hand. Unrolling the scroll it carried, he saw that the message was brief. In fancy handwriting, it read:

Will be there tonight. Sundown. You won't believe this. Party of two. A

Angela read the note over Richard's shoulder and said,
"It's something, I think, if not much. But it is something."
With a smirk Richard said,
"At least it gives you a reason to throw an impromptu party. I know how you love doing that!"
"Don't you know it," Angela said with that same grin on her face.
With that said, she smashed a blue bottle at her feet and said,
"Kitchens."
Richard shook his head, laughed at the smoke that was dissipating, and returned to his tea.

≈

Alieria had arrived on her griffon, and he was causing an uproar. He refused to go into the stall with the bars on it, and Rufus refused to let him roam free with the small animals running around. Finally, Alieria had to coax him into the stall with a couple of dead chickens. Rufus was mildly irritated, but they were more expendable than the other livestock.
"He's a meat eater, ma'am, and I just can't have him roamin' around my other charges," Rufus mumbled as he disappeared into a stall. Alieria turned to her griffon and said sweetly in her thick accent,
"Oh, now do as mommy says, or we shan't be allowed here again. Why must you be so stubborn?"
In a gruff manor, the griffon tucked his wings and adjusted himself fully inside the stall, looking slighted and a little proud. Zaphod stood wide-eyed in his stall with Chakra on his back.
Darkess heard her horse say to her cat,
"Should that beast get free, I'm going to Tanner's."
Chakra replied,
"Your back is the safest place out here, and that is where I am going to stay."
Darkess giggled to herself but kept her animals' secrets.

Alieria and Tasha were so similar in appearance that they could pass for twins. It was taking everyone a second look to figure out who was who. Alieria was dressed in all red, and Tasha in all blue, but it seemed that was the end of the differences, except for one small scar on Tasha's eyebrow. Everyone had been waiting for them in the small dining hall, but upon hearing the commotion outside, they had come out into the courtyard.

"Amazing, isn't it?" Alieria asked as she walked up the steps toward the castle.

Clearing his throat loudly to stop everyone from staring, Richard said,

"It is very nice to see you again...Alieria?" Richard questioned his assumption.

"Yes, my dear, you are correct. This, everyone, is my cousin Tasha," Alieria waved her hand towards the other witch.

Tasha smiled and followed Alieria through the door. In turn, the awestruck family followed suit.

Once they were all settled at the large dining table and everyone had something to drink, Darkess decided she couldn't contain herself any longer.

"Um, I hate to be rude, but could you tell us what you have found, please?" she pleaded.

Alieria smiled at her young friend then looked towards her cousin.

"I believe I will let you hear from Tasha. She did acquire the story on her own. Tasha if you please..."

Again, all eyes fell on Tasha as she began her tale.

"As you all know, I have searched for quite some time for the surviving wizard, and using my powers, I have finally found him. He did say he was the last surviving wizard, and that he had blood that extended from the original members of the Coven of Draco, the ancient protectors of the Eggs of Galdore. He knew little about the other two eggs, but he did have extensive knowledge of the egg he had been sworn to protect. He described the egg as rough surfaced, almost scaly, Most of it was black; however, there were several patches of red on it. He said the dragon itself should be red with black details, no wings, three toes and the ability to breathe a watery mist. She would have the ability to fly by means of magic and has the powers over passion, strength, and courage. Without evil magical influence, she would grow to be a good loving dragon but with a strong hand. Together with the other two dragons and controlled by a strong person, you could rule the world, unrivaled and untouched. And, as long as the dragons live, so does their master. The eggs were separated so none of them would be tempted to go astray and use the powers for what they think would be good but would ultimately not be. They have a magical pull, these eggs. One was strong, but endurable– however two or more could seriously test the will of the entire coven. They would tear each other up trying to control the eggs, so they are best apart. No one has been able to convert the egg back to its natural state, and he is unsure of the other two eggs. The man said the egg gave them all a boost in stamina. Each person who left their duty of egg watch wanted to do more than they had, as in work harder, clean more, or study harder. It has an odd effect. Essentially, it amplifies your personality. He said it even makes you want to love or hate something more than you had before."

Tasha looked around the table, took a large drink from her goblet, and continued with her tale.

"He also said if you were a thief before being near the egg, it made you want to steal more. The wizard also said he believed the power of the egg would make you lie or even kill to keep it if you allow its influence to control you. The last thing he said was that it gives you ideas you never had before, such as searching for the other eggs. At first, you believe it is so that you can protect them also, but that isn't it at all. It wants to be near the other eggs. They want to be born, and they are trying to use you to achieve their means."

The table was silent as Tasha told of the egg and its powers, but the last of her tale was the best part. It caused everyone to sit up just a little more as she spoke.

"The box in which each egg is housed hides the secrets of that particular egg. It seems there is a detector on each box capable of finding the other two eggs. The eyes of the detector dragon glow when the other egg is within a mile, which helps to narrow the search."

"Err, I hate to interrupt," Richard said, "but did he say anything about the demon that stole the egg?"

Everyone's eyes turned to Richard for a moment then swung back to Tasha, waiting for an answer.

"Oh, he got quite irate when speaking about him. George, the wizard's name was George, he didn't know who the demon was, but he said the demon resembled a demon the clan killed over a century before the attack. He remembered seeing an entry about a group of demons that had attacked the coven. Each one had died in the process, and each one had been drawn into the coven's family book, along with the powers each one had displayed in battle. George thought the demon looked familiar, and had looked him up. He believes our demon is the son of one that died one hundred years before, and is continuing his father's work. George says our demon had some sort of power of allusion and strong fireballs, but that was the only magic he saw the demon use.

"Evidently the demon made the egg's box appear to be on the ledge of the mountain to stop George from saving it. However when George reached for the box, it vanished as the air around it was disturbed. This gave the demon a head start. I am sorry to say, but that was all he had to tell. Trust me, if there was any more, I would have gotten it out of him," Tasha finished.

Darkess leaned forward before anyone else could get a word in and asked,

"Show us how your power works."

Surprised that the youngest person at the table had spoken first, an odd glint sparkled in Tasha's eyes, and a grin flitted across her lips. She cleared her throat and asked,

"On whom would you like me to perform this feat?"

Darkess leaned forward, getting very close to Tasha, and she grinned as she said,

"Me."

The grin slipped from Tasha's face for a moment then returned after some thought as to what she would ask the young lady before her. Chakra was laying on one of the large buffets on the wall of the room, and he flipped his tail in agitation as he watched his young master prod a woman she did not know. Angela eyed Richard with a small amount of worry. Everyone was waiting for what would happen next. Richard's look of concern deepened as the silence drug on. Silver had a grip on Daniel's hand, and he had a look of confusion on his face. No one had a clue about Tasha's power and how it worked. Tanner looked untrusting and ready for a fight. And Roxy and Alieria seemed rather normal, as if this was something that happened every day. The anticipation was thick in the room. All eyes were now on Tasha, and there wasn't even the slightest trace of fear on her face as she took a deep breath. The voice that issued from her throat was similar but not exactly the same as the one they had been listening to for the last fifteen minutes.

"The only question that I have for you is: What will you do with the eggs once you have acquired them?"

Everyone in the room relaxed, shoulders dropped down to normal calm positions, and frown lines vanished, not because the question was nonthreatening, but because of Tasha's voice. Darkess answered immediately, as if she had been thinking extensively on the subject.

"That depends on the demon, the eggs, and who is still alive when this whole fiasco is over."

Darkess smiled at Tasha with a trancelike look on her face, awaiting another question. Looking around the table, Tasha realized they all had the same look on their faces, and it was time to break the trance before there was a problem. She cleared her throat and spoke in her normal voice.

"Is every one alright? Back to normal?"

Shaking their heads and blinking, each person's head began to clear, and they looked normal again.

"That was extraordinary, my dear Tasha," Richard said rubbing his eyes.

"Does it work like that on everyone?" Darkess asked.

"Unfortunately, no. Beings with the ability to read or control minds are unaffected. And there is a potion I had made for anyone that I travel with. It makes them immune to my voice. And then again, there are wizened old wizards that know a spell to counteract my power or have the strength to override it. With demons, well, it is hit or miss," Tasha said grimly.

Tasha's last statement made Darkess think hard. Her powers may or may not work on demons either. She would have to learn that she could not depend solely on her powers, just as Jori always said. Darkess was lost deep in her thoughts when she felt a hand on her shoulder. When she looked up, she was surprised to see Tasha behind her.

"What is wrong dear?" Tasha asked in her normal voice.

"Nothing really, just making connections," Darkess answered. "It just seems that a lot more things are connected than meets the eye."

"What do you mean?" Richard asked.

"Just that I have heard in my lessons from several different people, from different places entirely, some of the exact same things said in totally different ways, but all amounting to the same thing. Stay calm. Use your head. Don't rely solely on magic. Things of that nature."

Richard smiled at Angela, and Silver at Daniel. She was truly growing up. She was listening to everyone and learning from what they said. Darkess was coming into her own, and they were watching it all happen.

Darkess was practicing spells in the tower with Richard. She had just turned a few well-measured ingredients into an owl, and it was flapping wildly around the room.

"Well done, my dear, well done," Richard clapped as he turned the owl into a raccoon.

"You try, make it into something else," Richard instructed excitedly.

Taking a pinch of herbs from the bowl on the table, she focused her energy on the raccoon and tossed the herbs onto it. With a small puff of fur, the raccoon was now a small monkey.

"Very good," Richard said pointing to the monkey, which promptly turned into a dust pile.

"I think that is enough for today. You are doing so well. I think we will try something new tomorrow."

Richard wiped his hand over the dust pile. When he removed his hand, the dust was gone.

"Thank you, Grandfather. See you later," Darkess said as she dashed from the room.

"Have fun!" Richard called after Darkess' retreating footsteps.

He smiled to himself as he put away his small spell book and mumbled under his breath.

"Amazing, that girl…" his voice trailed off as he retreated into his thoughts.

Absently he worked at clearing the lesson from this morning. His eyes flitted across the table but mostly seemed focused on something very far away. So far away, in fact, that his eyes began to glaze over. His mind was at the Red-Eye Tavern, and he was scanning the customers looking for a familiar hooded man. And again, he didn't see what he wanted to see.

"Where could he possibly be?" Richard said as his eyes began to return to their normal clear blue color.

Rubbing absently at his beard, he twisted the end into a point and wondered if his friend was dead. Or was he still searching? Or has he taken my money and stabbed me in the back? What in the world happened to him? It seemed Richard's mood had changed.

"Damn it all," he whispered to himself.

☼

The end of spring was nearing, and the storms were fierce once again. A knock on the door one evening was a surprise with such bad weather and the distance of muddy road between Vallencourt Castle and Crystal City. Roxy answered the kitchens side entrance, and Philineas was standing on the other side grinning broadly.

"Well, you old scoundrel. How are you?" Roxy asked, hugging Philineas.

He swung her around, then placed her gently back on the floor and quickly said,

"Fine, fine, and I'd love to talk, but I am here on urgent business. Is Richard here?"

The smile on Roxy's face slipped into a frown as she answered.

"Of course, follow me."

Roxy could feel it, and judging by Philineas' demeanor, she knew something was wrong. They made their way up to the second floor along the corridor to the library. When they arrived, they found Richard intently reading a parchment roll. His desk was covered in papers and small items of all kinds, including a few potion bottles.

"Philineas, old friend, how are you?" Richard said, standing to shake his hand.

"Fine, fine, and you?" Philineas replied.

"So what brings you here on this soggy day?" Richard asked.

Roxy shut the door and slipped down the hall.

Philineas' face became sober as he sat down, and he rubbed his forehead as he began.

"Something very bad is about to happen."

Richard's smile slipped from his face.

"What do you mean?"

"Well, now that is one of the problems," Philineas said. "We're not sure."

Richard sat down with a confused look on his face.

"We're not sure?" he asked.

"I am sorry, the familiars, we have been talking. Several different familiars have summoned me and they all described the same things, bad feelings by them and their masters. Some have seen signs of war or battle. No, more like dreams of them. And there is an uneasy feeling growing in the wizarding world, and if these feelings keep getting stronger, the humans will start feeling it too. Everyone is getting worried..." His voice trailed off, and there was a silence while he searched for the proper words.

"...worried that evil will destroy the world we know. That something evil will finish us off for good."

Richard's forehead smoothed back out, and he smiled a weak smile, asking,

"Have you heard this from an oracle or a seer? Was it a premonition? Repeated dreams?"

Philineas thought for a moment then answered.

"Come to think of it, no, I haven't heard it from a reliable source. But the feelings..."

"And have there been any actual events of violence yet? Or is it still just feelings?" Richard questioned.

Again Philineas thought and looked back at Richard to respond.

"No actual events, and yes, it is still just feelings."

"Okay then, we already know that there is going to be a battle of some kind. But unless we lose, the rest of the wizarding world should be relatively unaffected. The feelings they are exhibiting are only telling us that the inevitable is getting closer."

Philineas still looked uneasy, but he let Richard soothe his raw nerves with his calming voice and strong words.

"I do thank you very much for the warning. And I would like you to come again if you ever feel such a need. I think you should tell anyone you feel needs to hear that the Vallencourt Family is working hard on this matter. We have several people spread out around the world searching for this evil we're all feeling. We are getting closer, but we are not there just yet."

Philineas still had a concerned look to his face, making Richard add on another thought.

"I am sorry there is nothing more I can tell you, but the story is too long to tell, and at the end, we are not sure who exactly we are up against. I wish I could explain. But please do come to me again, for anything."

Smiling a sad smile, Philineas stood to take his leave and said,

"Thank you for your time sir. I know you are a busy man."

Turning towards the door, Philineas took a few steps before Richard said,

"Everything will be alright. Be prepared, but don't fret. Darkess will make sure we are all safe."

Turning back, Philineas' smile was a little brighter, and his shoulders stood up just a little more. He donned his hat and out the door he went. Richard went over to the window, pulled back the thick green velvet drapes, and peered out at the moon. It wasn't quite full, but it would be in a few days. Looking down into the courtyard, he saw Chakra slinking up a tree. Probably snooping, Richard thought as he closed the drapes. Returning to his desk, he looked at the pages spread out in front of him. When he sat back down in his chair, a burning sensation came from his leg. Quickly, he grabbed at the heat, realized it was the coin, and jumped back up again.

"It's about time," Richard said to himself.

Hastily he scribbled out a note leaving it on the top of the rest of his notes and trotted over to the potions cabinet. Richard scooped up a couple of bottles and pocketed them. Then he grabbed one last bottle and smashed it at his feet. As the thick blue smoke enveloped him, he pictured his friend's face, which only he knew. He held the coin tightly as he was transported to where he was not sure.

≈

Fanning the smoke upon his arrival, Richard was surprised to see that he had no idea where he was. He was in the alley of a city he did not know. The smells were new, different. Quickly, he backed up against the wall of some shop. He saw nothing moving and no animals sniffing for handouts. But he had the feeling he was not alone.

"Where the hell are you?" Richard whispered to what he hoped was his friend.

A shuffling sound came from the dark only a few feet away and a darkly cloaked figure fell to his knees in front of Richard. A gurgling sound escaped the cloaked man's mouth as he slumped towards the ground and landed on his hands. His arms couldn't hold his weight, so he collapsed on his face. In the starlight, Richard recognized his friend's cloak. He rolled the man over and leaned him against the wall. Bloody hands came out of his soaked cloak and groped for help. Richard's hands became greasy with blood when they clasped hands.

"Make haste…" gurgled from the hood of the cloak.

"What?" Richard asked.

"L-l-leave now…" the man stammered.

The bloody hands could be felt but not seen, and Richard finally realized that his friend was bleeding profusely and near death.

"What in hell is going on here?" Richard whispered quickly.

Richard felt along his friend's chest waiting for an answer and realized there were gaps in the cloak and there was wounded flesh showing. The cloaked figure was breathing raggedly and had begun to choke and wheeze with each breath.

"Trap..." the cloaked man whispered before a choking fit ceased him, blood and spittle flying.

Richard had not heard the man and was trying to comfort him when his hand was grabbed very tightly.

"Flee, now, get away," the man said and shoved with all of the energy he had left at Richard.

"Tell me what has happened to you," Richard demanded.

Further down the alley in the deepest darkness came the sound of boots on the hard packed earth, and Richard was alerted by the sound. Trying to stand up and confront this unseen presence, Richard looked up just in time to see a fireball flying directly towards his chest. To avoid a fatal strike, Richard fell to the side as quickly as he could and felt pain in both shoulders, one from the fall and the other from Takars' strike.

"I'll tell you what happened old man, you got too close. Looks like I found you before you found me. And now I have you. I win."

Scrambling to stand up, another fireball slammed into Richard's hip, rolling him over and nearly knocking him unconscious. His brain rattled in his head as he came to a stop up against some old wooden crates. Richard focused his eyes as best he could and managed to see his friend burst into flames. The cloaked figure didn't even move for he had already died before the flames consumed him. It was little consolation for Richard, for he was still alive. The pang of loss was brief as he tried feebly to get to his hands and knees. His shaking arm groped inside his cloak for a potion bottle.

"Your turn..." a singing voice came from the dark.

The bottle finally came free of the robes, and Richard smashed it under his hand.

"Home," he whispered.

As the smoke enveloped him, Richard was blasted broadside with a fireball at precisely the same moment he began to dissipate for his trip. Instead of bursting into flames, Richard was badly injured but slipped away back to his castle. For a moment, he could hear the demon screaming behind him then he was home.

"If you survive, you'll never find me!" Takar screamed at the blue smoke.

His breathing was tense and ragged as he dug through his cloak. Once Takar found what he was looking for, he tossed it into the air and sailed a fireball at it. As the fireball neared the object, you could clearly see the bronze coin flipping over, sun and moon, before it was incinerated. In the sky above the burning coin, Takar focused on the moon. There was a ring around it, an omen of bad things to come. But for whom, he wondered.

≈

Coughing and sputtering, Richard appeared in his bedchambers. He pulled a bottle of potion from his pocket and poured it on the floor. Crawling across the floor with all of his will, he dunked the bottle into the pitcher of water on the side table. He poured out the water and rinsed the bottle once more. In the middle of a choking fit that made him stop and wheeze, he nearly dropped the bottle. Clutching it tightly, he stuck the bottle into the wound on his ribs. Stifling a scream, Richard filled the bottle with blood, re-corked it, climbed on the side table, and sat down. Angela was not around. The room was silent with only one torch burning. Chakra had been in the tree outside when he had left, and since it had only been a few moments, Richard was sure the cat was still out there. He smashed the window with the hopes that it would draw the cat to him.

Shivering and losing strength, Richard pulled down the drapes and wrapped himself as best he could. Chakra was nosy enough to show up promptly once he saw the drapes ripped free from the wall. Panic struck Chakra, and he raced down the tree as fast as his claws would allow. He tore off around the castle towards the nearest entrance, yowling. Once he was inside the castle, Charka ran down the hall looking for Darkess.

'Where are you, Darkess?' Chakra spoke to his master.

'In my room,' came the reply.

Chakra was shocked that they could communicate given the distance between them. They had never been able to talk from so far away before.

'Your grandfather is injured. You must go to him. He is in his room,' Chakra said.

Darkess jumped to her feet, ran to her stash of potions, and slammed the blue one into the floor.

"Grandfather's room!" she yelled.

≈

When Darkess reappeared, she was in her grandfather's room. What she saw tore at her heart like nothing she had ever felt before.

'Chakra, you must find my Grandmother, and bring her here quickly.'

Richard had slipped off the side table and was on the floor. Darkess pulled the blanket from the bed and used it to cover her grandfather's bleeding and broken body. Tears flowed freely from her eyes, but her voice remained calm.

"What happened Grandfather?" Darkess asked, swallowing the knot in her throat.

"I met your demon. It was a t-trap," Richard wheezed.

His shaking hand held out a coin for Darkess. She had seen it before and knew what it was. Their eyes met, and the sight of his granddaughter's tear-stained face broke his heart. He handed her two bottles, one empty, the other full of blood, then he coughed hard and thickly.

"Take special care, Darkess. He is a powerful demon," Richard coughed, blood dotting his lips.

Darkess was so upset that she had forgotten she could channel her grandmother's powers, and she watched the light slowly dwindle in her grandfather's eyes. His eyes closed and his head slipped to the side.

"Grandfather?" Darkess pleaded in a squeaky voice.

She shook him gently, trying to wake him.

"Grandfather?" Darkess begged him to wake up and shook him a little harder.

"Grandfather!" Darkess yelled, collapsing on his chest in a fit of tears.

"No!" she cried into his robes.

The blood soaked blanket in her hands made her think, "Maybe I can heal him." Grandmother should be almost here. So she held her hands out over her Grandfather's side where the majority of the blood was. Nothing happened. Then, almost in a rage, she jumped up and squatted over the body, trying with all of her might to heal her grandfather. Again, nothing happened.

Footsteps thundered up the hallway towards the room, and Darkess yelled out.

"Help! Grandmother help!"

Chakra came running into the room with Angela and Roxy right behind him. In a flurry of robes, the two women took either side of the man on the floor. Angela's hands were out in front of her, and her entire body was glowing with the power she was pulling in trying to heal her husband. Roxy placed her ear next to Richard's mouth.

"He's not breathing, Mrs," she said with her lip quivering.

Darkess stood behind her grandmother, chewing on her lip with her jaw quivering, and tears streaming down her face. Silver and Daniel came thundering down the hall, and upon arriving at the door, Silver gasped, threw herself into her husband's chest and began to sob. Again, Angela took a deep breath and the glow around her became brighter as beads of sweat broke out on her forehead and upper lip. Darkess' eyes darted from Angela to Richard to Roxy and back again to Angela. She wanted some sort of response, anything. Roxy laid her head on Richard's chest, listening intently for a heartbeat. The tears that had been glistening rolled out the corners of her eyes and down her cheek and nose. Roxy swallowed hard at the knot in her throat and croaked,

"Still nothing."

Angela's glow decreased, and she grabbed Darkess' hand, yanking her to her knees.

"Help me child, give me a boost."

There was a quiver in Angela's voice that Darkess had never heard before, but the tears had not left her grandmother's eyes. She had it in her mind that this was not over yet. Sucking up her tears, Darkess closed her eyes and concentrated on the bloodied man on the floor. Both witches began to glow, and Roxy listened for a heartbeat or a breath. After a minute or so, Roxy looked up at the two witches. She sucked in a wet breath and said,

"Nothing. There's nothing."

But the two witches, wife and granddaughter, refused to give up. They squeezed their hands tighter, and the glow increased a little. Silver grabbed hold of herself and crept up behind them, holding Daniel's hand in a death grip. She reached down with her free hand and touched Darkess' shoulder. A premonition ripped through Silver, whose eyes clouded over, knocking her to her knees behind her daughter. She saw a funeral for a moment then she saw Darkess dressed for battle. Darkess was loading her pack with essentials, and just as quickly the vision changed, she saw Darkess in a new place, surrounded by sand, then all went black, and she was standing in a lavender mist. Silver knew what they had to do.

"Stop," she said. Her eyes had returned to normal but when she squeezed them shut, the tears rolled.

No one was paying attention, so Silver placed her other hand on her mother and squeezed the two witches' shoulders.

"Save your energy. It's over," Silver said miserably, tears sliding down her face.

The glow around Angela began to decrease, but Darkess' remained constant.

"Stop honey," Silver said.

"It's not over," Darkess said through gritted teeth in a very determined voice.

And as if to prove it, Darkess' glow became ever brighter, and her grip on her grandmother's hand became fierce. Her lips formed a sneer. She was angry. Angela had finally broken down in tears, but she knew Silver was right, so she tried to stop Darkess. Roxy's tears were rolling freely down her face, and she croaked,

"He's gone, Darkess. We've done all that we can. You can't heal the dead."

When she opened her eyes, the glow left Darkess, and she collapsed in tears once again on her grandfather's chest. She was crying so hard the only thing that could be heard was the air crackling in and out of her lungs. When she sat up, she whimpered,

"It's all my fault."

Angela grabbed her granddaughter harshly and pulled her close.

"It is not your fault."

"It is too, I could have saved him. I could have healed him when I first saw him. I could have stolen your power and saved him," Darkess wined in frustration.

Looking down at her broken husband, Angela saw the massive quantity of blood soaking the robes, blanket and drapes. She wiped his forehead and brushed hair away from his face. A tear rolled down her cheek and landed on his robes.

"I doubt if either of us could have saved him. Look at him, his wounds are extensive."

"It's still all my fault," Darkess said miserably, looking at her mother.

Silver smiled a weak, sad smile at her daughter through her own blurry veil of tears.

"Did you see what I saw?" Silver asked.

"A bit of it, and yes it is my fault. He is the one who had to die in order for the prophecy to become a reality," Darkess sniffed miserably at her tears.

Daniel was standing at Richard's feet looking down at the man, his eyes wet with tears.

"I should go and get Tanner. I will make the necessary arrangements," he mumbled as he squatted down and touched the old man's leg.

"An honorable way to go my old friend. But what were you doing?" Daniel whispered.

Wiping his tears away, Daniel stood up and silently walked from the room. Roxy and Angela pulled the quilt up over Richard's face, and all four women cried for their fallen leader.

"He gave me these. But why the empty one?" Darkess asked miserably.

"I know why," Angela said. Uncorking the bottle and holding it up to her eye, she caught tears inside.

☼

The shadows were deep and dark that night, darker than usual because of the shroud of pain that covered the inhabitants of the Vallencourt grounds. And in those shadows, Darkess crept through the castle, doing her best to allow her family the rest they needed. She decided to go to the tower. It was what her grandfather would usually do in these circumstances. When her grandfather had given her the blood vile, there had been a bronze coin stuck to the bottom of it. She intended to find the owner of the other half and get to the bottom of this as quickly as possible. When she reached the tower, she sat down in her grandfather's favorite chair and used her power to light all the torches in the room. Laying the coin on the table, she pulled out the maps her grandfather had kept for exactly this type of occasion and went to the cabinet to pull out their scrying crystal.

As she dug through the drawer for the crystal, she found several items that reminded her of her grandfather and the tears began to roll again. She slammed her fist down on the shelf in front of her and pursed her lips.

"No. I must not cry," she affirmed to herself. "I have to be strong."

Darkess took several deep breaths to calm herself enough to try to scry. She returned to the table with the crystal. Its end was capped in silver, and it hung on a leather thong. Tying the opposite end of the crystal to the coin, she swung the crystal's point over the map in front of her. Starting with her own country, she made small circular movements over the map and found nothing. Switching maps, she tried again on the Muscovatan and Asiattica maps with no results. Then, remembering that her grandfather had not been dressed nearly warm enough, she tried the map of Brumalia anyway. Once again, the crystal swung limply at the bottom of the cord. Nothing.

Darkess began to get angry and started digging for other maps of the lesser charted parts of the world. She knew there was a dreadful hot place where the rivers burn with fire and the mountains belched clouds of smoke and burning rock. Aha, she thought when she found a vague drawing of a few islands marked as the Isle of Ardor. She began to swing the crystal but felt no pull from it.

"How can that be?" Darkess said through gritted teeth.

Darkess had no idea that Takar had destroyed the other coin before her grandfather had even made it back to the castle, making it completely undetectable. She began to put all the maps back where they had been, and with slumped shoulders, she left the tower. The walk from the tower to her room seemed to take an eternity as the reality of her grandfather's death ate at the fringe of her mind. She kept trying to think of reasons why she couldn't find the other coin, anything to keep from thinking of her grandfather. That's when it hit her, and she stopped in her tracks.

"He destroyed it," Darkess whispered.

Somewhere in the back of her mind, she had known it all along, but the practice of magic and the search had kept her busy for a while. Now the busy was gone, and the quiet pain of reality was sinking in. She grabbed her forehead with her left hand and her mouth with her right hand in an effort to stifle the sobs as she ran to her room.

≈

After two life altering and miserable days, family and friends had gathered around the Vallencourt graveyard on the hill behind the castle. Darkess stood staring at the carved wooden box that would forever house her beloved grandfather. She holds a red rose. The setting sun shines brightly on the tears it has collected. Harlow is speaking eloquently about Richard, the patriarch of the Vallencourt Family and friend to all. Darkess stared for the longest while until she realized that Harlow was stealing thoughts from the minds in pain all around him. He had just stolen her thoughts to share with the crowd, ad-libbing some of it.

"The wisdom he takes with him will impact us all. He was a great man and wonderful patriarch, not to mention the most trusted friend a man or woman could have. He was a fountain of wonder, childlike at times, but still a true leader…"

Harlow's words turned to mumbles again for Darkess as she stared at the magically carved coffin draped in cascades of white roses. She felt wretched, and she wanted to scream and cry. Throwing a temper tantrum didn't seem out of the realm of possibility, and she clenched and unclenched her jaw in anxiousness and pain. Tears continued to stream down her face, but she made not one sound while others spoke about her grandfather. One by one, the mourners made their way back to the castle, but Darkess refused to leave. Daniel stood with his daughter and watched as the remaining grievers, followed by Silver and Angela, returned to the castle for some food and story swapping. Darkess looked up at her father, kissed him on the cheek and took his hands.

"Please, go join the family," she pleaded. "I want to be alone with him for a few minutes. Do you mind?"

"Are you sure you'll be alright?" Daniel asked, brushing his fingers down her cheek and grabbing her chin to get a good look into her eyes.

"Yes, I will be alright," she answered.

"I love you daughter, come in soon."

"I love you too, and I'll be in, in a bit," she smiled weakly and turned back towards the casket.

≈

Daniel made his way back down the hillside from the family cemetery, leaving Chakra as the only living thing with Darkess. His form retreated slowly, looking back occasionally to watch his daughter. The cat weaved around Darkess' legs as she interlaced the red rose into the white bouquet on top of the casket.

"Why didn't you take me?" Darkess asked the casket, her bottom lip quivering. "I could have helped you."

She played with the roses, rearranging them and pulling off the imperfect petals in an attempt to make them look better. She absently touched everything while her brain struggled to comprehend life without her grandfather.

"I need you. Why did you have to leave me?" Darkess pleaded in the most heartbreaking voice. The only answer was a couple of birds twittering nearby, and then she heard footsteps. Spinning quickly in her place, Darkess was surprised to see Oracle walking up the pathway. The Oracle was grace and beauty, stepping lightly as she walked towards the casket. Her white hair flowed around her head and shoulders like a halo, streaming down to her knees, and flowing white gowns obscured her petite form. Her eyes were a piercing blue, and her lips seemed to shimmer. Her body emanated a pale glow as she spoke to Darkess.

"We don't choose our birth," Oracle said taking another couple steps. "And we don't choose our death." She continued her path around the casket, her eyes locked on Darkess' with every word.

"But we can choose the forks in the path between those two points in life. You may choose to follow others down the path that is clear and easy. Or, you may choose to cut your own path. Easy or difficult is your choice. However you, my dear, are a leader, not a follower."

"But I'm not ready yet," Darkess said.

"Each path we choose has consequences. These consequences affect us as well the ones around us. You will do what is best. You are but a mere breathe's distance from it," the Oracle said.

"What?" Darkess asked.

"Free of the ties that bind you to youth. You'll now have the power to do what you must," Oracle said as she continued to walk slowly around Darkess and the casket.

"Look for the light, my dear, and follow the signs."

Darkess had a hundred questions burning in her mind, but she knew the Oracle didn't really answer direct questions. She merely pointed you in a better direction, sometimes giving you a clue, but never facts. Oracle had circled the casket twice, and upon reaching the path again, she started to walk back down the hillside. Turning back to make eye contact with Darkess once again, she said,

"The place of your birth will give you the strength."

Just as swiftly as she ascended the hill, she descended and was gone. The sun was setting on the side of the castle, which cast deep shadows on the valley. The glow was diminishing in the sky when Darkess turned to look at it. Brilliant pinks and purples painted the sky and ended in a deep blue that reached further and further, as the night claimed it. Darkess watched as the darkness closed in. She pulled her cloak tight and dug in a pocket. Pulling out a crystal, she said,

"Illuminate."

Following the path back down to the castle, Darkess walked quietly with Chakra at her side. Suddenly a bright light flashed overhead that caused her to stop and look for the source. Then everything was pitch black again.

"Lightning?" Darkess said as neither a question nor an answer, and they continued down the path.

They had taken several more steps before the bright light shone again. This time Darkess projected.

'That was not lightning.'

So the two of them waited for the light to show itself once more. Darkess looked up at the stars when the bright light beamed a third time.

It was coming from the locked tower, and it was aimed right at her. As quickly as it turned on, it turned off, and the tower was dark again.

'Did you see that?' Darkess projected to Charka, who growled and projected back.

'I think it is time we visit that tower once more.'

Speeding up their pace, they headed for the side entrance to the castle in order to bypass the mourners completely. The stealth of the cat was natural, but Darkess' was well learned as she and her cat made it to the tower without anyone noticing.

Darkess rubbed her hand on the wooden door she had tested so many times before. The knob was cold in her palm, and she gave it a good twist. Unlike all the times before, the door released from its jam and swung slowly open, creaking loudly. Her heart racing with excitement, Darkess looked at her familiar and said,

"Stay here. Wait 'til I give you the all clear. You may have to fetch help."

Chakra sat down and gave Darkess a very serious look.

'Please don't use the word fetch. I am not a dog.'

"Oh Chakra, you know what I meant," Darkess said as she crept into the room.

The room was completely dark except for the torchlight from the hall. Once Darkess was inside, a soft glow came from the crystal that hung in the window. As she made her way around the room, the crystal grew brighter with every step until it suddenly flared very brightly, shining a beam of light directly on her. She stopped and shielded her eyes from the light. There were torches around the room, and a chandelier above her burst into flame and lighted the room properly. The crystal went dark, or so dim it looked dark, as Darkess assessed the room. It seemed safe, so she called out,

"Chakra you have to see this."

As the cat bounded into the room, the crystal began to pulsate, and the light seemed to take a shape. The form coming from the crystal had tiny flecks for light, which grew bright then went dark, only to relight again. An odd swirling pattern began in the particles as they came closer to each other and tried to form a more solid shape. All at once, the particles converged and went black. The black shape swirled in a pulsating tornadic shape then converged again. Next, it exploded into a million dots of light. Standing where the shape had once been was the ghostly figure of an old wizard.

The wizard looked himself over then smiled at Darkess, who raised her hands, just in case.

"I'll be jiggered. It worked!" the old man said in an excited voice.

"What worked?" Darkess asked.

"Why, you did."

"Who are you?"

"I am Wolfbane Vallencourt, at your service," he said with a bow.

"The wizard who gave the prophecy of me…" her voice trailed off.

Floating forward, Wolfbane or rather his ghost, smiled at Darkess and said,

"You must be the correct age, or my crystal would not have awakened. Only when the time is correct will the crystal's light seek you out. The only view to my crystal is inside this room, the family cemetery, and the air. Oh, you don't fly do you? Oh dear."

"No, I can't fly."

"Good, good. Oh how rude of me, I am sorry for your loss. Who did you lose?"

Darkess looked down at her hands. Her pain had momentarily been erased by the excitement of the now unlocked tower, and now it came crashing back down on her.

"My grandfather," she answered pitifully.

"I take it he was a leader, your teacher?" the ghost asked.

"He was my best friend, too…" Darkess added nodding her head, a tear sliding down her cheek.

"There, there, it will get better. All things happen for a reason."

"But, I still have so much to learn," Darkess said, working herself up again. "We were supposed to be trying something new today, and I'll never know what it was. It could be very important."

"Focusing all of your energy on death will give you no time for the things in life that truly matter," said the ghost. "Focus on your demon, and on what you need to. You can't bring your grandfather back, and even if you could, it wouldn't be him. It would be an abomination, a sort of copy of the real thing, and it would be off, not right in the head. Let us focus on the job ahead. What sort of demon are we up against?" Wolfbane asked.

"I don't know really," Darkess said and looked blankly at him.

"You don't know…" Wolfbane cut himself short and started to think.

"Oh no, could I be here to early. No, it can't be," he argued with himself, looking very upset.

"Oh, I think you're here at the correct time. The prophecy said…" Darkess interjected.

Wolfbane cut her off quickly and said,

"This may not be the correct death. The crystal must have felt your pain and assumed it was the right time."

Fluttering around the room, he seemed to be searching for something.

"But, I am up against a demon. Only, I don't know who or where he is."

"Yes, yes, I see. Well, do tell me more," Wolfbane said, floating down to a stool as if he were sitting on it and giving her room to talk.

He pointed to another stool for her to sit on and waited for her to speak. Darkess told him everything she knew about the three dragon eggs, where they were believed to be from, why they were separated, and everything she knew about the demon, which wasn't much. She explained that she had seen this demon on two separate occasions, and that he had stolen two of the eggs already. She also said that she believed he was the reason for her grandfather's death, although she had no proof. She described his fire power and power over allusions, using your greatest fear or strongest desire. This seemed to intrigue Wolfbane. Next she told him about the weird symbols the demon had used to make his portal. This truly captivated Wolfbane, and he asked to see them.

That was when Darkess realized how long they had been talking. She knew she would have to go to her room to retrieve her pack, and her family would be searching for her. Jumping to her feet, Darkess startled Chakra who jumped from the table he had been investigating.

"What is it?" Wolfbane and Chakra chimed in together.

Taking a breath as if to speak, then exhaling with a miserable look on her face, Darkess wrung her hands.

"I really wanted to stay and talk to you, but I fear I must take my leave of you for a while. My Grandfather would have been the first person I would have shown this tower room, but since, well, he is gone…" Darkess choked back a sob. "I really have no desire to share this right now. I best go. I have to grieve with my family. When all of the guests have left, I will return."

"We have so much to do," Wolfbane said.

Thinking for just a moment, Darkess said,

"Yes, but I must wait until the blood moon, anyway. Can you leave this tower?"

"Oh, yes, but not the castle, unless…" Wolfbane answered, leaving off.

"Unless what?" Darkess asked.

"Unless you take a piece of me with you."

"Piece of you?" Darkess asked, wrinkling her nose.

"Yes. My bones."

"You want me to dig you up?" Darkess said with a clear note of distaste.

"Why no. Actually, I prepared for this very contingency," Wolfbane smiled and pointed to a small, plain wooden box on top of an ancient bureau.

Darkess walked to the bureau and cautiously took the box down. She examined it but didn't open it.

"Well, go ahead," Wolfbane encouraged.

Flaring her nose as if she had smelled something awful, Darkess slowly opened the box. To her relief, there was no stench, so she opened it all the way and peered inside. From the size of the box, she had assumed there was an entire hand inside, but amazingly enough, the box contained only three small bones and a golden ring. Darkess gave Wolfbane a questioning look, than reached for the ring. Upon inspection, she found the ring was the entire body of a dragon that wrapped around the finger. There were only two emerald stones for eyes, and the rest was solid gold.

"Are you a dragon keeper?" Darkess asked.

"No, but I knew you would have something to do with saving them. I had that ring made to remind me what I had to plan for. You probably don't know this, but I made that prophecy almost twenty years before my death. That gave me a lot of time to think about you…what you would be like, and of course, what you may be up against."

Putting the ring back in its box, Darkess closed the lid and replaced it on the bureau.

"I really must go now. I will be back in a day or so. I do have a lot of questions for you," Darkess said returning to the door.

"As do I," Wolfbane said as the door slipped shut and the autolock immediately engaged.

☼

For two days, family and friends laughed and cried, telling stories of their lost patriarch. Some ate with gusto, while others simply picked at their food. There were even a few outbursts of anger caused by the pain of

Richard's loss. At the end of two days, it seemed like everyone was dealing with the shock much better. Finally, Darkess decided to ask the members of the Order to stay for an extra hour or so. When the last guest who was not a member of the Order had left, Darkess called them all into Richard's library. All eyes were upon her as she stood in the front of them holding her grandfather's crystal-headed staff.

Darkess looked into the eyes of each person present, one after another, before she spoke. She nodded at Harlow, who nodded back.

"Before I tell you why I have asked you here, I have decided to change things a little around here."

Everyone gave her curious looks, and some exchanged glances.

"I am now the new leader of the Order of the New Horizon."

Before any one could say a word for or against her, she plunged on.

"With my Grandfather's death, I believe that I am the one who should take over the search for our demon."

"You're still too young to lead the Order. Don't be silly," Silver said.

Several people decided to speak at once, so Harlow, who abhorred the noise both mentally and physically, stood and raised his hands to silence everyone.

"Maybe we should take a vote for the new leader of our group," he suggested.

"No," Darkess said vehemently. "I am taking the lead."

"Now, Darkess, honey, you're upset. We should talk about this," Angela suggested.

Darkess' anger began to swell. She would have never thought that they wouldn't follow her. There was another mumble around the room as they began to talk amongst themselves. Darkess wasn't listening to them. She could only hear the buzzing of their voices, and she was beside herself. She thought she was the chosen one. She thought she was doing the best for everyone. They all seemed to have different ideas. Her eyes roamed the room, watching everyone talk, and she wanted to lash out at them. Why don't they trust me, she thought. Her head began to ache, so she closed her eyes trying to block the pain. It seemed the edges of her mind began to blur, and her image began to do the same thing. The image of Darkess slid across the floor, making a solid image in one place and a blurred image a few feet away. Darkess rubbed her head and exhaled sharply, which made the solid image slide back into the blurred, and they were one again. The entire room went completely silent, except for Silver, who gasped.

"What the hell?" Harlow muttered as he stared at Darkess.

"Are you feeling alright dear?" Janine asked.

Darkess gave no reply, and her eyes stayed shut. Angela had already begun to make her way to her granddaughter.

"Darkess, what is wrong?" Angela demanded.

Angela reached for Darkess and grabbed a hold of thin air. Her hands slipped right through the image. Shock rippled through the room at the sight of this, which caused Darkess to open her eyes and look around the room.

"What?" Darkess asked confused.

Silver had stepped forward and nearly everyone was standing closer trying to figure out just exactly what was going on.

"You're not here," Silver said.

One eyebrow shot up on Darkess' face.

"What do you mean, I'm not here? I'm standing right in front of you," Darkess said tapping on her own chest.

Silver reached out and put her hand directly through Darkess' hand and chest.

"Oh, we see you. You're just not there," Silver said turning to Angela.

"She's not a ghost. She's not cold," Angela said.

"Have you been messing with the black book?"

"No!" Darkess said sounding intensely hurt.

She began to think, and her image hovered back across the floor, the edges becoming blurry for a moment, then she was solid again, standing where she had been before. Angela grabbed again for her granddaughter, and found that she was indeed back where her image was. Angela and Silver grabbed Darkess holding her tightly. Darkess stood there with the most perplexed look on her face.

"What is wrong with you two?" Darkess asked almost angrily.

Harlow sat down slowly. Realization had just struck him.

"I know what it is," he said silencing the room again.

Everyone turned to look at him.

"I've heard of this power once before. She never left. She was here the entire time."

"But you saw my hand go straight through her," Angela defended herself.

"Yes, we all did. But I still say she never left. Did you see how she seemed to hover before her image blurred?"

Everyone shook their heads and mumbled yes.

"She has the power of displacement," Harlow said.

"What?" Darkess asked.

"Yes my dear. You have split yourself with your power. It is a defensive power, meant to hide your true self from pain or danger. Your body became invisible, and you threw off an image of yourself. Hypothetically speaking, we could have tried to kill you but only been able to hit your image, keeping you safe from harm."

Angela dropped down into the closest chair.

"Oh Richard, you would have loved this," she mumbled.

Silver grasped her daughter's hand and asked,

"Is this why you called us here?"

"No, it wasn't," Darkess said with a twinge of anger "But I think the argument spurred it on."

"I think you are correct, Miss Goodspeed. The opposition to you becoming our leader either hurt or angered you, which caused a split or displacement of your image," Harlow said.

"Beggin' yer pardin Missy Darkess, but why did ya want us ta stay?" Brutus' gruff voice rolled over everyone.

"I opened the locked tower," Darkess said.

Jaws dropped, and everyone stared. At once they all began to speak.

"How?"

"What's in it?"

"When?"

"What did you find?"

Darkess held up her hand as Harlow had done earlier.

"Let us go and have a look, shall we?" Darkess said, taking control of things.

☼

It took more than an hour to show them the tower and let them all ask one question of Wolfbane. And of course, he had one to ask in return. Roxy and Angela used their time to clean the tower after centuries of filth had accumulated, with Angela using the cleaning as a ruse to search the room in what she thought was an undetected method. The bed was remade with fresh linens so Darkess could sleep there, and each member of the Order was looking at the ancient magical supplies around the room. There were a few things here and there that remained locked, protected by the magic of Wolfbane and intended for the use only by Darkess.

The members of the Order inspected everything that would open, which kept them all quite busy. Janine and Darkess did a little altering of Wolfbane's ring with his permission. Delighted with her new ring and the fact that Wolfbane had convinced them all, even Harlow unbelievable enough that Darkess should be in charge of her destiny. Wolfbane promised he would do his best to help her in every way he could. That was when Darkess felt she had to get them all out and on their way. There were things she needed to do, places she may have to go, and a new power she had to test and practice. Considering how dreadful she had felt over the last five days, she felt pretty good right now, and she refused to let anyone ruin it.

Darkess stood on one of her new old chairs and cleared her throat loudly, trying to get everyone's attention.

"Excuse me. Everyone, I need you to vacate my tower if you would. I have much to do, and I have no clue about how much time I have to do it in."

Everyone eyed her, and a couple even laughed.

"I'm serious. This is very important to me. Please go. You can all talk about me downstairs."

Angela smiled at how she had taken control of the room. She really was in charge now.

"Okay, you all heard her. Tea and cookies anyone?" Angela asked as she opened the door to lead the way out of the tower.

They all filed out, closing the door with a clatter, and leaving the tower silent. There was a slight breeze at the window, purring from Chakra, and a sigh from Darkess.

"Whew, I thought they would never leave," Darkess said as a broad smile spread across her face.

≈

Working late into the night, Darkess used the teleport potion to pool all of her belongings into the tower room. Once during these trips, Angela had tried to enter the tower room while Darkess was away with poor results. It seemed that only Darkess had the power to enter that tower, and she alone could allow another entrance. Upon returning by potion, Angela heard noise once again inside the room and knocked on the door.

"Come in," Darkess said from the other side of the door.

Surprisingly enough, when Angela grabbed the doorknob, the door opened smoothly with no resistance.

"That's peculiar. Did you lock that door?" Angela asked.

"Why would I lock the door?" Darkess asked, slighted. "I have nothing to hide."

"It was locked only moments before, but now the knob turns freely."

"Maybe the room protects itself," Darkess suggested.

Angela had a small stack of journals and a few other small items from Richard's library in her arms and handed them to her granddaughter.

"Thanks, Grandmother," Darkess said and returned to her organizing.

She busied herself finding new homes for all of her most important things. Angela looked around the room and then at the young woman standing before her.

"Your grandfather would be so proud of you," Angela said with a slight tremble in her lips.

Darkess stopped what she was doing and looked out the window to the hill where her grandfather was buried.

"If it weren't for me, he'd still be here," Darkess mumbled. "I should have done more."

Darkess throat constricted, and her voice sounded thick with pain, which caused Angela to reach for her.

"You musn't blame yourself. He knew what he was doing. He did it for you."

"I miss him so much," Darkess said in a great rush of tears and hugged Angela tightly.

Finally reality sunk in, and a full torrent of tears hit Darkess, and she gripped her grandmother as if for dear life. Angela's eyes flooded and spilt over, and the two witches washed some of their pain away in the river of their tears. After, the two separated, and begun to clean up their sodden faces, Darkess apologized.

"I am sorry for that display."

"Don't be, you needed to let some of it out. I was wondering how long it would take before you broke. You've been very strong. Don't feel guilty. You do have a heart still, even though it may sometimes feel like stone, it is not. In time, we will both feel better. In time, the wound will heal over, even if it never goes away. Besides, he's always going to be with us, always watching us. He is a part of us."

≈

The next morning, Darkess awoke to the sound of Wolfbane's voice. "I found it young Miss. Please do wake up."

Rubbing her eyes and pulling her hair away from her face, Darkess sat up in bed.

"What have you found?" she yawned.

He hovered over the shapes Darkess had drawn in her notes on that long ago day at Alieria's and pointed to them, smiling a big toothy grin.

"The shapes, from the demons' portal, I've figured them out. Black magic of the most evil kind. These shapes are a location along with his family symbols. Together, they make a kind of key to space. Only his clan would know the correct ones to return to their lair. And you have to be a very strong demon, or in one's care, in order to handle the stress of the trip. From what I gather, your very particles come apart, and you are like a mist shooting towards your destination. Very painful I should think. Plus, you said there was a powder?"

"Yes. A potion?" she inquired.

"Umm, I expect so. Maybe to aid in the separation of the body? I don't know. I never delved deep into the dark arts. I found some of these symbols in Victor's old book. He seemed to be trying to make a portal for himself. Although I don't think he had the power to make it work. Oh, and don't get any bright ideas either. You won't be using the book. It's against the rules. You'll just have to find another way to find your demon," Wolfbane rambled like a schoolteacher.

"So you woke me up just to tell me that I can't use what you figured out?" Darkess asked, slightly miffed.

"I am sorry you see it that way. I saw it as one more step towards solving this mystery," Wolfbane stated.

"And I see it as interruption to the best sleep I've had in a week. Now, let me be for a while longer," Darkess grumbled as she pulled the covers back over her head and snuggled back into her new bed.

Wolfbane snorted his distaste towards her attitude, promptly swirled into stardust, and darted into his crystal.

☼

Darkess had taken to carrying Richard's old staff with her everywhere. She was on full guard at all times. All of the doors and windows had potions, talismans, and a crystal. She had prepared the castle for all out war. There were large bottles of potions stored in both towers now and in the kitchens. Everyone kept plenty of the potions that had a longer shelf life and a smaller amount of the more timely ones along with a back up pouch of ingredients for making more. Tanner and Rufus were doing regular rounds, checking on the castle's borders and its outbuildings. Darkess was checking all floors and sending out regular birds to check with the Order members on how the world was faring under the circumstances. It seemed that magic folk everywhere were feeling the upcoming battle. It was in the air. Takar had taken to harassing any wizard he came across in a futile attempt at finding the third egg or Darkess. It seemed that even a few mortals had felt the sting of Takar's wrath. The Void Commission had their hands full covering up the magical killings and disguising them as normal or accidental deaths.

The Void Commission is a group of beings who help hide good and evil magic from the world. This relatively new group was brought about by the death of all the dragons around five hundred years ago when humans began to resent and even hate magical folk. The humans' history is very different than the one written by the magic folk who know what really happened. Few mortals understand us or care to deal with the reality of what truly is. Or rather the reality as it is right now. Who knows what tomorrow holds.

Darkess insisted that everyone be on guard. Even her father had a small pouch of potions in case he was attacked. Still, Darkess didn't think she was doing enough. She poured through her grandfather's journals and notes. She did find some interesting things she hadn't known about her grandfather, but so far, nothing of any use in the hunt for the eggs or the demon. Darkess had a lot of pent up energy. All of this energy spent preparing for a fight that never came was making her very jumpy. She needed to blow off some steam. Deciding to practice her new power only angered her more. This new power had an odd trigger. She literally had to have the feeling that she needed to be in two places at once, or in a lot of pain, in order to make it work. Both were feelings she only felt occasionally and were difficult to trigger at will. Darkess paced the floor in Richard's office, thinking and not realizing that she was no longer touching the floor. She was hovering above it several inches. When she stopped pacing, she thudded to the floor.

"Ouch," she hadn't expected that.

☼

A week had passed since Richard's burial, and the castle was almost empty and quiet again. It seemed that Richard had been the one who initiated most of the conversations in the castle, and no one had very much to say. His chair still sat empty, a daily reminder of what was missing in their lives. Finally, Darkess plucked up the courage to say something at the silent dinner table.

"I'm going on a trip."

Silver clanked her fork on the plate in front of her.

"Oh? Where to?" she croaked.

"Zaphod and I are going to Crystal City to have a little look around."

"Do you think that you should go alone?" Daniel chimed in.

Darkess looked at her poor human father with a look of love mixed with a little pity.

"I'll be fine Father. Do not worry, this is my purpose."

Daniel's shoulders slumped down, and Darkess realized the pain she had caused her father.

"Father, I love you, but I must do this. In your heart, you know I will be alright," she assured him. "It's just the city. We don't even know where the demon is. I'll be back in a few hours."

Darkess hugged her father then her mother.

"Be very careful, and don't stay out too long," Silver said, hugging Darkess tightly, not wanting to let go.

Angela was waiting patiently to speak. Darkess went to her grandmother and hugged her, waiting for what she knew was coming. She whispered in her granddaughter's ear.

"The blood moon is not far off now. My guess is tonight or tomorrow. Watch for the signs and heed them."

Darkess nodded her head, pulled her cloak tight, and through the doors she went.

≈

The breeze felt good against Darkess' skin as Zaphod cantered off towards Crystal City. They had blinked only part of the way there so they could burn off some extra energy on a faster ride. Entering the city, Darkess had expected to see more people, because it was not quite dark yet. But the streets were nearly deserted. Curtains were all drawn everywhere, and all of the shops were closed and the carts gone. Darkess continued her ride through the streets. Even the taverns were locked up tight. Things were worse than she had expected. Why hadn't anyone told her it was this bad? Did they not think she was a good enough leader? It's my age, she thought. They all think I am too young. This spurred her on to visit with two of the members of the Order. Janine was the closest, so she decided to visit her first.

Once they reached the storefront of Janine's, Zaphod knew where to go, and he trotted down the alley into the stall that he considered his home when they were here. Ardimas' old gray mare was munching on hay in her stall, but Janine's white mare was missing. Jumping from Zaphod, Darkess made her way towards the door, and Ardimas appeared in the doorway.

"Pleasure to see you, young missy. What brings you here?"

Darkess smiled warmly at the old man and gave him a hug.

"I came to check things out for myself. What has been going on here?"

"Things seem to get worse every day. The humans think there is a band of marauders on the loose, and we all know what is about to happen. Some even say the world may end soon."

"Not if I can help it. Where is Janine?"

Ardimas' face drooped.

"She's at Alieria's. Seems that some of the magic folk have taken up hiding at her castle. Alieria said she needed help feeding and organizing them."

Darkess could feel the weight increasing on her shoulders, but she wasn't the only one.

"I am sorry to leave so quickly, but I must go and see what I can do."

≈

Arriving at Alieria's courtyard, Darkess found Prak standing guard at the castle door. There were no walls, only huge amounts of topiaries and shrubbery. In a gruff voice, Prak asked,

"Are you gonna save us, Miss Goodspeed?"

Darkess looked into his face, and for the first time, she saw fear in his eyes. Darkess patted Prak's huge hand and as she passed him on her way inside, she whispered,

"Or die trying."

Prak smiled weakly as she walked past. There were people and creatures everywhere, so many in fact that minus the music, it looked like there was a huge party. But one good look at everyone's body language and faces and Darkess could tell there was definitely not a party in progress. The music was somber and played by an old man trying to sooth the masses. All were wearing a mask of fear and pain, some cowering in corners, silently crying. Some were filthy and obviously half-starved. Darkess felt her stomach clench and turn into a knot. How awful. How silly of me, she thought. It is not only me who is affected here.

Her backbone stiffened, and she raised her eyes looking for Alieria or Janine. Scanning the room, she saw almost a hundred faces, and this was only the first room in this small castle. Darkess headed across the room and towards the kitchens. Maybe she could find someone who'd know where the mistress of the house was. A thick, accented voice was booming in a small room off the hallway that sounded like Alieria.

"But you must stay here, you are much too dangerous to have in a crowded room," came the voice again.

Darkess tapped her knuckles on the door, and it immediately opened, but only a crack. One bright blue eye stared back at her with a strand of blond hair trailing beside it.

"Tasha," Darkess said, relieved.

The door opened, and Tasha stepped out into the corridor, quickly closing the door behind her.

"Who is too dangerous for a crowd?" Darkess asked.

"He's a fire-breather with a bad case of the hiccups. He is a scared mess, and he ate a whole batch of pickled eggs. The combination is evidently deadly for a fire-breather and very smelly too, I might add," Tasha said, pinching her nose.

"Uh-huh," Darkess said, as if she had first hand knowledge, and waited for more.

"Oh, yes, you're here to see Alieria. She is just down the hall. She'll be glad to see you. Our food stores are nearly eradicated, and the city is scared to open their doors to anyone. Fear is rampant here. That pesky demon has come again. He looks for you and the eggs now. I'm so glad I am fire proof, or maybe I wouldn't be so calm. Follow me," Tasha said turning to go, and then added loudly at the door,

"You stay in that room, or you'll burn us out of our sanctuary."

The kitchens were bustling with activity.

"This is the last of the flour, mum," one short chunky woman with an apron hollered.

"Oh, very well then. I shall just have to find some more," Alieria huffed.

Turning to see who was behind her, Alieria smiled when she saw it was Darkess.

"I meant to send word, but as you can see, I have been a little busy. The demon came for you, here, this morning. Burned out my small barn to get my attention. He thinks you have the third egg. Why all of these people came here, I will never know. This is one of the worst places to be right now."

Alieria led Tasha and Darkess down the hall past all the other doors to a solid wall.

"Show me your secret," Alieria whispered, and the wall disappeared.

In the hidden room was Janine, who was writing a list of all the people who were now hiding here in the castle. Their homes were to be raided for food and magical supplies – if any of them was a wizard, anyway. There was a small pile of money on the table next to a list for additional items not found at the homes.

"This is what we collected for food and some more potion supplies. Oh, Darkess, whew, am I glad to see your face. You really must find this demon. We have to kill him, or…" Janine's voice trailed off, as a tear rolled down her cheek.

"I will find him," Darkess reassured her, "or I will die trying."

≈

The ride home was just what she needed. Zaphod ran until he was covered in white foam. Darkess' hair streamed out behind her, whipping in the wind. Tears rolled from her eyes. Whether it was from the speed or the pain was anybody's guess, because her face was set with pure determination. All she kept thinking about was the pain, the suffering, and the fear that had engulfed everyone. I'm not the only one scared half to death. Zaphod's hooves thundered across the hillside as horse and rider became one winding their way between the trees on their way home.

☼

The moon that night was almost full but completely normal in color. Darkess was exhausted from her trip. Nothing more could be done today, so she checked a few things around the castle. The rest of her family had already gone to bed, and she decided to let them sleep. She climbed up to her tower room and looked out her windows for one last check before climbing into bed. There was a torch burning between the large and small barns down in the compound. Wishing that sleep were an option, she put her pack back on and slammed a blue bottle at her feet. Reappearing at the mouth of the bigger barn, Darkess slipped around the corner to find Tanner talking to what looked like an awfully short person in a cloak. The crystal at the end of her staff began to glow faintly. Something evil was in that cloak but nothing too strong, or the glow would have been much brighter.

"I was just coming to find you," Tanner said.

The small person stepped forward and lowered its hood.

"We need to talk," it said.

"What's this?" Darkess looked at Tanner for an answer.

Holding his hand up in a calming gesture, Tanner said quietly, "Now don't get angry. He's here to help."

"What is it? And where did it come from?" Darkess demanded.

"He has been here before and spoke with your grandfather. We believe he may have some insight on our demon problem."

Before Darkess could speak, the creature stepped forward.

"Please, Miss Goodspeed. I believe I can help you. Please let us at least talk."

"Get him in the barn," Darkess said to Tanner.

"We'll talk, but if you lie to me, you'll meet a fate worse than death," Darkess demanded and marched into the barn.

Moments later, the two smaller of the three were sitting on overturned buckets on the floor of a stall. Tanner was on a stool sitting next to them.

"Well?" Darkess stared at the creature before her.

"I am Tuma, from a race of servants called Gilamen. I spoke with your grandfather several months back. I told him that I worked for a very bad wizard. I also told him I might be able to help him, your grandfather, and you save the world from certain destruction. What I did not tell him was that I worked for the half-breed demon Takar. The very demon you seek."

With that said, Darkess jumped to her feet, and using her power, clutched Tuma's throat, lifting him into the air. Tanner grabbed Darkess' arm.

"Wait. Let us hear him out."

When Darkess looked back, she saw the cloak hanging in mid-air, but Tuma had disappeared. Darkess set the flailing form of the lizardman back to the floor. Slowly, she opened her clenched hand, and Tuma sucked in a large breath. The cloaked form trembled violently, but color slowly started to bleed back into his face and hands. Tuma sat back down on the bucket, his tremors still coming in waves.

"Please, go on," Tanner prodded the lizard.

Tanner pulled gently on Darkess' arm, tugging her down on her bucket. When Darkess settled down, Tuma began to speak. With trembling lips and a definite quiver to his voice, he continued.

"I cannot do you any real harm. My magic is not for fighting with, but for service," Tuma swallowed the lump in his throat and rubbed his neck.

"Go on," Darkess said, folding her hands and settling down a little more.

Tuma looked at Tanner and then to Darkess.

"There are rules to magic, as we all know. Limits to your power, as well as consequences with that power, especially if you use it inappropriately. I have rules as a servant. I can't let you into my master's lair, and I can't give you any of his property unless he has instructed me to do so. Of course, if my master should die, the rules of protecting his lair and property no longer apply. Takar has no heir and no mate, so I would receive his belongings," Tuma stopped talking, letting his words sink in.

Darkess and Tanner looked at one another, both thinking the same thing. The eggs. Darkess' body language changed abruptly. Leaning forward, she spoke more sweetly to her prisoner.

"So, why have you come here, exactly?"

"For the demon that he is, even if he is only half, he is young and rash, more like a hormonal youth than the adult in human years that he is. And he's mad. No longer is he just using the dark arts, they control him. They live in his veins, pumping through his body. If he gains control of the third egg, I fear the end of everything. I see blackness, not just dark times, as if it could get any worse than this. No one will survive, not even my master. He will destroy all life everywhere with his ignorance and power," Tuma stopped speaking and looked down at his feet.

"That did not answer my question," Darkess stated slightly stiffer than before.

"I may work for evil beings, but I want to live. That requires getting the eggs away from him, which I can't do, because it requires his death. Now, about every three to four days, Takar goes out on an excursion. He searches for the eggs, and he searches for you. When he returns, he sleeps for a long time. I came here to tell you that he has searched faithfully, and he has to be near the last egg. But you must get to it first. That is where I come in. Hopefully, if he gets near the egg, he'll come home for supplies before going after the clan that holds it. Or, at least he should. Then I can tell you where he is going. If he comes home with the egg, well, we will all be out of luck." Tuma's eyes dropped down once again, and there was fear and sadness in his face.

Darkess thought long and hard before she jumped into some messed up situation she couldn't get out of. Her forehead wrinkled in concentration. This was one of the times she strongly felt the pain of her missing grandfather. His wisdom would be helpful at this point. Beside her, Tanner was also thinking, but more about whether she could make the decision and live with the consequences. Tanner looked at Darkess, and as she began to speak, he turned his view towards Tuma.

"Ok, here is the deal. You do what you normally do. Then, if you do find out where the last egg is before I do, you can come here and tell me. Do not come here for any other reason unless Takar is somehow killed. If you do help us, and it works out, I will insure you are left alone. Double cross me, and I promise you, you will beg me for death."

Tuma's color faded, but he didn't disappear, and a small shudder ran through him.

"You need not threaten me, ma'am. I believe you are true to your word. Besides, the fact that this is my second visit and Takar has yet to find you should prove that I am on your side."

"Well, we shall see," Darkess said as a large teary yawn overcame her.

"Tanner, take Tuma back the way he came. Take great care to reinstall all the defenses. I shall be on my way to my tower. And you," she said looking at Tuma, "best keep your end of the bargain."

≈

The next day dawned rainy and cooler than the previous. Darkess has slept fitfully, dreaming the entire night. She awoke with dry mouth and her linens twisted oddly around her body. Hair in her face made her rub at the sleep in her eyes. Climbing out of bed, she staggered half asleep to the table where she had a pitcher of water and her favorite tea. Holding her hand under her cup, the water bubbled quickly so she tossed in the ground leaves. The aroma helped awaken her more, and as she sipped, she looked out the window at the grounds below. Everything seemed normal for this sodden type of day. Returning to her seat, Darkess checked the color of the staff's crystal before returning to her steaming cup. Chakra purred around the legs of the table, circling Darkess with morning affection.

'What shall today bring?' Darkess projected to her cat.

Silently jumping up onto the table, Chakra sat down, wrapping his tail around him.

'Something is in the air today,' was all he projected.

They stared into each other's eyes.

"Have you heard something?" Darkess asked aloud.

Chakra licked his paw, looked at her cup, and meowed before projecting.

'I just feel it. Magically. Today, something will happen.'

Darkess poured a small amount of her tea into the saucer for her cat. The two of them sat sipping or lapping their tea in deep thought for some time.

≈

Dinner that night was the most boisterous since company from the funeral had left. Conversations flying around the table included everything from the city's troubles and the demon to the lack of food and the weather. New potions had been brewed all day, all the borders checked, and letters sent out. Food had been sent to Alieria's and nothing had changed. The city was terrified. Everyone was asking for some kind of relief from the demon attacks. The Void Commission had their hands full hiding magic, and most of them had quit trying. The outbreak of violence was too widely spread. It seemed to cover the entire civilized world, making it impossible to hide. Alieria, Tasha and Janine were dealing as well as they could. Tuma had not called again, or at least he hadn't tripped any alarms yet. Jori and Harlow had nothing new, and they said the Oracle felt only sadness and fear in massive quantities. Belthazor was overseas somewhere and currently unreachable. Brutus was on a job, procuring items for Alieria. Tanner and Philineas had heard that some kind of lower level mischief demons numbering in the thousands had been put to work by Takar and were attacking the city in his absence.

Takar was trying desperately to find Darkess, and he had been absent from all of the recent attacks. Where had he gone? Why had he left the troublemakers to cause such havoc if he wasn't around to enjoy it? A diversion? Darkess listened to everyone around the table talking and didn't say a word. Even Rufus had joined the family's dinner; an occasion Darkess could only remember happening a few rare times. This is the first dinner without her grandfather that everyone was talking. No one sat quietly, except for Darkess. It is odd, she thought, they don't seem to see me at all. No one is talking to me. It's like I'm not even here, like I'm not involved with the problem at all. Tanner looked back at her as if he had heard her thoughts.

"What troubles you?" he asked.

It seemed so weird to her sometimes that a non-mind reader could hear her thoughts.

"I was just wondering what my next move should be. I can't stay here and just expect Takar to come to me. I have to find him, or I must find the egg. Whichever I do, there will be a fight. The coven that holds the last egg will not part with it easily, nor will they trust an outsider to protect it. I feel so torn. I just don't know what to do next."

The table finally fell silent. Each person at the table knew they could help, at least a little, but when the time was critical, it would be entirely up to Darkess to make her own decision. Being non-magical, it was rather odd that it was Daniel who was first to speak. He placed both hands on his daughter's shoulders and stared deep into her eyes. He released his grip, pushed his chair away from the table, and stood.

"I may not have any magic blood, but I can tell you this – you are one of the most extraordinary people in the world. I'm not just saying that because I am your father. You have had the very best advisors, a family who loves and protects you, and to top it off, you are a very smart witch. Why, even as a babe, you learned to use your powers before you could even walk."

Daniel pushed Darkess' chair back and sat on the edge of the table in front of her. He grabbed her hand and squeezed it.

"My daughter, you are destined to beat this demon. I have heard it said many times how you are the greatest force for good this world has seen in centuries. I believe it, and now you must believe it too. Embrace it. Become what your ancestors believed you would. Look inside yourself. Really dig down deep. Behind your fear, you will find your greatest power."

Darkess looked at her father with a confused look on her face.

"What power is that?" she asked.

Daniel brushed his thumb across the back of her hand and said, "Courage, will and determination."

☼

After dinner, Darkess made her rounds of the castle and checked with Tanner to see how the Vallencourt borders were faring. Darkess checked her pack once again and decided to lighten her load to bare essentials for fighting. This took considerably longer than she had anticipated, because deciding what to take and what to leave behind was literally a life and death decision. She would put an item in then pull one out. Then she would return the item to the pack, go to add another, and end up dumping the pack and starting over again. Wolfbane was hovering near the ceiling, watching Darkess' frustration grow more intense with every item she picked up. Finally, he decided it was time to interrupt Darkess' futile attempt at packing. He slowly floated down to her level and placed himself on a stool close to her.

"You know, with your powers, you can call an item from halfway around the world. Or you could send Zaphod back with a note. Or you could just stop using your fear of being inadequate and shrink some of the items. Simple magic, child. You're trying to make this much harder than it has to be."

Darkess looked at Wolfbane with a flash of anger in her eyes.

"What would you know about it?" Darkess asked sarcastically.

"I heard your father tonight at the dinner table, and he was correct. You must stop doubting yourself," Wolfbane replied.

She knew Wolfbane and her father were right, but that didn't seem to steady the crackle she felt on her nerves. Darkess pulled out her oldest journal, looked in the spell section, and found just what she needed. She couldn't believe she had forgotten such an easy spell. This forced her to think one step further. What else had she forgotten? Quickly, she put a spell on the larger items so they would shrink upon entering the pack and return to full size upon exit. Then she knew what she had to do. She pulled a stack of leather bound books with blank spines down from the shelf and began flipping through her old journals, studying.

Every once in a while, Darkess skipped a large section in her journals, mostly the personal thoughts and things she had witnessed. In other areas, she thought herself to be quite proficient. She was deep into a section she had marked, *Detection of Magic, and Magical Traps*, when a knock came at the door. Darkess pointed to the door and turned her hand slightly to twist the knob. When the door swung open, Silver was standing on the other side.

"How are you doing?" Silver asked her daughter as she entered the room.

"Alright I guess. Just looking through my notes on traps and detection of hidden magic. Trying to check every angle. Anything could be the key to helping me find what I need…without dying," Darkess answered.

Silver stepped over to where Darkess was sitting and opened the box containing Wolfbane's finger bones.

"Taking him along with you?" Silver inquired.

Darkess looked up at her mother, marked her spot with a beaded ribbon, and closed the book.

"I was thinking about it, yes. What do you think?"

"Anything to give you the advantage. He may be able to help," Silver said.

Sticking her fingers down inside the box, Silver's finger brushed one of the bones. She gasped as her eyes clouded over, and her body went rigid. Darkess watched as her mother had an intense vision. It lasted for only a few heartbeats, and then it was over. Silver's eyes began to clear, and she took several deep breaths. Staring at her daughter with a frozen face, she said,

"It's time. I saw a bunch of weird rocks. And there was an opening with a glowing lavender light coming out of it. The mist rolled up on the ground, spilling out with a lavender life of its own. You and Chakra were standing near the opening pondering what to do next. The sun was setting between huge rock formations like I have never seen before. And then it was just gone. Darkess, we need to go to the Deadlands. That is where you will find the last egg."

Before Darkess could say a word, Wolfbane was standing directly next to her.

"Deadlands? Where is this place?" he asked.

Thankfully, Darkess had read a little about them and was able to answer.

"On the southern most point of Xyloidonia, there is a vast desert. As far as the eye can see, there is nothing but sand and more sand. No trees or grass, and only snakes and lizards seem capable of living there. The only birds are scavengers that prey on the poor souls who dare to try and cross it. There is no water. It is a death sentence to even attempt to cross it. Legend has it that there are stone cliffs in a multitude of colors at the other end, a few days journey to the ocean. And we all know that salt water will kill faster than it can save a life, especially when you are already dehydrated. No one has ever come back from trying to cross it, from either the desert or the ocean side."

Wolfbane seemed mystified as Darkess spoke.

"I have seen this place in my dreams," he said.

"Ghosts dream?" Silver asked.

"Ahh no. But when I was alive I had dreams, and I remember them vividly. The opening you described, is it the size of a man, like a silhouette?" Wolfbane asked quickly.

"Why, yes, have you been there?" Silver asked.

"No, just in the dreams. There must be a large concentration of magic beyond that door. Why else would I have seen it?" Wolfbane said excitedly.

"Show me, mother," Darkess said.

Silver took both of Darkess' hands in one of hers and placed the other hand back in the box with Wolfbane's finger bones. Both witches were rocked by the speed of the vision. Both sets of eyes clouded over. But the vision had more to it than the first time. Darkess had actually entered the cave's entrance and left her horse behind. When their eyes cleared, Darkess said,

"Well, wasn't that interesting? It was choppy. First I was with Zaphod then I was disappearing into the cave."

"It is too bad the visions aren't more clear," Silver huffed.

For some odd reason, Darkess felt she had to look out the window. When she gazed up at the sky, she saw that the moon was a deep red. The clouds were wispy, as if trying not to veil the moon too closely and hide its magnificent color. Darkess seemed almost in a trance as she followed her feet to the window to get a broader view. Shoving the windows open, she hung out and peered at the sky. A voice came very softly. It seemed to be coming from the sky. Darkess listened closely and felt no fear.

"Follow your heart, for it knows the way. Look closely at the signs, for they are meant to confuse you. Go to where the sands end and the stones begin. Choose your steps wisely, for some of them will be false. When you reach the treasure, bring it home. You are the only one that can do this with pure intentions. Go safely, and go quickly. Take salt of the earth and water from heaven, for these will be useful tools in your search. Go my child."

The voice trailed away, but Darkess remained staring out the window into the sky.

"Darkess, are you alright? What's the matter?" Silver asked worriedly.

"Didn't you hear her?" Darkess asked.

"Hear who?" Silver asked, giving Wolfbane a wary glance.

"The lady in the sky. She spoke to me. I wonder who she is?" Darkess said, continuing to look at the moon.

Silver made her way over to the window and looked for herself.

"I didn't hear anything," she answered.

"She told me to take salt of the earth and water from heaven with me, and that my heart knew the way. You really didn't hear her?" Darkess' voice trailed away.

Slowly she turned her back to the window and walked around her new room, picking up things that she needed. Turning to her mother, she looked at her blankly for a moment. Silver had learned over the years to wait until her daughter had formed the proper words for whatever she was about to say. Rushing Darkess only caused more trouble. Finally, she spoke.

"I know that you would rather I get a good night's rest, but I can't. I must leave now. Travel by night, and sleep by day, and I will take plenty of supplies."

Darkess continued plucking items from the tables and shelves here and there.

"Can I help you?" Silver asked.

Darkess knew that this was just killing her mother, but she was doing a good job of hiding it so far.

"I need salt of the earth and water from heaven. Oh, and if you could have Roxy make me some traveling food, I would really appreciate it." Darkess felt like she was condescending to her mother, but what else could she do. Her mother had already played her part for now.

"Not to worry, I will take care of it," Silver said, making her way to the door. "Is there any thing else I can do?"

Darkess went to her mother, gave her a hug, and whispered in her ear.

"Thank you, Mother. I love you."

"I love you too, dear," Silver said as she closed the door behind her with a sad look on her face.

≈

Sometime later, Darkess was heading for the kitchens when she noticed the crystal on her staff was glowing blue. Intruder! She dashed for the outside door. Running to the end of the stone landing, Darkess threw a potion at her feet and was gone in a billow of blue smoke. Arriving at Tanner's shack, she banged furiously on his door. Tanner did not answer.

"Oh, where are you?" Darkess said throwing another potion at her feet.

This time Darkess appeared near the large barn. Checking her crystal, the color had begun to pulse.

"What!" Darkess hissed.

Something had made it past the outer perimeter. Darkess scanned the areas she could see. Nothing was visible, so she closed her eyes and tried to sense what was out there and where it was.

"Take these human eyes from me that can't see in the dark, and replace them with the eyes of a cat, so I can see in light so stark."

Darkess opened her eyes, and it was as if everything was new. She could see unbelievably well. There was a flying squirrel scampering up a tree, and one of the barn cats was watching it with fervor. A field mouse ran around the corner. Then she saw movement down by the gates. Tanner was there. What was he doing? She walked swiftly towards him as he began to return to the castle.

"What have you got? Has Tuma returned?" Darkess demanded, nearly out of breath.

"Sorry for the alarm, it was just a skull rat. You know how they love to steal and eat magical charms. It had a hold of one of the talismans and was trying to tear it from the gate. He won't be causing any one any more trouble," Tanner said, wiping the blood off of his blade before putting it in its scabbard.

Darkess grimaced slightly, and her shoulders slumped. She had been hoping for news of Takar. No such luck. They walked in silence as Darkess calmed her nerves.

"I see you are ready to do battle," Tanner mentioned.

"I am leaving tonight. Much has happened since I saw you at dinner earlier. I would love to tell you all about it, but I haven't the time. I am going to the Deadlands. Travel by night, sleep by day, you understand. Mother will tell you everything," Darkess said.

When they reached the barn, Tanner turned to Darkess and grabbed her by the shoulders.

"I will have Rufus ready Zaphod. How long before you leave?" Tanner asked.

"I just need to grab a few things inside, and then I am going."

"I will meet you by the kitchens' side door as soon as we are ready. And Darkess, whatever happens…think first, then react. Use your heart, and most of all, be careful," Tanner squeezed Darkess' shoulders then hugged her.

Releasing her, he turned swiftly and slipped into the barn. That was the second time someone had told her to use her heart.

≈

In the kitchens, Roxy and Silver were wrapping up packages in waxed linen. Darkess had replenished her teleport potions, grabbed a couple more items they stored in the kitchens, and met up with her mother. Roxy had made her meals for seven days. Cheese, dried venison and beef, tiny loaves of bread, fruited paste muffins, dried fruit, and boiled corn balls called corn dodgers, one of Darkess' favorites. Roxy also hid a couple of candies at the bottom of the bag. Darkess would always be the baby of the castle to her, no matter her age or responsibility. If her food run out before her job was finished, there were a couple of bladders – one with water and one with a potion for strength and clarity. Silver had gone through storage and pulled out a leather bag of peter salt from a mine near the Copper Sands Desert. Then she had gone out to the rain barrels, something Roxy normally would have done, and filled three large bladders full.

"Salt from the earth and water from heaven," Silver said as she placed the items by the door for Darkess.

Angela and Daniel had been called down to say goodbye to Darkess. She hugged each one and said something special to all of them. She also gave her grandmother the crystal staff while she was gone.

"I hope to be back before seven days is through, but in truth, I have no idea when I will come home. Send me word if anything happens. The birds should be able to find me. Well, I guess I am off for the Copper Sands Desert then on to the Deadlands." Swiftly turning, Darkess grabbed her things and slipped through the door.

Quickly Daniel caught up with her and helped with the bags of water. When they reached the bottom of the short steps, Rufus and Tanner were bringing Zaphod around the corner. Zaphod had on a new saddle.

"Wow, don't you look dressed for battle," Darkess said to her horse.

Rufus, a man of few words, stepped up and handed her the reins. Darkess threw the reins on Zaphod's back, ignoring them. Rufus patted the horse.

"Tanner and I worked on this over the winter. Knew you'd be needin' a sturdy, lightweight one without the shiny stuff. Special made for you, Missy, to hold bladders of water, bedroll, pack, and extra feed bags. You like it then?" Rufus shuffled his feet a little as he spoke.

"Oh, yes, it's perfect," Darkess replied and hugged the shy man.

"Come back soon, Missy Darkess," Rufus said, turning a bright shade of pink, then he ambled off to the barn and was gone.

Tanner and Daniel both chuckled when he was out of sight.

"Poor man. He loves you, but you'd never hear it from him. Besides the animals, he loves you the most," Tanner said.

Darkess hopped on Zaphod and adjusted her cloak. Angela's lip was quivering, and Silver was crying quietly at Darkess' feet while Daniel rubbed their backs in a comforting way. Roxy was blowing her nose off to the side, and Tanner was giving last-minute instructions.

"The feed bags have enough food for one week and no longer. You will have to search for water, neither of you can carry enough for a week," Tanner said.

"Use my spells. They will help you," Roxy sniffed.

"Thank you, all of you. I will miss you. But I will be home as soon as I can," Darkess said.

Telling Zaphod to run to the gate, they turned on their heels and took off down the trail towards the road. Silver gave chase for twenty or so steps before she stopped. She was crying hard by this point, and her vision had turned to ribbons. Daniel caught up to her and held her tightly, letting her sob it out while he watched his daughter's back getting smaller.

"I'm sending my baby to do battle alone! What kind of mother am I?" Silver sobbed into her husband's chest.

Angela, Tanner, Roxy and Daniel all saw as Darkess reached the castle border gates. Zaphod turned back and Darkess waved goodbye to her family. From the distance, no one could see the tears threatening to spill over Darkess' eyes. And nobody could see the lump in her throat. She almost told Zaphod to go back. But she didn't. She knew what was at stake, and she knew she had to go. So she told her horse their destination. Silver turned back towards her daughter just in time to see her disappear.

☼

The sands were wind rippled, but she couldn't see it. The stars shone brightly in the sky, but the moon was nowhere to be seen. Everything was coal black around her. The wind was absent, and the air was hot and stagnant. Darkess jumped from Zaphod down onto the warm sand. Not a sound could be heard. She felt as if she had been packed in cotton and stuffed into a crate. Since she wasn't sure where she was exactly, she pulled out her grandfather's night shine and her golden egg. And though she was almost certain she was alone, she pulled her robes up around her head to shielding herself from prying eyes.

"Illuminate," she whispered.

The crystal began to glow, and in the palm of her hand rested her directional egg.

"Show me south, to the Deadlands," Darkess whispered.

The egg spun around in her hand half a dozen times before coming to rest. Darkess swiveled her body around so she was facing exactly the way the egg was pointing.

"Dark," she whispered again and flipped off her robes, which were threatening to suffocate her even more.

She stood next to Zaphod, facing south, and projected her thoughts to him.

'Can you see out there?'

Zaphod snorted, shook his head, and answered.

'It's quite dark, but if we walk, I can find our way.'

Satisfied with Zaphod's response, she returned to the saddle, and they started their walk across the uncrossable desert. They were silent. Only the muffled crunch of sand beneath four hooves could be heard. After a while, Darkess realized she had been staring at the constellation Draconian and finally recognized what it was.

"Of course," she said aloud.

Zaphod's ears twitched at the sound of her voice after the long quiet. She remembered what she had heard only a couple of hours before and what they had been teaching her for years. Watch for the signs. This has to be a sign, Darkess thought. She intended to follow it.

Minutes seemed like hours here in the silent desert, and Darkess found herself yawning with fatigue and boredom. A lack of stimulation allowed sleepiness to set in. Emotionally drained and physically exhausted, her tears flowed with every yawn. But she knew she must stay awake. Keep moving. Time was of the essence. She slapped her face and shook her head, twisting around in the saddle. But when she dropped her arms back down again, she began to slump again. She sat staring up at the stars, and slowly, they plodded on.

☼

Three fireballs exploded against the stones in the wall, leaving large black marks and cracked mortar. Takar was squatting down on the floor, clutching his head and rocking back and forth on the balls of his feet. He was spewing obscenities and spittle in his attempt to calm himself.

"Where could it beeee?" he screamed, slamming a fist into his own head.

"Think dammit, think!" he wailed, falling to the floor in the fetal position and sobbing like a child.

Tuma stayed invisible just beyond the doorway, watching his master fall into deeper chaos with himself. Takar had finally cracked into two separate beings: the skilled and calculating demon with no mercy and the sniveling half-human who craved power but wanted his mommy at the same time. He was incapable of dealing with the combination. Takar lay whimpering on the floor, mumbling to himself. Then, as if he were a new person, he sat back up, rubbed the tears and snot on his sleeve, and sniffed a couple of times. He sat staring at his map now dotted with flags. It seemed to be mocking his failure to find the third egg.

He looked around the room, and spotting a flag inches from his foot, he got an idea. His facial features changed from one of grief and madness to one of shrewd thinking. Plucking up the flag, Takar tossed it like a knife at the map. Its tip came to rest in the Deadlands. Takar had never been near this place. No one could survive out there, so he had deemed it an unlikely location for a coven of magical beings. Between the deadly sandstorms, the escalating 120-degree heat of day, and the lightning storms caused by the severe heat, it was fraught with danger. No food or water for hundreds of miles meant eventual death to those who tried the desert's patience, for it had an eternity to claim its prey. Victims only lasted as long as their supplies and their strength. So Taker knew he would have to be careful.

Standing up, Takar took a closer look at his map. Tuma watched his master's every movement from the doorway. Touching the map, he closed his eyes as if he were getting information through his fingers.

"I am not human. I will survive," Takar whispered to the map.

Suddenly, Takar released the map and began moving swiftly around the room, mumbling and tossing things about. Occasionally, he would keep a hold of something and toss the next item as if it were garbage.

"Tuma!" Takar roared.

A shiver ran through the small creature, and he slipped quietly away from the door.

"Tuma! Get in here now!" Takar demanded.

Knowing the pain he would feel later if he did not respond, Tuma reappeared and walked towards the doorway. He was pretending to be breathless as he said,

"Yes sir, what is your wish?"

Bowing slightly and looking apprehensively into Takars' face, Tuma held his breath.

"Make sure Crystal City is awake all night. Keep our little friends busy. Tear the city apart. I want the living hell scared out of everyone tonight. I want that little witch kept busy until I return with the last egg. Terrorize them until I return. Do you understand me? I don't care if I am gone for a month, do not let them stop. Give our friends whatever they want, just don't let them stop. Now go!" Takar ordered.

Tuma trotted off quickly to follow his master's instructions, but he planned on warning Darkess. Upon returning to the room Takar had been in earlier, he found his master had already left. The realization of what he was about to do made his color diminish to half-strength. A shiver passed through him as he ran from the room. His family would deem his actions traitorous, but he decided that possibly being called a traitor would be far more preferable than a world with no life at all. The color returned to Tuma as he ran quicker with his mission now set in his mind.

≈

The edge of the sky was becoming a lighter shade of blue, and Darkess realized morning was on its way. Soon the world would be visible to her. Finally. At first, Darkess was excited then a feeling of dread overcame her. The light could possibly bring prying eyes and would surely bring on the intense heat. They would need to find or make shelter. Walking further on towards the south, the sun slowly rose in the sky, finally spilling its full light upon the desert. The temperature rose quickly, and the only shadows were behind the small mounds of sand dotting the ground.

Darkess noticed how shocking she and Zaphod looked compared to the landscape. This is not going to work, she thought. Her sense of urgency was piqued, and she jumped off Zaphod and headed for the shade in a small dune. They were lower here than any of the surrounding area and temporarily shielded from the sun. Once she got Zaphod to lie down, they were also hidden from direct line of sight.

Pulling out two poles, Darkess rammed them into the sand. A large piece of muslin from her pack stretched out nicely over them, draping down behind them and leaving a large enough opening to see out for a short distance. Not only did it shield them from the oncoming sun and prying eyes, but it kept the sand off as well, which provided them a place to sleep. The first thing Darkess decided to do was write a spell that would change the color of her leather clothing and Zaphod's fur by day and return it to normal by night. Cover and concealment, she thought, my best way of getting to where I need without any extra trouble.

After eating a quick meal and making sure Zaphod was properly fed, she fell asleep with her back against him. Chakra had snuck into one of her bags and finally crawled out. He was lying in front of her, guarding the open lean-to flap.

'Finally decided to come out did you?' Zaphod snorted at Chakra.

'She can't send me back now, can she?' Chakra projected snottily.

'Wouldn't bet on it if I were you,' Zaphod projected.

Chakra whipped his tail around, annoyed. But Zaphod was glad the cat had snuck along and surprised that Darkess hadn't found him already. Soon Zaphod's head was lying on his leg and he was fast asleep. Chakra turned to face the opening and sat watching the sands blow slightly in the breeze.

≈

Tuma arrived at Vallencourt Castle shortly after daybreak, around the same time Chakra had crept from his hiding place. Tanner was making his first rounds of the borders. Riding his old horse, they trotted towards the main gates only to find the talismans swinging wildly although there was no wind. Taking a closer look, Tanner noticed the familiar yellow eyes of Tuma floating in the shrubbery next to the gates.

"Well, well, back again, are we?" Tanner said.

Mumbling a reversal charm on the gate, it swung open just enough to allow the small lizard in. Tuma let the color return to his body as he explained that Takar had gone again, this time to the Deadlands. Without a response, Tanner slammed the gates shut, re-establishing the protection charm. He jumped on his horse, yanking Tuma up by his collar, and dropping the small Gilaman in front of him. Yanking his horse's head around and digging in his heals, they thundered up the path towards the castle, dirt flying up behind them in great clods.

≈

Once Tuma was inside the castle, and he had told the remaining family about his plight, they all decided that Darkess should know that she wasn't alone in that vast desert. Angela immediately made her way to the tower, and sent out an urgent message to her granddaughter. Takar was on her trail, or right in front of her, either way she would have to use more caution. As the little bird made its way into the sky, message secured tightly to its leg, Angela whispered.

"Fly swiftly, Darkess' life may depend on it."

☼

Takar reached the desert when the sun had been in the sky for nearly an hour. The heat was already oppressive, but it was the light that seemed to cause Takar the most discomfort. He ripped a piece of material from the bottom of his grimy shirt and tied it around his head, cutting slits in the fabric to allow less light and still keep a good view. He scanned the land, turning slowly in place to see all the way around him. He saw nothing except sun, sand, and small shadows cast by the dunes that dotted the landscape. There was really nothing that caught his interest, so he turned towards the south and started walking.

Digging through his pockets, Takar checked his dragon egg detector but was disappointed when he got no response from it. Somehow he controlled his urge to panic and continued on. About an hour later, Takar had taken refuge in the shadow of a large dune. Hiding from the sun, he drank some water and realized he was getting quite hungry. As he dug through the pockets of his large cloak, he realized in his haste he had forgotten to pack food. Scanning the dune for signs of animals, he noticed the only prints were his. Nothing moved except for the shimmers of heat, even the breeze had died off. Not a lizard or even a bug was in sight, and Takar's stomach growled even louder. When was the last time he had eaten? He wasn't sure, and now he was getting really angry, and his stomach seemed to rule his temper at the moment. His heart thumped with increasing hunger, and he began to sweat more profusely. In an attempt to both cool and calm himself, he lay down in the sand. He closed his eyes for a moment. Slowly he gained some semblance of control and opened his eyes just in time to see a small bird fly over.

By reflex, he heaved a fireball at the bird. His aim was true, and the bird burst into flames, plummeting to the ground. Jumping to his feet, Takar crawled up to the top of the dune and looked for his fallen meal. He spotted a stream of smoke just over the next crest. The smoking, charred remains of the bird lay in a shaded area, and he leaped on it. Ripping the bird into two pieces, he gnawed at the tiny wings. The steam burned his lips and tongue as he devoured the small meal. Not until he was chewing on the minute drumsticks did he realize that there was a small melted silver tube attached to one leg. Licking his lips, he wished the bird had been larger. He looked at the leg and twirled it in his fingers. He wondered if it had been a messenger bird. As he wrestled with the idea for a moment, he questioned who could be waiting for a message way out here in this awful desolate place. His eyes shifted from side to side, and he realized he wasn't alone out here. He crawled up the dune and peeked over the edge at the top. His eyes darted across the skyline searching for the person who should have received a message. He repeated his steps and turned in place looking around and seeing nothing.

"Damn," Takar spat as he sat down in the shade again.

Now he regretted killing the bird. If he had let it fly, he could have found who else was out here with him. He slammed his fist down into the sand, angry with himself for his weakness.

"Fool," he whimpered, swatting sand in his fury.

Just as quickly as he turned to rage, his face straightened, and he climbed out of the depression he had dug. He began to slowly walk south and tried to keep his head above ground, trudging behind dunes to stay as hidden as he could.

≈

Dreams stirred Darkess as she slept, which woke Zaphod. Chakra had made a circle on their small refuge, looking for any signs of life and finding none. Upon returning to the opening, he saw Darkess twitching in her sleep and Zaphod nuzzling her.

'What's wrong?' Chakra asked Zaphod.

'Must be a bad dream,' came the reply.

A fireball appeared in Darkess' hand. Zaphod stood up and quickly tried to get away from it. In doing so, he pulled the small lean-to off its poles, disturbing everything and waking Darkess. Immediately she saw the fireball burning in her hand. Gasping, she squeezed her hand shut and extinguished the flame. She rubbed her eyes, looked around confused for a moment, realized where she was, and jumped to her feet. Zaphod was thrashing his head around, tangled in the muslin fabric. Darkess pulled her horse free of the fabric then scanned the skyline. The sun had already passed its apex, and the shadow that had shaded her lean-to was completely gone. The heat was intense and oppressive; making it feel like the air was low in oxygen. Darkess actually felt as though physical weight was holding her down. Heat waves rolled across the dunes. The light shone so brightly it almost blinded her. Darkess had never been to such a place, and it was daunting to her.

The time she had spent in Imhotepus was fleeting, but the structures there proved that life had indeed existed. But this place is barren. The land of heat and nothing, she thought as she replaced the poles and flipped the material out in an effort to recover her nesting area. She knew she still had a few hours before she should start back out on her search, so she crawled back inside. Zaphod also lowered himself back down into the shade.

"And just how did you get here?" Darkess asked, annoyed.

'I'm the day guard while you sleep,' Chakra projected.

"I didn't pack food or water for you," Darkess snapped.

'Never mind that. What was all that business with the fireball?' Chakra asked, and Zaphod perked up his ears.

"We're not alone. Someone near is using magic. I never felt the pull of magic before, at least not like this. Must be the remoteness of the area."

Not half a day's walk away, Takar was foolishly walking during the day. She never saw a thing, but she felt him coming.

≈

The sun was finally setting when Darkess began to pack up her things, readying herself to move on. Rolling up the muslin that had made up her temporary home, she smiled when she saw the fur on Zaphod begin to turn back to its original black.

"It's working perfectly," she said and shoved the roll into her pack.

Before the light became too dim, she pulled out her golden egg and reconfirmed her directions.

"Show me south" she whispered.

The egg spun quickly on her palm, stopping to point due south. Climbing up from the crater she had called home for a day, she peered over the edge in the direction that the egg had indicated. Ripples of sand rolled away from her as far as she could see. The vastness was overwhelming as she looked for something other than sand in the far distance. Seeing nothing, she drew a line in the sand that pointed the way then she returned to the base of the dune.

Zaphod was fully adorned in his black coat, and so was she. Darkess scanned the sand, checking to make sure they hadn't forgotten anything. She dug her fingers through the sand where she had set her pack to make double sure she didn't leave anything behind. Finally satisfied that she had all of her belongings collected and the light was no longer so threatening, she climbed aboard her horse. Chakra jumped up also, pawed the bag behind the saddle, and laid down for a nap.

Remembering the pull of power she had felt earlier, Darkess decided to use as little magic as possible. Zaphod had seen the line in the sand, and when she pointed to it, he understood. The three of them set off for a long night of walking with Zaphod kicking the line out of the sand on his way over it.

≈

Takar had rested now and again but had continued his walk all during the afternoon and on into the night. He had stayed to the shadowed dunes as much as possible, but that made walking much more difficult. Now that the sun had set, he could stay on more level ground. The temperature finally dropped to a more tolerable level, and he found that he liked the night here much better than the day. When darkness claimed the land, he no longer had to worry about being seen, and he walked more boldly. Once it became too dark for him to see, he decided to take a longer rest.

His stomach was growling again, and he had drunk most of his water. Takar found a small depression in the sand, and he crawled into it. Hungry and tired, he curled up in the fetal position and tried to quiet his squalling belly. Before too long, he was fast asleep.

≈

The stars were glowing brightly in the night sky. Darkess had never realized just how bright until she had come to this dark and desolate place. There was nothing else to look at here in the dead of night but the stars. So she concentrated on them, naming all of the constellations she knew, even spotting a few she had never seen. Darkess had never been so far from home on her own before, and she was doing anything to keep her overactive imagination busy. She wasn't afraid of the dark, per say, but what may be hiding in its useful black cloak. Every so often she would ask Zaphod what he could see, and his reply was always the same. Rolling sand and shadows.

Night two, she thought to herself, I wonder how many nights until I will see something? The rhythmic steps of Zaphod were a comfort to her as they trudged on through the soft sand.

"I'm scared Zaphod. What if I'm not the right person for this? What if I mess it all up?" Darkess asked.

Zaphod stopped and craned his head back towards Darkess and blew warm air out of his nose at her.

'Without fear, there could be no courage.' He projected.

'Couldn't have said it better myself.' Chakra added.

Zaphod pointed his head back toward the south and continued on.

≈

Stopping every so often to rest and check their direction, Darkess noticed a slight breeze. Small snakes of sand slithered over the dunes, but other than that, there was no movement or sound. She knew she should do whatever she could not to give away her position, so she hummed softly in an attempt to calm her tingling nerves and keep the wariness of the long dark night of travel at bay. Zaphod came to a stop and swiveled his head back and forth.

"What's out there?" Darkess asked, tensing up.

'Calm down, it's just a cavern. A deep one though, and we will have to find another way around. It is way too dangerous to try in the dark.'

'Do you think we should wait until morning, or try to go around now?' Darkess projected back to Zaphod.

'Would you like me to scout?' Chakra asked before Zaphod could answer.

'Since the only way for me to see would be to use more magic, I guess you better take a look.'

Chakra stretched and looked down. Silently, he jumped down to the sand.

'Give me a few minutes,' Chakra said, slipping silently down into the cavern.

'Glad you brought him along now?' Zaphod asked.

"Hmmph," Darkess' replied.

After a minute or two, the silence was becoming as maddening as the near blindness.

'Can you see him?' Darkess asked Zaphod.

'No, he was gone after a dozen steps or so.'

Darkess smirked into the darkness and jumped from her saddle. She was trying to scan the black hole in front of her, but it was no use. Moments seemed like hours as she awaited the return of her faithful familiar. Slowly, Darkess lowered herself down onto the edge of the abyss. There was a stone shelf under the sand, and she dug her fingers through it with anxiety. Just as quietly as he left, Chakra returned. Suddenly it seemed like he was just beside her, eyes flashing in the starlight.

'If he can follow my lead, I believe we can make it,' Chakra projected. 'But we will need to use your grandfather's night shine.'

Darkess smirked again. She hadn't wanted to use any magic.

'How long will it take to go around?' Darkess projected to her cat.

Chakra's tail flipped as he searched the landscape around them.

'We'll lose the rest of the night's travel, possible some of the next night's, too. And we will be exposed this close to the edge of a cavern. I don't think it would be a smart move, do you?' Chakra projected.

Darkess weighed her choices carefully. One way or the other posed the threat of being seen, by what she wasn't sure. Either way, there was a risk, but the day time exposure seemed the worst of the two scenarios.

"Well Zaphod, ole buddy, we're going in. Think you're up for it?" Darkess asked.

With a tiny whinny and a shake of his head, he snorted at her.

'I go where you go,' he projected.

Darkess exhaled sharply.

"This, boys, is where the journey really begins," Darkess said.

Pulling the night shine from her pack, she took a few tentative steps down, feeling her way with one arm and her feet. Once Zaphod had disappeared from her sight, she held the crystal out at waist height and whispered,

"Illuminate."

☼

Vallencourt Castle had become refuge for several magical creatures and people, but not near the amount Alieria was dealing with. Terror now ruled the city as well as the country. Everyone was tired, hungry, and scared to death. Silver had been pacing the castle, trying to look busy, but proving unsuccessful. Finally, when no return letter came from Darkess, she could stand it no more. Climbing the stairs to the tower, she went to the mirror and rubbed its frame, thinking. Did she really want to know what Darkess was doing? Did she want to know what was happening, even if it meant she had to watch her daughter die? Or even worse, find her already dead? Silver tapped the frame and considered her options. Deal with not knowing, or deal with knowing.

"Show me Darkess," Silver said in a trembling voice.

The mirror become black, then a glow appeared. Darkess was leading her horse down some sort of ravine. She looked safe. But why hadn't she written back? The load on Silver's shoulders lightened somewhat, but she was not fine by any stretch of the imagination. Her heart still felt heavy that her daughter was out there alone dealing with the weight of the world, but at least she could tell every one that she was still alive and trying to help. That would give some of the more distraught people something good to think about while they fought for their lives.

≈

Takar stirred in his sleep, restless with dreams. He saw his mother, his father, and his two eggs waiting at home for him, and he smiled. He saw a warm glow, just around the corner in another room, and he walked towards it. But every corner he turned brought him no closer to the light. So he began to walk faster. For some reason, he felt that he had to see the light, find the source of it. Finally he was at a dead run, and still the light eluded him.

"What the hell?" Takar mumbled and stirred in his sleep, his limbs twitching.

Suddenly he jerked so hard in his sleep that he woke himself. He looked at the pitch black all around him and momentarily forgot where he was.

"Dream, only a dream," Takar yawned and rolled back over, quickly falling asleep in the warm sand.

The dream began again, and the light with no source was there.

≈

Darkess couldn't believe her eyes. The coppery sands had given way to copper colored stones, even boulders after awhile. Gently placing each foothold, the threesome made their way down the steeply sloped cavern. Zaphod's hooves made the most noise, clopping on the larger stones and grinding on the smaller ones. Chakra, of course, made no sound as he led them deeper into the ground. The breeze they felt earlier was more of a wind deep beneath the sandy desert. Thankfully, the wind helped to cover the noise they were making. Unfortunately, Darkess thought, it could hide other noises that she would rather hear, like something laying in wait.

Darkess had to tear her eyes away from the spectacular stones and pay more attention to what may be out there. Six eyes shifted from the ground below to the darker shadows and back again. A small rockslide made them all freeze in their tracks, searching for what had started it. Darkess aimed her night shine where she thought she had seen movement. Clinging to the side of a large boulder was a six-legged skink, tongue lolling out, and it was panting quickly. Darkess closed her hand. She hadn't even realized that she had opened and clutched at the cloak on her chest. She had been so tense that she started to shake a little, now that the threat had passed without incident. Pointing at this curious creature, she started to giggle at her jumpiness. It was the first living thing she has seen since she left her family behind. The crystal's light shone brightly on its iridescent skin, yet the color was the same as the boulders it clung to – except for its eyes, which were a brilliant turquoise. Looking at Darkess, it cocked its head, maybe calculating its chances. It blinked at Darkess and its panting slowed. She decided she would try to talk to it.

'Don't be afraid, little one, I will not harm you,' Darkess projected.

The skink blinked again and slightly changed its position, still staring at the intruders.

'Can you hear me?' Darkess projected.

The skink licked its own eye and then around the rest of its face. Then it merely blinked once more, still staring at her. In what was more of a squeak than a voice, she finally heard an answer.

'Of course I can hear you. I've been hearing you the entire way. Haven't seen a witch in years. Didn't know what to make of it.'

Darkess looked at Chakra then Zaphod, who both had the same surprised expressions.

'How many years since you have seen a witch?' Darkess asked.

'Don't rightly know, to tell you the truth,' the skink replied.

Darkess thought for a moment then countered another question.

'Where was the last place you saw a witch?'

The skink stuck its tongue out, licked its other eye, and replied with a shiver, 'The Dead Lands, miss.'

Scampering down the side of the rock he had been on, he laid down on the stones below.

'Bad place. Can't stay there long. Too hot, no water.'

Chakra had settled down. He wrapped his tail around his feet and paid very close attention to the skink. Zaphod had lowered his head to get a closer look.

'Can you tell us how far until we reach the Dead Lands?' Darkess asked.

'Took me a week to reach this safe haven. Don't know how long it will take you.'

Darkess had to mash her lips together to keep from laughing.

'One more thing…is there anything else living here in this place?'

The skink looked nervous but only said,

'You should have nothing to fear, only small things to hunt for food.'

Darkess held out both hands.

'I have no intentions of eating you,' Darkess said to ease the skinks nervousness.

There came a small clicking noise. Darkess noticed a rock-like bug crawling along. The skink noticed too, and in a flash, he scampered over to it, lashed out his tongue, and the bug was gone.

'Only small things to hunt. Never let a meal pass you by out here,' the skink said, and with that, he slipped into a crack in the rocks and was gone.

'Interesting fellow,' Chakra projected, and he continued on down the path.

'His legs were short, but also very fast,' Darkess projected to no one in particular. 'I wonder how long the journey to the Dead Lands will take us?'

After a few more minutes, Darkess was glad to feel the ground level off. They had finally reached the bottom of the canyon. Darkess decided they should take a break while the terrain allowed for one. There were a few pieces of old wood lying about, where they came from Darkess didn't know, but she was sure glad they were there. She was suddenly excited. Collecting a meager pile, she thought it would be nice to have a small fire to look at for just a little while and maybe heat up some of the meat she had in her pack.

Darkess closed her eyes and cleared her thoughts. With all of her senses, she felt for magic around her. She felt her horse and her cat, but beyond that, she felt nothing. She believed she was alone and opened her eyes. Tossing a fireball at the pile of wood, it immediately caught life. Darkess crossed her ankles and slipped to her bum on the sandy canyon floor facing the small fire. It wasn't that she needed the warmth, but it was a comforting feeling to have a fire. Made any place seem less frightening. The flames tossed about in the wind, but Darkess found it perfect for making her dinner.

As she and her companions consumed their meals, they watched the flames and the show they performed on the rocks all around. The light was much brighter than she anticipated with the glittery reflections dancing all around her. She wanted to quench it, but in her heart, she knew the amazing show she was witnessing was something special. This was a thing of beauty in a world of desolation, in a place of death. It was a once in a lifetime sight. The stones almost came to life with the fire, and for a few minutes, she didn't want to leave. She felt as if she were in the most spectacular place for just a moment. There were no words to describe it, not diamond like, for it was much darker than any diamond. And not geode like, because there were no crystals. It was just beautiful, entertaining, alive.

But like all good things, this had to end. It was only a slight pause in their journey. Darkess finished her food and packled away all of the eating utensils. She looked back at the fire and saw it was dwindling quickly.

"We must press on," Darkess said.

Pausing to look at her companions, she added,

"When the fire burns down."

☼

The path up the other side of the canyon seemed much steeper. They had to weave around huge boulders, and the going was treacherous. They continued up the path for what seemed like twice the time it took to descend the other side. Darkess rubbed at her thighs, trying to alleviate the growing knots and tingling, but she did not stop. She fought the urge to use magic several times along the way. The closer they were to the desert floor, the closer they were to danger. She couldn't explain how she knew this, she just did. Something else was in the desert with them. What was it? The coven? The egg? A demon? Takar? Had he figured it out? Or is my imagination just eating at me?

The dark tended to narrow vision to the finest of points. She needed to concentrate on the trail. One slip, and she could get injured, give herself away, or worse die. One was just as deadly as the next. Looking ahead, she realized Chakra was getting further and further ahead. Get out of this pit and pay attention, she told herself then increased her pace.

The trail here ran level with the desert floor, maybe twenty feet or so from it. Chakra, being on the point, was looking for a trail wide enough for Zaphod to pass. After a few minutes, Darkess realized they were near the top when she could actually see the edge without light from the night shine. The sun was coming up. They just had to find a way out of the canyon. Somewhere there was an edge they could reach. They walked further towards the rising sun, which seemed to be in a hurry to start the day. Darkess knew they would have to find shelter before too long. Looking down, she saw that her clothes were now entirely tan, which meant the sun had cleared the horizon in its entirety. The hair on the nape of her neck was standing up. She was on full alert, and with the added advantage of daylight, she felt the need to move much more quickly. Then she saw it. A cave. A giant slab of the copper-colored stone had fallen from its resting place and landed on huge piles of rockslide debris. It was a little ways back down into the cavern, but it was hidden better than you would expect for its size.

'Shelter,' was the only word Darkess projected to her companions.

Chakra bolted towards it while Zaphod only pricked his ears toward Darkess and watched Chakra run to check it out. When Chakra reached the cave, he disappeared inside. Darkess wasn't too far behind and quickly projected to her cat, 'Wait for me!'

She slid to a stop in front of the cave and saw that it wasn't very deep, just big enough for the three of them. The floor was covered with fine sand, making it more comfortable. And there was a small ledge where she could put her pack. There were no signs that it was occupied by anything, man or beast, so they decided to make themselves at home. Darkess was exhausted, and so were her traveling companions, and the three settled in quickly. It didn't take long before Darkess' eyes began to droop, and she was asleep before the sun cleared the edge of the gorge.

≈

The sun had reached its zenith, unbeknownst to the weary travelers slumbering in their cave. After Takar woke up, he realized where he was and began to travel again. He walked farther than he should have before he stopped. He felt dizzy, and the sun blazed overhead, making him feel like he was being baked alive. Digging into the sand, he buried himself to escape the heat. His water was now gone, his head ached, and his stomach tormented him with its grumbling. He had to find food and water, and there was no way out of this place.

He felt scared every time he tried to draw his portal in the sand, and the shapes melted, making them too indistinct to get him out of the desert. He had to find some stone to write on, or he'd surely perish out here. At this point, he was too sick to conger up any real anger, but he held on to what little anger he could, because fear would overwhelm him, and then he would definitely die. He remained in the cocoon of his cloak, mostly buried until he thought the sand had cooled a little around him. Poking his head out, he saw shadows were starting to creep over where he lay. Throwing back his cloak, he lay fanning his shirt on his chest in an attempt to cool himself before continuing on his way.

Rolling over on his knees, Takar peeked over the small dune he was in. There was a ravine in the desert floor not two hundred yards from where he kneeled now. Why hadn't he seen it before? There has to be stones down there. He could collect enough stones to draw each symbol on a separate stone then he could get home. He would collect more supplies and figure out if this desert was worth coming back to or not. He checked his dragon egg detector, but it was unresponsive. He returned it to his pocket and staggered to his feet. He was in the beginning stages of delirium, and he stumbled towards the gorge he had seen.

When Takar had covered about half the distance to the ravine, he wobbled sideways several steps and collapsed on his knees. He looked towards the canyon and knew he must reach it. Clawing his way through the sand, dragging his legs forward slowly one at a time, he managed to make some progress. The sun made him squint, and his brain felt like it was boiling. His tongue was dry as the sand he clawed through, and if he had a tear to spare, it would have leaked out of his eyes from the exertion. The ledge of the canyon loomed ahead. With a few more handfuls of sand, he finally reached it. Looking down, he saw the shade below, and he rolled off the edge, slipping down the side into the blessed shadows beneath.

≈

The sound of sliding rocks roused Chakra from his sleep. He yawned and stretched, trying to shake off some of the fatigue from last night's jaunt. Taking great care not to wake Darkess and Zaphod, Chakra padded over to the ledge of the small cave to take a look. There were no sounds now, and he saw no movement. Staying in the shadow of the cave's mouth and trying to avoid detection, he skirted the entrance. Something had disturbed him, and now that he was fully awake, he knew there was something out there, but where? The tip of his tail twitched. His acute eyes were darting across and down into the cavern. Standing as close to the edge as possible, Chakra peered as far as he could into the valley. He saw nothing.

He walked the entire ledge, slowly searching a large area for the presence he now felt. Chakra held his tail low, and the tip now twitched ever so slightly. He had pinpointed some movement much farther up the canyon on the opposite side. The glare of the sun on the coppery stones combined with the black shadows of the deep canyon made whatever it was impossible to make out. He was going to have to investigate. Chakra's eyes began to glow red as he stared at the spot where he had seen movement. He must wake Darkess now and warn her before he left.

≈

Takar slid on his belly headfirst down the side of the canyon before he came to rest in the shadows more than a hundred feet below the desert floor. He merely lay there, trying to adjust his eyes and catch his breath. The stones beneath him were cooler than anything he had felt for some time. Shedding his cloak, he wiped at the sand on the rocks and laid his face on the cooler gravel beneath. He pressed his chest and neck against the stones in an attempt to lower his body temperature. He knew he must get home, but he was torn between the cool stones, his desire to sleep, and his need to travel.

He groped his way across the ground to his discarded cloak. Fumbling with it, he tried to locate the pocket that held his chalk and potion. Finally, he felt his chalk, and anger suddenly appeared, spurring him to draw his familiar symbols and go home to regroup. "Why haven't I received the power to blink?" he thought angrily. His father had told him long ago that he would get his powers in time, but he now realized his father had been wrong. Digging through the sand for large enough rocks to perform his task, Takar mumbled to himself. He crawled along the slope dragging his cloak behind him.

≈

Chakra pawed at the hair covering Darkess' face. She woke instantly. "What's wrong?" she whispered, clearing the hair from her vision.

When her eyes focused on Chakra, she could see the problem. His eyes were glowing red.

'Something evil is in the canyon. I'm going to investigate,' Chakra projected with a flick of his tail, and quick as a whip, he was gone.

'Not without me,' Darkess projected.

She quickly threw back her hair and tied it in a knot. She had slept with her boots on, so she snatched up her pack and crawled towards the cave's entrance. Looking to see where her cat had gone, she whispered,

"Stay here, and wait for me."

Zaphod exhaled strongly, acknowledging her. Peering over the edge, Darkess saw movement. It was Chakra. If she had been even one instant slower in her crawl to the edge, she would never have seen him as he was quickly enveloped in the darker shadows at the bottom of the canyon. Even though she feared that using magic would give her presence away, she didn't think it would reveal her actual location. So she closed her eyes and thought for a moment. Then she whispered an incantation.

"Connect mine eyes to thee, see exactly what Chakra sees, a portal your eyes will be, channeled directly to me."

The darkness behind her lids grew in intensity then suddenly; it was as if a star had burst inside her eyes. Opening them, she saw not the cavernous mouth of the canyon in front of her, but a path deep in the shadows below her. Instinctively, Darkess sat back on her haunches to protect herself from losing her balance in case the view made her dizzy. Concentrating on her new vision, her brow wrinkled and she squinted slightly. Chakra was moving quickly down the steep slope, his vision darting around and checking for secure footing. A human-like form appeared in the dense shadows. Chakra slowed his approach to avoid giving away his position. The figure appeared to be groping for something in its cloak.

Darkess recognized the figure when he lifted his face. Takar, she thought, narrowing her eyes. Chakra stealthily padded his way toward the demon. His eyes were sunk in, and his lips were white and cracked, and bleeding in some places from dehydration. He was dirty, sand-ridden, and scribbling something on the rocks in front of where he lay. Chakra skirted around the demon, approaching him from an angle just behind his peripheral vision.

Once again, Takar was digging in his cloak. Chakra crept closer still. Darkess' breathing was growing more intense as the seconds ticked by. With a great amount of effort, Takar pulled himself into the sitting position and began to sprinkle powder around him. Before Darkess knew it, Takar was nothing but a vortex of smoke. Chakra darted to the spot where the demon had just been, and he and Darkess saw the symbols burning away on the rocks. They were the exact symbols Takar had used when leaving Alieria's hidden room.

'That must be his lair,' Darkess projected.

Chakra scouted the area, but there was nothing left except some prints in the sand. Darkess held her hand over her eyes.

"Take these enchanted eyes, and return my sight to me, cancel the magic portal, and let me see naturally."

When she removed her hand and opened her eyes, she once again saw the ledge she was sitting on and the deep cavern in front of her. Moments later, Chakra popped over the ledge of the shelf and stopped to lick at his back foot. Darkess looked at her animal companions.

"He was ill prepared, but he will be back."

☼

Tuma had returned to his master's lair soon after he had warned the Vallencourts, but not before making sure that all hell was breaking loose everywhere per the contract with his master. He stayed well away from the room that contained the eggs as they made him feel greedy and anxious. Neither trait was normal for a Gilaman. He knew Takar was crazy enough to kill him for any reason, so Tuma was trying to avoid giving him one. Tuma stayed mostly to the small stone home above the lair or outside on the grounds where Takar was not likely to be seen. Tuma was in the kitchen nibbling on a fresh frog cake, one of his favorites, when he heard sobbing followed by a crashing sound. Tuma's stomach dropped to the bottom of his torso. The frog cake no longer looked so tasty, and he put it in a rag and wrapped it tightly.

Quicker than he felt like moving, Tuma made his way through the house towards the sounds. Upon reaching the bottom of the stone steps, he saw Takar laying on the floor and crying like a little girl. Takar heard his servant's approach and mumbled, "Water."

≈

With thirty minutes of daylight left, Darkess picked up her pack, checked the cave, and pushed farther up the cavern wall to get a good look at the land before it was impossible to see. This would be their third night of walking, and she was hoping to see something off beyond the cavern other than rolling sand dunes. Reaching the top, she stood with her back to the cavern and scanned the blackening horizon. She pulled her golden egg out, put it in her palm, and whispered,

"Show me south."

The egg spun gracefully for a couple of heartbeats then came to rest. Darkess started off in the direction it had indicated. Barely noticeable in the navy colored sky was something that looked tiny and pointed. Her heart leapt. Why hadn't she seen it a couple of minutes ago? Just then, lightning ripped through the sky and hit the point Darkess had just noticed. To the travelers, it seemed forever before the thunderclap finally reached them.

"That, my friends, is where we are headed."

For a while, they all walked side by side in silence. Night became deeper and deeper with every step. Darkess kept her hand on the stirrup for guidance as they walked. All three watched the lightning crash over and over above the obelisk they were headed for. There were quite a few seconds between the strikes, and it was mildly disorienting, even though it was so far away. Finally, the darkness became too much for human eyes, and Darkess climbed on Zaphod as Chakra jumped into his bag and curled up for a good nap.

≈

Takar slept on the cold stone floor all night, occasionally waking for large gulps of water. Tuma stayed on the steps all night watching and waiting, only approaching Takar when ordered. Morning brought the sun shining brightly at the top of the stairs. Tuma reached his scaly hand into the beam that reached towards him, wondering if this might be his last day.

"Water!" came his master's voice from behind him, stronger than before, and he cringed. Taking a platter full of food, milk, and water to his master, Tuma saw that Takar was in fact regaining his strength. Wolfing down his food, spilling half down his chest in his haste, Takar mumbled with his mouth full,

"Pack, me some…food, three days worth…and water."

Tuma was relieved at the request and scurried off to do as ordered.

≈

As the sun began to turn the sky from deep blue to a much paler color, Darkess finally got a better view of the obelisk they had been following all night. It was immense, still at least another night's journey away, and it seemed to poke a hole in the heavens. Having never seen anything so slender and tall, the obelisk took her breath away. She felt tiny, minuscule after seeing something so large.

"Did you ever imagine such a thing?" Darkess whispered, mostly to herself.

The sun was half visible now, and the obelisk glistened brightly. Darkess realized they must find shelter and quickly. The sand around her seemed scoured level. It was packed down, and there were no dunes here for shelter. Something was different. They walked on for maybe five minutes when Darkess finally decided to use magic. Jumping down from Zaphod, she realized he was completely copper, even his eyes. They hadn't stayed in the sun this long before, and it was pressing down on them like a stone. Kneeling, Darkess scanned the landscape, but the light was so intense she could hardly see without her eyes tearing up. She was not used to the desert, and it was antagonizing her, playing with her. Throwing out her muslin roll, she used her power to drive the stakes into the ground and then set up her lean-to. It took just a few heartbeats for them to be undercover, though Zaphod had the most trouble trying to crawl into a good position. The heat was increasing with every moment, and Darkess knew the material wouldn't be enough to shield them with no dune to hide in for the first and last parts of the day.

Darkess crossed her legs in front of her, put one hand to her chin, and rested her elbows on her knees.

"Wish I had power over the weather right now," she commented.

Zaphod snorted at her as he guzzled water from a bladder. Chakra tidied his fur and projected,

'Me, too. This sand in dreadful on the coat.'

"Let me see what I can do," Darkess replied in a sarcastic tone and with an arch in her eyebrow, said,

"Inside our hot little haven, where it is necessary to hide, we need a little cooling breeze, to help keep us alive."

A small wind picked up inside the lean-to, making it surprisingly cooler. Zaphod snorted at Darkess.

'Thought you were trying to limit your use of magic?' he said.

'Don't ruin a good thing,' Chakra replied.

"You know, I did say that. But since Takar probably already knows we are here, there is no point getting sick while we wait for him to return, is there? He will come back, you know. He was either trailing the egg or us, either way we must get there first. And we have to be alive to do that," Darkess said.

'Good point,' Chakra said smugly.

Zaphod shook his head at the cat and laid his head on his knee, closing his eyes. Even though it was early in the morning, Darkess couldn't help but yawn. She prepared a meal for each of them, which they all ate slowly together. When they finished, Darkess packed all of her things, laid out her cloak like a blanket, and crawled onto it. She stared at the top of the lean-to with her arms crossed under her head.

"I'll be glad when I can take a long cool bath and remove the sand from...everything," Darkess said, stretching, and yawning broadly.

Wriggling into the sand and trying to get more comfortable, she covered her eyes with her arm and tried to sleep. Zaphod was already napping. Chakra, however, left his sleeping companions to make a lap, looking for danger in any form.

≈

Takar was almost normal for the first time in weeks. It seemed that the combination of being away from the dragon eggs and being a completely unconscious, dehydrated, sick mess for twelve hours had made him his old self again. He was speaking much more clearly and intelligible than he had in a year. He ordered his food packed, his bath drawn, and he never threatened Tuma once. Tuma was happily shocked but worried that it would be short lived.

The hot bath made Takar tired once again, and unbelievably enough, he slept in his childhood bed in the family home above ground. He slept most of the afternoon away, waking only once for water. Evening was fast approaching when Takar's eyes snapped open. He knew what he had to do. Travel at night. He couldn't figure out why he hadn't thought of it before. But then he had the sudden urge to check on his eggs. Ripping the sheets back, Takar got swiftly out of bed. He felt much better now and threw on fresh clothes. He couldn't remember the last time he had changed clothes, and that seemed odd to him, but he pushed it to the side of his mind and took off for his underground lair.

Tuma was huddled against the wall in the kitchen when Takar sprinted past him toward the stone steps leading down. He looked and seemed almost human most of the day, but Tuma saw the glint in his eyes as he passed. Tuma stayed invisible. He knew the eggs must be calling his master, and he didn't want to be around for it.

≈

Hours later, once the sun had set, Takar bellowed at his servant. "Come here!"

Tuma's eyes were the only visible part of his body when he entered the room.

"Show yourself," Takar demanded.

Tuma's color showed up rather pale, but he was visible.

"Have you followed my orders?" Takar asked.

Tuma nodded his head.

"Good. Then I will be taking my leave. Stay away from the eggs. Be ready for my return. I will need food and water. Let no one in the house."

Takar rubbed the eggs and whispered to them.

"Fear not my babies, for I will find your sister soon, and you will be freed."

Tuma shivered and paled further in color. Takar refilled the pockets on his cloak, grabbed the leather bag with his supplies, and stepped over to his portal grid. He drew nothing on the grid but left it blank. Sprinkling the powder, he said,

"Return."

In a vortex, he was gone.

Tuma's color returned immediately, and he fell to the floor, clutching his head, breathing strongly, and sobbing quietly.

≈

Takar arrived in the desert precisely where he had departed. Deep in the canyon, the smoke cleared, and Takar realized just how dark it was. He had an idea there was someone out there from the bird he had consumed days earlier, but who and where he wasn't exactly sure. He had no idea Darkess was a full night's walk ahead of him or that she had started walking over an hour before he arrived in the desert. Not only did he need to cross the cavern's floor, he also had to climb the other side in the dark. Being half demon, his eyes were better than humans but not good enough. He stumbled and tripped, falling on a number of occasions and swearing harshly each time.

It took him almost the whole night to finally reach the top of the cavern's wall, and he crawled over the rim. Sweaty, filthy, and sore, he sat cross-legged and held his bag on his lap as he dug inside for food. A flash of light in the distance caught his attention, and he chewed slowly, waiting to see if it would happen again. He gnashed at a chunk of meat, but nothing more happened.

≈

The heat lightning was brilliant, and the sound took little time to reach them as they followed it like a beacon. They were getting close. The obelisk now looked more than twice the size it had earlier as it loomed overhead. Darkess had dubbed it Lightning Point, and it seemed appropriate. They walked for nearly an hour before the next strike of lightning almost ripped the sky open above them. Zaphod stopped in his tracks, Darkess ducked down, and Chakra let out a quick, startled, and pathetic sound. It had been so calm and almost peaceful until the lightning struck again. They had grown lax, and Darkess mildly chastised herself. She felt an odd mist of rain, and it felt wonderful. Chakra poked his head from the bag he was sleeping in, felt the wet, and retreated back inside. Darkess jumped down from the saddle for a short rest. Lightning strikes became more frequent, but the rain never came, only a light mist.

Darkess walked beside Zaphod and enjoyed stretching her legs, the illumination from the lightening, and most definitely the mist. They could now see the large stone formations down by the base of Lightning Point, which gave them a little incentive. Their pace increased, and the terrain changed a little. Tumbleweeds kicked up by this weird desert mist storm rolled about in the gentle breeze. Tumbleweeds meant there was life somewhere near here. This intrigued Darkess, because she had learned that there was no life here and that everyone who entered here also died here. Without the use of magic, this place was said to have no rain or water of any kind. Letting the mist collect and roll off their faces, Darkess and Zaphod walked side by side towards the hills in front of them, wondering what lie ahead.

≈

"Great magic dwells here," Takar said to himself in awe of the lightning he saw far in the distance.

He knew that was where he must go. Never before had he seen such a display of lightning strikes, all hitting the same spot. He quickened his pace towards the obelisk he could finally see. Not paying attention to the fact that his vision hadn't gotten any better, he fell into a dune and rolled to the bottom. Cursing his haste, he lit a fireball, checked his trail, and started climbing out of the dune. When he finally had view of the obelisk again, the lightning strikes had become less frequent. He headed in its direction, paying more attention to his footing.

☼

The lightning had completely stopped, and Darkess was again riding Zaphod. From the feeling in her back, morning wasn't far off. She was aching from the trip. They stopped walking, and Darkess climbed down, looked around, and found the skyline was becoming visible. It looked like maybe half a day's walk to reach the giant stones. They were incredible, shaped like nothing she had imagined would exist here. They were only a stark outline at this point, but they were there, and Darkess became excited.

"We're almost there boys," she said.

"Now where is that cave?" she asked herself.

Chakra made an appearance and was sitting in the saddle and looking off into the distance.

"I think that we'll camp here if that is okay with you," Darkess said to her companions.

'I'm going to have a look around,' Chakra said as he jumped from the saddle.

Zaphod pricked his ears towards the cat, watching him disappear into the darkness. Darkess unloaded and set up camp for the day. When Chakra returned, the sun had finally crept over the edge of the horizon. Darkess was chewing on a hunk of jerky while Zaphod happily munched on something that looked dry and unappetizing. Chakra begged for a piece of what Darkess was eating, having found nothing for himself. Darkess looked at her jerky, took one more bite, and tossed the remainder to her cat. Shoving a corndodger in her mouth, she asked him what he had seen. Chakra had found some scrubby cacti, and he said that they were very near their destination. He could feel the magic in this place. Darkess yawned and scratched Chakra behind the ears before laying down for a little nap. She fell asleep quickly, either from heat or exhaustion, and she had several short dreams – none of which she would remember later.

Suddenly, she awoke with a start. Looking around her lean-to, she saw Zaphod still sleeping and Chakra's back. All seemed well. But when Chakra turned to look back at his master, she saw that his eyes were completely red, and she scrambled to her feet, startling Zaphod. Once again, he stood too quickly, disassembling the lean-to and covering Darkess with sand and material.

'Sorry,' Zaphod said, taking the material in his teeth and pulling it off Darkess.

"What is it? Has he found us?" Darkess asked in a whisper, rolling the tarp up in haste.

'He's a day's walk from here,' Chakra projected. 'Saw him light a fireball before the sun was fully up. The magic I felt earlier was from the stones, but as you were going to sleep, I felt a small twang of evil. So, I looked for it. There are some boulders not far from here, and I stood atop one and watched him. The fool waved his black cloak around, trying to make a tent, which made it easy for me to spot him again. He hasn't moved since,' Chakra finished with an air of smugness as he turned back to watch for the demon.

"When, preytell, were you going to share this sweet little bit of information?" Darkess whispered harshly.

'You were in no danger. I saw no need to wake you. You will need your strength and your wits about you for the task ahead.' Chakra projected, sounding ever so much like a teacher again.

'That is for me to decide,' Darkess projected in a hostile tone. 'We must leave, and now.'

She was furious at Chakra. Once again, she felt like a child, and it angered her more. With the pounding sun on her head, she packed quickly, checking for stray items. The brightness of the sun on the coppery sand was irritating her eyes, so she ripped a strip off of the muslin she had used for a tent. Laying the strip in the sand, she cut two small slits about an inch apart. She tied the strip to her head and adjusted the slits over her eyes. The muslin blocked a large portion of her view but made it easier to keep her eyes open in the painful light.

Darkess scanned the horizon in all directions. She couldn't see Takar, but she knew he was behind her, and she intended to use every bit of her head start. They kept the pace slow, trying to avoid heat exhaustion. They had two bags of water left, and it may take all of it to get to the shade of the stones ahead. Pulling an empty vile from her pack, Darkess saved a small amount of pure water inside. Remembering her doubling spell, she made two bags become four simply by pouring from the full bag into the empty one until both bags were full. Sweat was pouring off her as she drank some water, set up her companions with some, and repacked the bladders.

She trudged on next to Zaphod, who was frothing a little around the edges from exertion. Chakra walked along in the shadow thrown by Zaphod, though the sand radiated so much heat that the shadow hardly helped. Darkess' mind began to wonder back to her grandfather then to the castle. How much she longed for its comforts and her family within it. Would she ever see them again? She hadn't even had her sixteenth winter yet, and she seemed to be the only thing that could save Crystal City, maybe even all of Xyloidonia. Chakra interrupted her thoughts.

'I think the fate of the world is in your hands.'

Darkess hadn't even realized she had been projecting her thoughts, and she snorted aloud,

"Gee you're a big help. No pressure there."

Chakra's tail twitched in irritation.

'It's all the same thing. Get this egg. City or world, you can't save one without saving the other,' Chakra projected, snotty as ever.

Darkess knew Chakra was right, and that made her more irritated. She swallowed a nasty retort, and said,

"You're right."

They walked on in silence. The sun was on a downward slide, and it was hitting the sides of their faces. Darkess could feel a burning sensation and pulled her hood up over her head, tugging it forward to hide her face. Her head began to pound, and her eyes streamed constantly, making her vision terrible. They had to take a break or find some shade. That's when she saw it – mountain debris, from a long ago rockslide. Darkess slowed her pace, and that's when Zaphod saw what caused her to slow.

'Do you see what I see?' Chakra projected, jumping on Zaphod's back.

'Yes,' they said in unison.

Darkess placed her hand on Zaphod's shoulder and grasped the reins in her other hand.

'You must take us to that shade,' Darkess projected.

'Takar will know we are here. We should keep walking,' Chakra projected.

'Damn that. We will all die out here if we keep moving in this heat. I believe you said that I should have my strength and wits about me if I am to fight Takar, and I can't do that here. Now you be quiet, and Zaphod is going to take us to that shade over there by those boulders,' Darkess projected as she pointed.

Zaphod knew better than to join this fight, and the three of them disappeared immediately. They reappeared more than an hour's walk away in shade that was much cooler than the open desert. Darkess dropped to her knees in the shade, digging her hands down to where it felt even cooler. She took slow deep breaths with her eyes closed. She was exhausted and needed more time to recover than she actually had.

After a moment Chakra crossed in front of Darkess, rubbing his tail under her nose.

"Thanks fur face. What was that for?" Darkess asked, rubbing cat hair off her nose.

'You were getting comfortable, and we don't have time for that,' Chakra answered.

Pulling her hands free of the sand and spraying Chakra a little in payment for the hairy nose, Darkess said,

"Just getting my head clear."

Sitting down in the sand, she took a better look at the stone monoliths. For the first time, she was getting a good and proper look at them, and they were magnificent. One of the most beautiful and deadly places, she thought, searching along them. She was looking for anything unusual then smirked, almost laughing for the first time in days.

"Boy, am I tired. Here I am looking for anything peculiar, when this entire place is peculiar. What could I possibly pinpoint in all of this?" Darkess said more to herself than her companions.

Zaphod and Chakra looked at each other then back to Darkess as she continued to scan the stones. Neither said a word as they awaited Darkess' next move. Spying something in the rocks, Darkess scooped up Chakra and pointed to the oddly shaped mountain she called Lightning Point. Slapping her hand on Zaphod's neck, she projected,

'The base of Lightning Point.'

Zaphod snorted, and again they teleported, this time into the shade of the largest stone formation in the area. Chakra jumped into Zaphod's saddle, and the three of them looked towards the heavens at the stone's zenith.

"Do you feel that?" Darkess queried as she moved along the base of the stones.

Since the sun was on its way down as Darkess circled the piles of stones, the shadows became deeper and, to her surprise, cooler. This helped to refresh her senses and quicken her pace a little.

"We're close boys," she whispered as she placed her hand on a large boulder.

A small snap of electricity jumped to her hand, shocking her enough to make her wince.

"Whoa. The lightning seems to live in these stones," she said and continued on, carefully picking her way around fallen rubble.

The shadows were thickest along a narrow strip that funneled between Lightning Point and the next of the massive rocks. Zaphod's ears were twitching back and forth, and Chakra's ears were doing the same, which caused Darkess to stop in her tracks. The three travelers listened intently.

'Good place for a trap,' Darkess told her companions.

Pulling off her eye cover, she silently treaded through the sand as close to the walls as possible.

'Good place for a hideout,' Chakra replied.

Fully expecting some sort of trap or spell, even a wizard on guard, they were all on full alert. Darkess was looking closely at any fissures in the stones, and Chakra was inspecting anything leading inside the stones that were too small for her. Both searched for an entrance. They could feel the magic, very strong magic, and its pull helping Darkess in her search.

Time ticked by quickly, and she had to calm herself lest she miss something. Stopping momentarily to look back and see how far she had come, she was surprised that she could no longer see the desert and that she was deep within the base of the cliffs. Hearing and seeing nothing behind her, Darkess looked back towards where her destination must lay. Up ahead, she noticed an area where larger stones had been cleared away. It seemed suddenly very odd to her eyes, very different from the rest of the base of the cliffs. She wanted to run to that spot and have all of this over and done with, but she knew it wouldn't be that easy.

Putting her fingertip to her lips, she signaled for her companions to be quiet and turned on cat's feet towards the clearing. She slowly placed each foot, scanning the area and cautiously moving forward. Zaphod stayed still as he knew he made too much noise, and Chakra moved to the opposite side of the path, helping her look for traps or movement. Step by slow step, she crept towards the stones. She was nervously apprehensive of the final steps. So far, nothing had happened. Only a small breeze swept overhead, creating an odd hollow sound in the small canyon. Darkess arrived at the stone base, and cautiously reached for it. The stone here held a small charge as well, zapping her. Pushing through the tingling feeling, she pressed her hands to the rock. It was a solid, seemingly normal stone. Rubbing her hands over the surface of what she was sure was something special, she felt sand cascade down to her feet. She noticed there was indeed something etched on its surface. She quickly began to rub the rock, scraping one of her knuckles badly enough to make it bleed, but continued to clear away more sand.

One single drop of blood smeared across a couple of the shapes as she wiped more sand away. This time, a stronger charge zapped her. She winced but brushed faster at the sand caked to the stone. Darkess wondered how long it had been since this gateway had been opened. Chakra and Zaphod approached and watched intently as Darkess cleared away more sand and made more shapes appear in the rock. Rubbing her hands side to side and top to bottom, she made sure that every shape or symbol was revealed. But when she stood up to read what it said, it was gibberish or a language Darkess did not know. It wasn't even one she recognized. The engraving was in slanted and swirling script, and it was fairly worn away in a few areas. Trying to take a closer look, her companions stepped up, and the crunch of Zaphod's steps made Darkess spin quickly in place. In her excitement, she was quite jumpy. She grabbed her chest and blew out sharply, "You scared me!"

She had intended to say more, but she saw a reflection in the metal on Zaphod's tack, the only shiny metal on him. It was a medallion that said Goodspeed on his chest. Sucking in deeply, Darkess dug in her pack for her rapier. Again, Chakra and Zaphod looked at each other confused. Swinging her pack to the ground, she followed suit, facing her horse with her back to the wall. Holding her rapier in front of her face with the blade angled just so, Darkess used the reflection to read the encrypted message inscribed on the stone. She angled the blade further with each word down to the bottom and found a small oval. She quickly turned towards the wall again and rubbed at the symbol, trying to completely reveal it. The storms must have ground away at it, but it seemed that it could possibly be a dragon's head. The damage was too severe to be sure.

'Well?' Chakra demanded.

"Oh yes, well, entrance demands the desert's greatest sacrifice," Darkess said, rubbing the word sacrifice.

She thought for a moment, could it be a life? No. Then it came to her.

"Water, you would never want to give up your water. That has to be it!" Darkess said excitedly.

Trading her rapier for something with a smaller blade, she also pulled out the small vile of pure rainwater.

"Get ready boys. There's no telling what could happen when this water hits the stone."

Darkess stood back from the wall a couple of feet, and using her telekinetic power, slammed the vile into the wall on the word sacrifice. For a moment, the water merely ran down its face. Then the stone began to shimmer as if in bright sunlight. After the shimmering, the stone vanished and revealed an elaborately carved entrance to a cave. Darkess immediately held up her hand in defense with a knife in the other, ready to strike if needed. Zaphod stood where he was, waiting. Chakra, on the other hand, was already creeping towards the opening, and Darkess held her hand up to stop him. He eyed her, and his eyes were their normal yellow with green slits. He sensed no evil.

Stepping forward, Darkess noticed her familiars' eyes, and this gave her a small boost of encouragement. Placing her hand on the carved arch, she felt its smooth texture. It had been rendered by magic; of that there was no doubt. Stepping cautiously into the entrance, she saw the first cavern seemed like a small room. It was almost square in shape, and perfectly centered were openings here and on the opposite side, both identically shaped and carved. The only light was coming from the entrance she now stood in. She needed light but must keep her hands free. It took only a second before she made a fireball and tossed it into the air. She held it in place a couple of feet above her head and a little in front of her, like a torch suspended in midair.

Darkess circled the room looking for something, anything that might give her a clue about what might lay ahead through the other opening. There were piles of sand, but none any deeper than a few inches, and none of them contained even the slightest clue. Deeming the room safe enough, she allowed Chakra and Zaphod to enter. Gulping down some water and even pouring some over her face, Darkess settled her companions.

"You must stay here. It is not safe to go on," Darkess said to them.

'I'm going with you. Zaphod can stay and guard the entrance,' Chakra said.

"No, I don't like it. You stay here and warn him if trouble comes," Darkess said and turned to leave through the next doorway.

'Takar will only think Zaphod is a horse. He's exceedingly rare, and he can get away any time he wishes to leave. But a cat in the desert, well, that would be deemed magical or food, neither of which I would survive. I am going to help you. I'd rather die in battle than end up on the dinner plate of some demon,' Chakra explained.

Darkess shook her head and pursed her lips at her cat.

"Will you be alright here alone?" Darkess asked Zaphod.

Snorting and nodding his head, he answered.

'The shade is nice, and Chakra is right. I have the best chance of survival here alone. Go on, I'll be ok. Just you come back, understand?'

Darkess clapped her hand on Zaphod's shoulder and stepped through the doorway. Chakra was next to her, and once they were through the opening, the stone morphed shut, locking Darkess and her cat inside. Spinning around, Darkess slammed her hand on the stone that had originally not been there, and it was solid. They definitely had to go forward, because backwards was no longer an option.

"Hellfire," Darkess said in a harsh whisper. "I guess we go on, better watch your step."

The fireball-floating overhead illuminated a much larger room, maybe three times the size of the first one they had found. It, too, seemed to be made by magic due to its odd shape, rectangular with a smooth surface. Standing just a few feet from the wall, Darkess looked around the cavern and took a couple of small steps forward, intending to investigate further. The air seemed heavier here, and with each step, it grew thicker. What at first was a thin veil of fog became thicker with each step. Darkess decided to stop a moment. She was having no trouble breathing, but the air smelled stale with a tinge of death in it. Chakra's tail twitched, and he froze next to Darkess. Both were unsure of what was happening. A swirling vortex of wind blew down from the ceiling, and it looked similar to the vortex Takar uses. The image of an ancient withered man stood before them. The man had an odd grin on his face, and he bowed to them. Darkess inclined her head for a moment and squinted her eyes, waiting for the specter's next move. Her hands extended, ready for a fight.

"Congratulations. You have just survived the deadliest desert in our world. However, your prize is not what you may have expected but rather a tragic death. For you have entered the home of the Handorf Family unannounced, and with only one exit and miles of tunnels and traps at every turn, you'll never escape with what you came here for."

Darkess knew honesty was best in this situation, so she tried to explain.

"I have not come here to steal from you but rather to help you. A demon is on his way here, now, to steal the one remaining egg and add it to the others. You must let me help you."

Darkess held her arms out in a pleading gesture. The old wizard only smiled, and his appearance shifted. He disappeared, reappeared, and shimmered, but made no response.

"I need to see your high priest, or someone. You must warn your family," Darkess pleaded with the image, her voice getting more urgent as she spoke.

The image of the old wizard shifted again, causing Darkess' brow to furrow. Stepping cautiously forward, she put her hand out to touch the wizard. Her hand passed directly through the figure, but unlike a ghost, there was no cold prickly feeling. It felt like the rest of the room. Stepping back again, Darkess pleaded with the old man.

"Please sir, let me help you."

As if he hadn't heard her, the swirl of wind came again, and the old wizard was gone.

"He wasn't a ghost. He was something else. Maybe a captured image…"

Before she could finish what she was saying, sand began to sift down from the ceiling, and a booming voice came with it.

"Let the journey to death begin."

The sand was falling quickly, filling the floor to her ankles in seconds. Darkess looked around the room. There were no doors, and the ceiling was falling in. Chakra was belly deep in sand and shaking off the piles on his back.

"I'm going to try to blow a hole in the wall. Hold on," Darkess said, scooping up her cat and opening her other hand.

When she produced a second fireball to throw at the wall, an amazing thing happened. Three doors opened in the wall they were facing. The sand was knee deep to Darkess now, and there was not much time to decide which door to take. Throwing a fireball into the first opening, she saw nothing. In the second one, she saw a tunnel leading forward, and in the third one she saw steps leading up. The first tunnel must lead down, she deducted, after seeing the other two more clearly. Trudging through sand that was now thigh high, she headed towards the doors as quickly as possible. She crawled across the top, sank in, and clawed her way towards the door that hopefully led to what she was after.

Chakra clung to Darkess' back; claws digging deep into the cloak, watching the door slowly get closer. The sand was spilling out of the room through the three openings, which helped her progression a little the closer she got to them. Once Darkess was within body-length of the opening, she pulled Chakra off her back and tossed him through the door. Twisting her pack around backwards, she held it close to her belly and dove with all of her strength towards the opening, rolling through it. As soon as she was through and in the squatting position, she took a quick look at the room she had just vacated. The opening slammed shut just as it had in the first room, but a peculiar thing happened. Electricity flowed through the rock, and for a split second, the room became visible again, and a small amount of sand trickled trough the stone barrier. Darkess stood and placed her hand on the newly solid wall when again a pulse ran through the stone.

"Ouch!" she hissed, and her hand slipped part way through the barrier.

"Oh," she sucked in air and quickly pulled her hand back.

Sand trickled through, covered the toes of her boots then stopped just as quickly.

"That's odd," she said as she turned towards the tunnel she had chosen.

Worn stone steps ascended into darkness. Darkess moved her fireball out further to get a better look. There were twelve steps leading up to something. What, she wasn't sure, but the way they were worn down suggested years of use. There were no markings on any of the walls or steps, so she took each one slowly, aware there could be traps anywhere. Chakra walked along the wall one step ahead of Darkess. When they reached the last step, the floor was marked with hashed lines, which made the floor look unlevel.

They followed the short corridor until they reached a set of stairs leading down again. Keeping the fireball lit above the stairs, Darkess heaved another down to the bottom of the stairs. The light traveled down and down, over dozens of steps until it finally hit the wall and burned out. It was a dead end, but she followed the stairs down, for there were no other paths to take at this point. The only sounds were the crunch under her boots and a small crackling sound coming from her fireball. After eight steps or so, Darkess heard a click under her heal, but before she could look down at what she had stepped on, the stairs flipped down to form a ramp. With her feet flying out from under her, Darkess landed sharply on her tailbone.

"Oof," escaped her lips, and her eyes clamped shut in pain.

Quickly she began to slip down the newly formed slide, Chakra yowling in fear beside her. Opening her eyes as she began to feel the rush of wind blowing hard in her face, she saw the wall at the bottom coming towards her at an alarming rate. Thoughts raced through her mind as she tried desperately to slow her descent. Clawing and kicking were her natural response, but after only a second or two, her training finally kicked in. Chakra's claws were raking across the stones behind Darkess' head, for he had also lost his grip and was flailing like a fish out of water.

In one fluid motion, Darkess kicked one foot furiously into the ramp, sending her rolling onto her knees and toes. She scooped up Chakra in one hand and threw one hand between her knees. She opened her free hand, and with all of her strength, pushed downward, gritting her teeth and groaning.

"Stooooop!"

Once she had finally come to a stop, only inches separated the soles of Darkess' boots and the floor. Her pack swayed heavily on her back. Chakra's eyes were wide and bright as he looked out from Darkess' shoulder and tucked himself close to her body. Darkess finally lowered herself to the floor with a gentle thud, and Chakra jumped down in front of her.

'Thanks,' her cat projected.

"Don't mention it," Darkess said as she looked around the small cubicle she was now stuck in.

"What now? Am I supposed to die of boredom, loneliness, or starvation?" she asked the walls as she rubbed them. She was feeling for a trigger to a hidden door, magic words hidden in sand, or even another trap door.

Moving her hands along the corners and the floor, she found nothing.

"There has to be a way to go further," Darkess said in frustration and slapped the wall.

Kneeling down, she rested on the incline behind her and glared at the wall in front of her. Her mouth felt like she had eaten a nice big bowl of dry sand, so she pulled out her bladder for a drink. Chakra mewled at the sight of the bladder, so she poured him a small bowl first. Looking at the ceiling as she took a long drink, Darkess noticed something very faint. An electric field was flashing just like the rock wall had earlier. Using much of her strength, she levitated herself up to the ceiling to get a closer look. She touched the stone and was zapped. The power seemed weaker, somehow drained. Maybe the depth of the passage caused it, Darkess pondered.

Placing her fingertips on the stone again, she pushed hard, but the stone was unyielding. Why was she drawn to this spot? Few would have been able to reach the ceiling, and that's if they had noticed the crackle of power flowing through it. She lowered herself back down and moved into the corner. She threw a fireball at the ceiling on the opposite end from her. It smoldered for a second then burned out. Drawing her lip up at one corner, she exhaled sharply at her failure. With a wave of her finger, the fireball that had guided their way went sailing into the same spot, leaving them in darkness. The ceiling looked a misty blue now and again as the power flashed over its surface. Darkess stared at the ceiling in the dark and began to see a pattern in the light. There were words in the surges running across the ceiling. The writing wasn't easy to read, because once again, it was backwards. She retrieved the same rapier from her pack that she had used earlier and told Chakra to stay back.

319

Getting to her feet, she held the blade down at her side. Levitating back up to the ceiling about twice her height, she stopped six inches from the ceiling. Darkess positioned herself where the words began to scroll across the ceiling. It was hard keeping steady, and she tilted her head down, staring into darkness until the blade finally caught the reflection from the ceiling above. She waited for the cycle to start again and slowly mumbled what was reflected in her blade.

"Only those with a human heart may enter, only the innocent can pass, in your veins lies the secret, of what is hidden in your past."

The ceiling went black for a moment then repeated itself. Lighting a new fireball, Darkess lowered herself again to the floor.

"Cryptic of them," she said mockingly as she replaced her blade. "Why didn't they just say, 'Put your blood here.'"

'Wouldn't do that if I were you,' Chakra warned.

"It's the only way through," Darkess protested and pulled a smaller knife from her belt.

'Don't say I didn't warn you,' Chakra projected.

"Warn me of what?" she demanded.

'You have no idea what is behind that wall, and blood is a very powerful ingredient, if you catch my meaning,' Chakra projected.

"You think I don't know that? We can't get out that way," Darkess said angrily, pointing back they way they had come. "And the teleport potions will only take us places we can see in our minds. What do you suggest we do?" Darkess said crossly.

'I actually have no suggestions at this point,' Chakra said snootily and settled down to stare at her.

"I'm doing it. Why else are we here?" Darkess announced.

Chakra did not answer.

"Well, I'm not just gonna sit here and wait for death."

Darkess gritted her teeth and drew the blade across the palm of her left hand. A small pool of blood filled her hand quickly, and she threw it at the wall in front of her. The beads of blood seemed to spray the stone in slow motion. Some clung to the wall, and others ran down it. The entire room lit up with bursts of electricity, and the room began to fill with sand. Just when Darkess was reaching for her cat to levitate them away from danger, a new door opened where her blood had spattered. Stepping through the passage, she thought she saw a glimpse of movement.

Inside of the next chamber, Darkess looked around for something alive or animated but couldn't see anything. This tunnel seemed more natural than magic with its gentle curves, coarse surface, stalagmites and stalactites. The ceiling here was much higher, and there were more shadows and places to hide. Darkess kept her right hand out in front of her at the ready. A small white, flying squirrel-like creature with glowing bulbous eyes scrambled down a stalactite and jumped at Darkess. Producing a fireball quickly, she threw it at the creature. Before it reached the target, the fireball's power diminished to a tiny glow. It smacked into the creature, which was burned badly but survived the attack, only to crawl off and nurse its wounds and call in backup.

"What the hell!" Darkess hissed, nearly at a loss for words.

'I told you not to give your blood to that wall,' was all Chakra said before continuing on his way down the tunnel with his ears and tail twitching in agitation.

Darkess made another fireball, which fizzled faintly in her hand. Then the fireball she made and carried with her and the one in her hand changed to a light blue color and burnt out. Silently, she thanked her grandfather for his night shine crystal and pulled it out of her pack.

"Illuminate," she said.

Luckily it worked. Though it was a little weaker than usual, some light was definitely better than none.

"Take these human eyes from me, that can't see in the dark, replace them with the eyes of a cat, so I can see with light so stark," Darkess whispered.

Her vision increased for a moment, then like a strobe, went brighter and darker. Darkess blinked her eyes, trying to clear her vision, but once she tried to focus on Chakra's walking form, her vision went from almost perfect to extremely poor. The spell wouldn't hold.

"Blast!" Darkess cussed but finally started to follow her familiar.

It was her own fault, and she knew it. The mountain had her blood. It knew her now, and it was overpowering her magic, especially magic she had used before. Nostrils flaring in anger at herself, she quickened her pace to catch her cat. Once again, she felt the child in her struggle. If she made ridiculous mistakes like this, no wonder they all thought she couldn't handle this yet.

There were scurrying sounds in the stalactites along the ceiling, but the little beasts had seen what happened the first time and had so far stayed back. She could see their glowing eyes now and again as they glided between the formations. The further down the tunnel they walked, the more scurrying they heard. The creatures were following, and more were showing up. The claw sounds increased, but they had kept their mouths silent so far. Darkess walked a couple of feet behind Chakra, since he was now the principal set of eyes for the two of them, both stepping cautiously. Several minutes had passed since the bulbous-eyed creature had first attacked them when the chattering sound began. Increasing quickly, it became a deafening noise.

Darkess' adrenaline started pumping wildly, and she was on full alert, pulling knives from several hidden pouches. Then it happened. Three of the creatures jumped Chakra. It was their last mistake. Quick as a flash, Darkess threw two knives in succession, each landing squarely on their target. Chakra's hair was bristled from head to tail, and he had one of the creatures pinned to the floor with his claws and his teeth sunk deep into its neck. Jumping back, Chakra sat on his hind legs, two paws up, claws bared, hissing at the carcasses on the ground. Batting at the creature he killed to make sure it was dead, he then checked the creatures with hilts stuck into their broken bodies. Darkess squatted down and pulled her blades from the creatures, wiping blood off the blades in the creatures' white fur. Anger swelled inside of her. She projected it through her thoughts, booming a warning at the little beasts but not knowing if they would hear her.

'I'm not here to harm you, but cross my path again, and I will kill you. This is not a threat, it is a promise.'

Crouching down next to Chakra, Darkess whispered, "Did you hear that?"

'It wasn't very loud, but I heard it. And by the sound of the retreating claws, I think they heard you, too. Wretched beasts. They got me all dirty again,' came the feint reply from Chakra.

The sound of claws scraping stone could be heard all around them, but the chattering had stopped. Looking back where the carcasses had been, Darkess saw that only one remained.

"Ulch, they eat their dead," she grimaced as she turned back towards the path and continued on.

The temperature of the cave wasn't exactly cold, but after the extreme heat of the desert, Darkess had the occasional shiver. Pulling her cloak up around her shoulders, she noticed the stone was dripping.

"So, that's how you have survived down here," Darkess mumbled at the few pairs of bulbous eyes still watching from a safe distance on the ceiling as she ran her fingers through the dripping water.

☼

Far above Darkess on the desert floor, night had fallen. Takar was dead set on reaching the mountains this evening, and finding the last egg was his only priority. He could feel the pull of magic in this area, and he plucked the egg detector from his pocket. Its eyes were glowing, so he quickened his pace. The moon was rising in the sky. Even at half-full, it helped considerably. Takar could see the trail of footsteps up ahead of him. Furrowing his brow and squinting his eyes, he scanned as far as he could see. He seemed to be alone, but he grew ever cautious. He had to get to that trail. There was someone here the last time he had been in this place, and he was sure this was his or her trail.

His heartbeat quickened, and he sniffed at the breeze. Since the trail had just begun out of nowhere, Takar was positive it was magic. He was in the right place, finally. He was so excited his eyes dilated like he had taken a powerful drug. Absently, he scratched at his groin as he walked briskly along, following his demon senses.

"Magic lives here," he said breathlessly.

Then he began to run, picking up speed the further he ran. He was too excited to wait. He had to get to that trail.

≈

The tunnel spiraled down in a long, lazy curve. Darkess stopped for a moment, digging for her water bladder. Chakra was drinking from a puddle he had found along the wall.

'Fresh as rainwater,' came faintly from Chakra.

Darkess found a place where the water was dripping quickly, and she put the mouth of her bladder under it. Far off down the tunnel came a crashing of stone and a roar of such magnitude that Darkess jerked involuntarily, causing water to spill down her leg. With her heart pounding, she looked towards where the sound had come.

"What the blazes was that?" Darkess asked, holding the night shine close to her face.

"Dark," she whispered, and they were plunged into blackness.

The only sounds now were the drips of water and the ragged sounds of Darkess' breath. Feeling her way along the wall, she moved slowly forward. Her heart was pounding up into her throat. She wasn't afraid of the dark, but instead, what was hiding in its protective cloak. There was little sand here, not enough to muffle her footstep anyway, and each one sounded like a crack in her ears. Darkess winced with each stride until she began to see a faint glow ahead. Dividing her attention between the glow and her footsteps, she nearly tripped on Chakra, who had stopped in front of her.

'Do you see something?' she projected.

'The cave is opening up ahead. There is a pit in the center now. Something is down there,' Chakra answered.

Getting on her knees, Darkess crawled to where the light ended. There was a hole in the roof of the cave, and moonlight was shining in. From the looks of it, the hole had been bored with magic. It was maybe the length of a man's arm in width but exceedingly deep. The moon would only be visible here for a few minutes each night, which would mean the same for the sun each day.

'How odd,' Darkess projected.

The moon had nearly passed the hole for it shed little light now, but she could see the tunnel was now more like a ramp, winding deeper into the stone cavern. The sound of tumbling rocks came from the pit, followed by a groan.

'Something is down there,' Darkess repeated.

Why haven't they tried to make some sort of contact with me, Darkess wondered. Standing up, she walked to where the wall still stood next to the ramp and continued down at an annoyingly slow pace. The light from the sky hole was waning, and seeing was becoming more difficult again. Wrapping her cloak around her night shine, she whispered,

"Illuminate."

It had the desired effect.

"Perfect," she whispered.

The only light was coming from the pointed tip, which she kept angled towards the ground. This enabled Darkess to quicken her pace. She made what she considered to be one revolution of the pit then crept to the edge to have another look. Shoving the crystal deep inside her cloak, she hid her profile as she poked her head out over the ledge. Nothing. Not a sound. No light. No movement. Nothing. Darkess grew suspicious. Maybe it had heard or seen her. She made her way back to the wall, uncovered her crystal, and followed the tunnel at a quicker pace than before.

Several long minutes passed as they walked. Chakra leapt out of Darkess' way as the winding path ran its jagged course. The wind outside the cave made strange sounds through the sky hole, making the hair stand up on her neck. The closer she got to the bottom, the more her senses seemed heightened. She mumbled the spell to see through Chakra's eyes and received a momentary glimpse of the pit's depth. She could see archways leading from the pit and stone rubble all around before her vision went dark again.

"Blast!" Darkess cursed.

Chakra ignored her and walked on. Using the night shine, she scanned a few steps ahead and realized the ramp leading down to the pit was unfinished. It was sheered off, leaving a distance of at least the height of two men between the ledge and the floor. Lying on her stomach, Darkess held her head over the edge. Not hearing anything, she chanced using her night shine to have a peek. Holding the crystal over the edge, point facing down, she saw a pile of boulders directly beneath her.

"Hmph," she grunted.

Her thoughts raced. What was all this rubble? Something trying to get out? An easy way to descend? A trap? She had to find another way down. Something just feels wrong about that pile of rubble. Darkess absently wiped away the hair from her eyes as she mumbled the spell again. She knew she only had mere heartbeats to see what she could and devise a way down. Her eyes flashed again, and for a moment, the pit was clear. There were seven archways leading from the pit itself and no stairs, ropes, ladders nor any other method of descent. But before she could look any further, her vision again went dark.

"Blast it all!" she hissed again.

'It's your own fault,' came very faintly from Chakra.

"Who asked you?" Darkess smirked.

Rolling over onto her back, Darkess thought for a minute or two. She stared at the hole in the cave's ceiling. She stared at it for a long time. Then suddenly, it was as if she were seeing it for the first time. Why was that hole there? What was its purpose? How deep was it? The hole was the only thing Darkess could see clearly. The stars and moon above let a small amount of light through. Was it an air hole? Maybe it was from a battle? Somehow it must be important. "Oh well," she thought, "right now, I must go down into that pit, curious hole or not." Rolling over onto her knees, she pointed her light around the edge and found a few small pebbles. Scooping them into her hand, she tossed one down to the floor of the pit. Clanking down on the stone floor, it bounced a couple of times then slid to a stop. Darkess waited and watched.

Whatever had roared earlier was no longer in range to hear the stone, and there were no traps a small stone would set off, anyway. Feeling extra precautious, Darkess threw three more stones all at once to the pit floor. She waited on pins and needles, thinking surely there would be a trap.

325

"Hear anything?" Darkess whispered.

'Only the wind,' came faintly with static from Chakra.

Darkess pursed her lips and wiped her hands on her legs. Securing her pack tightly, she looked at Chakra and whispered, "Here goes nothing."

Squatting on the edge of the pit and facing the center of it, she jumped. Tucking her legs, she rolled into the pit, landed on her feet, and spun out of her painful landing. Immediately, she jumped to her feet and scanned the room, listening for whatever lived down here. Several intense seconds passed as she waited to be attacked. The pit remained silent as well as the seven archways that led from it.

"Okay," Darkess mouthed and signed at the same time.

She looked up at Chakra and placed her pack on her head. Standing a couple of feet from the wall, she braced for impact. The weight on her head was brief as Chakra landed on the pack then leaped to the floor. Together, they made their way around the pit, looking for any indication of which way they should go now. Darkess then tried her golden egg.

"Point me towards the dragon egg," she whispered to it.

The egg only wobbled upon her palm then lay there, unmoving. Grimacing at the egg, she stowed it away. Once again, her powers were suppressed. Chakra sat still watching Darkess as she looked at the pile of rubble. Where had it come from? Darkess had no clue, because the pit had fairly smooth walls and seemed in perfect condition. Then she saw a flat edge sticking out from under one of the smaller boulders. Shining her crystal at it, she realized the rubble was meant to hide something.

"There's something under here," Darkess grunted as she pulled off a stone.

She pulled off every small stone she saw then tried a few of the larger ones. There was a huge stone directly in the center of what looked like an altar. She knew her powers were weak, but she was willing to take the time to try them out. This altar hides something important, but what, she wondered. Standing near the wall, she placed her hands on one of the larger rocks and her back against the wall. With all of her strength and every bit of magic she could muster, she managed to move the stone five or six inches. Darkess wiped her brow on her arm, and placed her hands on the rock for another try. This time, it moved almost a foot. Sweat was rolling down the sides of her face, and she took a couple of deep breaths. This time she knew it was going to fall and probably alert the thing that lived here. Her nerves were tingling at the thought as she gave the boulder one last shove.

Sure enough, the rock fell and slammed into the pile below. Darkess pressed herself up against the wall, watching one archway then the next in near darkness. Nothing appeared, but she was worried anyway. She circled the pit, listening at each opening. She shined her night shine down each one, but there wasn't enough light to see very far. After checking each doorway, neither hearing nor seeing anything, she made her way back to the altar. The wood surface was scarred deeply from the rocks that had been on it, but she could still see it had been beautifully carved and elegant at one time. There were a couple of smashed glass bottles and some scraps of parchment. Inspecting each piece, she found that their age had left them faded beyond readability.

"Nothing of any help," Darkess said, continuing her search.

Stacking the parchment pieces, she held them as she blew off the top of the altar, wiping away the heavier debris with her other hand. There was an engraved rectangle on one corner of the face. Darkess traced it with her finger, and the rectangle moved ever so slightly. She began to try to wiggle it loose. Bending over the top, she got a better look at the edge of that same corner. She saw the engraving lines followed over the edge. It was a secret compartment. Darkess gripped the top and side and pulled. It moved some but grew tight. She blew into the cracks, brushing them with her hand. Then she smacked the lid with the open face of her palm. There was a small popping sound, and she gripped the lid and pulled again. It moved but still not enough to see down inside.

Pulling a small knife with a slender blade from the back of her pants, she began to dig again at the cracks around the lid. As she pried, she again heard a popping sound, and off it jumped into the rubble on the floor. The soft light now poured into the hidden slot. Darkess could hardly believe her eyes. The amythest crystal from her dream came back to her in amazing clarity. The ancient leather strap tied to it had rotted loose. Darkess pulled the crystal out and laid it next to her night shine. She cut a slice of leather off her cloak and tied it to the crystal just as she had seen before.

Chakra jumped on the altar's surface and watched the arched openings as Darkess worked on the crystal. Her breathing became quicker as she held the crystal from its new tether in front of her face. She yanked the crystal up into her palm and scratched Chakra with her free hand.

"Ole buddy, you better hope this thing still works. Or better yet, works for me," she said.

Chakra purred and jumped off the altar to follow her. Flickering the night shine across the pit, Darkess eyed each opening and listened closely.

Centering herself as well as she could between them, she once again dangled the crystal in front of her face.

"Show me where the dragon egg is hidden."

The crystal merely dangled from Darkess' slightly trembling hand.

'You didn't really think that would work, did you?' Chakra mumbled faintly.

Darkess flared her nostrils at her cat.

"I have another idea. I just thought I would try the easy way first," she said.

Darkess sat down cross-legged where she had stood, placing her pack on her folded legs. Pulling out a velvet pouch and a small knife, she laid them beside the crystal on the ground in front of her. She secured her pack on her back and looked at her cat.

'What are you doing?' Chakra asked, his attitude coming through the quiet.

"I don't know why I didn't think of this before. I'm going to add my protection to the cavern," Darkess said quickly.

'Why would you do that?'

"If I add my protection, it won't feel I'm a threat any longer…and maybe if we're lucky, it will reveal its secrets to me. Whoever lived here is dead and gone. The magic here is dying."

'The magic here is strong,' Chakra countered.

Darkess pulled herbs from the pouch in front of her as she eyed Chakra and explained.

"The magic of the egg is strong. The family who lived here – their magic is dying."

'Then how do you explain the growl and the stone falling?' Chakra defended himself.

Cutting pieces of herbs with her small knife, Darkess prepared her meager potion.

"I can't right now. There is something down here, but it is not one of the coven. More likely, it's a creature left to guard the greater treasures."

Darkess continued to work on her spell and potion, once again annoyed that Chakra was questioning her every move. Hadn't she trained her entire life for this very moment? Or was it just that she wasn't ready yet? Cutting a couple of strands of her hair away, she tied the small bundles she had made with the hair. Hopefully, this added to the power of the potion and held it together.

'What's that?' Chakra asked.

"What's what?" Darkess answered abrasively.

When no reply came from her trusted but annoying familiar, she looked at him with a look of utter exasperation. But the look slipped off her face when she realized Chakra was serious about his question as he stared towards the ceiling. There came a glow above their heads that became more intense with each passing heartbeat.

Darkess lay down her bundles but gripped her knife as she stood up to her full height to watch what was unfolding above her. An odd design was etched around the ceiling that was now glowing. There were ovals, maybe twenty of them, each with eight squiggled lines evenly spaced around their edges. The light became so intense that she had to close her eyes for a moment. When she reopened them, the ovals began to pulsate. The stone was coming alive. The light again became so bright that Darkess shielded her eyes. Now the ovals were trembling, and the lines coming from them began to ripple like tentacles. On the face of the rock, each tentacle struggled to break free of its two-dimensional bonds. Darkess could scarcely believe her eyes when the lines on the rock became tube shaped tentacles, each reaching, stretching, happy to be free.

Just as suddenly as the lines became tentacles, they placed their tips near each oval on the rock and pushed, straining hard and shaking with the effort. The ovals were slowly released from their two-dimensional world with a cracking, grinding sound. Once free of the wall, the ovals turned into an ugly brown and tan gelatinous looking creature with eight tentacles gently glowing and floating in midair. Acid yellow spots appeared on the body of the creature and ran a pattern. Under normal circumstances, Darkess would have been curious and excited to see something like this. And although there was a look of awe on her face, Darkess' body was tense, and her hands were balled into fists.

"What are they?" Darkess said.

But when she looked down at Chakra, she saw his hair was standing up along his spine, and his tail was rigid.

'I have no idea,' his answer came faintly in her mind, 'but my guess is, it's not the welcoming committee.'

Darkess slowly rotated her feet, moving in a circle. She checked the distance between her and the newly formed creatures. They had her surrounded in a perfect circle. Not sure if she should act or not, she readied a second knife but only stood still, waiting. The archways leading from the pit remained black and silent. One of the creatures began to descend on Darkess, and she threw one knife, hitting it dead center. The knife went clean through the boneless body and crashed into the stone wall behind it. Sand poured from the wound, and it lost all of its brighter colors and turned back to tan. Just as the last few grains of sand fell from its slender wound, the flow went out of its tentacles, and it came crashing to the floor in a gelatinous heap to rest atop its own entrails of sand.

A tiny grin flickered across the corner of Darkess' mouth. Heaving a second knife and pulling two more, she watched as her knife again hit its target. Only this time, the blade stuck in place. It had the desired effect, at least for a moment. The luminescent blob stopped advancing. Darkess was stunned by this but heaved a third knife at the next creature in line. The knife hit it directly in the side, making a loud crack and breaking off the tip of the blade, sending it falling to the floor.

"They learn from each other," Darkess whispered.

The second creature she had hit was now using its tentacles to grab at the hilt of the knife imbedded in its side. Once it had pulled it free, the creature dropped it next to the other fallen blade and continued to descend on Darkess.

"We can't just stand here and wait to see what happens next! We have to get out of here!" Darkess said to Chakra.

Quickly, Darkess scooped up her bundles and moved towards one of the tunnel openings, ducking inside. The hovering orbs continued to descend on the pit as Darkess and Chakra walked down the tunnel farthest away from the lowest creature. Only a few steps inside the archway passage, Darkess realized her mistake. They were trapped. This wasn't a tunnel, but a storeroom meant to look like a tunnel. There were empty burlap sacks, broken wooden crates, and a few empty glass bottles. There had been food here at one point, but the stores here had long since run out.

"How could I be so foolish?" Darkess chastised herself as she searched for anything that might help her.

Barricade the door then finish the spell, was the first thing that entered her head. Don't get cornered, was unfortunately, the next thought. It came just a few moments too late, for she was, of course, already trapped. She almost yelled at herself. Going to the first pile of wood, she pulled only the whole crates first. She stacked all that she could; leaving only a small space near the top that wasn't large enough for the creatures to enter. As she placed the last broken crate on the top, one of the tentacles reached for Darkess' arm. She was quick at moving out of harm's way, but the tentacle oozed a drop of glowing acid yellow slime onto her arm. Even through her leather sleeve, she felt the intense heat. Pulling her arm up inside her sleeve, she cut off the extra material with a knife. When it hit the ground, the sleeve sizzled as the acidic slime burnt all the way through both sides and left a large smoldering whole. A tentacle whipped through one of the slots in the crates, narrowly missing Darkess' shoulder. A drip landed on the stone floor and sizzled, marring the stone.

"Back," Darkess told Chakra as the two of them retreated as far as the wall behind them would allow.

"Seems to be holding…for now, anyway."

Darkess knelt down, torched some debris for light, and pulled out the small bundles. She stared at them, working the spell out in her mind. She'd have to change it a bit. She no longer wanted to add to the protection of this pit, she wanted to control it. It was either over power the magic guarding this place or become dust in a cave never to be seen again. Her mind raced over the proper wording as the sizzling sounds returned. The creatures were trying to dissolve the wood that was barring their passage.

'You'd better hurry,' Chakra projected weakly to his witch.

"Working on it…" Darkess mumbled through clenched teeth.

She reopened the wound on her hand, and blood pooled in her palm. She dipped each bundle in the pool and saturating them. Then she laid them in a pile and poured the remaining blood over. Quickly wrapping her hand again, she grabbed a burlap sack and began stuffing it with other discarded items from the room. The burlap was old and rotten, and small tears were forming with each new item Darkess stuffed into it. Grabbing a second sack, she repeated the process.

'What are you doing…cleaning up?' Chakra pleaded with more static than before.

"I've got a plan," Darkess said as she rushed around the small room.

Laying the second sack next to the first, Darkess grabbed the blood-soaked bundles and rolled them into her shirttail in the front. Securing her pack, she squared her shoulders and looked towards the entrance. The wood was breaking down, and the sizzling became louder as several more globs of the acidic yellow goo hit their target. Darkess knelt down and took a firm grip of the two bags in front of her. Looking from the collapsing crates to her familiar, she warned Chakra,

"Stay here. Do not follow me."

The look in Darkess' eyes showed Chakra that she meant business, and he held his tongue. He stayed exactly where he was, watching the determination in her body language. Darkess stood up, flexing the muscles in her arms as she hefted one sack in each hand. With all of her might and all the magic she could muster, which wasn't much, she flung the sacks towards the passage. One broke open short of its destination, showering debris at the wall of melting crates but doing little damage. However the second sack hit hard. Wood exploded on impact, showering the pit's open floor with splinters of wood and scraps of burlap. Only one of the creatures was harmed by the blast; however, it had the affect that Darkess wanted. The rest of the creatures retreated several feet.

Darkess took off running when the second sack hit, knowing she would only have heartbeats to execute her plan. She waited until the last possible second to throw up both her hands, temporarily freezing the guardians of the pit. Unrolling her shirt, she pulled out the bundles and tossed one in front of each tunnel. When she counted to seven, she noticed the creatures had already begun to move again. Several were oozing acid and flipping it at her as they began again to descend on her.

"Lavender, lapis dust, and thistle, add the blood of the Vallencourt castle!" Darkess yelled.

Knowing a second freeze probably wouldn't hold, she dodged a couple drips of acid and tried again. Her hands flew up, and the creatures moved extremely slow, as if fighting a veil. It worked just long enough for Darkess to finish the spell.

"I call upon the power of my ancestors, to help me pass safely through these corridors."

Darkess blinked her eyes, not knowing what to expect. As she refocused on the closest guardian, she saw it was regaining its full strength and heading straight towards her. Instinctively, her hand went for the hilt of a knife when an arc of electricity shot up from each bundle she had thrown. All seven arcs converged at the top to make an enormous energy ball. It held its shape for an instant before exploding down into the pit. Darkess had no time to react. The ball was beautiful and horrifying as it advanced upon her. The shock wave blew her off her feet, slamming her into the floor. She felt the blast but not the floor. She was unconscious before the guardians of the pit smashed to the ground around her. Everything went black, right down to the night shine crystal.

☼

In a dark room somewhere, a man ran his fingers through the flame of a candle that's sputtering in the breeze. His fingers shadow his face so closely that his identity is kept secret. His breathing is deep and even, until an evil chuckle rumbles in his throat.

"Anyday now," he whispers as he pinches out the flame, a smile curls his lips in the dark.

≈

Takar sat staring at the spot where the footprints disappeared into the rock. He felt vibrations in the ground around him. A smirk crossed his face. Maybe she got the egg and did all the hard work for me, he thought to himself. Settling back down into the sand, he decided to wait here for the girl to return with his egg. He caressed the small shoe print in front of him in the sand almost lovingly. He hadn't felt this excited in a while, and his grin widened, sickeningly.

≈

Silver sat on a stool at one of the kitchens' tables weaving an unusually large basket. She seemed in a trance as she worked. Daniel had asked her to come to bed earlier, and her refusal made him sit in a more comfortable chair near her. He had dozed off and was gently snoring. Roxy and Tanner had long since retired for the evening, but Angela sat watching her daughter. The rings under both of their eyes were dark and deep. Worry and little food or rest hadn't helped, either.

Angela was worried about more than her granddaughter's life possibly being in peril, let alone the world. She was worried about Silver. Her eyes had never stayed clouded over for this long before. Occasionally, odd shapes would appear in the clouds of Silver's eyes, but Angela could not distinguish them. Her hands were moving skillfully over the form as she went, even though she had never produced this shape before.

"Silver, dear…" Angela tried once again to speak to her daughter.

Finally, the clouds in Silver's eyes began to retreat, and she blinked several times.

"I'm sorry, I must have been concentrating too hard. What did you say?" Silver said through a yawn.

It was not exactly the response she'd expected, but Angela was relieved.

"Are you alright?"

"I'm fine, why do you ask?" Silver replied but still worked on the basket.

"You've been sitting here weaving for nearly five hours. Everyone else is asleep."

"No, surely you're mistaken," Silver sloughed it off.

"Really, Silver. Look at the time," Angela said, not shocked at all.

Silver stopping her weaving and looked about the room. It was getting very late, almost morning.

"Oh well, I can finish in the morning. There's not much left to do. Have I really been sitting here for five hours?"

"Are you sure you are alright? Your eyes were clouded. I thought that you were getting a vision for a while, but you never stopped weaving," Angela said.

"My eyes were clouded? That's odd. Did I do anything different? Say anything?"

"No," Angela said quietly.

"Well, it must be the combination of concentration, worry, and not enough sleep," Silver said dismissively.

Standing up, stretching and yawning, Silver wiped at her eyes.

"Darkess is going to need this when she gets back," Silver said, gently patting the basket.

"Let's try to get some sleep," Angela said, eyeing her daughter uncertainly.

Waking Daniel, Silver started for her room and added a word.

"Tell me if anything out of the ordinary happens tonight. Something's got to happen soon."

But Angela believed something had already happened. She just couldn't say what.

≈

Alieria and Tasha had kept the Shadow Seekers at bay during the day, but at night it was a completely different story. When shadows were blanketing the world, they were nearly impossible to keep out. Fire and light helped to keep them back, but fuel sources were diminishing, and none of the wizards could sustain a fireball for such a long duration. It was a daunting task. Then there were the countless witches, wizards, and creatures now inhabiting the small castle. Even with this many close by, the night was unnerving, leaving everyone as jumpy as young children. The supplies were being used as quickly as they were obtained. Everyone was as exhausted as the supplies, and arguments between the refugees had broken out frequently. This many magical beings in the same place was not a normal occurrence. The state of affairs was keeping the elders and those with greater power very busy.

Windows were being exploded by rocks, bricks, even the Shadow Seekers themselves. Magic restored all but the largest section of windows overlooking the front. Poor Brutus was stretched thin over them, clinging to four knives jammed between the stones at the four corners of the windows. He was doing a better job than anyone at keeping the Shadow Seekers out of the castle. When they hit him, they simply bounced off instead of tearing through the room and destroying everything and everyone in their path with falling shelves or broken glass. Even though magic had restored the windows, it was becoming more and more upsetting and tiresome. Alieria had just repaired the glass panes in her library when one of the little buggers made it through, knocking over a giant shelf filled with books. No one had been in the room with her, and she decided to leave the mess when she heard screams down the hall.

"What now?" she roared and took off at a run.

Her brow furrowed as she turned the corner at the door. She was mumbling with her hands clasped in front of her mouth, tears entering the corners of her eyes. The snobby socialite was completely gone.

"Darkess, you must hurry back…we need you."

☼

The ground felt cold and gritty under her back, and her body felt numb. There wasn't a sound and it was dark, completely black. "Where am I?" she wondered. Her entire head hurt. She reached for her forehead and found a trail of blood running from her temple down her cheek. She must have been hit hard, she thought, as she tasted blood on her lips. Trying to sit up, her muscles screamed agony with every move. She sucked in air with the excruciating pain in her head and back. "Where the hell am I?" she asked herself. The straps on one side of her pack had ripped free, leaving one side tangled on her arm. She knew her pack inside and out, and she fumbled through it for her water bladder. She took a long drink then poured some on the corner of a rag and dabbed at her wound. She produced a fireball in her hand, and the light burned her eyes. She held it out in front of her to get a good look around.

She couldn't see very much, so Darkess levitated the fireball higher. Once the light fell upon the pit, she sucked in deeply, and the fireball fell a few feet before stabilizing. She remembered where she was, and the weight of the situation fell back on her. Nervously, she looked around the pit. The creatures had been smashed to sandy bits. Where was Chakra? Stumbling to her feet, she groaned and grunted her way to the storeroom where she had left him. The fireball floated ahead of her. There was debris everywhere around the entrance, both inside and out. It took careful steps, but the going was getting easier with each pace. Then, she saw Chakra's tail and back legs behind some broken wood.

"Chakra?" Darkess said, a quiver in her voice.

She pulled the wood off of her cat and gently touched him.

"Chakra?" she said again, this time her voice was thick with worry.

There was no movement. Darkess pulled the tiny limp body onto her lap. A tear escaped her eye and mixed with the blood on her cheek, rolling down and hanging upon her chin. There were no visible injuries to the cat, and Darkess rubbed his head with her fingertips.

"Wake up...p-please...w...wake up," Darkess mumbled, her throat tight and thickening with pain.

The tears flowed more freely, and each one dripped from her chin and splattered on her knee. One tear finally hit Chakra's whiskers, and he twitched. Sniffing hard, Darkess held still, waiting to see if he had really moved, or if she had imagined it. Several nervous seconds passed when Chakra sneezed and opened his eyes.

"Oh, you're a-alive!" Darkess said, hugging her cat close.

'You're choking me,' Chakra projected loud and clear into Darkess' head, as if he had screamed it to her.

"Sorry!" Darkess said.

Chakra looked at the fireball hanging in the air above them.

'Your powers...they're back. How did you pull that off?' Chakra questioned Darkess, the smugness already returning to his voice.

Absently rubbing at the bloodied tears on her face, Darkess turned down the emotions as far as she could, trying to return to the task at hand.

"I changed the spell," she sniffed. "I used the power of my family line to overthrow the dying, yet still potentially dangerous magic here. It must have worked. The blobs with tentacles are all gone, and my powers seem strong...stronger than normal."

'That is because you were without them,' Chakra projected.

"No...I don't think so. It feels...er...like I'm getting a boost," Darkess said, furrowing her brow in concentration.

Biting her lip, she stared at the blood on her hand. Then closing her hand tightly into a fist, she stood back up. She rolled her head around on her shoulders and stretched. She was trying desperately to relieve the soreness in her muscles, wishing her grandmother were here to help heal her wounds.

"There's no time to speculate now. We must find that blasted egg and get the hell out of here," Darkess said, quickly cutting Chakra off before he could say something snide.

Turning back towards the open pit, she waved her hand. All of the mess littering her way was swept aside, clearing a perfect path.

"Now that's more like it," Darkess said, her face hard as stone with determination.

As she walked back to the center of the pit, Darkess pulled out the crystal she had found earlier in the altar. With her newly restored powers, she levitated the larger remaining stones off the altar and approached it. There was a dragon's head carved into the wooden face. The stones had done serious damage to the carving, but it was still obvious what it was. She rubbed her hand across the marred surface. Returning to the center of the pit, Darkess held the crystal high and said clearly,

"Point me the way to the dragon egg."

The crystal hung limp. Darkess stared at the floor and whispered,

"Poorly phrased? Ah...yes. Show me your greatest treasure."

The crystal swung wildly on the end of its thong. Finally, it pointed to the archway directly next to the one she'd previously occupied with Chakra. Magically clearing a path, Darkess strode confidently towards the second tunnel. Several steps inside revealed a body, a hairy gray body about the size of a man. Darkess cautiously approached the prone form. It was perfectly still, so she flicked her finger, moving the arm off the face it was covering.

"What is it?" Darkess asked Chakra.

'Looks like a werewolf crossed with a human. Although that's not what it is, I don't think. I'm not really sure what it is.'

Darkess knelt down and touched its chest, feeling nothing. Next she tried feeling its mouth and nose for breath.

"It's warm but dead."

'Or so you think.' Chakra said, cautiously circling the body and sniffing the entire form, from large calloused feet to small hairy head.

"This has to be what we heard earlier. The grunting and growling, and it has human-like hands, perfectly suitable for moving rocks," Darkess said with relief in her voice.

Looking the body over more closely, she noticed a leather strap on its arm. Turning the band around to get a better look, she saw that it was very old. Nearly worn away from what must have been decades of wear was a dragon's head, exactly the same as the one carved into the altar.

"Another guardian of the egg?" Darkess asked.

Conflicted, she looked at the body one more time. On one hand, she was glad this thing was dead, but on the other, what could she have learned from it? Could it speak…or reason? Did it know the secrets of this place? Or was it just a mindless beast guarding its master's treasures? Unfortunately, she would probably never know. This caused her to clear her vision and return to her search. Swinging the floating fireball around to light the path ahead, she continued down the tunnel. Chakra was hot on her heels. A few more moments passed, and Darkess found herself standing on the edge of what looked to be a deep pit cut across the tunnel. There was no way over, not even a toehold at the edge. Darkess got on her knees and floated her fireball down. It hit something at floor level and stopped. Darkess pressed the fireball down and it extinguished.

"How odd," She murmured.

When she lit another fireball, she noticed more of that backwards writing. Pulling a blade, she lay on her back and held the knife over her head. It read, 'A leap of faith will help you on your way.'

"Leap of faith, huh?" Darkess said.

Standing up, she looked at her familiar, and without another word, jumped into the chasm. Instead of plummeting, she landed squarely on what felt like a stone surface. Instantly, the illusion vanished, and the floor became whole again. Witch and familiar looked at each other, grinning.

'You must be overcoming the magic as you encounter it. Best be on your toes,' Chakra told Darkess.

"You thought I was going to fall," Darkess said.

'You can levitate. Why would I think you'd fall?' Chakra said, embarrassed.

"I saw you as I jumped. You thought I'd have to use magic to get across, and you were worried. You thought I would fall," Darkess smirked at Chakra.

Letting Chakra's embarrassment sink in, Darkess turned on her heels and continued on down the tunnel. Chakra bounded down the corridor to catch up with his master, tail twitching in annoyance all the way. There was a spilt up ahead, and Darkess pulled out the clan's crystal.

"Show me your greatest treasure."

The crystal hung limply. That had worked last time, Darkess thought. Evidently, once someone had the proper tunnel, they should know where to go next. So she pulled out her own directional device: her golden egg.

"Show me the strongest magical source in this tunnel."

The egg spun and pointed directly at Darkess. She wrinkled up her nose and snorted at the egg.

"Show me the dragon egg?" Darkess asked as well as said.

The egg again spun around and pointed down the left tunnel in the split. Darkess followed the arrow down the tunnel. So far, the tunnel's shape had been consistently the same; however, the floor seemed to change periodically. The floor had been smooth until this point, except of course where it had been temporarily missing. Now there was a pattern. Darkess stopped. Something about the sudden change made her instincts flare up. The floor itself said nothing in writing as far as she could see. It just seemed ominous to her. She felt the hair go up on the back of her neck.

'What?' came from Chakra.

"Don't walk on that," Darkess said.

'Why not? What's wrong with it?' Chakra asked.

"Not sure," Darkess replied.

Darkess put her arm out over the floor in front of her. Nothing happened, so she touched one of the squares in the pattern. Nothing again. Digging into her pocket, she pulled out a couple of rocks she'd found earlier and tossed one onto the patterned floor. It bounced a few times, and each time it hit one of the squares with the wavy pattern across it, a dart flew out of the wall and smashed into the other side of the tunnel. Tossing a second stone, the same thing happened.

"Stay off the squares that look like waves of water."

Darkess threw a third rock, trying to hit other patterned stones. It seemed that only the water ones were booby-trapped. Gingerly, she stepped onto the diamond-patterned stones and was unharmed, so they kept going. Chakra stepped on the last water stone at the end of the patterned area, and nothing happened. Once again, the magic died once Darkess crossed it.

Darkess was beginning to think that she'd never reach the treasured egg, and she itched to move quicker but held herself in check due to the consequences. It was in these between places that her fatigue began to eat at her. She was tired and injured, and she just wanted to go home to her family and her soft bed and rest safely in her room. Then she saw the faces of all the hungry and scared people back in Crystal City and knew she must stay the course. Several steps after this thought, Darkess felt nothing when her foot should have hit the floor. She was floating but wasn't falling and could move neither forward nor back. She was stuck in midair. Trying to levitate, she slammed herself into the ceiling. The impact sent tears to her eyes and caused her to rotate in space. She was now inches from the ceiling and facing the floor, holding her head with her eyes pinched shut from the pain.

"Damn that hurt, sssssssss" Darkess sucked in air, rubbing the sore spot.

'Now what do we do?' Chakra projected from the floor behind the danger zone.

"Hell if I know. The last thing I tried nearly crushed my skull. Ouch," She said, gingerly rubbing her bloodied scalp.

'Well, do something,' Chakra demanded.

"Got any suggestions?" Darkess looked at her cat snidely but got no response.

"That's what I thought," she said, rolling over to face the ceiling.

"Whoa," she whispered.

'What?'

"It feels like I'm in water, only I can breathe."

Darkess grabbed a hold of the ceiling's roughness as well as she could and pulled herself along. Once she had half of her body past the energy field, she flipped onto the floor, landing on her feet.

"Well, come on. Or do you want to stay here and wait for me?"

'I can't levitate,' Chakra projected.

"Just swim across."

'Cats don't swim, or haven't you noticed?'

"It's not actually water, you furry chicken."

Not sure exactly what to expect, Chakra entered the zone of weightlessness and walked normally across the floor.

'Thanks,' the cat quietly projected once he'd reached his master.

Darkess smiled knowingly, and silence fell upon them as they walked down the tunnel and lower into the ground. She wondered how deep they were and if they would ever see the light of day again. Then she saw that the tunnel curved up ahead, making a blind spot. This caused Darkess to stop thinking, and slowly inch her way around the bend. A glowing lavender mist hung in the air. Unsure if the mist was innocuous or not, she skirted the bend on the far side, catching a glimpse of an opening that was human shaped.

'I think we found the treasure room,' Darkess projected to Chakra.

Waving her hand through the mist, she felt nothing but exhilarated, and she smiled. Slowly she stepped into the opening. When the light from her fireball reached the contents of the room, Darkess' jaw dropped. Easily, one hundred eggs were standing on pedestals on waist height cabinets that filled a room quite large in size but low in height. The single fireball wasn't enough to light the entire room, which made it difficult to see the outer reaches. Noticing a torch next to the door, Darkess lit it, and it sprung all the other torches to life.

'After all this time, I didn't think they would work,' Chakra projected to Darkess.

Still, Darkess did not venture into the room. She looked at the ceiling and found that there were no carvings here. And the floor looked clear also. Finally, she decided she could try a step or two and found her feet moving easily across the floor. Her eyes roamed the room to get a much closer look at the eggs. Lavender mist hung throughout the entire room. Dust and sand covered most everything in this old, unkept place. Brushing off one of the eggs, Darkess realized it was made of wood. Bugs had eaten into it, covering it with holes and marring the surface.

Checking the eggs in the first row, she saw that each was a decoy, a rotting, bug-eaten decoy. Darkess' heart jumped in her chest. This will make it easy, she thought, as she went to the second row of eggs. It was the same as the first, making her more excited. She almost ran to the start of the third row when she saw the skeleton. Squatting down next to the corpse, she recognized the clothes, or rather what was left of them. The bones, hair, jewelry, and tattered rags on the floor were the remains of the wizard who had greeted her earlier, or rather the recording she had seen.

"He must have been the last of his line. No one to take his place...or bury his body. He was taking his last stand. The egg is not in this row."

'Check anyway. He is lying next to his treasure,' Chakra projected.

"Haven't you been paying attention? This entire room is full of decoys. He is the last one. The real egg is in the last row. But we will check his body. He seems to be sitting on something."

Darkess lifted up the rags the corpse was wearing and found a book hidden under him. Shoving him over, she pulled the book out.

"Sorry," Darkess winced when the skeleton fell apart on the floor.

It was a little worn, but in much better condition than its owner. There was a dragonhead on the cover, just like the one on the altar and the leather band on the creatures arm.

"This looks important, better take it with us," Darkess said, scooping the book up in her arms.

She walked around to the fourth and final row of eggs and knew the real egg when she saw it. The colors were more vivid on the real egg. There were no fading dyes on its surface and no holes eaten through it. Also, its surface was much smoother. She moved over to the egg quickly but did not touch it.

'Well, what are you waiting for? Let's get that egg and get out of here!' Chakra projected.

Ignoring Chakra, Darkess looked around the base of the egg. It couldn't be this easy, she thought. There just has to be one more trap. She could feel it in her gut. She absently cracked her knuckles as she stared at the egg she'd come so far to find.

'Hurry up!' Chakra projected.

"Don't rush me!" Darkess snapped as she carefully touched the egg.

Lavender mist emanated from the egg. Darkess could feel the magic coursing through her fingers. Turning to the egg opposite it in the third row, she pulled it from its resting place. Levitating herself and the false egg into the air, she landed on the shelf next to the real egg. Bending down, she licked her lips nervously.

"Hold on to your hat," Darkess said.

Quickly as she possibly could, Darkess switched the real egg for the false one. For a moment, nothing happened, and she thought she was in the clear. Then, she heard a clicking noise, and the decoy egg began to lower down onto the shelf where Darkess was standing. Pulling her toes off the lower base, she jumped to the floor. Inches from where she landed, a trap door opened in the floor and just as quickly slammed shut. The egg was suspended in midair, and Chakra and Darkess were standing on solid floor. They had done it. Now all they had to do was get out.

Darkess took off her cloak and wrapped the egg in it. Then she used her damaged pack to secure it to her back. Taking one last look at the room filled with decoys, she felt a pang of sadness for the family line that had died out trying to keep this egg safe. As they walked past the end of the aisle where the skeleton lay, Darkess stopped and gave him one last look.

"You did not die in vain. I'll keep your treasure safe. Your job is done now. Go, rest in peace."

Without another look, Darkess left the room. The lavender mist had now dissipated. It was as if the egg knew it had been rescued.

Once Darkess reached the curve in the tunnel, it hid something new for her. She had to light another fireball to see, and that's when she realized the path was blocked by a newly formed set of steps. The only way to go was up. It was a long corridor up with occasional long stretches of level ground. The only sounds were the steps Darkess was taking, and it seemed like they were having a hypnotic effect on her. Completely worn out, more tired than she could ever remember being in her entire life, her mind wandered to what she would have to do next. She would have to check on Alieria and the refugees, get rid of the Shadow Seekers, and get herself home alive and with the egg. Then there were the other ones…and Takar to deal with. And then what in Merlin's name was she going to do with them? Darkess talked to herself, not realizing that some of it was slipping through to Chakra in her tiredness.

Her head hurt, her mind hurt, and a tear escaped her eye as she walked along yawning widely. They walked up yet another flight of steps and encountered a stone wall. Having felt so good just a short time ago in the treasure room, Darkess was amazed she could feel so horrible now, and this made it all worse.

"Stuck now? Not now…" she whined as she looked around for a clue to tell her what she needed to do to get out. There was no puzzle to solve, nor backwards writing, so she put out her fireball. In the dark, she looked for glowing letters or light coming from a crack somewhere, but there was none. Producing a new fireball, Darkess heaved it at the impeding wall. The only effect was a scorch mark. Rubbing her forehead, she clenched her jaw, feeling like she could blow the wall down with her anger alone. Going through her pack, she found several items that might help her.

"A potion for blowing things up. Useful, but it would either kill us or block us here with debris. Definitely not," Darkess said, replacing it deep inside her pack.

Cutting her finger, she hissed and pulled the offending item from her pack. It was her only bottle of teleport potion. Smashed beyond using, she pulled the pieces of broken glass from her pack, trying not to cut herself any worse. It must have broken hours ago when she had blown herself down. This sparked an idea. She threw a drop of blood at the wall. The only thing it did was run down. She stared at the flowing drop then returned to rummaging through her pack. There were things that made her think of home, and at the moment, it hurt to think of home, even with the victory of rescuing the egg. She longed to be back at her home again. Then she saw the bottle she had wedged in the corner of her pack. She had completely forgotten about it.

"Salt of the earth and water from heaven will help you on your way…"

Pulling the bottle from its cubbyhole, some of the sparkle returned to Darkess' eyes.

"That's it!" she gasped.

Darkess pulled the cork from the bottle and filled her hand with its contents.

"Please…let this work," she whispered with hope, flinging the salt at the wall.

She held her breath. Chakra stared from behind her. The salt hit the wall as if in slow motion as the anticipation pressed upon them. Darkess looked down at Chakra for a split second, and out of the corner of her eye, she saw movement of the stone. Turning back, she saw that an archway had opened where the salt hit its target. Relief washed over Darkess as she saw her beloved horse waiting on the other side.

☼

Dawn had broken above ground nearly an hour before Darkess reached the cave that both started and ended her egg search. Resting on the floor next to her trusted horse, Darkess fed the three of them and told Zaphod the tale of the long descent into the cave and its many passages.

'Why are we doing this here? We should be on our way home,' Chakra demanded.

"If we go home now, I won't get any rest for another day. And I'm not sure home is the correct choice. I don't want demons in the castle while I'm gone…and you know I can't stay home. I have too much to do. If Grandfather ever taught me anything, it was to be as prepared as witchly possible. That's what I intend to do. Now eat up, and think about what we must do next," Darkess said.

They ate in silence. Darkess was consumed with choices about what to do next. Unknown to Darkess, Takar waited on the other side of the stone. Her plans did not include using Zaphod's powers to escape from inside the mountain. She fully intended to leave this cave and mark the way so she could return again if need be. As Darkess plotted her new course back to places she knew, Takar was nervously waiting to alter that course.

≈

Darkess packed all of her things and checked the cave three times before she stood at the place where she had entered. Filling her hand again with salt, she smiled at her companions and tossed it at the wall. The arched entrance had only cracked its seal when Chakra's eyes began to glow a fierce red. Darkess could hardly believe what she was seeing. She had come so far, how could he have found her? Her thoughts raced as she yanked Zaphod around by the wall. Chakra felt Takar's presence and had already begun to back up, spitting and hissing as he went.

However, the figure that entered the cave was not Takar but Darkess' grandfather, Richard. The fireball Darkess held ready was fizzling in her tight fist. Her eyes wandered up and down the form of her grandfather's body, studying everything from clothing to jewelry. This can't be right, she thought. I saw his broken body. I watched him die. I saw his casket go into the ground. Darkess' mind was a blur. Her eyes darted from top to bottom of the figure again. Some little detail will be wrong, she thought, and I'll see the fraud in the disguise. But there was none. Every detail seemed absolutely perfect.

"How is this possible? I saw you die," Darkess said with a quiver in her voice.

"With strong enough magic, anything is possible," came from the figure.

"But why are you here?" Darkess' lip quivered, and she was on the edge of tears.

"You must get all three eggs."

"I know that, but what do I do with them once I have them?"

"Darkess my dear, when you have all three eggs, you will have the power to bring me back permanently. You will never have to fear losing anyone you love ever again."

Darkess' eyes dropped to her hands where she was interlocking her fingers and wringing her hands.

"Darkess you can rule the world. You can have everything you want...I will be your advisor."

That was when Darkess was sure this was not her beloved Grandfather.

'This is wrong. Grandfather would never want to be my advisor, and he would never want me to rule the world,' Darkess projected to her companions.

'Get ready,' she warned.

When Darkess looked at Chakra, she saw his eyes were still intensely red, yet her expression never changed. The image of her grandfather began to waver, because Darkess didn't want to see her grandfather any longer. Instead, she wanted to get at Takar. She knew he was behind this image. Closing her eyes, Darkess felt Takar's power coursing through her veins. An image of the egg she had just found wavered in the air in front of her. When she opened her eyes, she grabbed hold of it. The image of her grandfather was getting weaker as she drained Takar's power. This was what he most wanted. The egg was wrapped in the image of a velvet cloth. Darkess knew this would only buy her some time, but it was the only idea she had.

Laying the image of the egg down in the sand, close to the wall, Darkess mounted Zaphod. Chakra jumped on behind her. Darkess projected her thoughts to her horse.

'Jump to the bend in the cavern, just outside the cave's opening.'

Within the blink of an eye, they were outside – but the image of Richard and the egg remained. Darkess could just see Takar around the bend as he threw a fireball into the cave then raced in after it. A malevolent scream was heard inside the cave as Richard and the egg vanished, along with Darkess and her companions.

'Home,' Darkess projected, and they vanished.

≈

Arriving at the front courtyard, Darkess changed her mind and quickly said,

"My tower room."

Just as she said it, Darkess and her two companions were all in the tower room. Darkess dismounted and began dumping all of the clothes from her wooden chest, leaving a soft layer on the bottom. She gently placed the egg inside and covered it with all the clothes from the floor. Scribbling a note on a scrap of parchment, Darkess rolled it tightly and tied it to Chakra's collar with a leather strap.

"You need to take this to mother. Stay here in the castle with them. I haven't much time before Takar comes here or goes to Alierias. Now go," Darkess told Chakra.

She opened the door, letting her familiar go then latched it quickly. Scribbling something else on another scrap of parchment, Darkess folded it neatly and put it in her pocket. Jumping on Zaphod, she projected her thoughts.

'Alieria's home courtyard.'

In a flash, they were gone.

≈

The sun was hiding behind thick steely clouds as Darkess arrived at the courtyard of Alieria's castle. There were boards on many of the windows, and not a single soul was visible. All of the carriages were horseless and Alieria's griffon, Sugar, was the only creature in sight.

"Go. Hide in the barn. Listen for my call," Darkess whispered to Zaphod and patted him on the neck.

Darkess had to pound on the door. It was locked up tight. Even the guard was posted inside for protection.

"Prak! Let me in! I'm here to help!" Darkess yelled.

At the sound of Darkess' voice, Prak opened the door just a bit. Squeezing through the miniscule crack, she smiled at him.

"Thanks. Where is Alieria?"

Prak grunted and pointed towards the great room. Darkess bowed her head in acknowledgement, turned on her heels, and made her way towards Alieria. The room was packed full of humans, who were all in an odd sort of daze.

"What's wrong with these people?" Darkess whispered to Alieria.

"It's a form of your grandfather's befuddlement powder. Non-magic folks don't deal well with magical attacks, and then to see us fixing things and such, well, I had to do it. Things are bad here. Everyone thinks the city is haunted, and they're staying away or hiding. We must rid ourselves of Takar and his scores of Shadow Seekers," Alieria said, her voice tired from exhaustion.

"I know," Darkess said. "And we haven't much time. Takar could be on his way here now. This is what we need to do..."

≈

Darkess had no idea when or where Takar would attack, and she had thought about it long and hard. His first option was her home, Vallencourt Castle. She lived there, but the castle lacked wizards with major firepower. It would be a good place to start, but then there was Alieria. She had a house full of wizards, most too afraid to do much, and a lot of them were too old or young to fight. Of course that is what they think of me, Darkess thought. Takar also had Alieria under constant watch. Her place had to be the best place for him to attack.

All of the humans were sitting quietly against the interior walls. The magic folk, however, had work to do. Rain began to sprinkle the windows that were left as they made preparations for the attack. Everyone was doing one job or another – barricading windows, brewing potions, preparing food, and keeping lookout on every side and every level of the castle. Darkess walked from room to room, repositioning people and giving out jobs to those who seemed to need a little more direction. Some of the magic folk were left to guard the old, the young, and the humans.

Darkess had given explicit instructions on how everyone was to behave once the battle actually began, and this time, not a single person – wizard or otherwise – questioned her authority. Every person worked diligently at their given job, and they did it out of respect or fear. Not only that, they did their jobs well. When Darkess passed, there was a look of reverence on the faces of those who knew what was at stake. She was saving their lives, and each and everyone knew it. Darkess had changed while she had been in the desert. She had grown, and she knew it when she walked through the small castle, readying it for battle.

≈

As she stood on the roof of the castle and looked out at the land, the rain began to fall a little harder. One last check, Darkess thought as she made her way down to the second floor then the first. All was sealed up tight. Every sort of magic that Darkess and her band of hidden wizards knew was in place. Darkess was giving out some last-minute orders when the attack began. Something slammed into the castle, jarring the entire place.

"You all know what to do!" Darkess yelled as a massive amount of dust shook free.

This had been the hardest strike against the castle so far. The Shadow Seekers knew she was there, and that everyone had been preparing for them. The foundation shook with the second barrage. Any remaining windows shattered and shelves teetered, spilling their loads. Dust filled the air, and many people screamed as flying glass and debris cut them. Tasha shivered next to Darkess. Her only powers were defensive, not offensive really, and she was afraid. And she wasn't really the fighting kind. She worked quietly in the shadows, never out in the open battling demons. Darkess knew she was frightened, and it was hard on her, but she couldn't take the chance of Tasha being out of her power's range…she was important to the plan. In fact, she was vital to the plan. Tasha stared at the wall in front of her like she could see through it or into it. Darkess placed a hand on her shoulder and tried to comfort her.

"The plan will work," Darkess assured Tasha. "Just listen to the storm brewing out there. It will amplify our powers for sure. Trust in us. We can do this. We have to."

A third volley hit the castle, and there was a round of screams as a beam in the great room fell from the ceiling, crushing an elderly couple that had been sitting under it. Two other wizards had been pinned under it, and several people had gone to see what they could to. Darkess saw the poor old couple. It was a sad sight. Darkess took a closer look and saw that they were still holding hands. A tear slipped from her eye as she lifted the beam just enough to pull the groaning man free. The second wizard was lucky. His power was regeneration, and he grew back the leg that had been amputated by the accident. The first wizard was hauled away to the kitchens where they were also doing medical work on the injured. Darkess pulled a curtain off the wall and covered the deceased.

Darkess looked around the corridor and saw the rest of her rag-tag team assembled and waiting for the next step in the plan. She walked to the castle door and looked through the spyhole. Just when her eyes focused on what was out there, she saw Takar make a fireball and yell as he fired it at the castle. As she slammed the spyhole shut, the house was pummeled by the fourth wave. She had waited long enough, trying to attract as many of the Shadow Seekers as they possibly could.

"Now!" Darkess yelled as loud as she possibly could.

All around the castle, specially made spyholes were opened simultaneously, and potion bottles were shot, thrown, and projected into the shadows where the Shadow Seekers were hiding. Then the spyholes were locked shut again. Upon impact, the potion exploded into light so intense that it killed or mortally wounded nearly all of the Shadow Seekers in the immediate area. Takar was temporarily blinded and ducked behind some large bushes and rocks for cover.

Back at the spyhole, Darkess couldn't see a thing for a moment. There was muffled crying in the background, and she had to force it away, trying to hear any movement outside. Lightning ripped open the sky, giving Darkess just enough light to clearly see what was still hiding in the shadows. Most of Takar's army was out of commission, and he was hiding, waiting for reinforcements.

"This is it," she said, clenching her hands tightly to Tasha.

Thinking plainly about the fear she had felt upon her grandfather's death, Darkess felt her power working, and she projected herself to the other side of the door, directly in line with where Takar was hiding. Channeling Tasha's power, Darkess' voice dripped with a sickening sweetness.

"Come out Takar. We need to talk."

Darkess couldn't believe her eyes when Takar stood up and made his way around the barrier with a completely docile posture. Watching from spyholes and cracks in the shutters, the magic folk were shocked by this. Tasha, Alieria, and Darkess had known what to expect, and it was working splendidly.

"Don't let your guard down," Darkess whispered from her invisible body, still safely inside the castle.

Slowly walking towards the image of his enemy, Takar mounted the steps, stopping just feet from Darkess' image.

"Do you have the other two dragon eggs?" Darkess asked.

Takar nodded his head yes.

"Do you know what you need to do now?"

Looking confused, Takar cocked his head to one side.

"Kill you and take yours?" Takar said, more like a question, as if he wasn't quite sure.

This made Darkess wrinkle her forehead in confusion.

"No, you need to get the other eggs and bring them here. Do you know why?" Darkess said.

This time Takar only shook his head no with a dazed look on his face.

"Because this is where you will need to hatch the eggs. Right here in this very cellar is a hatchery especially made for dragons. It's the perfect place," Darkess crooned.

The attitude in Takar's stance changed. His head seemed to get smaller, more weasel like.

"Now draw out your portal," Darkess commanded.

With a devious grin, Takar took out his chalk and drew right on the stones he was standing on. Once he had finished, he stood up, grinning more broadly. But just before he looked at her image, she had levitated a small sachet around behind his heel, just inside his portal circle. He stared at Darkess, waiting for her next words.

"Go home. Retrieve your eggs. We'll be here waiting."

Takar's look changed to one of evil as he sprinkled the dust from his pocket, leaving in a vortex of smoke.

"Think it will work?" Alieria's thick accent whispered in Darkess' ear as she reappeared inside the doorway.

"It had better."

≈

None of them had expected Takar to return quickly, but after several hours, they were all beginning to think the plan had failed. Darkess was reading from one of her old notebooks, flipping slowing through it. Tasha was pacing up and down the hall, and Alieria had her eyes glued to the front spyhole.

"What was in that sachet you gave Takar?" Alieria asked without looking away from the courtyard.

Closing her book, Darkess looked at Tasha, who had stopped pacing to hear the answer, and then to Alieria.

"It had calming herbs, maybe to help keep him tame, and maybe help to continue Tasha's influence. And a coin to track him with. It's gold, so he'll keep it if he finds it. And if he doesn't, well, either way, I can find him now."

"Why didn't you tell us?" Alieria asked with a pained sound in her voice.

Darkess wasn't sure what to say, but the answer came to her.

"There wasn't time, and well, to keep the plan safe. The plan has been split up amongst participants. I fear there is more to Takar than we know. We can't afford any mistakes. The less each person knows, the better off we all are in the long run. Please don't take it personally," Darkess said.

Janine came down the corridor just in time to hear Darkess' last couple of words.

"Excuse me, did I interrupt?"

"Not at all dear. What is going on?" Tasha countered.

"How much longer, do you think?" Janine asked.

"Not sure," Darkess said.

"Well, some of the humans are waking up. We are going to need to do something. Some of the guards are getting antsy," Janine said.

"I'll take care of it," Tasha said, leading Janine towards the kitchens.

Prak stood quietly next to Alieria, who turned and looked directly into Darkess' eyes.

"So, who do you think Takar is partnered with?"

Shocked, Darkess hadn't expected anyone else to know what she knew.

"I can't tell you anything. I'm sorry," Darkess said.

"You don't trust us?" Alieria looked back out the spyhole.

"It's..." Darkess sighed. "It's not that. It's like I said before. We are all safer if we only know part of the plan. If one of us gets taken, none of us can jeopardize the entire scheme. If this doesn't work, we will all surely be killed, or worse, turned into slaves, or well, you can imagine what demons ruling the world would be like. That is, until they hatch the eggs and end life for everything," Darkess said, honesty staining every word.

Alieria said nothing, but remained watchful. Prak looked at his hands for a moment then sighed and returned to walking his rounds. Being Muscovatan, Alieria was usually hard and tough as nails. This was a side of her Darkess had never seen. It was getting to even the toughest of them, she thought as she opened her book and searched for something special.

☼

Darkess placed a cork in the last bottle of potion and smiled at Brutus and Philineas.

"Alright boys, back ups for the back ups. Better safe than sorry, am I right? Well, you know what to do if anything happens to me. Philineas, take the extras to mother. Explain what I told you. Merlin help us. Be careful."

"You be careful Miss Goodspeed. We're depending on you," Philineas said, smiling.

Slamming a potion bottle at his feet, he was gone in a cloud of blue smoke.

"Now whut?" Brutus asked.

"Think I'm going to go check on the tracking coin. Maybe I'm going to the demon's lair."

Brutus pulled the skin on his arm out, making a form of basket, and loaded the potions in it. He followed Darkess out of the kitchen to distribute them. All of the guards had reported no movement outside since the Takar's departure. Alieria was still watching the front when Darkess returned to the door. A few Shadow Seekers had begun more mischief, but few had come to help once they saw the corpses of all the others.

"Anything?" Darkess asked.

"Nothing," Alieria reported.

Pulling out a crystal and one of her grandfather's maps, Darkess began to scry for her coin. The crystal swayed on its thong, coming to rest on the map. She saw that it pointed to an area far outside of Crystal City. The coin had not moved since it arrived at that location. Just as Darkess was about to pull the crystal from its position, it skipped across the map. It landed on the edge of Crystal city, exactly where Aleiria's castle was located.

"He's coming!" Darkess yelled at the top of her lungs.

In a vortex of gray smoke, Takar appeared in the courtyard. He was carrying a satchel that was heavy laden with something. He seemed agitated, and he scratched at his head quickly, looking wildly around the courtyard. When he turned back towards the door, his eyes were filmy looking, completely glazed over. Tasha came running down the corridor towards Darkess. Alieria had slid to one side of the spyhole, allowing Darkess a look. Before Takar had a chance to behave in a deadly fashion, Darkess spoke to him, channeling Tasha's power.

"Bring the eggs to the door."

Scratching again at his head, Takar seemed thoroughly confused. Again, Darkess repeated herself.

"Bring the eggs to the door."

It looked like Takar was fighting himself, but he slowly brought the satchel to the door.

"Lay down the satchel, and back away."

Takar's body began to twitch, and his face was a grimace of pain as he lay down the eggs. He took two steps back then stopped.

"Ahhhh!" Takar screamed. "You can't do this to me! I've worked too hard!"

Grabbing his head, Takar fell to his knees, screaming and flailing with drops of spit flying from his lips. He was sweating profusely, and it dripped from his chin and nose. Every spyhole had faces shoved into it, eyes intently watching, potion bottles ready.

"Who is your employer?" Darkess demanded.

Trying to stand, Takar groaned loudly, and a fireball erupted from his hand. But he only stood there holding it.

"No!" Takar yelled as he squeezed the fireball, extinguishing it.

"Do you have a partner?" Darkess said with force.

Alieria looked at Darkess totally confused and raised her shoulders.

"Don't…" Takar groaned.

"Tell me!" Darkess barked.

Takar said nothing, he only groaned for a moment. Darkess was getting angry. Then with the yell of a man who knows he's about to die, Takar lunged at the barrier barring the door that Darkess stood behind. That was all that it took to send Darkess over the edge. She made a fireball and sailed it into Takar's chest through the spyhole. He was blown off the steps and down into the sodden courtyard. Lightning fractured the sky just as he was landing on his back in muck. He was injured but not yet out of fight. Huffing loudly, Takar tried to get up but was hit again by another fireball. Darkess ripped open the barricade and ran against protests out into the courtyard. Tasha and Alieria were following closely, demanding Darkess to stop. Janine slammed the barricade shut and watched from the spyhole.

"This is crazy!" Alieria screamed, desperately trying to catch Darkess.

"Just throw the potion and be done with it!" Tasha yelled.

"I want to hear him say who he is working for!" Darkess snarled.

Darkess reached Takar, who was now on his hands and knees.

"Tell me who is your employer!" Darkess demanded.

"Kkkk...ch, chh," Takar stammered.

He formed a fireball quickly and heaved it at the witches. Tasha screamed and fell to the side. Alieria dodged it as well as Darkess, who was narrowly missed. Producing a fireball of her own, Darkess fought back. Being off balance, she missed hitting her target broadside, but it still glanced off Takar's hip. He rolled over and threw another at them. Tasha was in the line of fire. Her dress was burnt away on the arm, but her skin remained pink and perfect. Now Tasha was mad. She mustered up her sweetest voice.

"Tell us what we want to know."

Takar's face turned a brilliant shade of red as he choked on words he refused to utter. Darkess held a fireball ready as the demon fought not to speak. He tried desperately to stand, sputtering and quacking all sorts of unusual sounds.

"Helpppp mm...mmeee," he said when he finally managed to form the words.

Takar was speaking to the air. An unseen ally? Alieria looked around for some other demon. Caught off guard by Takar's odd behavior, Darkess extinguished her fireball, giving him the perfect chance to produce one and heave it at them. There was demonic glee in his eyes as he watched it sail towards Darkess' chest. Darkess never moved. She didn't even blink. She only stared at the fireball as if it were coming in slow motion...as if she were beaten. Alieria and Tasha both screamed in unison.

"Nooo!"

Just as the fireball was a foot from hitting its target, Darkess deflected it. It slammed into Takar's shoulder, knocking him back to his hands and knees. And before he had a chance to collect himself and retaliate, Darkess threw the potion.

"Erase your power of illusion, burn away your firepower, eradicate you from this space, let this be your final hour," Darkess spoke from memory.

Black smoke billowed around Takar, and sparks of red began to burst inside the cloud. Then Takar did the most extraordinary thing. He reached out to Darkess. The pain was gone from his face, and the words flowed out free and easy.

"Thank you for my freedom," he said.

In the time it took for the words to find Darkess' ears, it was over. Takar exploded in a shower of black and red sparks, and the cloud began to dissipate. The three witches looked back and forth at each other. Speculation and confusion mixed upon their faces.

"Thank you? What demon ever thanked anyone for death?" Alieria asked Darkess.

"The kind that didn't want a partner and knew that death was the only way out," Darkess answered quietly.

Turning back towards the barricaded door, they saw Janine was opening the doors to let them back in.

"Is it over?" Janine asked.

"This part is," Darkess said.

Crowds had begun to congregate around the door and spyholes around the front side of the castle, and cheers went up all around. The noise was almost more than Darkess could handle. Even the storm had died down with the death of the demon as if it were trying to help her. She knew every one was happy, but she didn't have time for the pats on the back she would be receiving. Slowly, Darkess dredged her way through the mud towards the satchel lying on the steps. Alieria stopped and looked at her cousin. Tasha was staring back at her.

"This part?" Alieria asked, making haste to catch up.

Stooping down to check if there were indeed real dragon eggs inside the large satchel, Darkess began to mumble to herself, ignoring all around her.

"They're here. The real eggs are here," she said.

By rubbing the shells, Darkess could feel the power of them, and for a moment, she seemed transfixed by them. Her thumb caressed the texture but felt the magic from within. She was so intent on the eggs that she hadn't noticed them trying to get her attention.

"Darkess!" Janine yelled.

Darkess blinked her eyes and shook her head. She looked up from where she was squatted and focused on Janines' face.

"I'm sorry. What did you say?" Darkess stammered.

"What do you mean by, 'this part'?" Janine demanded.

"Oh, yes, well…" Darkess heaved the satchel over her shoulder as smoothly and gently as the heavy bag would allow and proceeded inside the barricade.

Everyone followed Darkess, those inside as well as those who had been outside with her. The doors were barricaded again, and they walked towards the kitchens. Darkess did not say a word. She waited for the crowd to thin as they walked further into the castle. And unbelievably it did. They all thought she wasn't going to talk at all, so they went back to where they had been hiding or stationed before except for those who had been in the Order, including Tasha and a few of the wounded.

"I feared this would only be half of the battle. Takar knew too much, Tuma was too willing to help; it was a number of different things. It got me thinking. How did Takar know where to find my grandfather? How did he know we were looking for him? I don't know exactly when I was sure, but I know he had a partner. And I'm not so sure he was a willing participant, at least not there at the end, that's for sure."

Alieria sent out new guards, and when there were even fewer ears in the room, she said,

"He was mad Darkess. Crazy with greed, but are you sure he had a partner?"

Brutus had lumbered closer to better hear what was being said.

"Who was he asking for help?" Darkess said, looking into Alieria's eyes.

"He was mad," Alieria returned Darkess' gaze boldly.

"It was too easy for him," Darkess said. "He was one step ahead of the Order every step of the way. I'm telling you, he had an inside man," Darkess said and turned away from them all. "Have you ever seen a clear glass filled with water, how when you place something inside, it changes shape? Well there is someone who is more crooked than a wand in water, and I intend to flush that someone out."

Darkess closed her eyes, and a pained look crossed her face before she opened them again. The room was dead quiet, and Darkess knew she was going to have to be the one to break the silence.

"Look, the way I see it, you are all in the clear. I would have known if it was one of you. I've been here. I've seen you all in action. It has to be some other member of the Order. And they may not be a willing partner, or even know what they've done. You saw what happened out there. Blazes, there could be a third party that I know nothing about, controlling it all. Like I said before, we are all safer with only pieces of the puzzle. Do you trust me?"

Darkess looked into the faces of those before her, and each looked hurt and confused. But they all shook their heads yes.

"Then you must trust me for a few more hours. For your safety and those you are protecting. I must keep you in the dark for now."

Checking all of her knives and adjusting her pack, she said one more thing.

"Before I go, I want to thank you all for what you have done. Now, stay inside, same precautions as before, and let no one in or out. I will contact you by bird when all is safe."

They all walked in silence to the barricade. Prak opened the door, smiling at Darkess. She slipped out onto the steps. The sound of hooves could be heard behind Darkess as she poked her head back through the door.

"Oh, and Janine, do me one more favor, will you?"

"Sure, anything."

"Melt every hinge on every outer wall, door, and shutter – every one. Stay put, and get some rest."

Without waiting for a reply, Darkess shoved the door shut and headed for Zaphod.

≈

Zaphod stayed on the cobblestones on his way around the small castle as they were leaving Alieria and her band of half-starved refugees. Darkess was yawning until she had tears in her eyes, but she had to move on. Thankfully the storm had died almost entirely. Only misty rain fell as they began the next leg of their journey. The coolness was helping to invigorate her, and the eggs thumped gently on her legs as she and her horse walked down the lane. She could feel the pull of the eggs, and she shoved thoughts of them to the back of her mind. She knew she was going to have to be clear in order to do what she had to do next.

Whispering a spell, her vision changed, and she could see much more clearly. The moon was hidden still behind steely clouds, and thunder rolled in the distance. Zaphod wandered through the back paths that led around the city. The warmth of summer was held back by these odd storms; however, this didn't keep Darkess from finding most of the plants she needed along the way. They took deeper paths, going further into the wilderness than many are willing to do alone. Still looking for one last plant, Darkess scanned both sides of the deer trail Zaphod was following. In a small clearing, Darkess spied the plant she had been looking for, and urged her mount towards it. The brambles were thick and surrounded the one plant she needed. She dismounted and hacked her way through with her rapier. Pulling a larger chunk than she needed, Darkess fought her way back out of the brambles.

'That's odd. I didn't see that cabin before, did you?' Darkess projected her question to her horse.

'No,' Zaphod snorted.

They walked quietly towards the cabin. There were no lanterns burning, and weeds had grown thick in the path leading towards it. A tattered hide fluttered gently in the breeze at the cabin's only front window.

'Do you hear anything?' Darkess asked.

This time, Zaphod only shook his head no. They kept moving towards the tiny dwelling, and Darkess crept upon the porch. Boards creaked with every step.

"Hello?" Darkess called out.

Only the breeze answered her with a large gust that whistled through the cabin. The door was closed tight. Darkess had to use her power to open it, because brut strength was not enough. The hinges screamed their reluctance to move. She tossed a fireball into the cabin and levitated it into the center of the room. Dust and cobwebs covered everything. Before entering, Darkess looked back over her shoulder.

'Stay close,' she projected.

An old iron pot hung over the fireplace. There was still dry kindling in the box next to it, but she would probably need some more wood. No one had been here in several seasons, but some dried herbs hung on the wall, although they were nearly unrecognizable from the years of dust covering them.

"Perfect," Darkess whispered.

Brushing dirt and debris off the small wooden table, she moved it closer to the fireplace. There had been a bench bed along the side wall, but now it had fallen from its perch. It would make excellent firewood. As she collected the wood, she inventoried all the ingredients she had picked and the ones she still had in her pack. Putting the wood under where the pot had been hanging, she tossed a fireball at it and it ignited beautifully. Darkess put the eggs behind the door, far away from the fire's heat. Laying her pack on the table along with the herbs she had picked, she tested the small bench. It held her weight, so she placed it just where she wanted and pulled the iron pot off its hook. The inside of the pot was full of leaves and soot from the chimney, but there were no holes. It would work just fine.

Knowing there was a creek nearby, Darkess set off for it. She washed the pot out with sand, rinsed and filled it, then refilled her water bladders. Carrying the pot and the bladders was not an easy chore, so she decided to levitate the pot back. Once she had returned to the cabin, she hung the pot over the fire. Pulling out a small knife with a short thin blade, Darkess began to cut, chop, and crush the herbs. Once she had finished, she pulled out a large maple leaf and unwrapped it. Inside was a piece of a dragon scale and powdered unicorn horn.

'We are not alone,' Zaphod projected to Darkess.

Standing swiftly, she walked across the floor to the door. She had left it open about a third of the way so she could slip in and out without making noise. Peeking out, she saw a cloaked figure walking towards the cabin.

"Who goes there?" Darkess yelled out the door.

Darkess had still been using the spell to see better, but the visitor had its face entirely hidden behind a hood.

"I came here to help you Darkess," a female voice floated through the air.

The fact that the woman knew her name really threw Darkess for a loop, but only for a second. Then she got a grip on herself. Just before she was about to yell out, 'How do you know my name', she decided to watch the approaching figure for just a moment. In the meantime, she pulled two knives and opened one hand to form a fireball. She intended to be ready to kill if the need arose.

"Who are you, and what do you want?" Darkess called out.

The woman stopped several steps from the porch and lowered her hood.

"You? How can you help me?" Darkess looked curiously at the old woman still hidden in shadow.

Darkess recognized the woman clearly from the city. She sold herbs, fruits and vegetables from a little cart.

"This cabin is mine," she said.

"I'm sorry for trespassing, but that doesn't explain how you can help me," Darkess said sternly, unwilling to give up her position.

"Please, let an old lady into the warmth. Lets have a cuppa, and I'll explain while you finish your potion."

How did this old lady know what she was doing, Darkess wondered.

"Go away. I'll be done with your cabin soon, and you can have it back."

"Darkess, put away the knives. You have more than enough fire power to kill me, and I intend to live past this evening, provided you pull off your mission."

Darkess' jaw dropped at the woman's words.

"Hold your hands where I can see them, and slowly come inside."

The old woman did as instructed. Once inside, she huddled close to the fire and warmed herself.

"This is your cabin?" Darkess asked the woman as she shoved the eggs further behind the door, trying to hide them entirely.

"Yes," was all she said then she turned around to warm her backside and smiled at Darkess.

"Why did you leave here?"

"That, Miss Goodspeed, is where you come in. I had a dream one night of you. You were here in my home, only it was dirty and forgotten. It was the night of the unbelievable storm. You made a potion, and you were one ingredient short. I know you didn't know that you needed this item until the potion didn't work properly. Even in the dream you weren't sure what item you needed, and you were crestfallen. You cried as you left this old abandoned shack. I had that dream every night for a year."

Darkess' eyes were glued to the old woman as she spoke.

"After that disturbing year, I met you in the square. You were much younger than in the dream, but I knew it was you. Your grandmother called you by name, and I never forgot it. After that chance meeting, the dream continued, every night, steady as the seasons change. This dream consumed me. Everyday I thought about you and your potion, and why your potion had failed you," the old lady said.

"Are you a witch?" Darkess asked tentatively.

"Ah, well, born to a witch, but I have no real powers. I do know what powers can do, and I also know plants very well, and I help out where I can. Where was I going with this? Oh yes, the dream. Then one day late in summer, I happened to be out picking through the woods and came across the most peculiar thing."

Darkess was intently listening and the old lady could tell she had the young girl's rapt attention.

"There was a hole in a tree, clear through it at my eye level. And it was at an angle, so I looked through it up towards the sky. There were no jagged chips, no animal or bird had made that hole, and I just had to know what had."

Darkess threw a couple more ingredients into the pot, and it smoked for a moment.

"When I looked down at the ground, I noticed a furrow in the dirt, almost a plow mark, only smaller, ending in a pile of mud. I got out my hand spade, dug the chunk of mud free from the earth, and broke it apart. At the center, I found a most spectacular stone. I believe it is metal from the sky. A meteorite. It is black, but when the light hits it, greens and blues appear on its surface. Of course I kept it. I finished my day as usual, but my sales were better than ever. I kept rubbing the stone in my pocket for more good luck. That night when I came home, I had made more in one day than I usually make in an entire week. I tucked the stone away in one of my hidy holes and that night, the dream changed. This time the potion worked perfectly, because I gave you the chunk of metal. The meteorite is the essential ingredient that you need. A special potion needs specialized components. I, myself, have used this stone's special properties, and now I have a better cabin with real windows and a cellar for keeping more over a longer time when there is bounty to be had. My time with the stone is over, but yours, well, it has just begun. In the dream, it was the last thing you put in the pot, and once the potion was poured off, you kept it next to your heart on a leather thong."

The woman unfolded her hand, and in her palm laid the stone.

"Take it. You need it. We all need it, I fear," she said.

Darkess felt a tingle when the old woman dropped the stone in her hand. It was warm to the touch. It was lumpy, but fairly smooth, and it felt magical in her hand. There is power in this stone, Darkess thought.

"Thank you," Darkess said as she dropped the unicorn horn powder and the dragon scale piece into the pot. Once again, the pot smoked for a moment, then it calmed down to a simmer again.

"I am sorry I threatened you," Darkess said.

"No need for that dearie. I know what is at stake here, beggin' your pardon, Miss Goodspeed."

"You can dispel the formalities. They do not matter here. But how do you know what is at stake here?" Darkess asked the old woman.

"I've been hiding at Alieria's castle. Being old and having no powers, I stayed with the humans and kept watch from a nice chair. Then, there is the dream I told you about. I have been with you in my sleep every night for six years. I have studied every detail in your face, your body language, your potion, your clothes, and actions, every thing about you. I feel like I know you as more than a customer at the square and of a considerably higher class than me, I might add. You best add that stone now," the old lady said.

"Why didn't you talk to me at Alieria's?" Darkess asked.

"Secrecy, only knowing part of the plan keeps us safe."

"You really were there," Darkess whispered in amazement as she dropped in the meteorite.

The potion popped and hissed and turned to a dazzling gold, like molten metal.

"I think it is done," Darkess said, pulling the pot from the flames.

There was a large stone off to the side of the fireplace for cooling purposes, and she put it there. Digging inside her pack, Darkess pulled out the only two empty bottles she had left. The old lady anticipated her needs and pulled loose a weak floorboard. Sticking her arm deep inside, she pulled out a leather bundle.

"Here you go. You can use these," she said handing the bundle to Darkess.

Unrolling the wrap, Darkess found six shiny new bottles inside, each with a good cork, a small ladle for dipping, and a pour spout. Darkess smiled at her in disbelief and said,

"Thank you so much. You know, I think you have more powers than you realize."

Darkess stirred the pot then made a funny face as she said, "I don't even know your name."

"My name doesn't matter."

"To me it does," Darkess looked at the woman pleadingly.

"Alright, then you can call me Dora."

"Well then Dora, on behalf of my family, I thank you."

"Thank you for trusting in a crazy old lady," Dora laughed a wild cackle.

Darkess fell into silence as she checked the temperature of the potion and began to ladle it into the bottles. She filled all eight of them, doubting that she would need that many, but one could never tell. As the bottles sat on the table, the color inside each turned more orange. Dora watched quietly as Darkess pulled out a piece of parchment.

"Do you mind?" Darkess asked.

"No dear. I rarely get to see magic in action, and I do love it so. It should do this old heart some good."

Dora tied a leather thong to the meteorite as Darkess uncorked a bottle. Raising her eyebrows, Darkess said,

"Bottoms up," and drank the potion.

"Ulch," Darkess grimaced, licking her lips and swallowing hard. Then she said,

"From now until it's now again, keep my secrets hidden deep, arrest my power of telepathy, allow no others thoughts to creep, seal off my mind completely, and make it as strong as meteorite steel."

Darkess had changed one word in her spell, from tempered to meteorite, but it felt like it was working. A warm glow began to radiate through her belly, and it raced through her body and throbbed in her head.

"Ahh," Darkess grabbed her head in mild pain, wondering if the meteorite had been a trick for a moment.

But after a moment, the pain passed, and she felt much better.

"Are you alright?" Dora asked.

"Yes, but for a moment there, I was beginning to wonder."

Darkess tried to project a thought to Zaphod, but it seemed to echo in her head. There was no reply from her trusted horse, so she took a couple of steps to the door and hollered,

"Zaphod ole buddy, you still there?"

A soft snicker came from the darkness just next to the porch.

"Just checking," Darkess said and returned to the table.

Rummaging through a large cloak pocket, she pulled out a gold coin and flipped it on the table like she had seen her grandfather do a hundred times before.

"I won't take no for an answer. Take the coin, for services rendered and use of the cabin," Darkess bowed to the poor old woman.

Dora blushed vividly in the firelight and smiled deeply into her cheeks.

"My mother always told me the Vallencourts were good people of position. Thank you much ma'am."

Darkess packed up the bottles and cleaned up her mess quickly.

"I hate to drink and run, but I must go," Darkess said.

"I take it the potion worked," Dora said.

"Oh, yes! I am sorry, it does work. But I really must be going now. It is getting late, and I know they are all waiting for me"

"Good luck deary," the old woman said.

"Thank you, again," Darkess responded.

Darkess grabbed the satchel full of eggs and books, hauled them out with her power, and loaded them on her horse. Climbing on Zaphod, she actually had to tell him where to go, and it felt weird to her.

"Home, boy. Take us to my tower room."

In the blink of an eye, horse and rider were gone.

≈

The tower room was dark until Darkess appeared. When the lights fired up, the exhausted Darkess felt exhilarated for some reason. The weariness she could feel all the way to her bones was being lifted. The power of the eggs was reunited. Finally, after centuries of being apart, they vibrated the room gently for but a moment. Lavender mist swirled out of the trunk where the third egg was hidden. The satchel fluttered, as with a wind, and ruby and sapphire mist came shooting from it. The tri-colored mist flowed around Darkess, making a vibrant purple. The entire room filled with a pulsating amythest colored light, which had a life of its own. Darkess climbed off of Zaphod and stepped on the largest table in the room.

The mist swelled and then began to converge. Darkess watched intently as the swirling air started to close in around her. Zaphod snickered a warning, but she only held out her hand and said,

"It's okay boy, stay back."

Suddenly the mist thickened and became ribbon-like, spinning around her body. One end of the ribbon wound around her legs as the other encircled her head. It was coiled around her but constantly moving and swirling. One end seemed to pierce her chest then quickly pulled back. As if it had a head, it seemed to be looking for something, searching for it before finding what it wanted. Darkess' mouth was open, and inside her it went until the entire ribbon was within. She stood still with her eyes shut and her lips slightly parted with her breath coming in short bursts. A small purple puff issued from her mouth with each exhale. When she opened her eyes, the purple glow was so intense that Zaphod had to look away. Shaking his head, Zaphod pawed the floor and snickered his worry. The connection between Darkess and her horse ran deep, and somewhere in her subconscious, she felt his pain. Clearing her throat and squeezing her eyes shut, Darkess shook her head and tried to clear her mind.

Once again, she opened her eyes, and the intensity of the light began to diminish until the center of Darkess' eyes finally returned to black.

"Whoa," she said as her vision returned to normal.

"Sorry there, boy. Thought you lost me, huh?" Darkess said, patting Zaphod's jaw.

"You're not that lucky pal." She grinned at her horse.

Zaphod snorted sharply, blowing snot at Darkess to show his annoyance.

"Gross. Thanks, but really I am fine. I was only kidding. I believe we are doing the right thing. Everything will work out, you'll see," Darkess reassured him.

Rubbing his nose up and down on the front of Darkess, he was feeling better. In the center of Darkess' eyes the purple light sparked brightly for a heartbeat and was gone.

☼

The small dining hall was prepared for a feast, but all the guests looked as if it were a funeral. Nervousness, worry, and exhaustion registered on every face, except for Tanner and Harlow. The Indian wore his normal expression of stoniness, as if he were studying something with no emotion. But Harlow's face was a mask of concentration, occasionally mixed with concern if he caught the eyes of another at the table. Occasionally, someone would say something trivial or get a little more comfortable, but mostly the room was quiet. It seemed the flicker of the candles had more to say than the waiting members of the Order. Thunder could be heard in the distance as a new storm approached.

Even though they were in different rooms, Darkess and Harlow simultaneously smiled when the thunder rumbled over the castle, for each knew that storms amplify powers. Harlow's smile quickly erased when he heard Darkess' approaching steps. He hadn't heard her mental presence. Darkess' smile remained on her lips, for she had a few magic tricks up her sleeves that Harlow didn't have, didn't even know he was missing, in fact. Darkess was born in this very castle, which also added to her strength. She had all three eggs, but she was pretty sure he knew already. However, what he didn't know was that the eggs had already chosen Darkess. He could kill her and take the eggs, but they would only attack and kill him at birth. Then there would be serious problems, and no one to command the powerful beasts.

A momentary look of fear crossed Darkess' face. Maybe he did know in a way. Tuma said he saw blackness when the world ended. Was that his thought or Harlows? Darkess questioned herself. Stopping several steps from the doors leading to the dining hall, she adjusted her newly arranged pack, clenched her fist in determination, and looked again at what she had over her enemy. The spell and potion to block her mind from penetration, the stone from the sky tied to her neck, her grandfather's teachings…then her mind went blank. He had Jori…or anyone else in that room. Clenching her lips, nostrils flared, Darkess shook her head once and pushed open the doors. Smiling as happily as she could, she said,

"I'm home!"

≈

Food was heaped upon plates and passed around. Everyone was acting normally. All seemed as usual, right down to Jori's fancy dinner goblet. Every one of them had questions for Darkess, and she a few for them, but Harlow seemed just one step more secretive than usual. It was obvious none of them had eaten much this week, and they were now eating heartily between questions. This helped Darkess believe that the food was safe and not poisoned, as she had wondered. Harlow chewed his food viscously as if he were attacking live prey, trying to kill it with each bite. Biding her time, telling her story, Darkess took stock of each person at the table. She searched for weapons and odd behavior with her eyes. She tried to pick up on even the tiniest clue to help her get an idea of what plans her newly formed enemy had made. Then she felt it. Her eyes prickled and produced tears from the pressure on her skull. Someone was trying to penetrate the barrier she set up on herself. Then, just as fast as it had hit, it dissipated.

Darkess stared at her grandmother as the old witch asked her another question, but Darkess wasn't seeing her. She was using her peripheral sight to concentrate on Harlow. Should she make the first move? Or let Harlow do it? How many lives would be lost if she made a mistake? That bastard, Darkess thought. How dare he bring such danger into her house? How could he even think of betraying her family's trust? Especially after all they had done for him. Before she wandered too deep into her own thoughts and it showed on her face that she was no longer paying attention to the conversation, she snapped back to listening to her grandmother and watching Harlow.

"Sorry Grandmother, I'm a little tired. Can you say that again?" Darkess covered.

"I know you're tired dear but a few more questions, and you can go off for a long night of well deserved sleep. You are sure Takar is dead?" Angela repeated.

Swallowing another small bite of food, Darkess said,

"Oh yes, he was badly wounded when I threw the potion, and I added a spell for good measure."

Shoving another piece of biscuit into her mouth, Darkess forced herself to chew. Her body was tense, and her stomach was tied in knots; but somehow, she managed to eat enough to suppress suspicion from either her mother or Harlow. Chakra rubbed Darkess' leg a couple of times, but when she ignored his projected thoughts, he snagged her leg with a claw. Under the table, she waved him away; however, concern outweighed obedience, and he clawed her again. Using magic, Darkess shoved Chakra out from under the table and up against the wall. This angered the cat, and with an air of attitude, he raised his tail, and left the dining hall.

"Anyone for desert" Roxy asked. Without waiting for an answer, she left to get it.

Darkess locked eyes with Harlow for an instant before he looked away from her and towards her mother. Darkess saw her mother's eyes clouding over. Everyone watched and waited for Silver to tell them what she had seen. As her eyes cleared, Silver realized that she was now the center of attention and said,

"Sorry for interrupting."

"Nonsense, do tell us what you have seen," Daniel smiled at his wife.

Darkess wasn't sure that her mother should reveal what she had seen, but to stop her could cause a serious problem. Even though Harlow could easily pluck the images right from Silver's mind, Darkess didn't know if the rest of the table should hear. So Darkess clenched her fists under the table and listened carefully.

"I saw this castle from the air. There was a dragon soaring over, and it was beautiful," Silver shared.

Angela looked at her granddaughter then her daughter.

"That is all that you saw?" Angela asked.

"Yes, a lone dragon, nothing else. But isn't that a good thing?" Silver asked.

"Could you tell how far into the future? Or past?" Angela asked.

"No, but it was spring, judging by the blossoms on the orchard trees."

Harlow smiled at Darkess, who smiled back confidently. That's when the pressure slammed against Darkess' head. Tears sprang to her eyes from the force. Darkess placed a palm to her forehead, stifling a moan. Jori flew into action. Before Darkess had a chance to move her other hand out from under the table, Jori had a knife at Daniel's throat. Jori's eyes turned purple and her fangs lengthened as she calmly said,

"Stop, or he's dead before your weapon hits its mark."

The infiltration attempts on Darkess' mind had ceased for the moment.

"What do you want?" Darkess asked, staring at Jori.

Only Jori didn't answer, Harlow did.

"You know very well what I want, or you wouldn't have blocked your mind from me. Impressive. But I am curious, how did you do it?"

"As if I would tell you," Darkess spat.

Doing her best to antagonize her guest without losing her temper and screwing up her own plan was proving to be a test. She wanted Harlow's attention to be on her and only her.

"When you die, I will know exactly how you did it," Harlow said with a sneer.

Darkess leaned forward in her chair, staring boldly into Harlow's eyes.

"I've always known I'd die. It is just a matter of when," she prodded.

Darkess stood up slowly and pushed her chair back with her foot. She grew a little louder of voice and said,

"But I don't think you know the time of my death."

Angela was sure Darkess had a plan of some sort, and she could see in Silver's eyes that she was about to ruin that plan. Putting her hand out to lengthen the fuse for just another moment, Angela said,

"Harlow, you have been a friend for so long. Do you really intend to kill one of us? We're like family. What turned you evil after so long?"

Harlow laughed harshly, but red stained his cheeks. Whether this was out of shame or exertion, no one could tell. Before Harlow could stop laughing to answer, Darkess interrupted to say,

"If evil had no allure, no one would do it. And he wasn't strong enough to fight it."

She glared at Harlow. She had stalled trying to save her family for long enough. Something she had not planned for happened just then. Not knowing that she would have been safest in the kitchens, Roxy returned with the dessert. It turned out to be the most perfectly timed diversion. Roxy barged through the swinging door with a large platter, and everyone in the room looked towards her at once. Darkess seized the opportunity and sprang atop the table. Jori threw Daniel out of her way. He slammed into the wall and crumpled to the floor. Silver screamed and ran to her husband. Angela knew she could best serve her granddaughter by removing the injured and easy targets, so she followed Silver. Tanner ran the opposite way, towards Roxy.

Harlow grabbed the pink-haired witch, who promptly dropped the tray she'd been holding, which exploded a berry tart everywhere. Tanner was there with a fist before Harlow realized he was in danger. Jori was pulling on Darkess' leg as Darkess was pushing on Jori with all her power. The struggle seemed to happen in slow motion as they wrestled. Darkess suddenly let go of Jori, and the force sent her sailing over the vampire's head. Darkess narrowly missed slamming into the wall by using her magic to stop herself. Inches from the wall, she spun around, landed her foot squarely on Jori's jaw, and knocked the vampire to her knees.

Harlow stopped Tanner from hitting him a second time, but Tanner was fighting Harlow's mind control. He was gritting his teeth and shaking, trying to break free of his mind's prison. Blood ran thickly from Tanner's nose with the effort. Roxy snuck quickly back to the kitchens to hide, sobbing as she ran. Angela was trying to heal Daniel, and Silver was trying to pull him from the room. Jori jumped up and slammed the palm of her hand into Darkess' chest. Once again, Darkess went sailing over the table, this time closer to Harlow. Stopping herself from a fatal landing on a stand of weaponry, Darkess grabbed a lance from the rack. Jori jumped onto the table, expecting Darkess' next move.

Tanner fell to his knees in front of Harlow, who now had a knife in his hand, as Darkess heaved the lance at Jori. The vampire caught it and smiled a devilish grin.

"Smart little witch, but it was I who taught you, remember? Do you think that I taught you all of my tricks?"

Darkess pulled another lance and heaved it at Jori. The instant she released the lance, she lunged at Harlow. The lance Jori had been holding ripped through Darkess' arm as she turned, but her lance had missed Jori completely.

"Aarg!" Darkess groaned with pain and pulled the lance free of her flesh.

Jori leaped at Darkess, and witch and vampire rolled across the floor, slamming into Harlow's legs. He was knocked to the floor but out of the way. It was just what Tanner needed to break free of Harlow's mind grasp. Tanner was now trying to help Darkess get out of Jori's hold. Jori grabbed Tanner's arm and hissed,

"Back off medicine man!"

Jori's distraction gave Darkess just enough time to pull a knife from her boot and jab it into Jori's back. The vampire growled in pain and arched her back, reaching for the blade. Darkess rolled out from under Jori's legs and tossed a potion bottle to Tanner. The side of the bottle had a small label that read, 'Drink'. He did not hesitate. Pulling the cork, he turned the bottle over and drank the contents down. Harlow being much older than he looked took considerable time to compose himself and realized too late what was happening. The knife he had been holding was lost in the shuffle, and he was cut on his leg and bleeding profusely. Jori had almost removed the blade in her back when Harlow saw the amber liquid running into Tanner's mouth.

"No!" Harlow yelled limping towards him.

Pulling the blade from her back had not been an easy feat for Jori, and Darkess exploited that time.

"Jori, do you ever wonder why Harlow refuses to become one of your kind? Why he won't let you bite him?"

Pulling the hilt free of her back, Jori cocked her head to one side and furrowed her brow in thought. Then the expression disappeared from her face as she looked at the blade that had injured her.

"Mine is not to question his motives," Jori hissed then threw the bloodied knife at Darkess, who immediately froze and turned the blade, all with the flick of her finger.

"Maybe you should do a little thinking of your own," Darkess said, sending the blade at Harlow.

Jori made it to him and caught it in the knick of time, not even an inch from his chest. It would have slammed into his heart had Jori not been there, and being that close to death made Harlow's heart race, which pumped more blood from the hole in his leg. Tanner had blood on his face, and Darkess' shoulder was bleeding thickly as well. Between Harlow's distraction from pain and near death, along with the substantial amount of blood flowing in the room, Harlow was losing control of his vampire bodyguard. Jori's face was one of confusion then arousal from the scent of so much blood. Jori still had the knife Darkess had sent at Harlow, but she was only holding it.

"He's tricking you, Jori. Don't be one of his pawns. Bite him. See what he is hiding from you," Darkess whispered, knowing Jori was listening.

Tanner went to grab Harlow, but Darkess held him back with her good arm. She shook her head no at Tanner, and he held his ground. Together, they watched Jori's face as confusion ate at her.

"No, now you know why we can't both be vampires…it wouldn't work," Harlow began to back away from his trusted bodyguard, but she was fast. Using all of her vampire speed, she grabbed him and hissed,

"Why are you pulling away from me? What are you hiding?"

She held him like she would a lover; close and seductive, and then she bent his head over and kissed his neck. Jori pressed her body up against Harlow, and squeezing him tightly, she licked his jawline. Fear was tearing at Harlow, and Darkess could see it in his eyes. For the first time in many years, this man was finally afraid of something. Spit flew from his lips as he grasped for what little air Jori's grip would allow.

"Show me your secrets," she hissed into his ear.

Rolling her head around on her shoulders, her eyes were a brilliant purple as she threw back her head. Jori bared her fangs and sunk them deeply into Harlow's neck.

"Go now, run," Darkess whispered to Tanner. "Get Roxy and my family to the tower. Lock it tight."

Tanner slipped through the kitchen door and was gone.

Harlow's body went into spasms for a moment, then he seemed to calm and his body went slack. After several long minutes, his body slipped to the floor. Darkess had already pulled out a twelve-foot long silver chain and the strongest befuddlement potion she could make. Jori swayed for a moment, hovering over the body of the man who had controlled her life for so many years. Her back was to Darkess, and her eyes were shut as she saw the blood memories of Harlow floating across her mind. The faces of many wizards and witches flowed through her thoughts. She saw demons and maps, Takar and Tuma. Harlow hadn't been on that ship when she met him all those years ago to learn his power. He was searching for the eggs even then. He had found the premonition for Darkess many years ago and had been controlling people for decades in his quest for the eggs.

Harlow had known all the while that he would have to use Darkess to get the final egg. The entire group he had called the Order of the New

Horizon had been his own personal search party. Each member was picked for his or her ability to help in the search. He had never killed anyone with his own hand, but he had arranged for many deaths in order to keep his hands clean. Even Richard, probably his only true friend, had gotten too close and paid the price. Takar had been one of his tools as well as Jakara and Sierra, his parents. Janine, Belthazor, and Brutus as well as the rest of the Vallencourts had been pawns in Harlow's sick little game to gain control of the eggs. Jori couldn't believe the amount of schemes, lies, and manipulation this man had been capable of. Worst of all, he had lied to her. She had been his lover, partner and protector, and it had all been because she had known a Vallencourt in her youth as a vampire. Blood tears ran from Jori's eyes when she opened them. Her heart had been broken.

As Jori turned back towards Darkess, she saw that the young witch was holding one fist close to her chest with a silver chain clutched in it, and her rapier, newly tipped in silver, for such an occasion. The blade was pointed at Jori's chest, then it was lowered a fraction of an inch and steadied. Darkess saw the tears rolling down the vampire's face.

"Do you really plan to try and kill me now?" Jori asked, calmly.

"That depends on you."

"On whether I plan to attack you next?"

Darkess raised one eyebrow and cocked her head in a slow and discriminate way.

"Are you my enemy," she asked, "or were you a pawn in his game too?"

"We were all pawns in his game," Jori said. "I just can't believe I didn't see it before. He has done so much good..."

Jori wiped at the blood on her face using an antique handkerchief.

"Or so he led us to believe..." Darkess added.

Jori pulled out a chair to sit, and Darkess moved smoothly around to face her, still keeping her weapons ready.

"Are you my enemy?" Darkess repeated.

"You could have killed me as I fed on Harlow. Why didn't you?"

"I wanted to know if I could trust you. I wanted to give you a second chance...if you were a pawn, too."

"That doesn't answer the question," Jori said. "You know that is when I am at my weakest, except for day. And you know that soon after feeding, I get a power boost. So answer my question, and I will answer yours," Jori said, staring at Darkess.

"I can kill you in self-defense, in battle, but if you are killing my enemy, why would I stop you? I am no murderer, even at the cost of my own life." Darkess answered. "Besides, I wanted to know what you saw. Okay, now, are you my enemy?"

"Lower your blade," Jori instructed, "and I will tell you the tale of evil that paraded through my mind before I killed our enemy."

☼

Satisfied that Jori was indeed a pawn in the same evil game, and that she was not a threat to her family, Darkess stowed her away in the cellar moments before dawn broke into the sky. The thought of climbing the stairs to the family tower made tears spring to her eyes. She had no energy left. She threw a bottle of potion on the floor and traveled that way instead. Reappearing in the tower, she startled her awaiting family. They had been watching on the mirror, but when she had used the potion, they had no idea where she was going. And they had missed most of the battle as they ushered everyone to safety.

"What happened?" Silver and Angela said in unison, rushing to her side.

Disheveled and bleeding through the bandage she had tied to her arm, Darkess limped to a chair and collapsed into it. She told the tale of the battle in the dining room and what Jori had seen in Harlow's memories. Angela healed the bloodied wounds and brewed a potion for the internal bruises and general wariness. Daniel was awake, but he had suffered near fatal injuries and was lying on a table listening. Roxy sat huddled next to Silver, the poor little witch was shaken to the core. And Tanner listened with his usual reserve as he carved on a piece of wood.

When the story was finally told, everyone in the tower was silent. Harlow had invaded each one of their minds and influenced many decisions they had made. It was an awful feeling to be manipulated so easily and so often. Every time he came to the castle or sent Jori as his conduit, he had violated their privacy and altered their lives to suit his search. He had been using teleport potion to come to the castle and spy on them while Jori slept. He had Silver make the basket in which the eggs were to be housed. He had even found the bounty hunter that Richard had been using and killed them both. But now he was gone. Jori had seen to that. And for the first time in their lives since Darkess had been born, they were finally free, and they hadn't even realized that they had been imprisoned. Everything was different now. And it was taking a moment to sink in.

Darkess' eyes were droopy as she drank her tea and began to slide in her seat. Tanner caught her as she almost fell to the floor.

"Oops, must have made it stronger than I thought," Angela said.

"What did you do?" Tanner asked.

"Mild sedative, she needs her rest."

≈

Darkess slept long and hard for over twenty hours thanks to Angela's potion and no sleep for almost three days. She dreamed many dreams during that day and into the evening. Some desolate and lonely, others bloody from battle, but when she awoke, they vanished like the night's mist in the morning sunlight. She remembered none of them. The storms from the day before had passed, leaving large chunks of blue sky with occasional patches of fluffy white clouds. The sun had just reached the mountains peaks and was flooding the valley with light.

A brand new day was dawning and it felt good to be alive, Darkess thought as she sat up in bed. She looked at the clouds floating past her windows. Wolfbane appeared and hovered over the table.

"Good morning, Darkess. Didn't need me on your trip, I see."

Blushing, she tore back the covers and pulled on her britches.

"Really, there was no time. I am sorry."

"It is quite alright," Wolfbane said. "I am here if you do need me."

Turning her back to the specter, Darkess yanked off her nightshirt, and Wolfbane spun around quickly to hide his face. She put on a more suitable shirt and turned.

"Thank you," Darkess said to Wolfbane's turned back.

"I'm done now," she said.

As he turned back around, Darkess bent down, opened her cedar chest, and began shuffling through the clothes. The eggs were still where she had put them. She closed the lid and sat on the chest's top, smiling. Her eyes had the tiniest point of purple light in them, and a ribbon of light flew from her parted lips. Instantly, it turned back into the mist and swirled around her. Wolfbane could only watch as the mist engulfed Darkess. It was moving around her then it shot into the air and made a cube. Some of the mist moved to make a panoramic scene of mountains. It zoomed in closer to a mountain pass, a long journey through the pass, and over the other side. There were dense woods and a cliff or gorge. Then there was an odd tri-shaped crystal and a pass through the stone to where a river led to an island. A small cabin was on the island, and then there was a ship. The ship docked in a snowstorm at the end, a blizzard by the look of it, and then it was a ribbon again. The ribbon made a corkscrew shape and shot back into Darkess' mouth.

When Darkess swallowed and blinked her eyes, she couldn't think straight for a moment. What the hell was that, she thought.

'Glad to see you home,' Chakra projected as he jumped up on the table.

"Hey, I heard that. Nice to see you, too," Darkess said, ruffling her cat's fur just to tease him.

Darkess picked up her cat and went to the window to get a breath of fresh air.

"Today is a new day, and it comes with a new challenge."

She looked out the window at the sky, and she knew what she had seen. She also knew what she had to do.

"Pack well boys. We have a long journey ahead of us. And whatever may come, we must be ready for it. We should leave near the end of the week to make it through the pass before the bad weather sets in," Darkess said.

She looked back out the window, ignoring the shocked look on Wolfbane's face and knowing that Chakra was dying to know what the purple mist had meant. An amber breasted black eagle soared by, screaming its delight at the sunny day. She had survived the hunt for the eggs and the battles with Takar and Harlow. She had saved most of her friends and family from death and manipulation. One story in Darkess' life was over, and the next was about to begin. She still had much to learn and even more to accomplish. The butterflies in her stomach seemed to tell her that she was doing the right thing. She stared out at the new day, wondering just exactly where her travels would take her. She wondered whom she should take with her on this trip, for things had changed. She could no longer take the road alone. Even with all of her strength, she would never make it that far on her own, not with the treasure she carried. Even the creatures that hide from humans will come out to find the eggs, now that all three are together. Could there ever have been a greater treasure? Demons and wizards alike will want in on this action. Who could blame them, Darkess thought. They think they can rule the world with these eggs, but they are sadly mistaken.

Whom could she trust? What should she do? Darkess went to her desk to plan her next move.

≈

Now, as they say, that is that. Darkess has saved the eggs from evil control, rescuing the planet from quick destruction. The story is over. Her destiny is fulfilled. The prophecy was correct. But Darkess is young, and she has other stories attached to her life. She has come of age and is ready to move forward. On that note: Do you remember the hidden passage in the castle from the first floor to the tower…the one neatly tucked away in the mop and broom closet? Well, my friend that is where the next story in the life of Darkess begins. Sometimes you must go down to get up. If you would like to see where the map in the purple mist leads, then you must find…the Citrine Crystal.

Acknowledgements

When I started this book, I was using a pen and notebooks. It all started with a journal given to me by a friend for Christmas. Later, I decided to type it all out, because I had no computer, and it was the cheapest way to go. I would like to thank Bob "The Ex" for helping me get a used school typewriter. I was really happy with it until another friend saw my archaic means of writing and donated an eight-year-old laptop. I was thrilled. She also lent a hand in editing this book. Thank you, Tracy.

During the writing process, I had a few friends who really spurred me along. I would say that Audrey, Darlene and Cheryl probably bugged me the most. But their prodding really helped, and I thank them for encouraging me not to give up. I also lost one of my biggest "cheerleaders" before I was half finished, but I believe he knows that he helped my confidence a lot. Dale, may you rest in peace.

When I finally started doing rewrites, and I thought this might really be a good story, something other people might like too, I remembered my chemistry teacher from New Bremen High School in Ohio. He told my parents at a parent teacher meeting that someday I would be somebody, and maybe he was right. Thanks for the vote of confidence, Mr. Miller.

I work at a small southern Indiana hotel and restaurant. My friends there have all read a page or a spell here or there, and I know that they are either sick of hearing about my book or they want to read it. So I would like to thank them all for their patience. Their names are too numerous to mention, but I remember their input.

My Dad also deserves an honorable mention, as he is responsible for the final edit on this book. And although he likes science fiction, he tends to lean more towards the sky — space to be more specific. And I have to thank him for staying on the ground for this book and dealing with a genre that he is not usually attracted to. Thanks Poppy.

I would also like to say thank you to my brother for helping with computer literacy and the illustrations in this book. His imagination helped to bring my words to life. Brad, you are the best.

And most of all, I would like to thank my husband, who dealt with my odd hours and weird questions. He was always there to help with whatever I needed. He was a huge inspiration, and I love him all the more for it, especially because he doesn't like to read! Thank you, Jimmy "The Shank."

I would also thank God for the creativity he gave me to come up with all of this. He has to be the inspiration for it all.

≈

Red Dobbs lives in a hundred and ten year old farmhouse in southern Indiana. She is happily married and has two rescued dogs and two adopted cats. She enjoys working in her yard and walking her dogs. She has loved animals and Native American history, including clothing, jewelry, and weaponry, since she was a child. She has tried to capture some of her favorite things in the life of Darkess, and she hopes you enjoy them too.

≈

This book is dedicated to all of my witchy friends:
Allison, Audrey, Cheryl, Darlene, Debbie, Suzie Q. and Vicky... the readers of the witchy tales.

Character and Location Pronounciation

Aleria	A-lear-ya
Brumalia	Broom-all-ya
Chakra	Shock-rah
Gilamen	He-la-men
Jakara	Juh-car-ah
Takar	Tuh-car
Tuma	Toom-a
Xyloidonia	Zy-loy-don-ya
Zaphod	Zaff-odd